EME

BOOK ONE

THE PROTOCOL

BY PJ LAMPHEAR

ISBN: 0615675964
ISBN 13: 9780615675961
Library of Congress Control Number: 2012950519
CreateSpace Independent Publishing Platform
North Charleston, South Carolina

FOR MOM
"Isn't this something!"

Europe

Brienz

Asia

frica

Indian
Ocean

Australia

Gerldton

★ Places of importance in the story
____ Eme's airplane flights

EME

BOOK ONE

THE PROTOCOL

CONTENTS

EME

BOOK TWO

AND NOW IT'S TOMORROW
(WORKING TITLE)

CHAPTER ONE
THE END

"What's in a name?"

The translucent fingers of his gnarled hands glowed in the eerie light of the monitors. He pounded the keyboard, unwilling to accept the inevitable, and desperate to discover the answer to his question—an answer that might save another world—her world—from the impending disaster.

"What's in a *name*?" the one-eyed man whispered again as his aching fingers flew across the keyboard, forcing the code of the evolving e-mail protocol. Perspiration dripped from his grimy face while he wracked his brain for the definitive answer that would jumpstart their quest.

A networked holographic interface and a bank of superterminals surrounded him. The CPU processor of his rig was running at capacity; internal cooling fans whirred, echoing off the stone walls of the underground munitions bunker, straining to keep up with the mass of information and digital encryption. With his teeth clenched in a nasty sneer, he wiped the salty sweat away from his mouth with the back of his hand. He knew the limit of his machines, but he kept pushing, adding more to the program, while the liquid coolant flowed throughout the system.

Three minutes elapsed when he remembered to blink; one bloodshot blue eye stung in the soft green glow of the monitors before him. He paused for a moment to scratch at the patchy stubble coating his face which hid some of the dreadful scar—a scar that stretched from under his right eye, across the bridge of his nose, under the hollow of his left eye socket, ending in the dimple at the corner of his mouth: a parting blow from an old enemy, or what had remained of him after all their jumps through the Cybernet. Three years on, and he regretted what he had done to the man and his partner the night he turned the full power of cyberspace against the traitorous Americans—a mistake of circumstance, nothing more, and many had died in worse ways since; he regretted it, nonetheless.

A warning message flashed across the main monitor; a calm female voice echoed off the stone walls: *"The change that you made in the NOAA 2015 name bank expended too much energy: forty-three percent risk of core rupture. Terminate all processes? Yes/No?"*

His stomach roiled. "No!" was the frantic cry, and then a whisper: "Not now—we're so close, and we have but precious minutes—increase the coolant flow to one hundred percent."

"Coolant cells are depleted, sir. Emergency override will activate in fifteen seconds."

"No it won't, QT," he told the voice of the Quantum Terminal. "Disable all emergency functions, and increase power to the system core; allow for variances of point zero two nine in the protocol's upgraded memory, and start filtering the processing memory from the botnets." *Almost there.* He shook his aching head; spots of filthy sweat sparkled on the monitor.

"*Emergency functions offline, variances equal point zero two nine. Available processing memory from the bot network is twelve million yottabytes. Another two hundred million zettabytes are available if we siphon the remaining continental US defense network. Proceed? Yes/No?*"

The man hesitated for just one moment, and then he remembered all that had been lost—all that had ceased to matter. He couldn't remember the last time he had used a computer for pleasure. Heaving a shaky sigh caused him to wince; he sat up as straight as his ruined spine would allow, glaring at the monitor. "Do it, QT, shut them all down, cut off information flow to the Internet, the Web, Twin-net, and all major bandwidth suckers; let them all burn!" He drew in a very long, deep breath; his entire body trembled at the thought of what he was about to do.

"*Affirmative. Health warning: Biometrics reports that your pulse rate is increasing, sir. Airflow to your brain is diminished; there is a forty-six percent chance that you will lose consciousness.*"

He exhaled and grinned—a rare event that made him appear younger, that made him look his actual age of twenty-three. "That's just old-fashioned excitement, QT. Don't worry, I'm not about to pass out. Thank you for your concern."

Several seconds later, a roar emanating from the network farm buried in the bunker beneath his feet shattered the silence; a wave of energy intensified the air in the room. A burst of some monumental, monolithic power swept through the banks of machines around the man. The ground shook, there was a muffled explosion, and several of his surveillance monitors collapsed under the glow of a red emergency light from overhead, impeding his ability to watch the UN forces advancing on his stronghold.

"Alert, sir," purred QT's ever-calm voice. "Transfer of memory is complete; worldwide networks have been terminated. The transfer destroyed ninety-three terminals in the network farm. There is considerable damage to the facility. Fire has been detected in the underground bunker. Emergency functions unable to respond. System is vulnerable to attack. I repeat: system is vulnerable to attack."

He choked out a laugh. "Perfect: all going according to plan. Activate the null field around the Singularity Matrix, QT. Prepare for overload of primary Twin-net, shut down all unnecessary functions, and prep for the program's final message transfer."

"Core rupture is now inevitable, sir. Without the core, the Singularity Matrix cannot shut down; it will escape the null-field. Estimated casualties from the collapse will exceed two hundred thirty-three million. Proceed? Yes/No?"

"Kill two hundred thirty-three million people for the chance to save one," he breathed. His face betrayed no emotion save for a glint of something in his bloodshot eye that may have been raw insanity. "Proceed, QT, full-steam ahead—Geronimo!" He began to chuckle, to laugh and scream, and then cry. Not too far from where he wept, a dark machine quietly activated. A sphere of unfeasible density hung suspended above a field of invisible energy and slowly began to spin...

"All systems online. Gamma bursts intermittent at point zero two nine variation. There is enough available memory to transmit one message of no more than twenty-two bytes."

He was silent for a moment. "All the processing power and memory on the continent, and all we can manage is twenty words." He shook his head at the absurdity. "So be it, QT. Send this message to the professor's e-mail account." Now that it had come down to the mark, what was there to say? What could be said to explain all that had happened—to make them all believe?

"*Core rupture in approximately ninety seconds, sir; I require forty seconds to transmit the message. Proceed? Yes/No?*"

"Yes!" *What's in a name? What's in a name?* He ran his hands over the thin wisps of white hair on his sweaty head. *There's no one left to e-mail for...* He hesitated for a moment, and smiled; his trembling fingers typed eighteen words; he heaved a sigh and chuckled, "I only wish I could be there to see their faces!" he whispered with a grin. "Now, on what date should it be delivered?" After a quick tabulation on his desktop calendar, he added the information to the message, and... "Here it is, QT; spell-check that, please!" he laughed, "And hit send!"

"*Affirmative, sir.*"

The man slowly exhaled, leaned back in his chair, and rubbed his tired eye. It was over—he had done it. It was undeniably the greatest accomplishment in techno-human history, yet no one would ever know. No matter. It didn't matter. *Nothing else will ever matter—for me.*

Forty-five seconds later, as the military converged on his fortress, he relaxed, sipping from a warm bottle of soda; he resigned himself to the inevitable as the computer core in his system gave a little splutter of defeat and shut down; the door to the command center shattered, and a heartbeat later, the monitor clock indicated a new day, September 11, 2021—perfect irony. A wave of tremendous heat washed through the underground bunker, and the man, the UN forces, and most of the continent were annihilated in a flash of blinding white light.

CHAPTER TWO
DIVISION

New York City
September 11, 2001
8:20 A.M. EDT (EASTERN DAYLIGHT TIME)

The rustling green leaves splintered the early morning sun's rays, casting dappled shadows on the bustling throng below. Anne Malone pushed the double-seated stroller across the busy plaza. Her twin great-granddaughters, Elaine and Erin, laughed happily together, fighting over Mittens, the blue rabbit. Each girl held the stuffed animal by a floppy ear, tugging back and forth and occasionally gazing up at the gleaming, impossible skyscrapers overhead.

"Mine!" Erin cried.

"Mine!" Elaine—Eme, for short—mimicked her sister.

Anne smiled. At fifteen months, the girls were coming along in leaps and bounds: walking, talking little ones, inseparable, of course, and identical down to the last freckle. Indeed, she had to look twice to tell them apart. The golden embroidery on the front and back of their blue fleece jackets, *Elaine and Erin,* was of little help, as the girls liked to exchange clothes, much to the irritation of their family and babysitters.

They could never fool their great-grandmother for long, however. Anne knew them down to their last freckles and then some. Erin was the older of the girls; they had been born prematurely to her granddaughter, at the tender age of sixteen, during an actual taping of the soap opera, *And Now It's Tomorrow.* The producers continued taping the show when Antonia went into early labor, and edited the tape to sneak it by the censors; however, they included enough of the real drama in the episode to catapult the new soap family to superstar status. This brilliant move also boosted the soap's ratings to the number one daytime drama; then, these same producers, in their infinite wisdom, "killed off" the parents nine months later, leaving the twins orphans. Soap fans mutinied, and the final decision to SORA (Soap Opera Rapidly Age) the twins, replacing them with ten-year-olds, resulted in a massive exodus of their fan-base, and the subsequent cancelation of the daytime drama.

The network's loss was a blessing to the young family; Mark and Antonia garnered movie contracts, and Eme and Erin, at the age of thirteen months, retired to a much calmer existence. With their great-grandmother overseeing the girls' welfare, their parents were free to pursue wildly successful movie careers.

Eme was the younger of the two by eleven minutes and could be more serious. While Erin liked to scribble color wildly across the page, Eme tried to stay within the lines. Eme was still a fan of sucking her thumb, a habit that Erin had never adopted. At an age when they were developing rapidly, Eme was more cautious in the way she turned her head and sometimes regarded Anne with eyes that looked far too old for a toddler. "That one's been here before," Anne had told Antonia only days after Eme's birth.

This daily stroll, to the heavy honking in the backed-up traffic along Liberty Street, was the favorite part of Anne's day. The sights and sounds of New York City were as familiar to the beautiful fifty-three year-old redhead as her two great-granddaughters. The heavenly aroma of coffee from the vendors along the route soothed her; however, many New Yorkers appeared stressed as they rushed to their jobs or meetings—thousands of feet keeping time to the frantic beat of the city's symphony.

Anne wove her way carefully through the throng, smiling at the twins and anyone who looked her way. She wound around Donohue's Donuts and past a giant billboard for the latest Antonia Malone and Mark Venture movie. She beamed at her granddaughter and Mark's tender embrace against the backdrop of a tropical sunset. Since the film, Deliver me From Paradise, was still in production in Bermuda, Anne had Eme and Erin this week. She adored them and cherished any opportunity to spend time with the pair. She sighed and tried to imagine what her life would be like once Bertie, Bogey, and she relocated to Malibu with the twins and their famous parents the following month.

The bells at St. Nicholas chimed the half hour—eight thirty. Her casual stroll had put her a few minutes behind schedule. Picking up her pace, she wheeled the buggy up the ramp into Building Five of the Trade Center complex. She proceeded to the bank of elevators crowded with anxious employees reading papers, eating the last of a hasty breakfast, or tapping impatient feet, waiting for the final leg of the journey to their daily grind.

After several minutes, and more than a few grumpy stares and heavy sighs at the inconvenience of sharing the elevator space with such an enormous stroller, she arrived at the third floor. She made sure her staff ID was clipped in place, and when the elevator doors opened, a well-dressed man wearing dark glasses was standing in her path; he turned to her and hesitated. Anne faltered, but then the man smiled, parting the crowd for them to exit. She flashed her most charming smile in return and quickly wheeled the buggy down the hallway to the Daycare center, unaware that the man had also exited the elevator.

As soon as she opened the door to the center, a mad rush of four newly-arrived toddlers overwhelmed her. Taking a few moments, she greeted their parents, acknowledged each and every child, and then shooed the children into the playroom before turning her attention to the receptionist.

"Good morning, Chantel," Anne greeted the young woman behind the counter. Even though the young blonde was still new to the job, her beautiful pink suit jacket had needed dry cleaning countless times from vomit or worse. "All accounted for this morning?"

"Hello, Anne. Aw, you brought the girls," she cooed as she leaned down to smile at the twins. She ruffled their curly red hair then straightened again and continued, "No, not quite. I'm still waiting on Sarah, Cody, and the new kid, Mallory. We also have quite a few toddlers absent or late, and Grace has called in sick: touch of flu."

Anne sighed. "We'll manage. Is Julie inside?"

"Yes, she's preparing the morning coffee and tea, and Olivia's in the pen." She gestured toward the glassed-in room to her right.

"Perfect." Anne wheeled the twins through the doors and into the huge, brightly painted playroom, smiling and greeting her young charges as they danced around her feet, begging for attention. Erin and Eme were already pulling at their straps; they were eager to join the fun and seek out their favorite toys from the cabinet in the playroom.

"Go on then," Anne said, unclipping the girls from the buggy. "Play nicely."

The twins were off like rockets, Mittens discarded for now. Anne smiled at her girls and set the stroller aside, waving to Olivia across the floor as she helped the younger kids navigate the plastic play slide. From where she stood three stories up, Anne held a commanding view over the square below and spent a moment admiring the city that never slept as it awoke for another busy day. She caught herself looking twice at a giant shadow flickering across the ground.

There was time to whisper, "Why can I hear jet engines?" before she stumbled. The scene before her switched to slow motion; the air tightened around her—she couldn't breathe. A rippling, intense scream of twisted metal and brick destroyed the normal atmosphere outside the window and across the entire complex. Her great-granddaughters continued to laugh and giggle five feet in front of her, while the nightmare of flaming debris and razor-sharp glass rained past the playroom windows on a journey to the World Trade Center plaza.

This was not happening: a dream, a nightmare. *I'm losing my sanity.* Rooted to the scene for what seemed like hours, Anne observed her coworkers do their best to quiet the now crying children when the building's fire alarm system activated. As if this were the starting gun for a race, Anne checked her watch and sprang into action. "Chantel, Olivia, Julie, grab the children and make your way to the stairwell, *now!*" She was sick with anxiety and fear as the enormity of her responsibility nearly crushed her.

The staff jumped into action and obeyed her orders. They were a whirling dervish; with Grace off sick and the three other helpers late, there were twelve terrified kids and an infant for the four of them to carry or herd down the stairs and out onto the plaza. Anne was already thinking five steps ahead: they would head away from the Twin Towers, across Vesey Street, and up Church Street as far as they could manage; she was certain that there would be EMT's and police to help her.

"Chantel, leave the backpacks!" Anne shouted at the young woman. "Just get the kids to partner up and hold hands. I'll bring the twins!"

Abandoning the stroller, Anne seized the screaming girls, one in each hand. She followed a pale, anxious Chantel, who held a howling infant over her vomit-stained shoulder, while wrestling with two-year-old Jason who was crying for his teddy bear that was stuck under a collapsed bookcase.

"We can get through this, we can get through this," Anne whispered to no one; no one could hear anything over the distraught evacuees, streaming from every office and shop on the third floor, making their escape to the stairwell.

Glancing at the sobbing girls on either side of her, Anne stepped into an open doorway and stooped down to embrace them both.

"G...G," Eme hiccupped, "make...stop! Make...stop!"

"Mommmmy!" Erin wailed.

"It's going to be all right, dears. Just stay with me, and I'll get you down safely—GG Anne promises," she croaked as the words stuck in her throat.

"Mit...ten!" screamed Eme. She struggled with Anne in an attempt to return to the playroom. Erin joined her sister in a tug of war with Anne, however their great-grandmother succeeded in gathering them into her arms, quieting them with a promise to return for their floppy-eared friend as soon as possible.

By the time she soothed the girls enough to get them back on course toward the stairwell, the hallway was empty. Anne heaved a sigh of relief at not having to battle the frightened throng. She took a deep breath and opened the stairwell door just as the second plane hit the south tower. A reverberating boom shook their building, throwing them to the ground. *This is not happening!*

Screams echoed off the stone stairwell from above and below her. Anne stumbled as she tried to stand. She tightened her grip on one of the terrified twin's hands and scooped up the other one who immediately had a death grip on her neck. Just then the exit door slammed open behind her and a new stream of evacuating workers pushed and jostled her on their way down the stairs.

Many minutes and several bruises later, she emerged on the plaza to utter chaos; throngs of people were fleeing in any and every direction, yelling about the two jet airliners that had hit the towers. Since Anne was so far behind the others from the day care center, she had no way of determining in which direction the group had gone. She paused to get her bearings, but was knocked about by heavy blurs. The noise was deafening, and the hazy air stank of destruction. Small fires spewing noxious clouds of smoke distorted the scene.

Anne gazed into the smoky sky at the burning towers. How much time had passed since the planes had struck? *Those poor people!* The entire world had gone mad. Sirens and flashing lights fractured the surreal landscape. Anne felt an immense pain in her gut, and then she heard nothing, as if the entire city was holding its breath.

Suddenly there was a catastrophic wrenching from above.

Oh, dear God!

The south tower was collapsing.

Anne turned and fled into the crowds scurrying away from the towers. Holding her twins tightly, one against her chest, the other by the hand, she ran. The fear of losing them in the mayhem caused her to tighten her grip more severely, prompting Eme and Erin to gasp and wail more miserably.

The fleeing masses battered and bruised her. Suddenly something clobbered her from behind. Anne tripped over the brick and glass scattered across the ground. At the last minute, she lost her grip on one of the twins and fell on her side to protect the other girl. Shock waves of pain tore up her arm, splintered glass ripped her skin.

A quick glance at the blue fleece jacket told her that Erin was still in her arms. Anne scrambled to her feet, struggling once again against the stampeding crowds. She cradled her injured arm against her body and snapped her head around for Eme. The noise was deafening. "Eme!" *Where is Eme?* For a split second, a blinding flash of blue light froze the scene.

Anne recovered quickly and spotted Eme running toward the north tower—toward Mittens. *Mittens? How did the rabbit get to the street?* She gaped in disbelief as Eme stooped to pick up her toy. *Could anything be worse than the present situation?* The reality of her plight hit her; she screamed for Eme to stop and to all the passersby for help. Anne struggled with the bawling Erin and ended up coughing on a mouthful of acrid smoke. She darted after the toddler, but found it impossible to cut through the horde of frightened people. When she reached out to stop a wild-eyed man for some help, he roughly brushed by her in a desperate attempt to save himself from the carnage.

Suddenly, a cloud of thick dust washed over everything; all sounds were muffled. Anne pulled Erin against her and crouched behind a parked car. Flecks of rubble and tiny chips of glass cut her cheeks and arms. She was screaming without realizing it, with a hand over Erin's eyes and her own squeezed tightly shut. *It was the end of the world.*

After a moment Anne heard only one sound: the deafening ringing in her ears. The wind shifted through the thick smoke; the stench of burning electrical equipment and scorched metal stung her eyes and throat. She cradled her great-granddaughter against her chest, holding her as she screamed and sobbed, while the wail of sirens cut through the air.

Screaming herself hoarse for Eme, Anne stumbled over the rubble for what seemed like hours. She remembered the other life she held in her arms and planted a dry, dusty kiss on Erin's forehead between her bright red curls.

"It's okay, sweetheart," Anne lied. "It's okay."

The toddler sniffed, entwining her arms around her great-grandmother's neck, and stuffed one thumb into her mouth. *Erin was sucking her thumb.* As she leaned back, Anne glimpsed the embroidered name stitched on the front of her fleece: *Erin.*

Her breath caught in her throat; she didn't have Erin—it was Eme. She had seen the girls switch jackets not an hour before. Eme was safe in her arms; it was Erin who had returned to the building.

Anne wept. The smoke was still thick, choking, and she had no idea where she was. She knew only that Erin had disappeared, and one of the towers had collapsed. She had felt the second plane strike the south tower. Had it been on purpose? If so, then what monsters had done this? Was the other tower still standing?

A stirring of dark fury mixed with the breathtaking anxiety Anne felt for Erin. She could just make out flashing lights on the rescue vehicles through the haze on her right, and she began to stumble toward them through the burning rubble; surely they had found her great-granddaughter.

She looked down at Eme's sooty, tear-stained face, and Eme stared back at her with frightened eyes. The toddler removed her thumb, choked down a sob, then threw her head back and wailed, "Eh-win!" just as the second tower began its collapse.

CHAPTER THREE
THE END JUSTIFIES THE MEANS

Malibu, California
Monday, June 1, 2015
3:10 A.M. PDT (PACIFIC DAYLIGHT TIME)

"Help us, Kevin!" Eme and Erin screamed as they turned to the armless man standing behind them. Miles of multicolored computer cable wound around the ankles of the man and the hundreds of howling armless people behind him, rooting them to the floor of the enormous underground bunker.

An ear-splitting screech refocused their attention on the computer, and the girls swore as the twenty-foot-high monitor burst with an undecipherable array of default errors. In concert, the teenagers ripped the keyboards from the terminal and threw them against the stone wall where they joined a mountain of destroyed computer peripherals; then they yanked a new pair of keyboards from the towering stack and resumed their frantic attempt at rewriting the code.

"It's not the code! It's not the keyboard! It's you! It's you! It's you!" The hideous hologram fiddler crabs taunted them from hundreds of holoports in the massive computer terminal. The girls covered their ears and swore in return.

"Focus, Eme, Erin; forget the Fiddlers!"

"We can't do it, Kevin!" the twins wailed in unison, running trembling hands through long red curls, tears streaming down their freckled faces.

"They're going to grab us!" cried Eme.

"And pull us into the computer!" finished Erin.

"Focus, girls; the keyboards recognize only your fingerprints; try again! The world is depending on you," the armless man pleaded.

"Too late! Too late! We warned you!" With the snapping crescendo of the crabs' hologram claws, the scene exploded in a cascading shower of ones and zeros.

"Aahh!"screamed the girls.

Claws dug into Eme's shoulder, and something warm and wet landed on her cheek. A clap of her hands illuminated the scene and erased the horror of the nightmare.

"Boomer? *Boomer!*" The girl hugged the two-year-old Lhasapoo, burying her perspiring face in his creamy white fur. He wagged his tail and licked her damp cheeks.

"You were expecting chopped liver?" A blue and yellow macaw danced across his perch by the window seat and continued squawking, "Chopped liver, chopped liver! May Day, May Day! Dive, dive, dive!"

Eme turned her head toward the bird, "Quiet, Bogey, you'll wake Mom and Dad!" One last squawk and the bird obeyed, hiding his head beneath his wing.

A glance toward the clock on the dresser between the twin canopy beds confirmed that there were still several hours until dawn. Turning back toward Boomer, Eme spotted a gigantic stuffed fiddler crab, poised to pounce, on the yellow Queen Anne chair next to her closet. Her stomach roiled at the sight of the Christmas present from her demented friends, Bailee Sue and Shaelyn. She gently pushed Boomer away and padded across the room, grabbed the crab by one of its menacing bloodshot eye stalks, hurled it to the back of the closet, and shut the door with a satisfying snap. Then, with one hand covering her mouth, she made a mad dash to the bathroom, where she purged her stomach of her pizza and root beer float dinner.

After washing her face and brushing her teeth, Eme returned to the bedroom. "That's the last time I watch any of those dopey *Fiddler Crabs That Ate...*," she paused and threw up her hands, "...*Wherever* sequels with Shae and Bailee," she told her two pets before climbing back into bed. "The first thing tomorrow, I'm deleting that Amazemail crab e-lert and replacing it with a parrot; Bogey will love that!" She flashed a smile at the beautiful bird. "Won't you, boy!" She chuckled at Bogey's cocked head and at the picture in her mind of his reaction to a macaw hologram.

After taking another few moments to think about her latest nightmare and shed a few more tears for her sister, she snuggled under the covers. Boomer licked her hand and circled five times before curling into a tight, furry ball next to her, optimistic that the drama of the night was over.

"Good-night, and in case I don't see ya..."

"Good-bye, so long, adios," she sang with the bird. Eme snapped her fingers, the room grew dark, and the three drifted off to a calmer, dream-free sleep.

The Venture Kitchen
SIX HOURS LATER

"We appreciate your enthusiasm for your hobby, Eme; however, you're not making it a career. You're ignoring all of your friends, and all we see of you anymore is the back of your head," complained her mother at breakfast.

"Here's lookin' at you, kid!" squawked Bogey.

With her back turned to her parents at the breakfast table, the fourteen year-old sat hunched over the Cybook computer on her lap, absentmindedly munching a dry piece of toast, while scratching Bogey's soft neck feathers, and nodded at her mother. She finished her Amazemail e-lert adjustments, whispered, "Good-bye and good-riddance, *Virginia*!" to the horrid fiddler crab as it disintegrated in a haze of ones and zeroes, and grinned at the hilarious multi-colored parrot that had materialized from the holoport. It was now sitting on her knee, preening its opaque feathers. She grinned at Bogey's agitation toward the funny little hologram. "Thanks, um...*Pandora*!" she giggled when her newly-named macaw gave her a sly wink before holding out the envelope clutched in its tiny wing. She clicked on it with her 3DX laser pointer to open the e-mail message; Pandora squawked a "good-bye," dissolved into a golden mist, and disappeared into the holoport. The message from Amazemail confirmed that the orange fiddler crab had been deleted. Satisfied, she closed the e-mail program and resumed her search for Southern California technical colleges, missing the parental glare, until...

"Elaine Mea Venture, I'm talking to you!"

"Answer your mother, Eme," her father mumbled through a mouthful of toast, not taking his eyes from his script.

"What we have here is a failure to communicate!" chimed Bogey.

Eme smiled at her pet's response and tossed him a piece of her toast, handing the rest to the fluffy white dog lying comfortably at her feet. Reluctantly, she saved her search, and with quiet resolve, turned to face her two famous parents. "OK, here's my face," she sighed, fluttering her long dark lashes over sapphire blue eyes.

Her mother, Antonia "Toni" Malone, was a typical Hollywood beauty: smoky grey eyes, long platinum hair, and a willowy figure that was the envy of all her friends. Her father, Mark Tomei Venture, was not much taller than his wife: rugged, with a well-chiseled face, curly black hair, and warm brown eyes that flashed golden when he laughed.

Since both of her parents were between movies for another week, they had decided to spend some "quality time" with their daughter. To Eme, this meant interfering in her well-ordered life.

"It's such a beautiful Saturday, sweetheart," exclaimed her mother as she rose and began clearing the table. "Why don't you invite the girls over for a swim and barbecue?"

"Smokin!"

"Took the words right out of my mouth, Bogey," Mark agreed as he finished his breakfast and returned the script to his briefcase. "Terrific excuse for me to break in my new grill, and have I got a surprise for you, my darling Eme!" He wiped the crumbs from his mouth, dropped his napkin on the glass tabletop, and rubbed his hands together; then he leaned over to the étagère and retrieved two large silver film cans. "Since you and your friends had such a great time with the Crab sequel last night, I persuaded the studio to let me preview the latest installment; the messenger just left these." He held up the round metal canisters: *The Fiddler Crabs that Ate Atlantis!*"

Eme groaned and lowered her head; long crimson curls hid her frown. She excused herself and darted to the guest bathroom in the hall, slamming the door behind her.

Toni put her hands on her hips and snapped, "Mark, I told you that the root beer floats were too much after anchovy pizza; no wonder she's so quiet this morning." Mark's face fell; he shrugged and returned the movie cans to the bookcase.

Several minutes later, Eme rejoined her anxious parents in the kitchen with a sheepish smile. "I think I'll pass on the barbecue, Dad."

"But, sweetheart, maybe after..."

As if by divine intervention, Alexander Graham Bell saved the day.

"E. T., phone home!" Bogey screeched his usual response to an incoming call.

Her father reached the phone on its second ring; his smooth baritone "Hello!" filled the kitchen. "Yes, Toni's right here—just a moment, Meghan." When her father turned his back to hand the phone over the counter to her mom, Eme took the opportunity to snatch up her computer and coax the twenty-five-year-old Ara macaw to her shoulder. Through the hall and up the curved stairway she scrambled, Boomer on her heels. After grabbing two antacid tablets from the bathroom, she slipped them into the pocket of her blue denim shorts, and continued to her bedroom.

Once the three were inside, Eme closed and locked the door, carefully placing Bogey on his perch next to the window seat that overlooked the Pacific Ocean. She paused to enjoy the breathtaking view of the summer sun sparkling on the surging surf just beyond their vast estate. Bogey patrolled his three-foot-long domain, screeching and squawking at a flock of blackbirds hopping along the sloping red-tiled roof outside her dormer window. Bogey's rant did nothing to scare the little birds; however, it did prompt Boomer to jump onto the blue and yellow striped cushion. When the birds took flight at the sight of the dog, Bogey snapped at him, "Aw, go lay an egg!" Boomer turned toward the macaw, growling in response, and Bogey answered with some choice expletives, intermingled with his usual squawking, dancing tirade.

Eme grabbed her pillow, climbed onto her bed, sitting cross-legged, and laughed at their banter for a moment before the familiar icy stone of regret and loss dropped into her stomach. Tears flooded her eyes. *Erin would have adored these two, this life; she should be here with me, with us.* She buried her face in her pillow and allowed the hollow feeling to thoroughly engulf her. *Why did it have to be Erin? Where is she now? Alive? Dead?*

Tired of Bogey's persistent noise and insults, Boomer shook himself and leaped onto the bed, lying down beside Eme, interrupting another of her incessant guilt trips. She sniffed and stroked his soft, creamy white fur, scratching behind his long beige ears, and then grabbed a tissue to wipe her nose and eyes. "What's… the matter, Boomerman?" she hiccuped. "Bogey didn't appreciate you…taking over his job?" Bogey squawked louder. Boomer jumped up and barked at him, turned back to Eme, licked her tear-stained cheek, and then curled up next to her. She sniffed again, glancing once more at the empty twin bed across from hers. After a few more sniffles and a heavy sigh, she gazed one last time at her two beloved pets before returning to her computer and her cyber search.

Eme was not the beautiful extrovert her parents had hoped she would become. Because of Erin's loss, they held Eme close and limited her contact with the outside world. Surrounded only by her parents' Hollywood friends and their children, they were expecting her to grow into a clone of Toni and never expected a "geek," the title given to her by her friends, or "genius, the first in a generation," as her extended family anointed her. She called herself Eme, and Eme was beautiful. Hey, if no one else could see it, that was their problem! She did agree that her penchant for computers and her straight A's could be misconstrued, leading to the nicknames. The mirror, however, agreed with her.

OK, maybe she was a bit short: five feet, four—in two-inch heels. Maybe her long red hair was a smidge too curly.

Nonetheless, her eyes were beautiful: sapphire blue—as clear as a summer sky. Moreover, were not the eyes the windows of the soul? What was more admirable than a beautiful soul? Not one darn thing, as far as she was concerned. She would insist, however, on rating her Cybook (her constant confidant and very best friend) as a close second. In fact, she had poured most of her heart and soul into her personal blog which now resided in bits and bytes on its partitioned hard drive.

As Eme approached school age, her parents realized that their hectic schedules necessitated hiring a nanny to home-school her—also to keep her from the prying eyes of her parents' adoring fans and from the paparazzi who were still hounding them about Erin. Nanny duty, thankfully, fell to her GG Anne, whose house was situated at the end of a wooded cul-de-sac which bordered her parents' Malibu estate.

Spending time with her quirky great-grandmother was one of Eme's favorite pastimes. Anne Malone was an excellent teacher, and Eme's meteoric advancement through the California standards allowed her to bypass the middle school curriculum. Now, with the commencement of her senior year courses only two months away, she was eager to find a college that was close enough to home, where taking some advanced courses during the summer would not be a burden to Anne.

Eme fantasized about zooming to college on the hot pink moped she had found hidden in GG Anne's garage—the one she had asked for and knew she was getting for her birthday. She was an expert at driving her dad's motorcycles, and she could not wait to earn her motorcycle license once she turned fifteen. Her parents did not know it, but she was planning on majoring in computer technology, and she was not relishing the argument that was certain to ensue once she gave them the news.

She often wondered if Erin might have shared her passion for technology. Such thoughts about her twin, especially when she was alone, always drove her into a deep depression. Bogey and Boomer would eventually lighten her mood and bring a smile to her face; however, survivor's guilt plagued her every thought of her sister. The twin canopy bed next to hers, and the identical presents on birthdays and Christmases from her parents, were constant reminders that they expected Erin to appear out of thin air one day, and they wanted to make sure that she knew they had never given up that dream.

A few minutes of intense concentration on her computer search passed in relative quiet when Eme's sudden cry of "Eureka!" startled Boomer off the bed. He hit the floor with cat-like grace, but barked at her for interrupting his nap which provoked Bogey into another squawk and dance routine.

Eme bounced off the bed and smiled at her pet, "Sorry, boy!" With her left hand she patted her sweet rescue dog (a Christmas gift from her great-grandmother), slammed her computer closed with her right, tucked the notebook under her arm, and bounded toward her bedroom door.

"Houston, we have a problem!" Bogey quipped after ceasing his rant.

Eme skidded to a halt against the door and turned to see Bogey flaring his tail feathers in irritation. "I'm sorry, Bogey; I've been so preoccupied lately, I've not paid much attention to you or Boomer. Do you want to come to GG's with me?"

"That's what I'm talking about!"

"Woof."

She chuckled and rubbed Boomer's ears once more while placing her shoulder next to the perch for the blue and yellow macaw to hop aboard. With Bogey situated, she skipped out the door, stopping in the bathroom just long enough to place a hand on the mirror and greet her reflection with the usual, "Hi, Erin, I love and miss you," run a comb through her crimson curls, and apply an uneven layer of "Crimson Carousel" to her lips.

She then grabbed two more antacids, just in case, batted her lashes at Bogey's customary wolf whistle, and dashed out the door and down the stairs—dog on her heels, yapping merrily, bird on her shoulder, squawking, "I'm king of the world"—through the hallway and out the back slider to the glorious Southern California morning. She answered her parents' command from their pool-side lounge chairs to "Stop and talk about the barbecue" by yelling an airy "Good-bye" over her shoulder.

If anyone would appreciate her splendid discovery, it would be her GG Anne, not her parents. To them, the latest technology was their reel-to-reel movie projector with its wall-to-wall screen; her mother and father had renounced television once they'd all been written off their soap; instead, they had showered their daughters with a wealth of classic books and fairytales as soon as they were able to hold one in their hands.

As far as computers were concerned: "Fuh-get about it!" as Bogey would say; they had neither the time nor the inclination for the technology. In fact, she would not have a computer today if it had not been a gift from her great-grandmother, once she'd passed her Elementary and Intermediate School Standards, two weeks before her twelfth birthday. She was still the only kid in her small circle of home-school academy friends without a TV, but at least they all knew she had her very own Cybook. When her new high school academy friends learned of her computer-age debut, they'd bombarded her with requests to join them on all the internet blogging and social media sites.

"If all of us unite to stop global warming, it *will* happen, Eme," pleaded Bailee Sue.

"We have to save the animals from abusive kitty and puppy mills, Eme!" Join your blog with ours; the poor animals are suffering, and Boomer will be so proud of you!" Shaelyn implored.

"Recycling *is* the most important issue facing us today, Eme; our combined blogs will convince the world, and our planet will become a pollution-free reality!" Judy insisted.

"We must stop the war in the Middle East! Add your blog to ours, Eme; they *will* hear us!" begged Patty.

All were extremely compelling arguments; however, Eme was not an activist, nor was she a socialist; she was a realist. Her personal blogs were just that—personal. No one needed to read her thoughts, learn of her political or social ideals, or know she felt that half of her was missing. Let her friends save the world, Eme would just save herself. To her friends' dismay, she had, instead, immersed herself in online computer classes, secretly pleased that they called her a geek.

It was Anne, once again, who had realized how adept she was on her notebook. She had hired Kevin and Jim Burke, young software designers, and the grandsons of her great-grandmother's best friend from college, to teach the teenager programming during her last summer break. Eme had spent the happiest eight weeks of her life attempting to understand the complex world of writing, testing, and debugging the source codes of computer programs.

Now she was ready to take it to a whole new level.

Eme (with Bogey still clinging to her shoulder) cleared the low garden gate to her great-grandmother's back yard while short-legged Boomer charged through his custom-made puppy door. They bounded around the sparkling pool, through the French doors, and into her sunny kitchen. Eme yelled, "GG, I've found it!" to her surprised GG Anne.

"What's new, Pussycat?" squawked Bogey, much to Anne's delight.

"Good morning, you three. Sit down, dear, and tell me what you've found!" Anne laughed. She set down her coffee mug and recovered from her great-granddaughter's assault on her home.

Eme placed Bogey on his old perch, and Boomer yapped before jumping onto Anne's lap, rolling over and giving her access to his tummy for the customary massage.

"Be it ever so humble," began Bogey. Eme and Anne chuckled, joining him for the well-practiced refrain, "There's no-o place like home."

Eme turned away from the bird and plunked herself down at the cluttered kitchen table, clearing a place for her computer. "I've found my summer college!" she announced. "It's a brand new private technical institute located only a mile from here. I can ride my mo...er, bike," she beamed. "And look at all the programming classes they offer! They even have one on 'Bridging the Carbon/Silicon Gap.' It's a class in human thought/computer interface. Kevin and I disc..." She started to turn the computer to Anne when a thought struck her. "GG, I had the wildest dream about fiddler crabs and an armless people last night. I wonder if it's because of the discussions I've had with Kevin and Jim about this evolving technology."

The older woman scanned her great-granddaughter's face in concern. "It's entirely possible, darling; dreams are the filter for all your unspoken fears and desires." She paused. "Maybe it's time to focus on more pleasant fare; go to the beach with your friends; forget about computers for a day or two." Anne stroked Eme's hair and searched her beautiful eyes.

Eme thought about her words and then dismissed them with a grimace and a shrug. *It was just one dream...*

"Ha, I can see that's not an option," Anne surmised. Eme grinned and shook her head; Anne laughed and turned her attention to the College webpage.

While Anne scanned the course list, Eme studied her beautiful face and curly red hair, almost a carbon copy of Eme's hair, except that her great-grandmother preferred a shorter hairstyle and had acquired a bit of grey at the temples; however, at sixty-seven, Anne Malone had more energy and vitality than most of her friends' parents. When a tragic auto accident claimed the lives of her husband, daughter, and son-in-law, twenty-one years ago, Anne had assumed the role of parent to her ten-year-old granddaughter, Antonia. She'd dealt with her grief by throwing herself into promoting the young girl's acting career.

Once she was certain that Toni's life was secure, Anne had found some measure of happiness with Toni's talent agent, Bertie Bernard, who had moved with them from New York to Malibu after her parents' three-year long search for Erin had ended. Because Bertie was wheelchair-bound, it had been difficult for him to travel, so he and Anne had spent most of their time teaching movie one-liners to Bertie's pet bird, Bogey. However, now that Bertie was gone, Eme was afraid Anne would never find her "happily ever after." She had given Eme the macaw to help her great-granddaughter with her depression, but also because Bogey was a constant, bitter-sweet reminder of her time with the dear man.

Eme heaved a sigh and returned her attention to the computer. Anne had finished studying the admission requirements and smiled at her great-granddaughter. "It's perfect, darling. Now we just have to convince your parents."

Eme snapped out of her reverie and made her plea: "Do you think you could tell them, *please?*" she begged. She smiled and batted her eyelashes, a ploy that nearly always got her what she wanted.

"Ha! I may be old, but I'm not ready to die—I was planning on living at least another few years," Anne replied with a smirk.

"I see dead people!"

Anne laughed at Bogey's remark and the pout on Eme's face. She sighed and finally relented. "OK, you win; I'll talk to them tonight at dinner." She held up her finger for emphasis. "Before I embark upon this suicide mission, however, let me show you where I keep my will." Eme's delighted face turned to terror and then back to delight when Anne started laughing. "You know, they'll probably be ecstatic that you've found a goal for your life."

Eme's eyes widened. "You're kidding, right?" She tucked a loose curl behind her ear and pouted. "They hate that I tote my notebook everywhere I go." Eme suddenly stood up and walked to the cupboard for a glass. After filling it with water from the tap, she turned to face her great-grandmother. "They told me this morning that they're tired of looking at the back of my head; they wanted me to invite all of my friends over for a barbecue and swim party this afternoon. Most of those girls are all so full of themselves; I can't relate to anything they talk about."

Her great-grandmother looked up at her in surprise at that comment, and Eme quickly explained, "Oh, they're all OK, and I love Bailee and Shae, don't misunderstand, but all they know—or *want* to know—about computers is how to e-mail, blog, and play games." She popped an antacid tablet into her mouth, took several swallows of water, and put the glass in the dishwasher. At the concerned look on Anne's face, Eme waved her hand and responded, "Just an upset stomach from breakfast, GG."

"Oh, I see, your dad was cooking again." Anne smirked.

After Eme stopped laughing, Anne continued their discussion. "I'm afraid that when we skipped you from elementary to high school academy courses, we put you in this position, honey. You're not on the same..." she hesitated, "well, the same emotional level as your home-school peers." Eme walked back to the table and plopped down on her chair, folding her arms in disgust across the USC logo of her crimson and gold T-shirt. After a few seconds of contemplation, she raised her head to argue, but Anne cut her off by patting her on the knee. She smiled and continued, "It's true, and things may not get any easier at this technical college, you know." She stood up and put an arm around her shoulders.

Eme leaned into Anne's embrace and wrapped an arm around her tiny waist. "At least I'll be with people who have the same interests," she mumbled. She looked up at the woman, who was more like a mother than a great-grandmother, and pulled away. "You have to convince my parents, GG," she pleaded. "If I can't get away from here this summer, I'll die of boredom." She leaned back into Anne's side, and a frown creased the older woman's forehead as she placed her hand on an envelope inside her pink jacket pocket.

Anne cleared her thoughts, patted Eme's shoulder, and returned to her chair. "I'll do whatever I can to convince them, dear." She paused for a moment at the hopeful look in Eme's eyes and grabbed her hand. "However, you may have to turn on the waterworks if things get dicey."

Shocked at these tactics, Eme raised her head to protest, and then she saw Anne's smile. "I thought you seriously wanted me to cry," she laughed.

Eme froze when Anne squeezed her hand, gazed into her eyes, and in a solemn tone replied, "If you're serious about this, Eme, be ready to do whatever it takes."

"I love the smell of napalm in the morning!" was Bogey's ominous warning.

Eme's House
7:35 P.M. PDT

The sun was dancing on the western horizon, and the cloudy spring sky was awash with brilliant oranges and pinks, by the time Anne and Eme returned to the girl's lavish Malibu home. After thoroughly discussing their story and tactics and researching Southern California college entrance requirements, curriculum, and class schedules, the two felt confident with their elaborate battle plan.

Neatly groomed and attired in her favorite blue silk dress, Eme entered her family's elegant dining room, followed by her great-grandmother. The teen, however, felt somewhat naked without her favorite accessory; part of their strategy called for no computers anywhere in sight—she had even gone so far as to hide the Cybook in her closet. Bogey and Boomer were also tucked away in her room.

"Well, don't you two look lovely this evening," her father commented as he rose from his chair, giving his daughter and Anne the once-over. Eme and GG smiled politely, saying nothing as they proceeded to the chairs Mark had pulled out for them. He turned his head at the approaching footsteps from the kitchen. "How can a bloke get lucky enough to be dining with three such gorgeous ladies?" he continued when his beautiful wife joined them at the long dining room table. She placed a bowl of scalloped potatoes on the silver trivet and smiled at her husband before sitting in the chair Mark had ready for her.

The glorious beams of the setting California sun cast a golden halo on Eme's long curls when she took her seat. Anne winked, and placed her napkin on her lap. The two parents were oblivious to the sly looks passing between the youngest and oldest members of the family.

Toni gave her daughter an approving smile; it had taken only a few seconds for her to notice what was different about her appearance. "It's lovely to see you without that computer glued to your hip, darling," she commented, passing the steaming vegetable platter to her daughter.

Eme smiled at her mother, took the platter, and said nothing.

"Does that silent smile indicate the possibility of a new hobby or summer project you're about to spring on us this evening?" her father inquired, grinning at Eme and Anne.

The smile and silence continued.

Toni and Mark looked from Anne to Eme and back again with confusion on both of their faces. The last of the sun disappeared below the straight line of the blue Pacific horizon along with the last of their patience.

Several drops of chicken Marsala sauce splattered on the snow-white tablecloth when Toni abruptly laid down the serving dish, placing both hands on the table. "OK, enough of this silence, young lady; you're up to something, and if I'm not mistaken, my grandmother has something to do with it!" Toni and Mark stared expectantly across the table.

Eme and Anne grinned. Anne was the first to break the silence. She calmly folded her hands on the table, winked at Eme, and looked innocently at Toni. "We're not up to anything, my darling Antonia. What gives you that idea?"

Mark looked at his wife and back across the table. "Something's up," he stated. "You look like two cats that have just swallowed a whole flock of canaries." His brown eyes flashed and flicked between the coconspirators.

Five more seconds of silence and…"OK, here's our big secret: I met this really cool guy today when GG and I went to the mall!" blurted Eme, grinning at her parents. (This was a lie; the two of them had spent the entire day in Anne's kitchen formulating their subterfuge.) "He's twenty-one and wants to take me to a Flash Bang concert next week—on his motorcycle." She turned a beaming face to her parents.

Two jaws dropped, and one crystal wine glass spilled its burgundy contents across the white linen.

"He's very nice," intoned Anne, trying to control her laughter and mumbling into her napkin, "...once you get past his tattooed face and arms and multiple piercings."

Anne and Eme could barely contain their glee at the complete stunned silence on the other side of the table. Anne kicked Eme as a prompt to remember her next part.

"Oh, and, Dad, he's an actor!" Eme exclaimed with a huge smile.

Her parents recovered from their shocked stupor; Toni began mopping up the spilled wine, and Mark took a deep breath. He pasted a sickly smile on his pale face and squeaked, "Really, honey, TV or movies?"

Anne slowly placed her hand in her maroon jacket pocket and, not taking her eyes from the unfolding drama, silently activated her phone.

Eme moved in for the kill. "He's been in one movie! Let's see, it's called..." she stopped and put a finger to her temple for dramatic effect. "Oh, yeah..." She reached into her pocket and pulled out a small piece of pink paper. She squinted and read, *The Spy Who Came in from the Black Lagoon...*"

"Oh, that's..." began her mother.

Eme looked up and turned the paper over, interrupting. "There's more—let's see, oh yeah, *and Stayed for Dinner.* He and his brothers, Madman and Thor, wrote and produced it, but it hasn't been released, yet." She hastily added, "I know how you and Mom love acting in spy movies, so you'll have lots in common," she grinned. "Maybe we all can be in some movies together; you know how you've always wanted me to forget about technology and get interested in acting. I can't wait for you to meet him!" She stopped for a breath and beamed at her parents who had once again stopped breathing. "Can he come by tomorrow after dinner?" She opened her eyes wide and then held up her index finger. "Better yet, can I invite him *to* dinner? He's a vegetarian."

There it was—the catalyst that galvanized her parents into action. They expelled their collective breath. "We don't think you're ready for dating, sweetheart," stated her mother in a shrill voice, flashing imploring eyes and a grimace at her husband.

"You're not even fifteen!" Her father's face was as crimson as the wine-stained tablecloth.

And right on cue, the phone rang. Eme grinned at GG's timing, and the angry whispers behind her, as she ran into the hallway to answer the call.

"Bruno!" Eme's voice boomed down the hall. "GG Anne and I were just telling my parents all about you." Eme put a hand over her mouth to keep her laughter at bay. "Yes, and they can't wait to meet you!" She could hardly contain herself and needed to cross her legs to keep from wetting her pants. "How about tomorrow?"

I'm not going to make it to the bathroom.

"OK, I'll call you later with details. Me, too! Bye."

Eme slammed down the phone, made a mad dash for the guest bathroom, closed the door, and turned on the fan, laughing herself silly while she relieved her bladder. She couldn't wait to unroll the rest of their plan.

A minute later, she stood outside the dining room, composing herself before making her grand entrance, to discover...an empty room. Stunned, she hurried into the kitchen and spotted her family through the wide expanse of windows, standing by the pool. The deepening glow of the sky was nothing compared to the angry red of her parents' faces. They stormed at her poor great-grandmother. *This wasn't part of the plan.* She started to rush to GG's defense and then noticed the waving hand behind Anne's back, warning her to stay away. Biting her lip, she seated herself on the stool by the breakfast bar to watch the fireworks.

After a few minutes of animated talking, yelling, and arm waving, her parents' body language relaxed, and they smiled.

What is going on now? Eme wondered. Then, there it was—another signal from her great-grandmother. Once more, Eme composed herself, plastered a smile on her face, and walked toward the patio doors. *Here goes nothing!* Opening the slider with a flourish, she advanced on her family.

GG Anne was standing between the house and her parents; all turned toward Eme, huge grins on their faces. "Darling, we were just talking about how fast you're growing up," GG began. Her parents nodded. Anne winked.

"Yes, sweetheart," continued her mom. "We're so proud of all you've accomplished with your lessons—and with your...uh, computer studies," she added with a faltering smile, "and thought you might like to go abroad to a computer camp this summer."

Eme froze. *That definitely was not part of our plan.*

Her father continued the dialogue. "GG has been telling us about this wonderful technical school in Switzerland." He nodded at the two women and added, "We were wondering if you'd like to enroll in their summer classes."

Anne moved slowly behind Eme's parents and nodded emphatically. Eme finally caught on to this unexpected development in their well-thought-out strategy and managed to close her gaping mouth. "Uh, sure, but isn't this rather sudden?" She gathered her courage and walked forward to face them, searching her great-grandmother's eyes for some clue about this detour in their plans.

"We know how much you loved studying computer programming during your last summer break; we thought you would really enjoy attending a school with kids who share your affinity for technology." Her father smiled at her.

Eme's head swiveled from one smiling face to another as they unveiled this wild idea. "What do you say, sweetheart?" continued her mother. "We wouldn't be far away, either; our location shoot is on Gibraltar and some remote islands in the Mediterranean, on and off, for most of the summer; we could meet you on a weekend or two."

Eme was stunned at this totally unexpected turn of events. Why hadn't GG told her about this school earlier? In fact, how and when did she even learn about it? "What about GG?" she blurted. *What am I doing?* She couldn't blow this fabulous opportunity; however, she also couldn't bear to leave her beloved great-grandmother here by herself.

Eme's parents turned to face Anne who raised her hands and replied, "Don't worry about me, darlings; I have plenty to keep myself occupied while you're away." She gave Eme a pointed look and shook her head when her parents whirled around at their daughter's next words.

"Why can't you come with me, GG?"

Anne rushed to Eme's side, wrapping her in a hug while whispering in her ear, "This isn't the time for the waterworks—trust me, I'll explain later."

That snapped Eme out of her indecision. She surrendered a tiny smile. "What's the name of this school, and when does it start?"

The three adults breathed quiet sighs of relief and grinned at her. "We were just asking GG those very questions when you joined us, honey," explained her father. "Let's go back inside, finish dinner, and then we'll discuss the details."

9:06 P.M. PDT

The lights of Malibu were twinkling through the evening mist by the time Eme's family finished their reheated dinner. She had never known a meal to last so long. Eme gulped her food and tried nudging Anne to follow suit; however, like most things, Time moves slowest when urged to do the opposite, so she bit her tongue and waited for the adults to excuse her from the table.

Once Toni had swallowed the last bite of the raspberry sorbet in her crystal dish, the teenager established a table-clearing, kitchen-cleaning speed record.

So engrossed in their own summer plans were her parents, that they hadn't once mention summer school, taking little notice of their daughter's anxiety. Therefore, when Anne and Eme quietly took their leave, neither of them commented.

Up the stairs and into Eme's bedroom, the coconspirators fled. Once inside, Anne closed and locked the door. Eme retrieved her computer from the walk-in closet, and joined Boomer, Bogey and her great-grandmother by the small desk next to her bed. "No wire hangers!" squawked Bogey.

"That's right, old boy—plastic only for this girl!" Eme chuckled, scratched his head, and bent down to receive a kiss from Boomer. She then set down the computer, flipped up the top, rebooted, and turned to Anne. "OK, GG, what's the name of this school?" she asked, rubbing her hands together, eager to begin her search for the miraculous school.

Anne answered her with a shrug and a grin.

Eme's eyebrows disappeared under her curly bangs. She was at a loss for words and sat down on the corner of her bed. Anne burst out laughing at the startled look on the teen's face and sat down next to her, wrapping her in her arms.

"After you left to answer the phone, your parents were ready to kill me." Eme peeked up at Anne's face, concern in her blue eyes. She continued, "Your father stormed out of the room with your mother and me in hot pursuit." Anne pulled back and peered into Eme's eyes. "Afraid all the neighbors within a mile-wide radius would call the police, I came up with my brilliant backup plan: an outstanding school in Switzerland. They would have you away from 'Bruno,' and you would have your techno-summer! Voila!" Anne blew on her brightly painted fingernails and buffed them on her velvet jacket, an air of smug satisfaction shining in her grey eyes.

"That's it, man, game over, man; game over, man! Game over!" Bogey chirped as Eme hugged her great-grandmother again.

Then she snapped her head up with urgency in her eyes. "We have to find this school you've invented," she declared and bounced off the bed, hastily grabbing the computer from her desk, and resituating herself next to Anne. "OK, where are you, my beautiful Swiss summer school?" she cried.

With the new flurry of activity, Boomer barked at Eme and Anne, and began chasing his tail, while Bogey anxiously danced across his perch, squawking, "Yippe-ki-yay! Get along little doggie!"

Eme and Anne laughed at their antics, and then Eme settled into search mode while Anne, watched over her shoulder, fascinated by the ferocity of the teen's Internet search skills. After a few seconds, the older woman chuckled and reached into the pocket of her jacket, pulled out a light blue and green envelope, and leaned it against the screen of the laptop. Eme looked up, startled by the interruption. She stared at Anne who nodded, urging her to open the envelope. Eme obliged with haste.

One glance at the flyer and registration form, and Eme's mouth gaped, her eyebrows disappeared under her bangs, and she squeaked, "You've had this all this time and didn't tell me!"

Anne smiled at her while Eme read the ad. "It came in the mail this morning; it's from Kevin and Jim. I didn't want to use this unless it was absolutely necessary and, since your parents weren't exactly *thrilled* about you attending a local technical college with Bruno lurking close by..." Eme nodded absently as she continued to read the flyer. "Well, I didn't show you, because... I didn't want you to go so far away for the whole summer." Anne's eyes glistened.

Eme looked up and saw the tears in Anne's eyes. She tossed the letter on the bed and threw her arms around her great-grandmother. "Oh, GG, here I've been so involved in my own drama, I didn't even stop to think how you might be feeling. I'm so sorry—I won't go; I can't leave you all alone."

Anne pulled away from the teenager, wiped her eyes on the lace handkerchief that had been tucked into the cuff of her jacket sleeve, and glared at her. "Now you listen to me, young lady, of course I will miss you terribly, but you will go to this school, and you will have a good time—or else!" she scolded. Then she folded into Eme's arms, and the two females laughed and cried for several seconds, until...

"Women: can't live with 'em and can't live without 'em!"

Eme and Anne broke apart and collapsed on the bed, roaring with laughter.

"Leave it to Bogey to bring us back to reality. Now that we have that all settled, let's find this wonderful school on the Internet," laughed Anne, and she brushed the remaining tears from her eyes.

Several seconds later: "Here it is, GG: St. Bruno's Academy!" Eme smirked at the older woman. "Bruno! I wondered how you'd come up with that ridiculous name." Anne winked at her, and the two sat mesmerized by the photos of the magnificent old school nestled in the snow-covered mountains of the Swiss Alps. A picturesque lake sparkled in the foreground of the college town; it looked too perfect to be real.

Once the introductory video ended, they bent closer to read the information on the Website. "Kevin called me last week and reminded me about their summer exchange program. That's the school he and Jim attended the summer before entering MIT seven years ago. He said that you'd love it, so I asked him to send me the..."

A sudden knock on the door interrupted Anne's explanation. Pulling herself together, Eme got off the bed and opened the door to her parents.

"What's so funny up here? We heard you all the way down by the pool," her father questioned, looking from Eme to Anne.

"Yes, let us in on it! We could use a good laugh after...well, you know..." Toni looked sideways at her husband.

Eme chuckled and wiped her eyes, "Oh, it's just some e-mails that Bailee Sue and Shaelyn sent me," she fibbed. "We were about to come down to talk to you about this school in Switzerland." She reached down, winked at Anne, and picked the computer up from the duvet. "Let's go, GG!" She gave her a hand up from the bed and grinned.

Anne wiped away a few tears, gave a small chuckle, and followed her family down the stairs, Boomer bringing up the rear.

As the bedroom door slowly closed, they heard Bogey's parting words. "Good morning, and in case I don't see ya, good afternoon, good evening, and good night."

Brienz Switzerland
8:02 A.M. CEST (CENTRAL EUROPE SUMMER TIME)

"We have an agreement, and you know what happens to people who disappoint me, yes?"

Pause.

"I don't want to hear your lame excuses; get him soon, or suffer the consequences from my associates."

Click.

Malibu
Tuesday, June 2, 2015
10:56 P.M. PDT

Eme stroked Boomer's soft fur as she gazed at the peaceful view from her hilltop home and sighed. The Pacific Ocean, sparkling beneath the full moon, was indifferent to her concerns. Why did she want to leave such a beautiful place? More importantly, she'd be leaving GG, Boomer, and Bogey. She looked down at her two-year-old buddy and kissed the top of his head. He looked up at her with his big black eyes and licked her cheek. She knew that her great-grandmother and her beloved pets would be just fine while she and her parents were gone; however, a little voice in the back of her mind kept bugging her, nagging her to rethink this trip that she'd be taking in a week—the day before her fifteenth birthday, to be exact.

She shivered as a sudden cool breeze swept across the patio. Fastening the top two buttons of her USC sweater, she shook her head to clear the nagging voice and thought back to the previous day's events. Her great-grandmother's plan, although not quite the plan they had originally hatched, had succeeded beyond their wildest expectations.

St. Bruno's Technical Academy, her soon-to-be home for the next two months, was a minor miracle. All she had wanted was to attend a local technical college a mile down the road; instead, she would fly halfway around the world to a prestigious school in Switzerland. *Thank you, Bruno!* How her parents had missed the significance of the name just added to her and GG's delight.

They'd had a huge laugh over the whole turn of events that morning once they'd found some private time at Anne's house. She'd called Kevin and was reassured that she'd have the time of her life and learn technological wonders she never dreamed possible. He was even jealous that he was too old to return as a student himself.

"Some of the top software designers have been students and instructors there, including many from your favorite, Amazemail."

"Seriously? Amazemail programmers may be instructing there?"

"I don't know if they'll be there this summer, but they've been there in the past, including yours truly—two years ago. Maybe Jim and I'll surprise you and meet you there as instructors—just to keep an eye on you," he teased. She groaned but was excited about the prospect of actually meeting top designers in her chosen profession.

Now, here she was dreading—no, not really dreading—*reevaluating* her plans. *Oh, grow up, Eme. It's only two months.* She would meet kids who actually knew more about computers than how to e-mail and add blogs to *Top Topic*. She may even have some fun hiking those fabulous mountains or boating on that glorious lake, and who knew what other adventures awaited? Besides, her mom and dad wouldn't be too far away for most of her term. *What could possibly go wrong?*

After several more minutes of arguing with herself, she was convinced that she had put all her doubts and fears to rest. She and Boomer made their way into the family room, where her parents were arguing over a reel of their latest movie. Her attempt to slip by unnoticed failed, and she knew they would drag her into another nitpicky debate about costumes, dialogue, and anything else associated with the film. Sure enough…

"Sweetheart, you're just in time to settle a little disagreement about my hairstyle in *The Muddy Marauder*," her mother cajoled, spreading her arms wide to enfold her daughter in a hug. Eme shuddered at the thought of how this discussion would end. Stealing a look at her father's frown from over her mother's shoulder, she decided a direct approach was her best and most expeditious option.

She pulled away from her mother and pointed at the frozen scene projected on the immense screen. Her beautiful mother was unrecognizable; her entire body, including her long blonde hair, was drenched in mud, blood, and swamp grass. "Since you were in the jungle during the monsoon season, Mom, how could you even call what they did to your hair a hairstyle?"

Mark nodded in agreement and spread his arms toward his two favorite women. "See, Toni, Eme agrees with me: you can't be expected to look like a—well, you know, a beauty queen during any of those jungle scenes!"

While Toni studied her muddy appearance on the ten-foot-tall screen and pondered their words, Eme took the opportunity to escape her parents' arms and inch closer to the hallway. Her father, thankfully, gave her the cue to leave while he wrapped both of his arms around his wife. Eme did not need to be told twice; she and Boomer were up the stairs and ensconced behind her locked bedroom door in ten seconds flat.

"Here's Johnny!" Bogey welcomed their sudden appearance in the room. Eme walked over to stroke her pet's beautiful feathers.

"Honestly, my parents' whole existence revolves around their careers," she announced to her pets while getting ready for bed. She couldn't believe that it actually used to annoy her. With a squawk and a woof in reply, Eme was satisfied that Bogey and Boomer agreed with her.

Now she thanked her lucky "movie" stars that their own lives took too much time for them to get involved in hers. GG Anne's guidance was all she needed; her great-grandmother truly understood her and wanted Eme to do whatever made Eme happy. In fact, it was Anne, who hated the name Elaine Mea, and had nicknamed her Eme before her first birthday, much to her parents' dismay. Anne was the only one who found the joining of the first letters of her first and middle name a clever idea. When Eme was old enough to understand the name change, she was grateful for her great-grandmother's creativity. They both positively crowed when they set up her latest e-mail account with eme_please@cybersleuth.net.

That thought reminded her that she needed to buy her great-grandmother a new notebook and printer before she left for Switzerland. She also needed to set her up with a high speed account and e-mail address—gg_eme@cybersleuth.net would be perfect. Eme flipped the lid of her pink Cybook and winked at the iris scanner; it awakened and purred in response. She launched her shopping network, and scanned in; ten minutes later a spiffy new printer and laptop with all the features (including an Amazemail 3DX laser pen scanner and holoport) had been ordered and would be in transit to Anne's home by morning. One more stop to Kevin and Jim's company website, cybersleuth.net, and her GG Anne had a new high speed account, modem and wireless router, set for installation in two days.

It was midnight before Eme finished her to-do list. She snuggled into the soft cotton sheets, Boomer in a ball beside her, Bogey on his perch, head tucked under his wing. All thoughts of her busy week ahead were pushed back to the far reaches of her mind; therefore, the dreams of fiddler crabs and airplane crashes, that kept her tossing and turning all night, were surprising. Eme laughed them off the next day. *How silly to worry about these same ridiculous nightmares.*

CHAPTER FOUR
SO, SO LONG!

Los Angeles/Atlanta
Tuesday, June 9, 2015
7:00 P.M. PDT/10:00 P.M. EDT

"Any sign of a breakthrough?

"Nothing, yet—same old routine: he thinks he has it, and then he revamps the entire sequence."

"Well, we can't wait much longer—too much heat on the other side to get this done before the kid takes flight."

"What can we do? It's a process."

"Process this: you move tomorrow, and it had better be done before I arrive!"

Click.

Malibu
7:03 P.M. PDT

"Surprise!

How her parents had pulled this last-minute birthday/going-away/end-of-lessons party together, without rousing her suspicions, was beyond her! However, here it was, and here they were: Bailee, Shaelyn, Linda, Alison, Judy, Patty, and, *oh, no*—a frown briefly crossed her brow when she spotted the much-despised Cynthia in the crowd of well-wishers.

She shrugged her shoulders and smiled, realizing that her mother must not have received the memo about their falling out over—whatever—she had forgotten, anyway.

Bogey must have noticed her brief frown, because he greeted her from his perch in the breakfast nook, echoing Eme's exact feelings: "Hang on; it's going to be a bumpy ride!"

Eme smiled at him and plunged into the crowd of her teenage friends while her family and a few of their friends stood off to the side, smiling at the brilliant fifteen-year-old.

10:55 P.M. PDT

As the last of the partygoers bid her good-night and good luck, Eme closed the stained glass door and smiled. It certainly had been fun to see them all one last time before her departure. Kevin and Jim Burke had given her one of their recent programs on bridging the silicone divide, plus a flash drive containing tips on how to make the most of the St. Bruno curriculum and information about places to visit and things to do on the weekends. She had even made up with the not-so-awful-after-all Cynthia. After a tenuous beginning, they had shared a good laugh over the fact that neither one of them could remember what had caused their rift.

She smiled and sashayed into the kitchen, where her parents were cleaning up the party mess. Surveying the scene, she snickered at her father sneaking another piece of carrot cake behind his wife's back. Boomer was licking up the crumbs, as they fell on the blue limestone tile floor, while Bogey danced on his perch, chanting "Feed me! Feed me!"

Eme chuckled again at her wacky family. Not wanting to bother them, get roped into cleanup duty, or witness the argument that was sure to ensue once her mother turned around and caught her dad cheating on his diet, she silently slipped through the patio doors to join her great-grandmother by the pool.

Anne folded Eme into her arms and gently kissed her on the cheek. "So, are you all ready for your big trip?" she asked, stepping back to survey her great-granddaughter's smiling face.

"Ha, I haven't even started to pack; I was going to do that tonight, but..." she made a sweeping gesture toward her parents who were now in a heated discussion in the kitchen over the piece of carrot cake in her dad's hand. She laughed at their predictability and turned back to Anne. "Don't get me wrong, GG, I loved the party. Jim and Kevin gave me a pep talk about St. Bruno's, and I even made up with Cynthia—go figure!"

The two sat down, side by side, on the soft blue chaise. The older woman grinned, shook her head, and caressed the teenager's cheek. "Do you want me to help you get your things together tonight?"

"Thanks, GG, but I'm going to bed. It won't take me long tomorrow morning; I'm not taking that much, and Bailee and Shae are stopping by to help."

Anne reached into the pocket of her green cotton jacket and extracted something printed on a sheet of pale blue paper.

Eme cocked an eye at her and asked, "What's this?"

Anne looked into the redhead's brilliant blue eyes and winked. "This is from St. Bruno's." She handed it to Eme who quickly scanned the information her great-grandmother had printed on her personalized stationery. "It arrived today in my e-mail to confirm the enrollment application we e-mailed them a week ago. You'll find the name and picture of the woman who is to chaperone you and a few other American students to Switzerland."

Defiance replaced Eme's smile. "What chaperone? I don't need a chaperone!" Then curiosity replaced defiance. "What American kids?"

"I thought that would get your attention," she laughed. "Evidently there will be two other girls and two boys."

Eme laughed and exclaimed, "Boys! I bet you haven't shown this to Mom and Dad!" She tapped the letter on Anne's head. "Is there anyone named Bruno attending this school?" She smirked.

They both chuckled at the absurdity of that question. "Not that I know of; however, as I said before, I haven't written my will, yet." The girl and the woman roared with laughter, drawing attention from the kitchen.

They rose from the lounge, great-grandmother and great-granddaughter, embracing one another under a starlit sky.

Slowly, they walked through the wide glass doors into the house, past the bickering movie stars, Eme's fabulous cache of birthday presents in the living room, and into the ornate hallway. Anne headed toward the front door. "Good-night, sweetheart," she said. "You have a big day ahead of you tomorrow!"

Eme glanced over her shoulder toward the living room. "Thank you again, GG, for the awesome moped. I'm sorry I won't have time to test it out before I leave tomorrow. How did you know it was just what I wanted?" she asked, with a mischievous grin.

Anne threw her head back and laughed, "Ha! Ha!" Then she leveled her gaze at the smiling redhead. "Don't give me that innocent look, missy; you can't kid an old kidder; I've seen more than one of those *Motor Scooter* magazine ads floating around your house and mine for the last two months." She laughed again and wrapped her arms around her blushing great-granddaughter. "You'll have plenty of time to test-drive—what did you name it?"

Eme peeked at her. "Maud."

"Oh, yes, short for Marauder, right—something to do with your parents' movie, *The Muddy Marauder*." Eme laughed at her perceptiveness and nodded her head. "I like it, but I don't want to see that beautiful, custom pink paint job splattered with mud, young lady." Eme snickered and nodded again before she left Anne's embrace. She kissed her beloved great-grandmother on the cheek. Anne opened the door and stepped out into the balmy, starlit night.

"See you bright and early, GG," Eme called. Without a backward glance, Anne raised her hand in farewell, and Eme closed the door quietly behind her. She glanced again at the shocking pink moped, with its huge pink polka dot bow wrapped around the handlebars, and the temporary license tacked to the back of the long black leather seat. Taking one step toward the scooter, she noticed that a remote control door opener was already installed and thought, *one spin around the neighborhood wouldn't hurt, and then I can park it in the garage.* She glanced at the paper in her hand, realized all the work she still had ahead of her, and turned back to the moped; she patted the seat and whispered, "Sorry, Maud, we can get better acquainted in two months."

Eme turned away from her scooter and trudged up the curving staircase, reading her letter and becoming familiar with the picture of Mrs. Murphy, her assigned protector during the next day's transatlantic flight to a new land—a new adventure.

LAX Runway
Wednesday, June 10, 2015
4:15 P.M. PDT

Pandemonium!
  Exasperation!
  Discombobulation!
As Eme reclined in the window seat of the Stargate jetliner, several minutes before take-off, replaying in her mind the hours

that preceded this moment of tranquility, she couldn't decide which term was most fitting. With a smile and a sigh, she chose all three: one to describe each of the well-meaning, crazed relatives who had been responsible for her departure.

6:03 A.M. PDT

Pandemonium: her mother.

Bailee and Shae stopped by to help Eme pack, move Maud to the garage, and wish her Bon Voyage one last time. When the girls reentered the house from the garage, it was all they could do to keep from laughing out loud: Eme's mother, in mudpack and rollers, was dashing from room to room, first seizing and then discarding pieces of clothing, going-away presents, cosmetics, and sports paraphernalia, until the entire house looked like a department store fire sale.

"Eme, have you packed your jacket? Where is your tennis racket? Oh, and don't forget the book of poetry and silk scarf Shaelyn and Bailee Sue gave you last night."

"Of all the gin joints in town, she happens to walk into mine," earned Bogey a treat from her dad and a thumbs-up from three teenagers and one great-grandmother.

6:47 A.M. PDT

Exasperation: her father.

While her mother was in full combat mode, her father paced by the front door, glancing at his watch, and exclaiming every few minutes:

"Toni, do you realize the time?"

"Have you any idea what the traffic will be like this time of day?"

"You do understand that the security lines will be out the terminal doors!"

"Skis! Are you kidding, Toni—it's *summer*, for heaven's sake! *Women!*"

"One's too many, and a hundred's not enough!" earned Bogey another treat from her dad and glares from five females.

7:43 A.M. PDT

Discombobulation: her GG Anne.

Eme walked her friends to the gate that led to the woodland path bordering her parents' estate. They hugged a final good-bye and Eme turned to walk home. After all the drama of the morning, her family was miraculously ahead of schedule.

Halfway to the L.A. airport, Mark reminded Anne to give Eme her ticket. "Mark, you didn't give *me* the ticket!" was her great-grandmother's surprised response.

Eme thought her dad had surely sustained whiplash when he jerked up his head to look in the rearview mirror at his wife's grandmother; however, before he could retort, Anne sucked in her breath and shouted, "Oh, no, just a minute, I do remember laying it on the kitchen counter when the phone rang this morning."

At 7:45 a.m., her father swerved the black sedan onto the next on-ramp and beat a hasty retreat toward home.

"Insanity runs in my family; it practically gallops," were Bogey's welcoming words to the whole family when they stormed into the kitchen in search of the forgotten ticket, which Eme found sitting on the counter next to his perch. No one gave Bogey a treat, but Eme blew kisses to both of her pets before she flew out the door.

Anne apologized all the way home and back through the murderous traffic; everyone believed Eme would surely miss the 10:30 a.m. flight. Ironically, thanks to Bruno (this time in the form of an upgraded tropical storm), several of the inbound planes from Florida were delayed, and Eme and her family found themselves with hours to spare.

Finally, after a long, tedious afternoon spent in the airport's VIP lounge, Eme's flight was announced. With more apologies for harsh words of retribution, tears of sorrow and farewell, and reminders to look for Mrs. Murphy in Atlanta (but to keep a low profile with her dark glasses in place at all times), Eme boarded Destiny Airline's Vestige 645 Stargate to Atlanta International Airport—the first leg of her journey to Switzerland, and her first trip away from her family.

CHAPTER FIVE
OH, NO!

Destiny Flight 44
Wednesday, June 10, 2015
4:20 P.M. PDT/7:20 P.M. EDT

"He's changed the name to what?
    Pause
    Why?"
    Pause
    "But it's still the same program? And you've got all the equipment?"
    Pause
    "OK, it's about time! See you in a few hours."

10:45 P.M. EDT
Exhausted from the party, her sleepless night, and the harried trip to the airport, Eme had slept beneath her sunglasses most of the way to Atlanta.

A half hour before their scheduled landing, Pilot Rick Calonico's smooth baritone voice awakened her with a harsh warning: "Ladies and gentlemen, the remaining ride into Atlanta promises to be turbulent. Please return to your seats, fasten your seat belts, stow your gear under the seat in front of you, and return all seats to their upright positions. These are only precautions; Tropical Storm Bruno seems to have changed course again, intensified, and is approaching Atlanta. If necessary, we'll also change course and head up the coast to South Carolina; however, all indications so far put us into Atlanta just ahead of the storm. We'll keep you updated as we approach the airport."

The passengers seemed to be taking this announcement in stride. Eme and a lanky teenage boy, sporting a blond crew cut, and sitting across the aisle from her, looked around nervously. She removed her glasses; they locked wide eyes and grinned at one another.

"Is this your first time flying?" Eme asked the boy.

"No, but it's the last time—at least after my return trip to L.A.!" He paused while Eme pocketed her mini disguise and unbuckled her seat belt to slide over to the aisle seat. "I didn't want to spend a hot, muggy summer in Atlanta with my mother and her punk rocker husband," he continued, "but my dad's got a hot new wife, and they needed some 'alone time' to get better acquainted." He wrinkled his freckled nose and grimaced. "*Ha!* So here I am, about to die, just so they can christen every room of the house without an audience." He looked straight at her with twinkling blue eyes and continued, "But they'd better stay out of my room...I've got it booby-trapped!" he finished with a wicked smile and a wink. "How about you?"

Eme wasn't quite sure how to respond to this boy's sarcastic outburst about personal family business; however, she leaned across the aisle and was now only a foot away when she answered, "No, but it's my first time flying alone. I..." she hesitated, patting the sunglasses in her pocket. She paused again, threw caution to the wind, and finished, "I'm Eme Venture, by the way."

The boy stopped for an instant, cocked his head, and studied her face. Then he shrugged and answered with a cheesy grin, "Glad to meet you, Eme Venture By-the-Way. My friends call me No...No Henderson. Are you as adventurous as your name implies?" He stuck out his hand and wagged his eyebrows.

Eme blushed and cocked her head at the intriguing nickname. "No...No, I'm not adventurous at all—rather shy and reserved." She laughed and gripped his large, warm hand in return, forming a new friendship.

They were in the middle of their handshake, grinning at each other, when the plane hit the first of the promised turbulence, startling Eme. She lost her grip on No's hand and fell to the floor.

"Are you all right?" the boy gasped once the plane had stabilized. He quickly unbuckled his seat belt to help the red-faced girl return to her seat. A furious blonde flight attendant rushed up the aisle at the sounds of the distressed passengers. All eyes were now concentrated on the commotion caused by the two teenagers.

"What do you think you're doing?" she reprimanded No in a fierce whisper as he helped Eme to her seat. "You were warned to stay seated and to keep your belts tightened; you could have been seriously injured!"

Eme flushed, but No stood his ground, returning the woman's glare. "Eme's seat belt wasn't fully fastened, and she fell because of the air pocket. I was just helping her get resituated." He turned back to Eme as she strapped herself in, testing the security of the belt. He stretched to an imposing six foot three. "OK, bedlam, panic, and disorder—my work here is done," he sneered at the flight attendant, wiping his hands together, and returned to his seat.

The boy's vehemence stunned the woman, so she turned her steely gaze on Eme. "You've got to stay seated and securely fastened; we're not finished with..."

Eme was certain she knew what the woman's next words would have been, had the plane not plunged two thousand feet into the second, and much deeper, air pocket. The drop forced the attendant and No, who had not had time to secure his seat belt, skidding down the aisle, landing with a thud against the bulkhead jump seats in a tangle of arms and legs. Cabin lights flickered, oxygen masks descended, passengers screamed in terror. No slowly rose from the floor, blood streaming from a gash over his right eye, cradling an injured right arm.

The flight attendant wasn't moving.

Eme unfastened her seat belt and was about to rush to her friend's aid when an older woman in front of her grabbed her by the arm. "Sit down, young lady, and stay put! This wouldn't have happened had you followed instructions," she hissed.

Chagrined, Eme did as the woman bid. Passengers from the first row rushed forward to help the disabled pair; however, a male flight attendant admonished them to return to their seats.

"Help up front!" he called to the attendants at the rear of the plane; but, before they could comply with his request, the plane hit several more air pockets, tossing No and the entire crew to the floor; chaos ensued inside the storm-tossed plane.

"Ladies and gentlemen..." The deep, mellow voice of the clueless pilot was barely audible over the pandemonium on the other side of the cockpit door. "It's been a bumpy ride; nevertheless, we're making our appro...what's that commotion?"

Suddenly the cockpit door slammed open, revealing the mayhem to the horrified copilot. Eme watched as the tall, dashing redhead, green eyes blazing, rushed to the aid of the closest flight attendant, shouting at the passengers who were desperately trying to help the others. "Return to your seats; secure yourselves for landing!"

In his rush to help the injured, the copilot had not closed the cockpit door; it swung violently, becoming unhinged, as the Vestige 645 Stargate fought against the crosswinds of the tropical storm. Wild-eyed passengers clung to the seats in front of them; some hung on to the dazed crew members who were sitting or lying in a heap on the floor at their feet. The flushed copilot sat next to his unconscious flight attendant, and No, pale and bleeding from his head wound, could do nothing but sit and brace his body with his long legs against the empty crew seat in front of him.

Eme prayed that the storm-battered plane would make it to the ground without further injury. She held her breath. Through the rain-streaked window, she could see the airport and emergency vehicles, bright lights rotating, speeding toward the runway. No one dared breathe as the ground rose to meet them. A wobble, a thud, a screech, a collective sigh of relief, a cheer; they were down; it was almost over. Eme watched, fascinated, as the rescue crews raced the aircraft to its final destination.

"Ladies and gentlemen, due to the injuries suffered by a passenger and crew member during our flight, and to expedite their immediate evacuation, I've asked the emergency crew to meet us on the tarmac away from the congestion at the terminal. As soon as the injured are off-loaded, we will taxi in. Even though the plane will be stationary, I insist that you remain seated and firmly belted. On behalf of the Destiny organization, this is your copilot, Dean Brody. I apologize for the inconvenience. It is now 11:15 p.m. Eastern Daylight Time. We welcome you to Atlanta and wish you a pleasant stay."

"A pleasant stay! Is he kidding? Actually, how could it get any worse?" Eme mumbled, but she decided to play it safe and tightened her seat belt.

The inconvenienced passengers continued their grumbling while Eme sat back in her seat, watching a pretty brunette flight attendant examine No's arm, splint it, and then clean and bandage his head wound. She situated him in one of the jump seats fastened to the bulkhead. He looked so young and vulnerable with pillows behind his head; his bright blue eyes peered at her over the edge of a light blue Destiny blanket. Slowly, pulling down the corner of the covering with his uninjured hand, he gave her a cheeky grin. She responded with an enormous smile and was about to wink at him when a flash of light outside the window caught her eye. By the time she turned her head, it had disappeared.

"Attention, ladies and gentlemen, we have just been informed that our plans have changed again and we will be taxiing to the ter…"

Boom!

The plane shook, lights flickered, and the cabin filled with cries of alarm. Beyond the turmoil inside the aircraft, Eme witnessed several more flashes of lightning, followed by even louder crashes of thunder. The lights continued to flicker, and a few claustrophobic passengers were out of their seats. Dean Brody was still standing next to No when he resumed his now frenzied speech:

"Please, everyone, stay seated and belted. It looks like the hurricane has arrived, and…" The remainder of Captain Brody's speech was quashed by the screaming passengers.

Tweeeeeet! Tweeeeeet! Tweeeeeeeeeeeet!

Instant silence.

Eme's head swiveled in the direction of the whistle, and she was rewarded with a kink in her neck. A burly gray-haired man in a blue polyester suit, flashing a badge, and knocking people out of his way, marched down the aisle to the front of the plane. Grabbing the microphone from the surprised copilot, he announced:

"Gunter Dexter, CIA, here. I've commandeered this plane, and the next person out of his or her seat will be arrested under FAA Regulation 341A. Now *sit down* and *shut up!*" This was punctuated by another flash of lightning and rumble of thunder. Several people were ready to scream again, but the look on Agent Dexter's rage-filled face kept the cabin silent.

"That's better!" he growled. "We're stuck here for a few more minutes, so remain calm and stay in your seats!" He smirked and then flashed a wide, toothy grin, the warmth of which was not evident in his beady brown eyes. "You don't want to see me get angry, now...do ya?" he finished with a sneer.

The passengers slumped in their seats; many were grumbling, while the rest were looking out of the windows at the fury of the full-fledged hurricane. Eme watched tree branches and other debris skid across the runway, propelled by Bruno.

With a flourish, Gunter returned the microphone to the nervous copilot, nearly losing his balance due to the severely rocking plane; then he plopped down in the jump seat next to a bemused No.

"Thank you for your help, Agent Dexter..." No began.

"No problem, son; you can call me Gun—happy to be of service." The smile he flaunted at No, Dean Brody, and the passengers exaggerated the deep scar that ran down the right side of his face, but again, there was no warmth in his eyes. Eme shivered. There was something about this man she didn't trust. No, on the other hand, seemed thoroughly entertained by the brash government agent.

"Yes, uh, thank you, Agent Dexter. We're all grateful for your, uh, assistance," the copilot continued. He fiddled with the microphone, stalling for time, pondering his next instructions. "Uh, well, as I started to say, there's been a change in planes—er, plans; we are now headed for the terminal and should be moving soon, so, uh, stay calm." He flashed a nervous smile and took his seat next to No—as far away from Agent Dexter as the confines of the airliner would allow. Gun plastered another one of his fake grins onto his flabby face.

The plane continued its rocking and rolling, but it did not begin its journey to the terminal. An ominous silence fell over the eerie tableau, with Bruno supplying the background music. Every cough or sneeze caused passengers to flinch and glance toward Gun and Dean.

Sirens suddenly blared through the howling category one hurricane; the tension in the plane seemed to relax. Eme could see the lights of the emergency rescue unit approach the left side of the plane; the original plans were back in place as evidenced by the uninformed copilot's red face.

Rotating lights continued flashing while copilot Brody approached the door, battling to open it against the relentless wind. He lowered the stairs and waited until two drenched male medics entered the cabin—followed by Bruno's wind and water. The lead man carried a long red stretcher. After a whispered conversation between the medics and copilot, they advanced toward No and the semiconscious flight attendant. The roar of the wind drowned out No's response to the medic's question, but his body language made it quite clear that the teenager wanted no help and would not be leaving the airplane. Eme giggled when No smiled and winked at her. The medic shrugged and continued to place a brace around the flight attendant's neck. The two men carefully placed the still body on the stretcher, strapping her securely. They made their way down the steps, struggling against the torrential rain and seventy-mile-an-hour wind gusts, to the waiting ambulance.

No and Gun continued their conversation. The teenager pointed toward Eme and made a few more comments; Gun sobered, asked another question which No answered, and the agent's face paled; he jerked his head toward the girl.

Unexpectedly, as the copilot was about to close the cabin door, Gun jumped up from his seat, grabbed a surprised No by the uninjured arm, and forcibly escorted him to the door and off the plane. He glared one last time over his shoulder at the redhead and disappeared through the door. Eme watched, horrified, as No, protesting all the way, was dragged down the stairs and loaded into the back of the ambulance with the paramedics and the injured woman. The doors closed, and with sirens blaring, the flashing lights disappeared into the raging storm toward the terminal.

"What was all that about?" she heard the old biddy in front of her ask her companion.

"Maybe the kid's a spy!" an elderly male voice replied. Laughter followed this remark, and Eme sank down in her seat, fear for her friend bringing tears to her eyes, anxiety about her obvious involvement knotting her stomach.

After several agonizing minutes, the plane began to move. "Ladies and gentlemen, thank you for your patience. We've been cleared to dock at Gate 34. Estimated time of arrival…"

Crash!

Several people screamed.

The plane shuddered and jerked to a halt. Eme didn't envy the maintenance crew's job of cleaning the seats once this group of passengers departed the plane.

"Ladies and gentlemen," boomed the voice of the pilot, "not to worry, a large tree branch has become lodged under our wheels. The maintenance crew will have us on our way again in a few minutes."

Why did I think this trip was such a brilliant idea? Eme asked herself. *I could be home right now, with GG Anne, Bogey, and Boomer. I wouldn't even complain if my parents made me re-watch all of their old movies.* She sighed. *I hope No's all right.*

Several minutes later, the maintenance truck arrived to rescue the hobbled airliner. Eme watched as four men and one woman labored against the thirty-foot branch of eucalyptus and the hurricane force winds of Bruno. One of the men grabbed the radio, presumably to call for more help, as she couldn't see how so few could possibly remove the debris without a chain saw or a few more hands.

As if he'd heard her thoughts, or was the recipient of the radio message, the cockpit door flew open, knocking it off its last hinge, and Rock Hudson emerged; at least Eme thought he was a dead ringer for the 1950's movie star, and she was surprised that Doris Day wasn't right behind him. She chuckled at the thought. He relocated the disabled door to the galley, then turned a dazzling smile on his passengers, gave a small wave that said, "All's well, because *I'm* now in charge," and made his way to the jump seats. He whispered to Dean Brody while two flight attendants approached from the rear of the jetliner. The noise level escalated as several male passengers rose from their seats, attempting to get the attention of the conclave at the front of the plane.

Once again Dean announced on the microphone, "Ladies and gentlemen, so that we don't waste any more time calling for extra help with the tree removal, we..." he indicated the small group, "will exit the plane and assist the ground crew. No, thank you," he indicated to the passengers who were standing, "thank you, but we won't ask for any passenger help, so please remain seated and securely belted; this won't take long." Relief was evident on the faces of some of the volunteers as they returned to their seats, secure in the knowledge that they had shown their bravery simply by offering their assistance.

With that, a flight attendant, once again, opened the door to the fury of the wind and rain and deployed the emergency stairs. Eme watched the crew battle the forces of Bruno while they filed out of the crippled plane. She was fascinated by their speed and competence as they successfully wrestled the enormous impediment away from the trapped wheels. The moment it was clear, Hurricane Bruno urged the branch to continue its journey across the tarmac, the median, and an adjacent runway, where it ended its destructive journey smashed into the side of a hangar. There was a collective sigh from all on board. Eme watched with bated breath while the tree-removal contingent reentered the plane. Cheers greeted their arrival, and the dripping, disheveled heroes smiled at their charges. "Rock Hudson" and Dean Brody returned to the cockpit, and the flight attendants resumed their stations.

"Without further delays, we should be docked in five minutes," the baritone voice of the pilot crackled through the overhead speakers. "Thank you again for your patience." More cheers followed this announcement, and the conversation level of the cabin returned to a happier timbre as the aircraft resumed its slow journey behind the maintenance crew to Gate 34.

Eme grinned when she thought about seeing No again. She couldn't wait to talk to him once they were inside the terminal. She wondered what he had said to Agent Gun for him to glare at her, and then suddenly yank him from the plane. *My parents would have loved to star in this soap opera,* Eme mused while she watched the lights of the terminal come into view through the rain-streaked window. *How much more drama could possibly occur on this trip?*

She would ponder the irony of this thought many times over the next few days, beginning with the mysterious disappearance of No and CIA Agent, Gunter Dexter.

CHAPTER SIX

ALL THE WORLD'S A STAGE

Atlanta Airport
Thursday, June 11, 2015
12:02 A.M. EDT

"You've got him?" The CIA agent lurked in the hallway outside the airport infirmary and gruffly whispered into his cell phone. He paused for an answer, and then satisfied by the reply, drew in a deep breath and continued. "We've got another situation—one that might throw a monkey wrench into everything or solve a major problem." He paused again for the reply and then cut in, "No, it's not from their end; it's here. We've got to bring down the transatlantic flight on the island."

Pause.

Speaking in a louder whisper, he said, "Quit the theatrics; we'll just tell them it's a possible security breach—it's in our best interest to bring it down.

Pause.

"No, Bruno's not headed that way; in fact, we may have a delay here. Where are you?"

Pause.

"Well, hurry up; I don't know how long the airport's going to remain open and communications are shaky. We've got to try to get out of here, now. I'll meet you by the plane in five minutes, and we'll decide then if we go or stay. And make sure he's totally out, and out of sight, by the time I get there; we don't want..." Agent Gun didn't finish as his call was dropped; he snapped his phone closed, pocketed it, and stalked into the infirmary to collect his prisoner.

12:51 A.M. EDT

"This is a security announcement: All outbound passengers are reminded that bags and suitcases must not be left unattended at any time. Do not accept any packages from unknown persons. Hartsfield-Jackson Atlanta thanks you for your cooperation. Have a safe flight."

Although all flights had been canceled, the public address system chimed the obligatory message for the third time since Eme had entered the terminal. Tired of her confinement aboard the airplane, she had spent much of the time since her brief meeting with her chaperone and three of her traveling companions wandering alone through the airport food court. Nothing tempted her, so she decided to sit down in one of the many generic airport seats: molded plastic, bolted to the floor, complete with a thin, worn hardboard-backed cushion. It was next to impossible to sit comfortably, yet Eme saw many travel-weary passengers, using their carry bags as pillows, laid out along the belts of chairs. A glance at her watch confirmed that it was late: nearly one a.m.—ten o'clock in California—her bed-time; however, it didn't appear as if she would be getting to sleep any time soon.

Mrs. Murphy had told them all to remain near Gate 14 until she found her wayward charge—some boy named Rafael Romero—and already Eme was growing tired of the situation. The turbulent flight into Atlanta and ensuing drama of their docking had drained her of any desire to board another airplane; Switzerland seemed more than half a world away. Still, it would be fantastic upon arrival; St. Bruno's promised a world of technological delights and experiences that the community colleges back home couldn't hope to match. A tingle of excitement vibrated through Eme's body. It was that excitement that had made parting from GG Anne, Bogey, and Boomer just bearable.

She had tried calling her parents as soon as she'd entered the terminal to let them know that she had arrived safely; how-ever, the phone lines and towers were reported to have gone down when Bruno was upgraded to a category two hurricane a half hour earlier; the storm was also hindering satellite visibility. She'd considered unpacking her laptop and booting it up just for one more glance at the St. Bruno's course list she had stored on her hard drive; however since Mrs. Murphy could return at any minute, and Rafael had already caused enough lost time with-out her adding to the problem, she'd decided against it.

Although, Eme thought, glancing across the concourse, past the food court and retail shops, and out at the rumbling storm clouds over the runway, *that hurricane will keep us here for quite some time since the airport is officially closed to all flights.*

Eme took in a deep breath and slowly exhaled. She consid-ered chatting with the other kids seated nearby, but they had already formed a clique, happily chatting about the flight to Switzerland and the wonders of St. Bruno's Academy while playing games on their tablets. Mrs. Murphy's pretty blonde assistant had just returned from her search for Rafael and was tapping her foot, keeping one eye on the young boy and two girls and one eye on the latest celebrity gossip in her Hollywood Trivia magazine. She assumed there was no hope of conversation there, about St. Bruno's or otherwise.

Eme took another deep breath and exhaled just as slowly. So this was how she would be spending her fifteenth birthday: alone and bored in the international terminal of the Atlanta Airport— and worried about the strange disappearance of No.

She had peeked in through the infirmary door, on her way to her meeting with Mrs. Murphy, but hadn't seen the tall blond teenager, and didn't want to bother anyone to ask about him, assuming he had been taken to a hospital or picked up by his mom. But why had he been escorted so abruptly off the plane by Gun? And what was the meaning behind the agent's menacing stare? Since he was CIA, maybe he had recognized her due to her parents' fame and the much-publicized disappearance of her sister. Maybe not, since she had been out of the public eye for the past ten years, and no one knew her nickname except family and friends. So, why the evil stare? What did he know? And why take it out on No?

She reached in her denim jacket pocket for her glasses and then chuckled—there weren't many passengers who were still awake, let alone interested in her. She patted her pocket, and then wondered if she should check the airport infirmary again. But that would anger Mrs. Murphy when she found her missing. She should have given No her contact information. Shaking her head to clear these thoughts, she decided to boot up her notebook and compose e-mails to her parents and GG Anne; she could send them once the storm cleared.

Just as she flipped up the lid to her Cybook, the public address system chimed in once again. "This is a security

announcement: all outbound passengers are reminded that…"
There was a warble of static and feedback over the system; a
younger voice, male, cut through the announcement: "…There
are more things in heaven and earth, Horatio, than are dreamt
of in your philosophy…" The cool, soft voice of the automated
announcement lady cut back in, "…Hartsfield-Jackson Atlanta
thanks you for your cooperation. Have a safe flight."

Eme blinked and swiveled her head. *What?* She saw that
most of those who were still awake had heard the impromptu
announcement. Passengers and airport staff alike gazed around
in confusion, some with curious smiles. Eme giggled and brushed
a soft crimson curl behind her ear.

At least someone was having fun with the stormy delay.

Unable to bear the plastic chair a moment longer, Eme
closed her notebook, stood up, and stretched her legs. She felt
bruised all over from the bumpy landing, and now that her mind
had had time to settle, she was hungry and thirsty. She eyed the
colorful Venetian style pizza parlor across the atrium.

After biting her lip for about three seconds, she made up her
mind, picked up her laptop bag, and waited until Mrs. Murphy's
assistant—Kala something or other—was totally focused on her
magazine; then she darted across the concourse.

*Might as well break my last twenty while I'm still in the coun-
try,* she thought.

A large slice of vegetarian pizza and bottle of soda later
found Eme sitting at a table in view of her travel group, under the
bright hanging lights of the food plaza. Nearby, the departure
board displayed all the flights that were canceled due to the
storm, and a stream of scrolling red text updated the terminal:
*Severe weather warning in effect—all flights are canceled until
further notice; Destiny apologizes for any inconvenience.*

Eme noticed a boy, about her own age, sitting one table
length away, under the fronds of a giant potted palm; he was

sporting a flashing wrist device and tapping away on an ancient Cybook computer. With brow furrowed, his dark blue eyes, partially hidden by shoulder-length dark hair, were totally focused on his computer. It was his notebook that had initially caught Eme's attention. Old and battered as it was, she admired it with a curiosity that bordered on envy.

It was colorful, to say the least. There was so much hardware clipped to it, and through it, that Eme wondered how the boy could lift the thing, let alone make it work and keep it powered. Two of the gadgets and gizmos she recognized: a CyPod bay and a GPS screen. An external multidrive was strapped to the cover (complete with a sticker that read, "When Shall We Three Meet Again?"). There were also about a dozen mismatched USB ports protruding from the device, along with a retractable 3DX laser pen and a holoport. Eme had no clue as to the function of any of the other flashing devices.

Her eyes flicked back to the boy's face, and she started—he was staring at her.

"Did my heart love till now? Forswear it, sight," he laughed, "for I ne'er saw true beauty till this night." At the gobsmacked look on Eme's face, the boy winked and pointed up and across the plaza at the increasingly dismal departure board. "Wait for it," he said. He pressed his thumb to the Enter key on his customized keyboard.

Eme watched as the large board with the red scrolling text darkened, all of the canceled flights disappeared. What took their place in the same electric red light was: "For I ne'er saw true beauty till this night" (*Romeo and Juliet,* Act 1, Scene 5).

Eme's head swung back to the boy who had a self-satisfied smirk on his face, emphasizing the cutest dimples she'd ever seen. She giggled as she winced at the renewed spasm in her whiplashed neck. He'd changed the board. "You messed with the message system, too!"

The boy attempted to look affronted while tapping a finger to the side of his nose and raising one eyebrow. "All the world's a stage, fair Juliet."

"Is that...Shakespeare?" she asked.

"None other."

Eme sipped at her lemonade, both curious and a little shy. Was he trying to impress her? "How'd you do it?"

He shook his head. "A better question, perchance: *Why* did the Cyborg do it?"

She smirked. "OK, *why*?"

The boy's blue eyes flashed. He cocked his head, smiled, and stated simply, "Because he could."

In spite of her outrage that this boy could be so cavalier at breaking the rules, Eme was impressed. And she was enthralled with his hacking skills. She rose from her table, grinned, and approached the boy, her hand outstretched in greeting. "Hi, I'm Eme...Eme Venture, and you must be the boy that Mrs. Murphy is looking for—Rafael?"

The boy stood. "The one and only, at your disposal, fair Juliet, but please, call me Rafe!" Instead of taking Eme's hand, he doffed his purple plumed Yonkers Shakespearean Festival cap. He then bowed with a flourish. Remaining in this pose, he looked up at her with a cheesy, dimpled smirk and winked at her through long-lashed, glittering blue eyes.

Before Eme could respond, there was a screech from across the terminal: "There you are, you naughty boy! I've been search-ing this entire..."

"Rafael Romero, please report to Security next to Gate 9. Rafael Romero, report to Security."

Before the announcement had finished, a red-faced Mrs. Murphy had erased the distance between them, and her right index finger pointed an inch from Rafe's nose. Her blazing brown eyes squinted at the boy, and she screeched, "Do you see what inconvenience you've caused me and airport security! We have been combing this entire terminal for you." Rafe remained calm and smiled as the stocky, graying brunette continued shaking her finger and railing at him. "Wait until I call your grandfather! I've half a mind to send you home—now! What do you have to say for yourself?"

Rafe bowed. "The Cyborg humbly begs the professor's forgiveness and vows never to cause her further pain or anguish." He raised his head a fraction, grinned, and winked at her.

Mrs. Murphy, taken aback by his charm and etiquette, retreated a few steps, ceased her rant, blushed, and finally smiled.

Composing her demeanor, she responded, "Well, since you've apologized so nicely," Eme turned her head to cover her quiet chuckle, "I'll give you another chance." She returned to her authoritative stance, complete with shaking finger. "But if you so much as place one toe out of bounds again, young man, it's back to Yonkers you go."

Rafe grinned and winked at Eme as his counselor patted him on the shoulder and turned to the remainder of her open-mouthed charges. She continued in a much more subdued voice, "OK, children, we're going to be in Atlanta until tomorrow, and the airport is sending us to a hotel for the night; so, gather your things and follow me." With that, she bustled toward her assistant and the younger students to answer questions and supervise their departure.

A few groans accompanied by some enthusiastic comments and smiles greeted this change in plans as the small group of students followed these latest orders.

Eme turned to face Rafe; her cheeks colored as she asked, "Were you serious about staying out of trouble, or were you just placating Mrs. Murphy?"

Looking offended, he pouted then responded, "The fair one wounds the Cyborg and cuts him to the quick with her skepticism. Was it something the Master of Cybermatter did that caused the crimson goddess mistrust?"

If Eme hadn't known better, she might have fallen for the wounded puppy dog look on the quirky teenager's handsome face. Rafe must have realized the futility of his sham, and they both burst out laughing. A strong bond of friendship cemented in that moment of shared mirth while they gathered their belongings. Still chuckling, they followed the troop down the escalator and out the front doors to face Bruno and to locate the waiting airport bus.

They had no way of knowing that the next thirty-six hours would severely test their camaraderie.

Somewhere Over the Atlantic
1:05 A.M. EDT

"We've got him; quit worrying."

Pause.

"We're on our way to Base Two, Bermuda—should be landing in two hours."

Pause.

"We had a slight security leak; I'll tell you more once we have the coconspirator in custody."

Pause.

"It's nothing we can't handle, and we've got clearance from headquarters."

Pause.

"No, the storm's not headed this way."

Pause.

"Yes, we have the protocol, the programmer, and all of his equipment. We'll have answers for you in a few hours."

Pause.

"We're not barbarians; we won't hurt him. This time tomorrow, the plane will be on its way to Switzerland again, and we will have infiltrated the World Bank; we'll all be in the clear and filthy rich. I'll be in touch."

Agent Gun closed his satellite phone and flashed his partner a toothy grin. "Revenge is sweet; they'll never know what hit 'em."

Brienz, Switzerland
7:06 A.M. CEST

Another phone snapped closed, the sound echoing off the stone walls of the cavernous weapons storage facility. Rack after rack of missiles and other weapons lined one cinderblock wall. A sinister female laugh soon joined the echo. "I'll soon have you all to myself, my darling. Revenge is sweet. Good-bye, America! They'll never know what hit them!"

Atlanta Airport
1:25 A.M. EDT

Mrs. Murphy's weary group wasn't ready for the sight that greeted their terminal exit at half past one: umbrellas, turned inside out and abandoned to the winds by frustrated owners, deserted cars, drowning in a parking *lake*, and Bruno, proclaiming its upgraded category three status to the entire Atlanta airport. They rolled up their pant legs, and, with their counselor in the lead, plodded through half a foot of water while dodging wind-propelled branches and other debris on the way to their hotel bus.

Through the open door of the yellow airport shuttle, a bald, portly man with a British accent greeted the drenched troupe of would be-passengers. "Sorry, ducks, we won't be going anywhere tonight; the highway's just closed, and the entire downtown's flooded."

Mrs. Murphy blanched. "But...but what am I to do with all of these...these...children?" she yelled with a thumb pointed over her left shoulder.

A shrug and smile were her only answers, and the bus door closed in her dripping face. The demoralized group watched in disbelief as the bus driver turned off his lights and prepared a bed on the rear passenger seat, settling in for a warm, dry, comfortable night.

It took a few more seconds for the counselor to grasp the situation and compose herself enough to face her shivering students. Anger clouded her face. She opened her mouth to speak—instead, she pointed toward the terminal doors. The teens needed no further instructions; they waded as quickly as the water allowed, half carrying, half floating their bags toward shelter.

The moment they stepped through the doors, the power failed. "This can't be happening," breathed one of the girls and her twin sister burst into tears. A few seconds later, the emergency generators kicked on, launching Mrs. Murphy into action. With determination etched on her tempestuous face and murder blazing in her brown eyes, she flew straight to the nearest passenger counter, ready to blame the first airport employee for Bruno, the rude bus driver, the unfairness of the high gas prices, and any number of the world's injustices.

When banging on the annoying silver bell for a full minute brought no response, she whirled in place, pausing just long enough to select a target, and then launched herself at the first uniformed person unfortunate enough to enter her line of sight.

"Where are the counter people? Who's in charge around here?" she howled at the elderly man clad in extremely loud orange overalls.

"I'm terribly sorry, Mrs." he replied, not the least bit offended at the portly woman's overbearing demeanor. "After the last shift left for the night, the next shift was unable to get through the flood. A few of us were lucky enough to have come in early, but from the looks of things, we may not be going home when our shifts end at nine. You must have just missed your last window of opportunity to escape when Bruno was upgraded," he checked his watch, "about thirty minutes ago."

At that, Mrs. Murphy eyes widened and she whirled on Rafe. Once again she jabbed that nasty index finger within an inch of his nose.

"Now, do you see what your gallivanting has caused? This is your fault!" she shouted.

Rafe had the clear sense to hang his head, not in shame, but to hide the grin that tugged at the corners of his mouth. Eme, standing behind her counselor, had to turn her head and put a hand over her own mouth, once again, to stifle the laugh threatening to escape.

As soon as Mrs. Murphy was convinced that Rafe was thoroughly chastised by her reprimand, she turned on her heel, thanked the bemused airport worker, and commanded, "Follow me," pointing the way toward the escalators.

Not certain what she could have in mind to rescue them from their immediate discomfort, the half-drowned teens followed their leader up the escalator and down the dimly lit, deserted concourse. They stopped abruptly when they arrived at the same departure gate they had left fifteen minutes earlier. In that short amount of time, the scene had dramatically changed; several exhausted, disgruntled passengers were either camped out in corners on the floor, slumped on the uncomfortable plastic seats, or, in the case of one enterprising young man, curled up and snoring on top of an abandoned ticket counter. The teens gaped at the sight before them; then the realization of their fate hit them head-on.

"All right, you lot, what are you waiting for? Claim a space and go to sleep."

"You can't be serious!" whined Carly.

"What about blankets?" moaned her sister, Cassidy.

"I need a pillow!" wailed Michael, the only other boy.

And so the complaints continued until…

"That's enough! There's nothing more that can be done tonight; you're all old enough to fend for yourselves—go to sleep!" That said, the plump woman opened her bag in the middle of the vast unfriendly room, removed her hair net and bathrobe, and proceeded to ready herself for sleep. Her students looked on in horror; the terminal windows were now their only protection from the fury of the ferocious night.

With no options remaining, the demoralized teenagers slowly followed suit, claiming spots on the cold, hard terrazzo tile, as close as possible to Mrs. Murphy—without actually touching her. Eme and Rafe found a quiet stretch of carpeted floor between two rows of plastic seats, far away from their group.

While they were removing their shoes and drying their freezing cold feet: "This looks cozy," chimed a cheerful Australian accent. Rafe and Eme whirled around to discover that the voice belonged to Mrs. Murphy's amber-skinned, blonde assistant. "Mind if I join you? I'm bushed just listening to the whiney ankle biters," she thumbed in the direction of the conclave of the three distraught teens and their counselor.

Eme and Rafe smiled at the newcomer. "Ah, another fair damsel in distress; alas, the accommodations are sorely lacking," Rafe made a sweeping gesture with his hat toward the floor, "but Juliet and the Cyborg would be most gratified with your esteemed company." He finished with a smile and a wag of his eyebrows.

"Yeah, what he said," laughed Eme.

"Rafael, you're just too funny!" Rafe bowed to the girl with a grin. "Hi, Elaine, we haven't been properly introduced—it was a bit hectic when you arrived, to state the obvious; I was busy chasing down our wanderer." She looked pointedly at Rafe who smirked in return. They all laughed. "I'm Kala Weston." The pretty blonde stuck out her hand, which Eme clasped.

"I'm happy to meet you, Kala. But, please, call me Eme."

"And you may address the Cyborg as Rafe, or, if the lovely one wishes, His Most Esteemed Master of Cybermatter!" Kala and Eme laughed at Rafe's wagging eyebrows and rakish pose.

"I think I'll just use Rafe," grinned Kala, and he winked.

"Wise choice," laughed Eme, and then she continued, "Isn't that Mrs. Murphy an old biddy? Do you think we're ever going to get to computer camp?"

"At this rate, I doubt it's going to happen *before* summer is over, but I'm not going to summer camp." Eme and Rafe were surprised by this statement. Kala continued, "Mrs. Murphy is my Aunt Mayrah." Eme blanched and stammered an apology, which Kala waved off. "Don't apologize; she's always been that way—kind one minute, a tyrant the next—a bit of bipolar, if you ask me. In fact, from what I remember of her brother, my deceased father, she's got the same temperament."

Eme relaxed a bit while Rafe looked thoughtful. "Anyway, I'm going to visit her family in Switzerland on my way home. I've never met my cousin, the headmistress of the school."

"Oh, so that's the connection to Mrs. Murphy," Eme responded, nodding her head in understanding while pulling on dry socks.

"Yep, her daughter sent her on this mission and had to sweeten the deal with a first-class ticket to placate her. I overheard Aunt Mayrah's side of a very heated phone conversation after Rafe went on his walkabout." Kala gave the boy a pointed look and smirked.

Rafe shrugged, finished, slipping into dry loafers, and smiled at her. Eme stopped her unpacking. "You don't sound like an American; what are you doing here?" Eme asked. Kala frowned. Eme covered. "I'm sorry, that didn't come out right. What I meant…"

Kala laughed at Eme's red face and answered, "I've just come from a trivia competition in New York and jumped at the chance to accompany all of you on this trip to Europe, before I return home, down-under—Australia, for my first year of college."

Eme and Rafe stared at their new acquaintance while she rooted through her bag for dry clothes. Their eyes were wide, as the realization of her remark set in.

"You were invited to take part in the Annual International Trivia Competition? Wow, that's quite an honor! How did you do?" asked an awed Eme.

"I don't mean to big-note myself—brag," she added at the confused expressions on the faces before her. Kala fished around under her red rain jacket. "I'll have to remember not to use my Aussie slang around you Yanks," she smirked, flashing her beautiful amber eyes at them; then she produced a glittering golden medallion hanging from a purple ribbon around her neck and added simply, "I won!"

The normally unflappable Rafe was stunned, as was Eme, and they both stared open-mouthed at the beaming blonde. Recovered from his shock, Rafe looked sadly at Kala and shook his head. "So wise so young, they say, do never live long."

It was as if Bruno had reached through the protective glass barriers of the terminal and doused the girls with his icy fury.

Kala recovered first; she chuckled when she replied, "It has nothing to do with my wisdom, you goof; the one good thing I inherited from my, uh," the girl paused, her face became clouded, she cleared her throat, and continued, "well, my father had a photographic memory; I seem to retain whatever I read." Her face brightened and she added, "Dead useful for trivia games."

Eme wondered what had been left unsaid, but she dismissed it when Kala's next words brought her and Rafe up short: "For instance, I know all about you, Elaine Mea Venture!" Eme instinctively reached for her dark glasses, and then stopped at the absurdity of pulling them out now that she had been recognized. "You're mentioned in many of my Trivia Books." She faltered at the looks on the faces in front of her. "You didn't know?" she continued in surprise.

"No," Eme whispered.

"Wh-why?" Rafe stammered.

A slow smile spread across Kala's face as she looked first at Eme and then Rafe's shocked faces, and then she burst into peals of laughter, until she was shushed by several of the passengers trying to sleep nearby. She covered her mouth and continued to laugh until the two pairs of eyes in front of her grew dark with anger. "OK, OK, I'll stop, but the looks on your faces..." She started to snicker again, but Eme pushed her gently on the arm.

"What does it say about me?" she asked in a fierce whisper, her face flushed.

"Why is the crimson goddess even mentioned in a book of trivia?" Rafe demanded.

"Rafe, don't you read or watch the telly?" asked Kala, astonished.

"Yes, the Cyborg reads the works of the Bard and the exploits of comic superheroes, and no, we've never allowed the idiot box into our home; the only news the Master of Cybermatter seeks is found on Persephone." He smiled fondly and patted his dilapidated computer in response to the puzzled looks from the girls.

Kala looked thoughtful for a moment, finished changing into drier clothes, and then turned her attention to Eme. "Well, our new friend, Eme, is a celebrity." Eme began to squirm as she was sure she knew what was coming next. "Or at least she was until she and her twin sis, Erin, were written off the soap opera that made them famous." Kala faltered before revealing the more pertinent facts. "Her sis was lost during the World Trade Center attack on September 11th and has never been..." She stopped when she saw the raw pain on Eme's face and the tears welling in her eyes.

Kala's smile vanished, replaced by a concerned frown. "Why don't you kick me in the arse, Eme? I'm such a big mouth!" She put her arm around Eme's shoulders, which were now shaking, and Eme turned and softly cried in Kala's arms. Rafe stood by in confusion and then joined the girls, wrapping them both in his long arms.

After a minute, Eme pulled away and wiped her eyes with the sleeve of her damp jacket. The three moved closer to a ticket counter. Kala and Eme took a seat, while Rafe sat cross-legged on the floor facing them. "I'm all right, Kala, it...it was just a shock realizing that my family's story made the pages of a...a trivia magazine. I'm used to the tabloids, but...but a trivia magazine... that's just wrong on so many levels." She sniffed, shook her head, and held up her hands at another attempt by Rafe and Kala to hug her. "I'm ok... really. What other information is in these books?"

"Are you sure you want me to tell you more?" Kala asked with raised eyebrows.

"Yes, I...I want to correct any misinformation," Eme answered, raising her chin bravely.

Rafe sat in silence, watching the exchange between the girls.

"Well, OK, let's see. Your parents are famous movie stars—we all know that." She turned to Rafe shaking his head. "Ha, everyone who reads *real* books and newspapers or watches movies and the telly, that is!" she laughed.

"You and..." she checked to see how Eme was reacting so far and continued at the redhead's urging, "and Erin were born during the actual taping of a soap opera." Eme nodded, and Rafe shook his head rapidly with wide eyes.

"Your maternal grandparents and great-grandfather were killed in an auto bingle—accident —when your mom was only ten and your great-grandmother raised her." Eme nodded, and Rafe's eyes grew wider still.

"That's about it!" Kala finished with a shrug.

"So there's nothing about my nickname, or where we live, or that my great-grandmother homeschooled me, or...?" Eme asked to a slow shaking of Kala's head.

"No, nothing that hasn't been reported in the mainstream media; however, your sis's name was one of the questions in the trivia competition. No, the question was not directed at me," she added at Eme's questioning stare, "but my opponent bungled it, and I answered it correctly on the redirect," she smiled.

Eme frowned. "Well, good for you, Kala, but I think I want to redirect this conversation to another topic." Rafe and Kala nodded in agreement. They sat in silence for a moment until the wide expanse of terminal windows was illuminated by lightning; they were then shaken by volleys of thunder loud enough to reawaken all the sleeping occupants of the room.

"Mars and Zeus approach, m'ladies! Bruno's fury is nigh!" Rafe grinned. The girls shuddered.

"Eh, that reminds me, did you know that this hurricane is misnamed?" Kala beamed, happy to have a new trivia topic, at least one less painful for Eme. "Another one of the categories in the trivia contest was storms. I studied hurricane history quite extensively, and this one was supposed to be named Bill. Besides, Bruno isn't a name used for Atlantic hurricanes—it's in the rotation for Pacific typhoons."

Rafe and Eme looked at each other in amazement. "Please go on, wise Kala," Rafe encouraged.

"Yeah, I had no idea the names were set ahead of time; I thought the weather people just pulled names out of a hat," Eme added.

"Oh, no, they're set six years in advance and recycled; the only way a name is taken out of rotation is when its storm has been responsible for major death and destruction. Bill was up for this hurricane, but someone at the NOAA buggered it up, and no one knows who released this new name to the media; by then it was too late and too confusing to rename it. It was on all the newscasts—didn't you...?"

Eme felt a sudden shiver run down her spine and blanched. *Bruno. What's with that name? And why would anyone deliberately change the hurricane protocol?*

Eme began to tremble; Kala and Rafe grabbed her hands and knelt before her. "Eme, what's wrong? Are you ill?" asked Kala.

Eme couldn't answer; she had no idea why she had this feeling of foreboding; she couldn't stop shaking. "I...I'm just, uh, surprised." She took a deep breath and slowly exhaled. Her two concerned friends rubbed her hands and arms, and some warmth crept back into her body; the trembling stopped. "Don't you find it strange, considering where we're going?" She stared into the concerned faces in front of her.

Rafe broke the tension with an enormous smile followed by a raucous laugh that, once again, brought contemptuous shushes from the many stranded travelers around them. Kala giggled, and Eme managed a sheepish smile.

"You've been reading too many mystery novels," Kala admonished.

"The Bard would love this farce; Bruno is the tempest, ordered by the banished sorcerer, Prospero, to drive his enemies to an island where Ariel and Caliban were to commit the ultimate heinous deed." Rafe rose and finished his speech with one foot on his bag, his arm raised high in the air: "'As you from crimes would pardoned be, let your indulgence set me free.'" Applause from the girls, more shushes from the unappreciative weary passengers.

"You do enjoy your drama, eh, Rafe?" Kala whispered with a giggle.

Rafe winked at her, doffed his Shakespearean hat, and bowed. "Many lessons can be learned from reading the plays of the great Bard," he ended, donning his purple plumed hat once again.

"Well, we can rest assured this play will not come to pass— we're not headed to any island," Kala responded.

"Thankfully," Eme added.

Without another word, the trio finished unpacking their belongings and attempted to prepare for an uncomfortable night's sleep.

After unceremoniously emptying his bag of its contents, and with a wave of his hand, Rafe proclaimed, "Good night, fair ones, the Cyborg takes his leave; it will be morrow soon, and yours truly will be there to greet the dawn." Without waiting for an answer, he dove beneath his makeshift bed and, from the snuffling sounds emanating from beneath the pile of clothing, seemed to fall asleep instantly. The girls looked at each other, giggled, and returned to their bags.

Several more minutes of preparation and louder snores broke the silence. Eme and Kala turned toward the sound and broke into fits of giggles at the sight before them: Rafe had reemerged from his 'bedding' and was lying spread-eagle in the midst of what looked like his entire wardrobe. His head was precariously perched on his laptop, and he was dead to the world, mouth wide open. The girls' laughter increased in volume until Rafe awakened.

"Morning breaks?" he yawned, gazing at the hysterical girls.

"No, however, if you don't find a better resting place for your head, your laptop or your neck will be in a world of hurt when it does break." Eme answered, and the girls continued to giggle while Rafe reverently patted his laptop.

"Point taken!" He saluted the girls, tucked his computer under his bag, and burrowed beneath his clothing once again; the tip of his freckled nose was the only indication that something human inhabited the space.

The girls made themselves as comfortable as possible under the glare of the generator-powered lights. The hum of the cleaning crew's vacuums and the roar of the misnamed category three hurricane lulled all but one traveler to sleep; Eme's thoughts of Bruno and the mystery behind No's sudden departure from the plane kept her awake long after Kala's breathing relaxed in slumber.

CHAPTER SEVEN

WOUNDED DIGNITY

Atlanta Airport
Thursday, June 11, 2015
5:55 A.M. EDT

Before morning did break, Rafe woke with a start and a huge kink in his neck. *Eme was right about using Persephone as a pillow.* He glanced at the two girls, sleeping peacefully beside him, and then turned toward the window; the storm outside was anything but peaceful. *No hope for escape from Atlanta today; however, the Cyborg has two new friends and an uncertain adventure ahead. The Bard would write a most excellent play based on this premise.*

He spent a few seconds on isometrics to remove the kink, then moved his laptop aside, and grabbed a sweatshirt among the wardrobe that made up his bed. After wadding it into a roll, he tried to get comfortable on the cold, hard terminal floor.

Several attempts at finding a painless position failed, and he gave it up as a bad job. With a sigh, he gathered up his make-shift "bedclothes," stuffed them into his bag, relocated to a nearby seat, and booted up his computer. With no internet con-nection, he opened his e-reader application, and with a smirk at the girls, selected The Tempest; however, by Act 2, Scene 3, he realized he hadn't comprehended much of the story; so, he closed Persephone to devote his full attention to his distraction: his last day at home with his grandfather...

"Rafe, hurry up, we're going to be late for the festival!" He remembered his grandfather's plea drifting upstairs that sunny summer day, as if it were yesterday. (He shook himself and laughed; *it was yesterday.*) He had saved his search, and closed Persephone's lid, stashed it lovingly, as always, into his green camouflage bag, and dashed out of his bedroom door, stop-ping in the bathroom just long enough to run a brush through his wavy black hair, before barreling down the stairs of the home he had shared with his grandfather for most of his seventeen years.

"Fear not, Paternal One, the Cyborg wouldst die rather than be tardy to a festival honoring the Bard," he laughed, as he rounded the bottom of the elegantly-curved staircase.

Bill Rafe was waiting for him by the front door, keys in hand. He clapped him on the shoulder in greeting. "What are we wait-ing for?" The two grinned at each other, and the teenager led the way to the waiting red sports car parked in front of the steps of the two hundred year old stone manor house.

"What kept you?" Bill asked as he started the car.

"Alas, I have yet to discover any more information regarding the history of St. Bruno's Academy. Something is rotten in Denmark...or in this case, Switzerland."

Bill Romero guided the racy convertible expertly down the sweeping curved, tree-shaded drive and onto the quiet upscale New York avenue. The summer morning sun glinted through the magnificent ancient oaks lining the street in front of the stately homes that made up their neighborhood. He turned briefly to his grandson and studied his worried frown. "You're really serious about this; just because you can't find a detailed history of the academy, you feel there is something "rotten" afoot? It has the most prestigious accreditation in all of Europe, if not in all of the world. Its technical school is second to none."

"It's not that, Grandfather. Why is there no history available anywhere? It's like someone has erased everything regarding St. Bruno's, before 2001, out of cyberspace. Don't you find that troubling, since it has been in operation since 1990?"

The older man was silent, as they approached down-town Yonkers. At the first red light, he turned to his grandson with a smile. "I have an idea: in your free time between classes you can research the archives that I'm sure you'll find in the basement of the school, and then tell Dr. Murphy that you'd like extra credit for updating their website."

This seemed to intrigue the self-proclaimed Cyborg of Cyberspace, and he returned his grandfather's smile. "It shall be done!" The light turned green, and the remainder of the trip was spent in happy banter about the upcoming trip and subsequent summer sojourn to Switzerland.

Anyone who knew Rafe marveled at his devotion to his grandfather, especially since the death of the man's wife of forty-one years. It took the two of them years to recover from Amy Romero's death from breast cancer and resume a fairly normal life. Rafe had thrown himself into Shakespeare and computer science as an escape from the pain.

The majority of his grandfather's day was spent managing his international fitness centers. In his spare time, when he was not with Rafe, he practiced Buddhism and wrote; in the four years since his grandmother's passing, Bill Romero had penned six books on meditation, Buddhism, martial arts, and physical fitness;

garnering him the title of foremost authority on the subject of grief-counseling through meditation and writing. His world-renowned fitness clubs also hosted free grief-counseling seminars, led by the man and by many other experts in the field.

To say that Rafe was proud of his grandfather would be an understatement. Ever since he could walk, talk or think coherently, he had adored his grandparents. Never knowing his own parents, Janine and Christopher Wilkes, Bill and Amy Rafe were his whole world. They had rescued him from an abusive home when he was only five months old, changed his last name to Romero, and very lovingly made him their own. His parents had not objected to his removal from their drug-induced lives, and had silently vanished leaving their belongings in the beautiful home that had been given to them as a wedding present. He knew that his grand-mother had grieved for her daughter, but his grandfather had been too concerned with his grandson's health and well-being to worry about Rafe's mother and worthless father.

Consumed with guilt that their lack of guidance had led to their daughter's disastrous choices, his grandparents had enjoyed every moment possible with him. They took turns home-schooling him, and introduced him to the great authors. Numerous trips to museums and extensive travel broadened his thirst for and love of knowledge.

Since he was home-schooled (all but the two disastrous months he had spent in a public high school), he had very few friends. Television was never allowed in their home, so the inter-net kept him informed of current events, and books—books, books and more books, including Bill's extensive collection of superhero comics, were his constant companions. With his grandfather's vast library at his disposal, he had read all the clas-sic novels. And, when he discovered Shakespeare at the age of seven, he was hooked. He spent hours at a time reading Shakespeare's plays, even imagining that the Bard's characters were his friends; he spent much of his time conversing with them, much to the horror of his grandparents. After several trips to Dr. Friedlander's Office of Psychiatry, they finally acquiesced to the good doctor's pronouncement of the soundness of his mind and left his quirky personality alone to grow and flourish.

His prowess as a martial arts student also became evident at the age of seven, when he began training with a master of Shaolin Kung Fu at the Romero Fitness Center in Yonkers. In keeping with his study of Buddhism, he and his grandparents became experts in the discipline. He became obsessed with the history of Buddhism, martial arts, and soon reveled in the historical research of any and all of his interests, which included computers.

Persephone, his Cybook 2095 notebook computer, was a gift from his grandfather on his twelfth birthday. It was a bitter-sweet parting with Shylock, his techno-buddy of four years, but it didn't take long before Persephone had his heart and all but erased the memories of his clunky old pal.

With the extra money he earned as an instructor and physical fitness coach at the fitness center, he outfitted his new lady love with all the latest in computer peripherals. He had laughed at his grandfather's questions when he unveiled the myriad of devices he had installed on Persephone the night before he left for Switzerland. He had promised to give him a lesson in their operation once he returned from his summer at St. Bruno's Academy in Brienz.

However, computer peripherals were not on Rafe's mind as his grandfather parked the car in the lot of Yonker's beautiful two-year old convention center. Attending this festival with his grandfather would be their last outing before he bid him farewell at Kennedy International Airport later that afternoon. He would certainly miss the man; this would be their first time apart, and Ethan knew it was more of an important step in his grandfather's emotional, rather than his own educational, growth. Dr. Friedlander had suggested it for both their sakes.

He turned to his grandfather once he had closed the car door, and flashed him a smile.

"OK, Romeo, let's find out if there's a Juliet in there who can tear your mind away from Persephone!" the older man joked.

With a wave of his hand, Ethan made a mad dash toward the other brightly-dressed festival participants entering the sprawling convention center. He stopped to wait for his grandfather at the first of many vendor booths, hawking everything from pointed plumed hats to room-sized posters of the Bard and many of his memorable characters. However, by the time the older man had caught up with him, Ethan was already wearing one of the hats: a lurid pink model, sporting a garish purple plume, and advertising the 2015 Yonkers, Shakespeare Festival in gold old English script. He knew his grandfather had vowed then and there to hide the 'monstrosity' before Ethan could pack it for Switzerland.

Ethan was grinning at the memory of the fight he'd had with his grandfather about his pointy little hat, when a particularly loud crash of thunder interrupted his thoughts and brought him to his feet, while waking nearly every one of the terminal's weary travelers, including...

"Oh, my back!" complained Kala, stretching and trying to rise from the floor.

"Your back and my right hip! I feel like I've been sleeping on a bed of rocks," countered Eme as she also made a move to stand.

Rafe stood over his new friends, hands on his hips, smiling down at their tortured expressions and disheveled appearances. "Morning has broken, fair maids, but it's without hope of an escape from Atlanta. In fact, it appears that Bruno's ferocity has intensified; the eye wall must now be over the Georgia coast," he finished, thumbing over his shoulder at the rain-streaked terminal window.

"Who died and made you the weatherman, Rafe?" Kala groaned as she gave up trying to stand and sat back on the floor, with her chin on her knees, and arms over her head.

Eme finally made it to her feet with a hand up from Rafe, and they both reached out to their blonde friend. With a giant tug from them and a loud grunt of thanks from Kala, the Australian teenager joined the land of the vertical.

After gathering their belongings and taking care of their personal hygiene, to the extent afforded them by the terminal restroom, they joined the rest of their group.

Because the terminal was still running on emergency power, many services were still not available to the stranded passengers—a hot breakfast and, most importantly, satellite service to Rafe's computer. "Food is sustenance for the body, but an Internet connection is sustenance for the *soul!*" he sighed.

Sleep helped to placate Mrs. Murphy's demeanor; however, with no news and no airport employees available to answer questions about their flight, she gathered her band of sleepy travelers to prepare them for another day of uncertainties.

"Well, ladies...and gentlemen," she began, her smile dimming a trifle when she glanced in Rafe's direction, "we find ourselves in no better shape than last night." Groans greeted this announcement. "However, we are a bit drier," nods greeted this decree, "better rested," more nods, "but," and she searched their faces, "we're also a lot more hungry." Eager smiles and enthusiastic nods made her chuckle. "So it's to the vending machines we must turn." Faces fell at this, but brightened at her next remark: "Whichever one of you finds me a cup of *hot* coffee will be awarded my first-class seat to Switzerland!"

All six faces expressed surprise and then delight when the implication of the prize registered. No one needed further prodding—the six teens took off at a run in search of the machines.

As Eme, Rafe, and Kala dashed down the concourse, Eme yelled at her two friends, "I still don't think it's fair that she got a first-class seat while we're confined to coach."

"As I said, it was the only way the school could coerce her into taking the job of chaperone to a bunch of 'sniveling teenagers;' that's what I overheard her tell my Aunt Leura!" was Kala's response as they rounded the first corner.

"Oh, right!" was all Eme could answer before they came skidding to a halt in front of "breakfast." They quickly raided the candy, soda, and chip machines, but they were disappointed at the lack of cups in the hot beverage dispenser.

"First-class is highly overrated, anyway," Kala responded to the disheartened faces of her friends. Besides, now we'll all be able to sit together, eh!" she beamed.

"Witty as well as winsome, Wise One!" Rafe replied with a cheeky grin.

The girls laughed at Rafe's alliteration and sprinted back to the waiting area, eagerly anticipating their junk food meal.

By the time they returned, Mrs. Murphy was happily sipping her cup of steaming coffee while the smallest member of their group, Michael, was grinning at the first-class ticket he held high for all to see. The trio chuckled until Eme realized that the young boy with the ticket was to be her seatmate.

Horror replaced Eme's smile when that thought sank in: she would be seated next to Mrs. Murphy for the seven-hour trip across the Atlantic. She turned pleading eyes to her friends who had come to the same realization. They held up their hands, violently shaking their heads at her unasked plea.

Resigned to her fate, she joined Rafe and Kala who were headed for the painful plastic seats; she took solace in the fact that their departure was delayed for quite some time. She hoped for some miracle to spare her the coming agony of the long flight and sadly munched on her high-fructose breakfast in the murky morning light. If she had only known then that her wished-for miracle would, in fact, turn into a tragedy.

Atlanta Airport
11:45 A.M. EDT

The three new friends spent the morning getting better acquainted and staying away from the wrath of their minder who was riding constant herd on the three younger students. All spirits had improved now that Bruno was wending its way over the Atlantic. It was still a category three hurricane, but now it was someone else's category three hurricane. Normalcy returned to the airport, as did the workers and passengers who were lucky enough to have spent the night in a proper bed.

A check on their flight revealed that they would be stuck in Atlanta another night and all the next day, only this time it would be spent at a local hotel. Kala and Eme expressed the burning desire for a hot shower and clean clothes. From the look of Rafe's wardrobe upon awakening, Eme and Kala doubted he'd have much luck in that department. They expressed their curiosity over a vegetarian pizza.

"So, Rafe, what exactly do you have left to wear after sleeping in all your clothes?" asked Kala.

"Yeah, Rafe," continued Eme, "I've never before seen anyone wear an entire wardrobe at one time." The girls snickered at the Cyborg's wounded expression.

Running his hands down the front of his rumpled red "Take a Byte out of Cyber Crime with Hacker Hawk" T-shirt, he gave the girls a wry smile and replied, "You rebuke the Ruler of Cybermatter's fashion sense?"

"No, just your decorum and cleanliness!" giggled Kala.

With a sneer, Rafe stood up, grabbed his bags, and stalked away from the table, leaving two shocked girls in his wake.

They looked at each other, and Eme whispered, "Was it something we said?"

"No dramas!" responded Kala. "He's just throwing a mini wobbly; he'll be back shortly." She reached for another piece of pizza; Eme took another sip of her soda. A few seconds later, one and then the other burst into gales of laughter; Kala choked on her food, Eme sprayed the table with her soda. After recovering their composure and mopping up their mess (under the disapproving glares of nearby patrons), they decided to search for their missing friend; however, before they could rise from their chairs...

"This is a security announcement: all outbound passengers are reminded that bags and suitcases must not be left unattended at any time."

"Nor should friends criticize a friend's belongings."

"Do not accept packages from unknown persons."

"Nor hurt said person's feelings."

"Hartsfield-Jackson Atlanta thanks you for your cooperation. Have a safe flight."

The two girls jumped up from their table and grinned at each other. *"Rafe!"* they shouted together as they scanned the concourse for the source of the interruptions.

"You go left, and I'll go right; in ten minutes we'll meet back here, whether we've found him or not!" commanded Kala.

"Right on!" Eme flashed a wicked grin, grabbed a "Reserved" placard from the nearby kiosk, and placed it on their table; then they separated to begin their quest.

Ten minutes later, after searching the entire upper floor of the terminal, they returned to their table—no Rafe in tow.

"He's playing with us—probably sitting in some store window laughing his head off." Kala sat down and continued eating her stone-cold pizza.

Eme joined her, sipping her watery soda. "Let's just give him a few more minutes; he'll return." The fifteen minutes that passed proved Eme wrong. Disheartened and ashamed for hurting Rafe's feelings, they returned to the waiting area and Mrs. Murphy.

"There you are! I've just been told that we can go to our hotel. Get your things together, and meet us in baggage." She looked left and right, put her hands on her ample hips, and glared at the girls. "Where *is* he?"

Eme and Kala gave each other a sad look, which Mrs. Murphy interpreted as "He's gone!" And off she went: "What's the matter with that boy? Did he learn nothing from last night?" She threw her hands in the air and was about to storm off toward security, but stopped dead in her tracks; right in the middle of her projected path stood Rafe. "Small miracles!" Mrs. Murphy exclaimed and breathed a sigh of relief. With her right hand on her hip, she pointed at him with the left and bellowed, "You, over here, now!"

Rafe obliged with a cheeky reluctance that earned him another glare. He had his bags slung over his shoulder, his laptop bulging beneath one arm, while he nursed a double scoop of chocolate ice cream in an enormous waffle cone.

Eme was relieved to see he hadn't gone far, after all; the thought of another night in the airport was more than she could bear. Her new friends were awesome, but she hadn't abandoned GG Anne, Bogey, and Boomer for a bed on the cold, hard airport floor. That reminded her: the delay would be on the news, and she should try again to e-mail GG Anne and her parents.

"Fair Juliet and oh, so kind Kala..." Rafe gave the girls a chocolaty smile. "What wound did ever heal, but by degrees?" He doffed his hat.

The girls looked at each other and then back at Rafe. "You're saying all is forgiven, eh?" Kala asked.

"Ah, ice cream doth soothe the savage soul, and thus I clothe my naked villainy," he professed with a sly smile.

"Rafael! Come along!" Mrs. Murphy demanded, pointing to a spot on her left. "You stay by me until we get to the hotel."

Rafe sighed dramatically. "How poor are they who have not patience. Lead on, madam, lead on!" He winked at the girls.

Eme and Kala giggled at their friend. It seemed that Rafe wasn't one to hold a grudge, although he had a temper that could flare up and result in some rather intense hacking of allegedly secure airport systems. Eme was a little dismayed to think that if a teenager could do it, what was to prevent someone with more malicious intentions? Not much, all things considered.

But then, no harm done, she supposed.

Atlanta/Los Angeles
1:15 P.M. EDT/10:15 A.M. PDT

"Oh, it's you, gov'na! Norma just left to pick up the kid!"

Silence. Then... "*What?* She just left *now!* His plane got in twelve hours ago!"

"Well, your lordship..."

"Don't get smart with me, you two bit has-been! Where is my son?"

"Don't get your knickers in a twist, I was..."

Click.

At that same moment, a battered black sedan zipped in and out of the heavy traffic on the northbound Atlanta freeway, heading toward the airport. The forty-year-old bleached blonde behind the wheel was in a panic; she had passed out during the

Hurricane Bruno party, that she and her rocker husband had hosted the night before, and had not been in any condition to pick up her son.

"Well, it really wasn't my fault," she reasoned with herself. "We had this party planned for twelve hours, and if his plane had been on time, I would have been there on time. It was all Bruno's fault, after all." She was laughing at the irony of that statement when her cell phone rang.

Throwing caution to the wind, and breaking several traffic laws, she reached into her bag in search of her worn-out cell phone, cursing as two bags of marijuana and her last stash of cocaine fell to the floor. Further rooting in her bag caused her entire CD collection to follow, landing on top of the drugs. The CD case of her husband's one and only recording managed to split the bag of cocaine, sending clouds of white powder throughout the cramped interior of the car. Coughing violently, she cursed her husband for pawning her Cellpoint adapter for his new guitar.

After rolling down the windows to clear the air, she put the car on cruise, unfastened her seat belt, and took her eyes off the road for a brief moment to assess the damage on the floor. That was all the time needed for the small car, traveling seventy miles an hour, to swerve onto the concrete median, flip once in the air, and land upside down in front of an SUV in a southbound lane.

The phone call went to voice mail.

CHAPTER EIGHT
ROOM SERVICE, PLEASE

The airline had arranged for two cabs to take the group of students under Mrs. Murphy's care to the hotel a mile north of the airport. The travelers piled into their appointed vehicles and settled in for the short trip to the hotel, happily anticipating their hot showers and soft, comfy beds.

Two minutes later, as the last of the cabs pulled away from the curb, the airport speaker crackled with a special announcement: "No Henderson, please report to airport security. No Henderson, to security, please."

This call from his father, like the call to his mother, went unanswered.

Atlanta Freeway
1:22 P.M. EDT

The worst of the hurricane had moved east over the Atlantic and beyond, yet Bruno's destructive footprint was evident; trees were bent at odd angles or torn from the earth, flooded cars were abandoned on the side of the road, and giant pools of muddy water punctuated the storm's story.

As they crossed the overpass on their approach to the freeway, Eme saw swarms of emergency vehicles surrounding a recent accident in the southbound lanes. She was thankful their hotel was north of the airport; traffic was backed up for miles behind the tangled mess.

She was also thankful that the turbulent flight into Atlanta hadn't had to contend with the full fury of Bruno. It was a name that had been both fortuitous and frightful in the last few days, and her thoughts drifted once again to No; she wished she'd thought to get his phone number before he left the plane. "Woulda, coulda, shoulda!" she whispered sadly.

"What's that, Eme?" asked Kala.

"Oh, nothing, just thinking about missed opportunities."

Kala patted her on the knee, nodded her head, and grimaced. "No worries, I know exactly what you mean."

The two girls smiled at each other and returned to their private thoughts while Rafe continued to demonstrate the features of his new computer peripherals for Michael, a small boy with a shock of impressive sandy hair.

Ten minutes later, there was a mad dash from the cabs and into the sparkling interior of the airline's twenty-five story Stargate Hotel—six teenagers diving under cover out of the lashing rain, wheeling suitcases and carrying bulging bags of belongings for a summer in the Swiss Alps. Eme saw Rafe stuff his massive customized laptop beneath his shirt and under his belt, a feat she didn't think possible with such a hefty piece of hardware.

The hotel lobby was packed with passengers being rerouted there for the day and night as Bruno's storms ended and the clean-up began. Mrs. Murphy wrestled her way to the front counter, keeping a firm grip on Rafe's arm and advising Kala to keep an eye on the younger kids. Eme stayed near Kala, feeling tired but anxious to send her e-mails.

In the end, the airline had managed to get the Bruno Academy party four separate rooms, all of them doubles; with the size of the group, they would fit perfectly. It meant Mrs. Murphy got a room to herself; no doubt she was hoping for a break, however short, from her needy charges, not to mention her one mischievous flight risk, Rafael Romero.

Speaking of the devil...

"Fair Juliet," Rafe began as the entire group crammed into an elevator and made for the nineteenth floor, "shall we share a room?"

Eme blushed, the girls snickered, and Mrs. Murphy barked a quick command: "Boys and girls will not share rooms! Rafael, you're with Michael; Kala, you go with Elaine; Cassidy and Carly will take the last double. All of you will have lights out and be in bed by ten."

"So early!" Rafe exclaimed. "One's work has barely begun; midnight, oh professor, the outpost of the advancing day! Suffer us not the citadel of the night."

Eme watched Mrs. Murphy struggling with herself not to scold Rafe then and there. The elevator doors pinged open on floor nineteen, and the group spilled out into the corridor. "By ten," the elderly counselor barked, brooking no room for argument. "That's the schedule you'll have once we finally reach St. Bruno's, and that's the schedule you'll have tonight."

"Very well," Rafe sighed and slapped his hand down on the shoulder of thirteen-year-old Michael. "To the minibar, young Michael; such stuff as dreams are made on...and so forth, so forth..."

"Don't you dare, Mr. Romero," Mrs. Murphy warned, shoving a key card for the nearest room into his hand. "One drop, and you'll be on the first flight back home; I *will* be in to check."

Both Eme and Kala giggled as Rafe shrugged, winked, and steered Michael into the first room on their floor. Mrs. Murphy watched him with a steely gaze until he disappeared into the room; she then swiped a card against the pad on the room directly opposite. "Elaine and Kala, you're in here. She then turned to Carly and Cassidy and commanded, "You two follow me, and we'll get you settled in."

Kala and Eme watched as Mrs. Murphy bustled off with the two younger girls in tow, no doubt contemplating the minibar in her own room: much-needed medication after suffering through the adventures of the last few days.

Once they were thankfully in their own room, Kala threw down her bag on the perfectly made bed closest to the door and asked, "Do you think Rafe knows how to communicate in anything other than garbled Shakespeare?"

Eme walked across the room to the wide rain-streaked window and admired the stormy view of the airport in the distance before she collapsed onto her own bed. "He can be a bit much, can't he?" she replied. "He's giving your aunt a headache."

Kala grinned. "Too right about that; he wanted to share a room with you!"

Eme fought the blush that rose to her cheeks. She shrugged her shoulders and grinned. "He was just playing around."

Kala raised one blonde eyebrow and said nothing. Around her neck the trivia medal glinted in the soft light from the lamp on the bedside table. "So what shall we do for the rest of today?"

Eme shrugged and patted her laptop case. "I should catch up on some e-mails."

"Well, I think I'll take a shower," Kala responded. She began rooting through her bag.

Eme settled down on her bed, booted up her computer, and read the texts from her parents, her friends, and GG Anne. GG expressed concern about the hurricane, letting her know that she had called the Atlanta Airport and had been assured that she and the St. Bruno party were safe and secure. Her parents' text message asked that she call her GG Anne as soon as possible, and reminded her that they would be en route to Gibraltar and out of reach for the next few days. Since her cell phone was still only transmitting intermittently, she resorted to e-mail:

***

Dear GG,

So you've heard that we're stuck in Atlanta because of Bruno. That name has been getting me in and out of trouble all week! Apart from a bit of a bumpy landing, I'm OK and missing you, Boomer, and yes, even Bogey.

I'm in a hotel just outside of the airport with the school group. We should be flying out tomorrow afternoon—I know, we're only two days behind schedule.

I've made friends with an Australian girl named Kala (we're sharing a room) and a boy named Rafe (who may be insane), so I'm not totally bored out of my mind, waiting for the flight out!

I'm not sure when I'll have phone service again, but I'll e-mail again before I leave tomorrow, GG.

All my love,

Eme

P.S. Give Boomer a hug and a treat from me! And tell Bogey, "Toto, I feel we're not in Kansas anymore!"

***

After shooting off shorter e-mails to a few friends and to her parents, Eme jumped into the shower that Kala had just vacated. The jets of steamy hot water felt lovely against her skin and relaxed her aching muscles. After the excitement of the last few days, sleeping on a hard floor, and battling torrential rainfall, Eme imagined all her travel woes being washed down the drain. She spent about ten minutes longer than necessary under the stream.

Wrapped in nothing but a towel, she stepped back into the main room to find that Kala had invited in a few friends; Rafe sat on her bed, his monstrous laptop balanced on one knee, grinning from ear to ear. Michael was with him, flicking impossibly fast through the channels on the T.V.

Eme shrieked, heat rushed to her face, and she dove back into the bathroom. "Kala!"

Snorts of laughter from the room turned Eme's faint blush crimson, and she huffed as Kala brought in her bag, an apologetic grin on her face. "Sorry, Eme."

"Give that here," Eme grumbled, but with a hint of a smile. "And tell Rafe he'd better wipe that grin off his face, or I'll toss his beast of a computer down nineteen floors of stairs, or worse, down the elevator shaft."

5:15 P.M. EDT

Dinner that night was delivered to Eme's and Kala's room, where all the St. Bruno's students had gathered, but their feast wasn't much healthier than the previous evening; since it was on the airline's tab, Eme, Kala, Rafe, Carly, Cassidy, and Michael, had ordered huge club sandwiches, milkshakes, pie, and ice-cream sundaes. Mrs. Murphy popped her head in every hour or so to make sure that all were behaving, the Cyborg in particular, and reminded the entire party that *lights out* was still ten o'clock sharp.

Kala talked the others into playing her travel trivia game, which Michael found extremely boring. Rafe's solution to that: his laptop plugged into the back of the television set, streaming the latest movies (some yet to hit the theatres), freshly ripped off the internet. Michael's demeanour changed in an instant once the new *Harry Potter* movie remake began to play; it was clear that Rafe had become the boy's new hero.

While Michael took over one of the beds, the others sat on the floor, laughing, eating, and taking turns playing Kala's game. Rafe mumbled his answers through most of the games while watching the movie out of the corner of his eye.

"Shall we order more ice cream before the evening draws to a close?" he asked as Kala won the final game, making her the undisputed champion.

"None for me," Eme said, patting her stomach. "I've eaten enough to see me through to Switzerland." Carly, Kala, and Cassidy held up their hands and shook their heads.

"I'll have some!" Michael exclaimed, jumping up from the bed. "Chocolate, strawberry, and chocolate chip cookie dough, Rafe!" he exclaimed with a huge grin.

Eme snickered. "He's going to be bouncing off the walls all night. Good luck getting to sleep, Rafe."

"Curses!" Rafe ran a hand back through his wavy dark hair and chuckled. "Room for one more tonight, ladies?" He raised his eyebrows in anticipation of their affirmative answer.

All four girls glanced at each other and shook their heads as one. "Nice try, but you're out of here at ten, Mister," Kala sneered.

Rafe sighed with faux dismay. "Surely you know that the Cyborg will depart, wise Kala, but the wild one shall remain!"

They all turned to watch the thirteen year-old bouncing merrily on Kala's bed while laughing hysterically at the bootlegged Harry Potter movie. This was going to be another long and sleepless night—but not for any of the girls.

Stargate Hotel
Friday, June 12, 2015
11:20 A.M. EDT

The next morning found the worst of Bruno well and truly gone, with only a light pattering of spent rain to mark the hurricane's passing—that and the flooded roads and uprooted trees, the muddy buildings, and the swath of broken glass littering most of Atlanta.

Eme was just glad that the airport was nearly caught up with the backlog of canceled flights, and their flight was on for that evening; all runways had been cleared, and Hurricane Bruno would soon be nothing more than a bad memory of an inconvenient delay. Mrs. Murphy was organizing everyone into groups for the return trip to the airport, pairing up the younger kids with the older ones in order to keep everyone together. She seemed remarkably back in her element after a good night's rest, and most of the St. Bruno students couldn't muster up much strength to argue with her; they were all feeling bloated from the large amounts of food the previous night.

Amazingly, Rafe seemed to have found a way of sleeping through Michael's sugar-high. "Cleared for take-off," he exclaimed, with his Shakespearean hat firmly in place, as he typed away at his laptop. "The Cyborg shall be swimming in chocolate waterfalls amongst the mighty Alps before the sun rises once more."

Atlanta Airport
9:35 PM EDT

After a day of wading through the logjam of inconvenienced passengers anxious to board their long-awaited flights, and trying unsuccessfully to keep tabs on the teenagers (who took every opportunity to sneak away from their chaperone to ride the airport's underground tram), it was with immense relief that Mrs. Murphy herded her charges through the security checkpoints and onto the waiting aircraft. There was the usual struggle of cramming bags into the overhead compartments; however, Eme eventually managed to take her seat, relaxing into the headrest, looking forward to their departure. She struggled a bit fastening her seat belt, but she had no qualms at all about bidding Atlanta farewell.

As the engines whirred to life, and the plane taxied onto the runway, Kala swapped her seat with Carly so that she was sitting next to Rafe, across the aisle from Eme and her aunt. Both of them giggled as Mrs. Murphy assured Eme that this would be the last time she would ever collect the international students and, quite possibly, the last time she would ever board an airplane. Eme nodded along politely, wondering how soon she'd be able to check her e-mail and send another text to GG Anne as promised.

Maybe not until they landed in Switzerland.

With five hundred grateful passengers on board, the mighty aircraft roared down the runway, soaring into a bleary black sky, shooting for the clouds. There was a round of applause from Rafe, which Eme and the rest of the passengers soon adopted.

At long last, Bruno was long gone, and St. Bruno's was on the horizon.

CIA Secret Command Center, Bermuda Airport
10:45 PM ADT

A distraught man bent over a sophisticated computer setup; intricate scanners, immense lasers, and other hardware occupied the large work surface upon which also sat several flat-screen monitors. As he frantically typed in codes, which he just as frantically erased, two large, menacing figures loomed behind him, watching and recording his every move.

"Hey, what about that code, Edelman; you're moving too fast—slow down!" yelled Gun, his hand raised to hit the man cowering in front of him.

Ed grabbed his arm. "Leave the poor guy alone; you're not helping him, you know."

"Yeah, well, the 'poor guy' is costing us time we can't afford." He glared at his partner and continued, "If we don't get this program perfected before our colleagues from Washington arrive, we might as well kiss our money, freedom, and lives good-bye. And our overseas connection is threatening to send in foreign goons armed with the passports and CIA IDs—that we heisted for them—how'll we explain that?" He turned back to the visibly shaking computer technician. "Now get on with it, Edelman, before I decide I don't need you anymore and send you to join our crustacean friend."

Tim Edelman took out a handkerchief and mopped his forehead before returning to the stressful job of pretending to perfect his e-mail protocol. He had envisioned what this program could facilitate when he was a student at St. Bruno's summer tech camp twenty years before; however, if he had known then what his revolutionary experiment would cost him, he'd have shelved the entire insane idea. Instead, he pursued his wild dream, and then these federal goons took him away from his wife, two kids, and his CEO position at Amazemail in Atlanta. He had no idea how the CIA had learned of the protocol or how they had managed to infiltrate his house, putting it under surveillance, but from what he could gather from their discussion after their flight from Atlanta, it had been going on for years. Too late to worry about what-ifs now; he couldn't let them learn the last piece of this protocol puzzle. It may cost him his life, but if stalling for time kept this discovery out of enemy hands, it was the least he could do for the security of his country and the lives of his family.

After another thirty minutes of monitoring Edelman's progress on the protocol's "fabricated" glitch, a disgruntled Gun grabbed the man by the scruff of the neck and dragged him from the computer toward the hallway to the left of the central command center. The man remained silent, believing his ordeal was about to come to a bloody end. Instead, Gun unlocked his cell, throwing him unceremoniously toward a toilet and the lone piece of furniture that occupied the eight-foot-square enclosure. As he fell, his right foot snagged the leg of the cot, causing his loafer to fly across the floor.

"Hey, what's this, Edelman!" exclaimed Ed as he bent down to retrieve the small black device that had dislodged from the shoe. "Holding out on us, eh?" Tim forced an air of nonchalance, while his insides screamed in horror at their discovery; his whole life was on that flash drive, including his computer-hacking program and the key to his protocol.

"Hey, those are all my family's photos!" was the man's lame response.

Ed smirked and turned the shiny black device over in his hand. He held it up for Gun to examine. "What do you think, Gun, look like a family photo album to you?"

Gun grabbed the key chain clip from his partner and dangled the USB device close to his face. "Yeah, it does," he sneered at Ed, "and I love looking at baby pictures; let's go check it out." He turned back to Tim who was still sprawled on the floor, doing his best to remain calm. "Let's go, Timmy boy; we want you to tell us all about yer *lovely* family." He reached down and yanked Tim to his feet, shoving him back through the door toward the computer room.

With his thoughts in overdrive, Tim slouched in the computer chair while Ed jammed the flash drive into the USB port. Instantly the encryption screen appeared, requesting the pass code. One glare from Gun, and Tim typed ten keys and waited while the screen went black, then flashed a red "Fatal Error" message, followed by the distinctive sound of a bugle playing "Taps."

Stunned, then furious, Gun hoisted Tim from his chair by the back of his shirt and slammed his meaty fist into the side of his face, followed by, "You little piece of...!" which Tim didn't hear. Nor did he feel the subsequent punches he received on the return trip to his cell.

Meanwhile, Ed took the key chain flash drive and clipped it to his belt loop, for safekeeping, before following his partner and their meal ticket.

CHAPTER NINE
BERMUDA TANGLE

Destiny Flight 65
Saturday, June 13, 2015
1:22 A.M. ADT

Illuminated by unrelenting streaks of lightning, the Vestige 645 jetliner trembled on fragile wings to the beat of the inevitable thunder. For ten minutes, Destiny's Flight 65 had executed an intricate tango with Hurricane Bruno ten thousand feet above an angry sea; her brutish partner showed no signs of tiring, until the plane met Bruno's eye; it blinked and the jetliner plummeted three thousand feet into the void.

Destiny's pilot had warned everyone on board of the impending turbulence; as a result, no injuries occurred during the precipitous drop into the air pocket. Nevertheless, nerves were strained to the breaking point until the swept-wing jetliner stabilized. Most of the five hundred Europe-bound passengers had regained their composure and anxiously followed the crew's orders to prepare for an unscheduled landing in Bermuda.

The *Island* of Bermuda.

One teenager had been unfazed by the nervous clamor of her fellow passengers until the announcement of the impending detour. She wished she were sitting closer to her friends so that Rafe could reassure her that his account of the Tempest, the island, and the renaming of the hurricane was merely a hilarious coincidence. She pressed her freckled nose to the porthole window and shuddered at the ferocity of the approaching storm's outer eye.

"Elaine, how can you watch? Doesn't it make you more nervous?" asked her seatmate.

"Actually, this isn't quite as scary as our flight into Atlanta, Mrs. Murphy," the girl answered, checking her seatbelt for the third time that hour.

The older woman shook her head at her student when several bursts of light reclaimed Eme's attention.

Lightning coursed through clouds that resembled giant rippling brains engaged in menacing thoughts. In the next streak of light, Eme noticed that the left wing of the plane had tilted toward the earth; their descent continued with no sign of Bermuda below—only lashing rain and mountainous storm clouds. Another flash illuminated something on the wing that was glaring at her.

Mayrah Murphy gasped when Eme suddenly reared away from the window. The woman gripped her shoulder. "Dear, maybe you shouldn't watch."

She shook her head at the summer school counselor and resumed her focus on the sight beyond the window, but the reflection of her two frightened eyes were all that stared back.

The plane continued to shake; it then listed farther to the left as it continued its spiraling descent toward Bermuda. Her last meal threatened to reemerge; however, morbid fascination forced her continued voyeurism. Lightning again revealed a long, thin eyestalk slithering toward her window; it pressed its hideous, but vaguely familiar, bloodshot eyeball against the pane. Was it trying to break in? *I spoke too soon—this flight is definitely scarier.* The lightning faded, and the eye disappeared.

Here comes lunch! She slammed the cover over the window and put her head between her knees, nearly paralyzed with fear.

It's trying to get inside.

Mrs. Murphy patted her shoulder in sympathetic understanding, totally unaware of the visions that were upsetting her. Eme was relieved that she made no further comments.

For several more minutes, the aircraft toiled with its descent through the storm. Eme burrowed into her seat and tried to put the image of the eye out of her mind.

It hadn't been real.

It couldn't have been real.

She was just overwrought from the turbulence and the last few days in Atlanta. She quickly located the airsickness bag, just in case, and took deep, calming breaths.

Suddenly a sound of twisting metal, of something being crushed, permeated the window. She quickly turned her head to observe the reaction of Mrs. Murphy who now had her eyes closed. She glanced across the aisle at her fellow students who merely smiled and waved when she caught their attention. Curiously, no one else seemed alarmed.

Didn't they hear it?

Her heart skipped a few beats. In her mind she envisioned a hideous tentacle tightening around the wing of the plane, biting and tearing, as the eye stared at her through the window cover.

The suspense was more unbearable than the possible reality. Making an immediate decision, Eme leaned back slowly then snapped up the window cover. There was nothing—nothing but the relentless storm lashing her window and washing away her foolish fears.

Just then the plane leveled against the storm, and the rattling of the fuselage subsided. Mrs. Murphy and the other passengers breathed sighs of relief; Eme released a greater one—there was no eye, no tentacle attempting to rip off the wing; it was merely her recurring nightmare encroaching upon her imagination.

The trip monitor embedded in the seat-back in front of her indicated that their plane was at two thousand feet and descending rapidly. Rain lashed Eme's window; once more, lightning tore apart the sky.

No eye. No tentacle.

Good.

A minute passed, maybe more, and with only the sound of the blood pumping in her ears, Eme waited with five hundred nervous people for Destiny to touch down.

Wham!

Something slammed into her window. The outer pane cracked, and fractures spider webbed across the glass.

Eme's scream and the passengers' frightful chorus joined the screech of tires biting into Bermuda. She could see nothing outside; all the same, she knew...

A rush of utter terror and impending doom bathed her in a cold sweat, and she tried to stand, to get away from the window, but her seat belt was on so tight.

An ear-piercing screech of wounded metal renewed the terrified screams in the Destiny cabin. The plane careened down the runway, its brakes squealing for purchase on the tarmac. A flash of lightning once again lit up the world beyond the window, and Eme saw nothing.

Nothing, as the left wheel fell away from the fuselage, torn from its housing by the ferocity of the storm...or worse.

A shudder rippled through the aircraft, and for one brief moment, the crippled airliner balanced on one good leg, until gravity and Bruno intervened. Eme cried out as her world tilted left.

A crash.

Then, darkness.

Bermuda Airport Tarmac
1:45 A.M. ADT

Am I awake or in that incessant nightmare? Eme thought upon regaining consciousness a few minutes after the landing. The muffled moans and cries around her were not enough evidence that this was reality, nor was Bruno's relentless pounding on the hull of the crippled plane. When she tried to unfasten her seat belt and winced at the excruciating pain in her shoulder and back, she was convinced—this was no dream. *Why am I wedged sideways in this seat?* She reached behind her to discover that someone's carryon bag must have fallen from an overhead bin and was now lodged between her and Mrs. Murphy. Even though her belt was all that kept her from falling into the cracked window, she worked through the pain, trying unsuccessfully to remove the bag and release her restraint.

Without warning, oxygen masks descended from the alcove above her head, erratically bobbing in time with the undulating, storm-pummeled plane. The lights flickered and stark terror trumped her frustration when acrid smoke attacked her nostrils. Panicky screams and wails now filled the cabin as row by row of passengers realized that the plane was on fire.

The Vestige 645 shuddered and shook; it perilously balanced on its damaged left wing at the end of the runway. Both aisles of the wide-bodied jetliner were strewn with luggage, pillows, blankets, and other debris ejected from the overhead bins during the horrific landing.

Eme squirmed against her seat restraint. The angle of her body in the tilted plane made it difficult to see anything that wasn't in her direct line of sight; however, she could hear the pilots as they battled the electrical fire in the floor near the cockpit and see the frantic flight attendants as they cautiously picked their way through the debris, assisting and comforting the more frightened and injured passengers. The violent jerking of the jetliner intensified in concert with the passengers' screams, increasing the crew's frantic efforts to assuage their fears.

Eme continued her struggle with the belt when a heavy weight fell on top of the carryon bag behind her right shoulder. Slowly she wiggled her body enough without crushing her unconscious seatmate's head, and, with a trembling right hand, managed to check for a pulse. It was faint, but at least Mrs. Murphy hadn't died during their terrifying landing.

Even though the pilot had informed them that the landing would be rocky, Eme couldn't understand what possible emergency had warranted an unscheduled stop on Bermuda with a category one hurricane battering the island. She could only imagine the number of lawsuits the airline would incur if anyone were seriously injured just because someone had an impulsive desire for a tropical vacation. Grimacing at that ridiculous thought, she rechecked Mrs. Murphy's pulse, heaving a sigh of relief that it was slightly stronger.

The noise level in the cabin increased as the smoke from the fire continued to drift toward the rear of the plane. "Mrs. Murphy, please wake up! Please, we have to get out of here!" The young girl prodded her summer school counselor. "Please, Mrs. Murphy!"

"Attention, folks," crackled the copilot's shaky voice from the damaged intercom. "Please relax, keep your belts tightened, and rest assured that your Destiny crew has the situation under control.

The electrical fire in the collapsed wheel well is out; there's no immediate danger." Cheers from the passengers who had not donned their oxygen masks, greeted these words. "Stay calm for a few more minutes; use the oxygen while we ready the plane for evacuation."

"Eme, are you OK?" Kala asked.

With difficulty Eme shifted in her seat but failed in an attempt to see her two new friends.

"I think so, Kala, but your aunt lost consciousness when we crashed; she's still breathing, but she's got a huge bump on her forehead—probably from one of the falling bags. How are you and Rafe?"

"I'm fine..." Kala's voice became much clearer when she loosened her seatbelt and leaned across the aisle to examine the injured woman; she gently righted her in her seat and placed the oxygen mask over her mouth. "Do you want one, too, Eme?" she asked. Eme coughed but shook her head. The lights ceased flickering. Kala surveyed the rows of people behind them. "From what I can see from all the open overhead bins and bloodied heads, I assume that most of the injuries were caused by the falling bags; many who are sitting in a left-hand window seat, like you, also appear to be unconscious."

"I think a bag may have knocked me out for a few seconds," replied Eme. She felt the knot on her forehead. "And now it's crammed into my back."

"I can't reach it, Eme; you're going to have to wait until we're cleared to evacuate."

Eme twisted her body as far as she dared and responded, "That's all right, I can wait, but can you see..." She was interrupted by a litany of obscenities, accompanied by the loud clacking of computer keys, drifting across the aisle. Kala smiled at Eme's frown and remarked, "Our Shakespearean wannabe is disgusted that he can't reach the blokes in the control tower to complain about our less-than-stellar landing."

Eme smirked at a vision of Rafe giving his beloved laptop a furious pounding. "Can you see Michael and the twins?" she asked.

Kala craned her neck to see into the First Class section. I can't see Michael, but the girls are waving to me that they're all right." Kala returned the wave and gave them a 'thumbs up.' She turned back to Eme. "As tenacious as Michael seems to be, I'll bet he's fine, too."

The wail of sirens signaled that help had arrived and silenced the passengers. Kala resumed her upright position, retightened her seat belt, and added her "Hallelujahs" and cheers of relief to the impromptu chorus.

Flashing lights from the flotilla of rescue vehicles and buses on the tarmac cast eerie patterns on Eme's cracked window, punctuating the surreal scene. She took the opportunity to check whether the eyeball remained attached to the wing and smiled at the alien-free surface. She shuddered, chuckled, and muttered to herself, "It's all your imagination, Eme."

The copilot resumed his position near the partition. He wiped his brow with a Destiny Airline handkerchief and continued, "Due to the angle of the plane, there are only four exits available to us. Please, all capable passengers locate the exit nearest you and make your way there calmly and carefully; a flight attendant will help you down the slide." He added in a lower tone, "No, sir, please, you cannot take your carry-on bag." Eme could see the copilot, three rows in front of her, brace himself against the bulkhead between First Class and Coach and pause in his announcement to contend with a disgruntled businessperson about his briefcase.

"Please, everyone," he continued more emphatically, "leave your belongings on the plane, even if they're in the aisle; they will be delivered to the terminal." He glanced again at the same man who was now swearing at his cell phone, and added, "Also, your cell phones and Internet connections are inoperative because of storm damage to the airport's communication towers and lack of satellite visibility."

A loud snap, accompanied by a few colorful words, drifted across the aisle, indicating that Rafe had given up his quest to contact the control tower and had slammed the lid of his laptop.

"Just follow the red aisle lights to your exit," the pilot continued. "If you're injured, stay calm and remain seated, with your seat belts and oxygen masks securely fastened, until all the other passengers are off-loaded and the medics are able to board."

The businessperson huffed but followed orders, joining the listing queue of anxious passengers who were bracing themselves against the seats, as they stumbled over bags and debris toward the exit. The crew won their struggle against the hurricane's savage strength and threw the doors open, granting access to the raging storm. The exiting passengers buffeted themselves against Bruno's encroachment on their cabin sanctuary.

Eme squirmed and fidgeted with her seat belt buckle. When Kala and Rafe appeared in her field of vision, she stopped her struggle long enough to focus on her two friends. Kala removed the bag behind Eme's back, much to the redhead's immense relief. "Ahh, thanks, Kala, but I still can't unfasten my seat belt," she complained as she leaned back in her seat.

After checking her aunt's pulse, Kala shook her head at Eme who had resumed fidgeting, frowning, and fussing with the belt release button. "Since she's still unconscious, you won't be able to get out until the medics move her, Eme," Kala shouted over the roaring wind and escalating chatter from the apprehensive passengers.

"Fair Juliet is much safer here than the Cyborg and the Wise One will be sliding into the jaws of the Tempest!" Rafe added in a low roar.

Eme sighed, giving up her quest for freedom. She pouted and turned sad eyes to her friends, then noticed a rectangular bulge under Rafe's jacket, and scoffed, "I see you're following orders about leaving your belongings on board."

Rafe's eyes widened and he frowned. "The Cyborg resents the fair one's insinuation!" The slap he gave his very hard, flat stomach resounded with an emphatic thud. "Persephone and her... *ahem*...peripherals," he wagged his eyebrows, "are not belongings—they're as much a part of the Cyborg as his...his spleen!" He raised his arm for emphasis and nearly lost his balance.

The girls laughed as he regained his footing. "That's for sure," added Kala, "he hasn't let it...er, *her*, out of his *lecherous* grasp since we left Atlanta." She smirked and added, "Actually, it's his sixth appendage."

Rafe opened his mouth to object and then his face reddened. He gave her a cheeky grin and winked. "Wise Kala is as perceptive as she is beautiful."

Eme's laughter followed Kala and the self-proclaimed Ruler of Cyberspace as the faltering flow of motivated passengers swept them toward freedom.

"See you in a trice, fair Juliet! Ariel and Caliban await— *Geronimo!*" was Rafe's parting salute before he and Kala slid into the stormy night.

Eme frowned at Rafe's repeated reference to Shakespeare's *The Tempest*. She shuddered, shook her head at her irrational fears, and wondered, not for the first time, how he had come to speak in the third-person vernacular.

One more check on Mrs. Murphy convinced her that the woman was in no immediate danger. She returned her gaze to the chaos just beyond her cracked window; because of the wing and the angle of the tilted plane, she wasn't able see the crews clearing the last passenger from the slide and removing it, but she could hear the sirens of the fire trucks approaching. She assumed it was a matter of minutes before the stairs were installed for the medics.

With a few more calming breaths, she resigned herself to wait patiently for the rescue teams. Since she was seated so far forward, she could see only a few of the injured who were also waiting for help to arrive; however, even over the roar of the wind, she could hear the soft cries and moans behind her. Then she heard something more ominous—a strange splintering noise outside her window. *It's coming from the wing!* She had just turned her head to check when...

"I'm sorry it has taken so long for us to reach you, Miss," a calm southern voice drawled. "Are you injured?" he asked, bracing himself against the seat with one hand and checking Mrs. Murphy's pulse and injuries with the other.

Eme redirected her attention and strained to see the flight attendant behind her seat. "No, but my seat belt is jam..."

Crash!

"Aahhhhhhh!"

Eme's world collapsed onto its head.

Bermuda Airport Tarmac
2:12 A.M. CET

"Oh, no—Juliet!"

"Aunt Mayrah!"

Rafe's and Kala's frightened cries joined those of the other freed passengers. The thunderous crash of the plane toppling onto the runway eclipsed the roar of Bruno. Thankfully, the deplaned travelers were too busy navigating the Bruno-driven debris, guided by the rescue workers, and were nowhere near the plane when it crashed onto its cracked wing and caught fire. Still, many people were attempting to return to the plane—to their belongings, to their loved ones.

"Stay back, folks, we have everything under control! Board the buses, please! Let us do our jobs!" hollered the flight attendant, holding his arms out to block a few of the more motivated passengers. With help from the flames that were now shooting from the gaping hole, caused by the collapsed left wing, the rescuers succeeded in driving the anxious passengers toward the waiting buses.

While the crew members were urging the passengers to move faster, a firefighter radioed for the ladder truck that would allow them to reach the only available exit doors—doors which were now located near the *top* of the fuselage. Several of the crew battled the flames, while two men used giant saws to cut a new door in the roof of the plane—the section of the fuselage that was now facing them.

The only option open to Kala, Rafe, and the others was to follow orders; they were ushered onto the buses, but not one person could tear their eyes away from the unfolding rescue of their friends and relatives. Prayers issued forth from many in the group, intermingled with expletives from many others

Bermuda Airport Terminal
2:15 A.M. CET

Two CIA agents, in nearly identical polyester suits, were standing at the expansive terminal window, waiting for Destiny Flight 65 to land, anxious to finish their mission. When the plane's wheel fell off upon impact with the runway, they were dismayed, but when the wing broke and caught fire, they were afraid—for themselves.

Many minutes later, after fretfully discussing contingency plans in case their target was delayed or died, they watched the first of the passenger buses begin its journey to the terminal. Gun was the first to recover his composure; he led his trembling partner to a nearby lounge seat.

Ed Turner, a tall, thin man in his early forties, with brown eyes and curly black hair, sat with his back hunched, elbows on his knees. He watched the green door to the hangar corridor, fiddling with the photo gallery on his phone, and breathing heavily. "What if she's still on the plane? She could be dead—lots of people could be dead. You and I will have a lot to answer for after this disaster, Gun!" He turned his head and glared at his partner, beads of perspiration glistening on his forehead.

Gun leaned back in his seat, sipping his beer, and continued to stare out of the terminal windows, watching the rescue efforts at the far end of the runway. He took a deep breath and finally glanced at his partner, chuckled, and addressed his concerns. "Oh, calm down, Ed, my boy!" He slapped his partner's back. "We may get a chewin' out, but we'll just stick to our story: 'It was in the best interest of national security, *sir*!' That always works. He returned his gaze to the rain-streaked window and continued, "Then Dvorsky can work his magic and clean up the mess. By the time they figure it all out, we'll have our hard-earned dough aboard our fishing boat, heading toward our Cape Verde retirement." He sighed, plopped his feet upon the table in front of him, and grinned. "Just think, we'll soon be reading all about the aftermath of our exploits in the tabloids, surrounded by white sand, Creole cuties, and cases of booze. We'll be National...no," he paused, his eyes brightened, he raised a finger in the air, and continued, "*International* celebrities!" His eyes were wide and glistening when he lifted his cup to his partner. "Here's to our happily ever after, Eddie boy!" While his partner sank lower in his seat, Gun chugged the contents of his cup, smacking his lips, and silently blessing non-extradition treaties.

The commotion caused by a team of medics and triage units streaming into the nearly vacant passenger lounge, ended Gun's reverie. By the time the first passenger bus arrived in the hangar, the two agents had grabbed more beer and relocated their stakeout operation to a bank of plastic seats at the far end of the lounge. They continued their vigil in silence: Ed was lost in thoughts about his twenty years of faithful CIA service, now blown to smithereens, and of the worst possible consequences facing them for their actions; while Gun—no doubt inspired by the potted palms directly behind him—spun fanciful vignettes of tropical nude beaches and beer.

Meanwhile, the medics worked feverishly, stocking the triage stations with the medical supplies and devices that would soon save many—but not all—victims of Ed and Gun's greed.

Terminal Hangar
2:20 A.M. CDT

"Hurry, Rafe," urged a tearful Kala when the bus doors opened.

Rafe gave up trying to patch into security cameras or terminal news feeds about the crash; he stowed his computer and followed the blonde from the bus, anxious to watch the rescue work from the vast lounge window he had noticed on their short drive to the terminal; although, he first needed to attend to other pressing matters.

They followed their swiftly-moving fellow passengers down the corridor that connected the hangar to the waiting area. Once through the door, Rafe grabbed Kala's arm. "The Cyborg is in need of the facilities, fair one; I'll meet you and the runts in a trice."

With a nod from the girl, he doffed his hat to the tearful St. Bruno contingent, located the sign to the restrooms, and made his way through the throng of passengers and medical teams.

At that same moment, Ed and Gun had begun their search for their target among the fourth group of passengers who were now streaming into the lounge. Ed was busy studying the photos of Eme that Gun had requested from the surveillance cameras at the Los Angeles Airport, periodically glancing toward the door.

"Just look for a redheaded teenage girl, Ed; there can't be too many of them—forget the photos!"

Rafe was walking past the agents at the time Gun made this last comment. "Redheaded teenage girl" caught his ear; he glanced at the two men and caught a glimpse of the photo on Ed's phone. Without missing a step, he made an immediate detour around the cluster of palm trees that bordered Ed and Gun's bank of seats. Unbeknownst to the CIA agents, he squatted between the back terminal wall and the huge planter, removed a small plastic device from his computer bag, stuck it behind his ear, and remained as still as a corpse. Several seconds later...

"She's not with the St. Bruno group. See that blonde with the three younger kids." Gun pointed in Kala's direction. "She's the assistant to Leura's mother, who's also not with them; they're probably both trapped on the plane. If they're injured, it might make it easier for us to grab the Venture girl when they bring them in."

"Well that means we're going to be stuck here for an hour or more." Ed sighed, rose from his seat, and stretched. "I'm going to get something to eat; what do you want?"

"Get me another beer and a pastrami sandwich on a sourdough roll—lots of mustard and horseradish. I'll keep watch on our group."

Ed walked toward the food court which had remained open for the convenience of the late arrivals.

"Come on, missy, where are you? We don't have all night!" Gun grumbled, "Your little boyfriend will be happy to see you," he cackled and crumpled his empty beer cup, throwing it toward, and missing, a nearby waste receptacle.

Rafe's head was spinning—*what boyfriend?* He was anxious to hear more, but he used Ed's brief absence to finish his original mission; he returned to his stakeout behind the palms just before Ed returned with their food.

The agents continued to discuss their plans while they ate. What Rafe heard over the next ten minutes would forever alter his universe.

CHAPTER TEN
OUT OF THE FRYING PAN, INTO THE CLOSET

Destiny Flight 65
Saturday, June 13, 2015
2:15 A.M. CDT

Drip.
　Drip.
　Drip.
　The warmth of the crimson fluid pooling in her open palm was Eme's first sensation when she awoke with her face smashed into the ceiling of the airliner; she winced at the excruciating pain in her shoulder, forehead, and cheek. The latest disaster had broken the final link in the seat belt that had held her captive, and she groaned as she struggled from under the unconscious, bloodied body of the flight attendant. The blood dripping from the man's split skull beat a soft tattoo on the shattered

plastic windowpane. Was he still alive? With extreme care, she knelt by his side and checked for a pulse. A larger pool of blood was forming under the six-inch gash in his forearm, but he was still breathing.

Once she was on her feet, she fought to maintain her balance on the rocking wall of the plane and located a package of cloth napkins that had fallen from an overhead bin. After folding one of them in a triangle, she tied it tightly around his arm. Then, pulling the belt from his slacks and the handkerchief from his jacket pocket, she applied the temporary dressing to his head wound.

Satisfied with her handiwork, she turned her attention to Mrs. Murphy who hung limply from her seat just above the girl's shoulder. Eme checked her pulse, which was faint but steady. *It's a good thing she wasn't conscious through this ordeal*, she mused.

The plane's fuselage was no longer resting on its broken wing, which had finally given way under Bruno's relentless assault. Eme could only guess that the plane was now flat on its side—a crumpled heap on the Bermuda runway.

A *burning* crumpled heap.

The pilot had informed them that the fuel had been jettisoned before they attempted a landing. Since fuel is stored in the wing, the electrical fire would have, otherwise, turned this disaster into a catastrophe.

Violent coughing met the thick smoke that was filling the cabin once again. All of the passengers were hanging helplessly by their seat restraints, and not one of the six crew members, lying smashed against the walls and ceiling of the aircraft, was moving. The crackling flames, cries, and moans of passengers inside now joined the howling wind and screams of rescue workers and passengers outside. Even though she had suffered various scrapes, cuts, and bruises during the collapse of the wing, Eme was the only mobile person on board.

And the flames were rising.

Once she realized that no one was coming to their immediate rescue, Eme's adrenaline launched her into action. After placing blankets over the flight attendant, she scrambled as quickly as the tilted, rocking cabin and her injuries would allow, toward the source of the fire near the cockpit. By the time Eme spotted the fire extinguisher next to the cockpit door, the flame-resistant plastic wall covering was a blistered sheet of Destiny blue.

With her jacket buttoned over her mouth and nose, she inched her way through exploding soda cans, plastic cups, and peanuts; then she tripped on the outstretched arm of an unconscious crew member near a bulkhead seat, propelling her head-first into the valve stem of the red metal extinguisher.

Dazed but determined, she ignored the renewed pain in her head, neck, and right shoulder, and the salty sweat and blood pooling in the corner of her mouth; she yanked the extinguisher from its housing and attempted to twist the hot, slippery valve. After several seconds of struggle against the stubborn knob, Eme succeeded in releasing foam on the growing electrical fire in the tilted floor, presumably caused by the shorted wires in the shattered wing. The sizzles and pops from the dying fire were quite possibly the most satisfying sounds she had ever heard. *But what if there is fuel remaining in the wing? Could the fire reignite?*

The shouts from the rescue workers outside filtered through the walls of the fuselage, as they launched a new plan to release the trapped passengers, and refocused Eme's thoughts. She could hear the giant saws attacking the top of the plane near the cockpit. She tossed the empty canister behind her and crept slowly, carefully along the cracked walls of the fuselage, placing blankets under the heads of the unconscious crew members.

The teenager unbuttoned her jacket that had been covering her nose and mouth and continued to help those she could reach and offer words of comfort to those left dangling just above her head. "The medics are almost here, stay calm," she repeated to all who could hear her. By the time she arrived at the tail of the plane, the first of the rescue teams had broken through the ceiling in the first class section, and most of the crew members had regained consciousness.

The wind and rain that accompanied the entry of the rescuers cleared much of the smoke and gave welcome relief to the first class passengers. However, another round of violent coughing erupted, caused by the smoke redirected toward the rear of the plane.

As Eme retraced her steps, she rechecked the condition of each person she could reach, but she didn't dare release any from their seat belts.

"Ello, Miss. You all right?" bellowed a slim, bronze-skinned man with an English accent.

Eme had just finished checking Mrs. Murphy and the flight attendant she had helped earlier; both were still unconscious, but alive. She stood and wiped away the blood dripping into her eyes and mouth, and yelled, "Yes, I'm fine, but at least fifty passengers and crew are injured and suffering from smoke inhalation and worse."

She approached the man; the name tag on his work shirt boldly introduced him as Ben O'Reilly. He turned toward the front of the plane and back to Eme, raising the empty fire extinguisher. "Good on you, Miss; those electrical fires can cause a right bit of damage." He then paused for a moment, appraising her, his smile replaced with a look of absolute seriousness. "Miss...?"

"Eme," she answered his implied question.

"Well, Miss Eme, you may have saved everyone on this plane, plus the lives of us blokes trying to rescue you."

Eme blushed and was about to respond when the emergency door, located above their heads, flew off, followed by the remaining three hatches—four more toys for Bruno to juggle. With five openings, the hurricane was able to clear all of the remaining smoke from the cabin while the rescue crews dropped rope ladders and emergency medical equipment into the plane. Eme was mesmerized by the fearlessness of the first rescuer, a woman, who slid down the ladder closest to her, rather than taking the time to use the rungs. The medic smiled at them as she passed, working her way toward the rear of the plane—toward the passengers most affected by the smoke. Ben grinned at the awe-struck teen, grabbed her hand, and carefully led her through the scores of ladders, medical supplies, and other lifesaving equipment. Emergency workers helped them pass through the huge opening they had cut in the roof of the fuselage.

Eme glanced one last time at the chaos behind her, praying that Mrs. Murphy and the remaining passengers would soon be rescued and safely inside the terminal. She and Ben stood on the brink of the plane's gaping wound, pausing to get their bearings, while they braced themselves against the storm. She refastened her jacket and surveyed the damage to the once proud airliner. Then, with one leap into the storm, she cleared the small chasm between the plane and the stairs that would lead her away from her near-death experience.

Once Eme was on the ground, she accepted a wet towel and ice pack for her bloodied head but waved off further medical assistance. After a short argument with a persistent medic, he relented and accepted her logic that there were people in more need of assistance than she.

Taking her arm and guiding her farther away from the medical staff, Ben had to shout to be heard over the storm. "It looks like it'll be awhile before all of the injured passengers are evacuated. Would you like to ride in the crew bus with us, Miss Eme?"

"Yes, thanks, Ben, I really don't need any immediate help, and I don't want to take a seat away from someone who does," she replied.

Ben nodded and directed her to a crew bus where she could wait until he and his crew finished their mission.

The sticky plastic seats and relative quiet of the van were a welcome relief from the Destiny death trap; her breathing and heart rate slowed. She watched the injured passengers as they were removed one by one and transferred to the myriad of waiting ambulances. As she waited, she drifted off to sleep, thinking about the "dastardly, cruel fates," as Rafe would call them, that had led her to this place and time.

Alexandria, Virginia
2:30 A.M. EDT

"No, I did not give the OK to bring down the plane on Bermuda, sir."

Pause

"Yes, that is exactly what I am saying, Agent Dexter acted alone."

Pause.

"Yes, sir, I will be at Kennedy as soon as possible, and I *will* take care of the situation."

Click.

Agent Stuart Dvorsky sat on the edge of his bed, running his hands through his thin gray hair, gazing at the beautiful woman asleep beside him—his wonderful wife of forty years who had asked him to retire the year before. What would he do if this incident cost him his career and pension?

Damn you, Gun!

Bermuda Runway
3:33 A.M. ADT

An hour after the crash, Eme awoke to the violent rocking of the crew bus; the hurricane had increased its ferocity and was pummeling the van with debris from the plane and vegetation from the island. Her attention was drawn to the rescue workers who had finished their task of removing the injured and, quite possibly, dead passengers. Her thoughts drifted to her friends and the condition of Mrs. Murphy.

When the last ambulance departed from the grisly scene, sirens blaring, the battered crew battled Bruno to their waiting buses. Twenty solemn faces told the tale of their life-saving mission. On the tarmac behind them, the sleek Vestige aircraft lay crumbled on its side, its right wing waving frantically in the early hours of the stormy morning like the leg of an enormous drowning beast.

As five of the crew came closer to her bus, Eme recognized Ben O'Reilly's face beneath several layers of grime mixed with sweat, blood, and rain. He glanced up and gave her a smile and small wave. After successfully wrestling open the door, allowing access to a huge blast of Bruno, he slid in beside her, splashing her with mud, blood, and more of the tropical storm.

"Sorry about that, Miss Eme. Dreadful storm, that Bruno! How're you holding up?"

Before Eme could answer, three more doors were yanked open, allowing the hurricane full access to the interior of the van. The crew heroically fought the storm's insistence at keeping the doors open. Eme shivered. Finally, the last door slammed, the young driver glanced into the rearview mirror, gave her a wink, and turned over the engine; they were on their way away from the crash site.

Fifteen seconds later, the sky ignited, and the earth shook.
Boom!
Kaboom!
Boom! Boom!

It was a good thing all passengers in the van were belted, because it skidded to a screeching halt. The raging fire was reflected in the eyes that were now turned back toward the plane, or what was left of it after a bolt of lightning struck the tip of the right wing. An inferno occupied the runway site where moments before stood the wreckage of Flight 65.

Bruno was propelling the flaming debris toward the crew bus, and the driver didn't hesitate a second longer; into first he jammed the transmission, and with screeching tires, he was now racing the devil itself toward the hangar. Eme couldn't take her eyes off the burning wreckage, thanking God that all the passengers had been moved to safety and the entire crew had evacuated before the explosion.

The teen wondered what morbid thoughts occupied the minds of these heroes. Ben's hand reached out for hers, squeezing it gently, as if he'd read her thoughts.

Once they were safely in the terminal's equipment garage, the crew let out a collective sigh of relief. Ben opened the door and helped Eme from the bus as several other exhausted fire crews raced toward their vehicles. Ben and his team turned to watch as new sirens blared into the night for one final visit to the doomed aircraft.

The bright light of the enclosure blinded her for a moment; the metal building magnified the roar of the storm and sent a chill down her spine. Without a backward glance, the six men and two women headed for the underground tunnel that led to the passenger section of the terminal. She watched as the driver stopped for a moment beside a small cabinet next to the door;

he deposited his keys then sprinted to catch up with his crew. Ben led Eme to the same green door.

"It looks as though your belongings are gone, love." The realization of his words hit Eme like a battering ram; her computer, money, passport, and clothes had just disintegrated. The horror of these thoughts must have shown on her face, because Ben patted her shoulder and added, "I've got to see to it that all the other vans are attended to. Just follow the tunnel; it will lead you right to the terminal's waiting area." He opened the door and pointed down the brightly lit corridor. "Report to the first agents you see. Tell them who you are, and they'll take care of you." He smiled at her and finished, "You're a real hero, Miss Eme. Just remember that belongings can be replaced, lives cannot!"

The girl blushed again and shyly responded, "I did nothing compared to what you all did tonight." She couldn't help her curiosity and blurted out, "Did anyone die?"

Ben studied her face for a few seconds, as if trying to decide whether he should answer her question. Finally, coming to a decision, he answered, "I can't tell you that, darlin'; you should ask security inside." He hesitated, and then added with a smile, "You can clean up in the staff restroom right there, if you like, before you meet your travel mates." He indicated the first door on the left side of the corridor.

At first, Eme was surprised at this comment, but then she touched the dried bloody patches on her grimy face, gave him a lopsided smile, and nodded. "Thanks, Ben, I must look like something that's been dragged through a war zone."

He chuckled and responded, "Battle scars of a hero, Miss Eme!" He smiled at her muddy blush and added, "I've got to go; you take care; it's been a real pleasure knowing you," He patted her shoulder one last time, turned on his heel, and disappeared behind the crew buses.

Just as she passed through the doorway, another battalion of fire fighters streamed down the corridor. Eme jumped aside to let them pass, and with a sigh, entered the restroom.

When she saw her reflection in the mirror, she nearly fainted and understood why Ben had suggested stopping here before she made an appearance in the waiting lounge. *I look worse than my mom in that Muddy Marauder jungle scene.* A sad smile played about her lips and tears glistened in her eyes as she washed as much of the rain-streaked grime and soot from her face and hands as she could without reopening all her wounds. *I miss my family.* She wallowed in her misery for a few seconds, shook her head, straightened up, took a deep breath, and rechecked her appearance, confident that she wouldn't scare the daylights out of the children in the waiting room. "It's time to grow up, Eme! Realize that the world is full of trials and tribulations, and accept some responsibilities! You're fifteen—a grownup, well almost. You've been shielded and babied far too long!" she lectured her reflection. Then, with quiet resolve, she turned away from the mirror, and, with head held high, walked bravely into the toilet stall.

Bermuda Airport Terminal
Seven minutes earlier

"Well, that's the last of the injured, Gun," Ed remarked when he joined his partner at the lounge window, "and there's no curly redheaded teenager that resembles..."

"Yeah, yeah, I see that, and here comes that last crew bus." Gun wiped the perspiration from his meaty forehead and turned away from the rain-streaked window. "We might as well move her little boyfriend back to the command center then recheck the airline manifest and..."

Boom!

Kaboom!

Boom! Boom!

The tropical night was suddenly electrified; lightning had struck the upright wing of the disabled airliner, igniting the remaining fuel, disintegrating the plane, and cratering several hundred feet of runway in a towering inferno.

The ear-splitting boom of the explosion, accompanied by the instantaneous volleys of thunder, reverberated throughout the terminal, shaking the floor, and throwing Ed and Gun into the fronds of a potted palm. Then the fiery glow of Destiny's "last flight to oblivion" was the only light illuminating the lounge—the power had failed.

Screams from the passengers erupted and panic ensued, disrupting the work in the triage centers. By the time the generators kicked in, relative order had been restored, and the two agents had regained their footing. They returned to the window with most of the able-bodied passengers and airport staff. All were spellbound by the ball of fire that now occupied the end of the runway—mesmerized by the horror that now engulfed their belongings and the airliner responsible for their present nightmare.

When the last of the fire crews streaked by en route to the crash site, Gun tore his eyes away from the disaster and yelled over the chaos, "Let's get out of here!" He turned on his heel; Ed nodded and followed his partner down the hall that led to the office where they had left their prisoner.

A few moments later, at the opposite end of the lounge, a curly redheaded teenager emerged from behind the green door.

Bermuda Airport Terminal
3:50 A.M. ADT

Pandemonium greeted Eme when she opened the green door to the waiting room; passengers in tears and triage stations littered the lounge. She stood framed in the open doorway and quickly searched the sea of distressed and dismal faces for a sign of her friends and schoolmates, while a huge mob of the horrified, uninjured gathered along the bank of windows, watching crews battle the wind-driven inferno at the far end of the tarmac. Periodic yells and obscenities punctuated their morbid fascination when Bruno slammed a flaming piece of debris into the window.

"Everyone, please, for your own safety, stand back from the window!" announced a terminal speaker. Very few passengers heeded the warning, but several others with children sought the relative safety of the waiting area.

Suddenly a hand grabbed her shoulder from behind, wheeling her around to come face to face with...

"Rafe! Kala! No! *No?*" Her eyebrows disappeared under her dirty, disheveled bangs. "What are you...?" But she didn't have time to finish her question as all three pulled the stunned redhead back through the doorway.

"Wh-what in the..." she stammered and rubbed her bruised arm while No slammed the door behind them.

"Follow us; we have no time to lose," whispered Kala, and they hustled Eme down the deserted corridor to a maintenance closet several yards from the hangar she had just left.

After a few attempts with Rafe's bent paperclip, the lock clicked, and they were in. No quickly locked the door behind them and flipped the light switch while Kala threw her arms around the stunned girl.

"What...what is...?" Eme tried to ask.

"We were so worried about you, Eme!" Kala interrupted; she pulled away to look at her friend and frowned. "Oh, your poor face. What took you so long, we were beginning..." she began, lightly touching Eme's bruised and lacerated face, but Rafe grabbed Eme's shoulder and spun her around to face him.

"Make yourself comfortable, for what we are about to tell you will add curl to your beautiful..." he flipped her long curls with his hand, "albeit," he grimaced and shook his head, "slightly tousled locks—Mr. Negative has a story to spin."

No one made a move to sit down; they stood close together in the cramped closet, anxious for No to launch his tale.

Grabbing her cold, trembling hands, No began, "Eme, it's all my fault...if I had known..."

"Time is of the essence, here, Mr. Negative, Eme needs the facts, not apologies," Rafe interrupted.

"Right! OK!" No dropped Eme's hands and paced in a small circle, then he came back to face the redhead and took her hands again. "Where to begin..." He leaned down to look at Eme's face; their blue eyes locked: two, deadly serious; two, wide with fright. "OK," he began again, "after we left the plane in Atlanta, Gun—you remember the CIA agent?" Eme nodded with eyes still wide. "Well, he forced me off the plane to get medical attention for my arm—you saw him grab me off the plane, right?" Eme nodded her head. "Well..." Eme's attention was drawn to his bandaged right forearm and orange overalls. No shook his head and answered her unasked question, "Oh, no biggie, it's only slightly sprained, nothing compared to your injuries, and I'll get to this latest trend in fashion design later." He studied her injured face. She just smiled and shook her head. "Anyway, while we were still on the plane, waiting for the medic to check me over, we chatted about the accident—you know where I went into the bulk..."

"Yes, yes...go on," encouraged Eme, nodding her head to speed up the story.

"Well," No looked deeper into Eme's questioning eyes, "I told him why my seat belt was unfastened, and as soon as I mentioned your name—Eme—he looked startled and asked for your last name. When I told him, I'm not kidding, Eme, his face turned white—he looked like I'd just told him that beer caused baldness!"

Rafe and Kala snickered at that, but Eme's mouth dropped open, and her world began to spin. "Why?" she cried, "What does my name have to do with anything?"

"A rose by any other name..." began Rafe with a wistful smile.

"Not now, Rafe!" No and Kala shouted together.

"Right!" retorted a chagrined Rafe.

"That's what I wanted to know, Eme, since Gun's whole demeanor toward me changed, from warm and fuzzy concerned citizen, to CIA operative, in the blink of an eye. He clammed up and yanked me off the plane—you saw that." Eme nodded her head, and No continued, "He didn't say another word to me—just left me off at the first aid station to get my arm wrapped. I figured that was the last I'd see of him. But...and here's the really scary part," No shuddered, "as I was about to head back down to the baggage claim area to find my mom, he grabbed me, pulled me into a doorway, and stuck a gun in my back." Eme drew in a deep and very loud breath. "He told me to keep quiet. He then steered me in the opposite direction, down this long corridor toward some private offices, through a door at the end of the office corridor, down some stairs, to a private hangar. A guy named Ed—I assumed that he was another agent—met us there. I tried to find out what was going on, but neither one of them would answer me—just told me to shut up. I was taken—handcuffed and gagged—to a small government plane and flown here, to Bermuda."

Eme could stand it no longer. "So let me get this straight, the CIA kidnapped *you* because of *me?*"

No looked into Eme's wide blue eyes. "Yep, but it gets more bizarre. These two agents—and, I don't think they're *good* guy CIA agents..."

"What could have possibly brought you to that brilliant conclusion?" interrupted Kala who now had her arm around Eme's trembling shoulders.

"OK, OK, I *know*, they're not on the right side of the law. How's that, Kala?" he sneered at the amber-skinned blonde.

"Better!" she gave him a smug smile.

"Good. Now let me get on without any more sarcasm from you—that's my department." Kala and Rafe looked at each other and smirked.

No leveled his gaze at Kala and Rafe. "Hey, there's nothing more discouraging than unappreciated sarcasm, except maybe our current predicament," he replied with a sneer.

Kala sighed, "Yes, No, we know! Is there ever a time when you're not sarcastic?"

"Every other Tuesday," he snapped with a straight face.

Kala rolled her eyes and replied, "Oh, just get on with it!"

"So, these baboons..." Rafe prompted, giving a "wind-it-up signal," trying to refocus No's attention to the matter at hand.

No stopped staring at Kala and concentrated on Rafe. "Yeah, that's a good moniker to hang on 'em, Rafe; there's really nothing wrong with them that another five billion years of evolution wouldn't cure." He paused when the other three laughed in spite of their circumstances. Satisfied that his sarcasm was finally clicking with his new friends, he grinned and continued, leaning down to look into Eme's concerned eyes, and taking her hands once again. "These *Neanderthals* blindfolded me and escorted me at gunpoint, from what looked like a private hangar, through a few doors, to a cell somewhere in the airport."

"They have a jail, here, at this airport!" Eme was stunned, but anxious to hear what happened next. "So, you must have had some idea where you were...how did Rafe find you?" she asked, turning to Rafe then back to No.

"That didn't happen for quite some time," he shook his head and shuddered, "and in the meantime, the gruesome twosome chloroformed me and left me on this cot, gagged and shackled." He made a face, straightened up, and started pacing again. "Anyway, when Gun returned with his buddy—it must have been a good twenty, twenty-four hours—I lost track of time since I was out for most of the day and night, and I was a mess—I couldn't get up to use the...you know."

Eme was ashen. "They left you with nothing to eat and no chance to use...?" The redhead glanced at the solemn faces of her other two friends.

No stopped, laughed, and stared at the three teens, "Yep, and believe me..."

Eme shook her head, made a face, and held up her hand. "That's all right, you don't have to explain." The other three chuckled at the disgust on Eme's face. "So, go on..."

No shrugged, "Well, the taller guy did apologize...said they'd forgotten all about me, what with the hurricane and some sort of emergency—I assume it was your plane crash." He looked at Kala's and Rafe's nodding heads and turned back to a white-faced Eme.

"Right!" No started pacing once again, head down. "They didn't say anything more. The tall guy started to clean up the mess on the cot while Gun unshackled and blindfolded me, stuck a gun in my back again, and marched me through a couple of doors to a bathroom, where I was able to shower and change into some spiffy new duds." He stopped pacing and indicated the way-too-short, baggy orange maintenance overalls he was wearing."

Eme let out the breath she hadn't realized she'd been holding. "That must have been a relief!"

"You got that right!" continued No. "But I'd have traded my fashionable new wardrobe," he sneered as he executed a sloppy pirouette, "for what happened next."

"What could be worse than what's already happened?" asked Eme, eyes wide.

He walked back to Eme. "Well, I was blindfolded once again, marched through more doors and up some steps to an unused office—not really an office, more like hell with florescent light-ing," he sneered, "where they left me again. At least he took the blindfold off, and since I hadn't had anything to eat or drink, except for shower water, for a day or so, I wasn't as worried about...well, you know." He shuddered again and continued, "Anyway, I waited, slept a bit, and then Rafe rescued me, and here we all are, together at last! Tada!" He finished his story with a little tap dance and bow.

Eme looked at the other two teens for confirmation, a million unanswered questions sparkling in her tear-filled eyes.

"How...?" she began as the tears started to fall. Kala put an arm around her shoulders again.

Rafe interrupted, "The Cyborg had desperate need of the facilities around that time; wise Kala and yours truly had just entered the terminal. I left Kala with the runts and was walking past the evil ones when I heard the words, 'redheaded teenage girl.' That, plus the suspicious demeanor of the two foul felons, flashing a cell phone photo that resembled the fair one, prompted this crime fighter to adopt his Bruce Wayne persona." He posed for dramatic effect. The others laughed, and Eme took the opportunity to dry her eyes on her bloody jacket. "As the caped crusader is the most revered of all the superheroes, and stealth is the Cyborg's second nature," he wagged his eyebrows, "I hung a right, squeezed behind some potted palms, whilst the dastardly duo engaged in whispered intercourse." He winked at the girls. "With Puck, my trusty magnified listening device," he pointed to an earpiece hidden behind his left ear, attached wirelessly, Eme presumed, to Persephone, "yours truly was able to intrude upon their private conversation." He stopped to look at Eme. "What the Cyborg heard curled his very toes: fair Juliet's name was mentioned in conjunction with another's, a bloke by the name of No Henderson. The Cyborg recalled the decidedly negative name mentioned by the fair one in Atlanta." He paused to sneer at No and continued, "Then they said something about a project, Venture: Eme."

"Wha-what!" stammered Eme, her eyes as large as half-dollars, as she looked to each of her nodding friends for confirmation.

"The story gets more ominous, Eme. Evidently the Central Intelligence Agency...the CIA," explained No at Eme's confused expression, "has some e-mail protocol program they named Venture: Eme." No nodded solemnly at Eme's raised eyebrows. "When I mentioned your name, he must have been shocked at first, but then decided to hatch this scheme to implicate the two of us as espionage agents, using that as an excuse to fly to Bermuda; what I know for sure: we're the reason your plane was brought down here."

"*What!* That's...that's the most ludicrous thing I've ever heard!" Infuriated, Eme balled up her fists and stamped her foot in furry and frustration. "Let's just go tell them the truth!"

No extended his hand toward the girl to stop her from dashing to the door. "I tried telling them the truth during our flight here, Eme; they know we're not spies; they're only using us as scapegoats."

"Why the dirty, rotten, twisted..."

No grimaced. "They're not so much twisted as totally mangled." Eme calmed her rant and managed a brief smile. The others nodded in agreement with No's characterization, and he continued, "Evidently, *they* are the double agents, working for some foreign agency. They've somehow convinced the CIA that they needed to track you down here in Bermuda and arrest you before *you* could sell their secret project to European terrorists. That's why they risked bringing down the plane during the storm here in Bermuda. From what I could understand from their conversation, their project is based at CIA headquarters in Atlanta and here, on the island. Whatever it entails, it must work between the two places."

Eme was incensed. "You mean they risked everyone's lives on that plane just to…"

Rafe interrupted again. "As the Cyborg listened in on their plan, it became clear what their dastardly intentions entailed: to capture you, then kill you and Mr. Negative, dump your bodies from a fishing boat, and charge you as traitors and fugitives. Once the feds discovered the project missing, the heat would be off of them as the suspected double agents, and they'd have the protocol, free and clear, to pass on to their foreign coconspirators."

Eme dropped her head in her hands. "This is impossible!" She jerked her head up and glared at her friends. "This is America!" She shook her head and smiled. "Well, it's Bermuda—close enough." She frowned and plowed on, "But we're Americans! We have rights!" Her anger turned to shock. "Oh, no, I sound like one of those blogs my activist friends are always bugging me to post on the net." She shook her head sadly at the nervous smiles from the other three teens, and then turned her full attention on Rafe. "How in the world did you ever find No?"

Rafe put a hand on her shoulder. "Ah, my fair Eme, once yours truly understood their sinister plans, it was merely a matter of booting up and replaying the video of the airport's intranet security cameras on Persephone," he patted the computer bag slung over his shoulder, "to locate Double Trouble's prison. Without hesitation, the caped crusader swung into action." Rafe posed with hands on hips, head turned at a jaunty angle, nose in the air. "With a mighty dash down the correct office corridor, a pick, a click in the lock of Mr. Negative's 'hell with florescent lighting,' and the captive one was freed." He bowed and paused for Kala's and No's applause.

The replay of the daring rescue, however, did not register in Eme's brain—she was in shock. Her nightmare had taken on a whole new perspective; dying on a plane in a hurricane seemed painless compared to being charged as a spy and killed by the CIA. Once the applause died down, the silence in the tiny closet was deafening. What was she, or were they, to do? The others watched Eme's face pale; her shallow breathing quickened.

The three teens rushed forward to catch Eme when she stumbled. "You'd better sit down," Kala cautioned.

They gently led her to the only space that was free of brooms, buckets, and mops; all four of them sank to the floor, exhaustion replacing their adrenaline-fed high.

"What can we do; who can help us?" Eme whispered to the now grim faces in front of her. "Are they looking for me now? Why didn't they come to the plane when I didn't show up with the St. Bruno group?"

Kala was the first to answer. "They must be waiting for you to be brought in with the injured passengers."

"Maybe they think you died in the plane crash," No offered with a smile.

"Oh, that's a pleasant thought, No, just kill her off and our problems are solved?" Kala sniffed and tears sparkled in her brown eyes.

"Well, what I meant..."

"Actually, that's a great idea. With No missing, and me not showing up..." Eme began with a smile.

"They may be thugs, but they're not totally bereft of brains... they'll figure it out, eventually...the fair one and Mr. Negative are not safe here," Rafe retorted.

No one spoke for a few minutes, each immersed in his or her plans for escape. Finally, Rafe summed it up: "If this were played upon a stage, the Cyborg could condemn it as an improbable fiction; it is abundantly clear that approaching the unlawful ones will come to no good end; likewise, we are hunted by the very ones upon whom we depend for protection; suffice it to say," he paused for dramatic effect, "we're screwed!"

"Now, that's a friendly thought," Kala moaned, "We're just going to do nothing?"

"We have to tell Mrs. Murphy!" Eme ventured.

Three faces fell.

"What? You don't think she'll believe us! Why, that old biddy! I'll convince her!" Eme scowled and tried to stand, but Kala grabbed her before her bottom left the floor.

"She's dead, Eme," Kala croaked.

Eme froze.

Bermuda Airport Terminal
4:11 A.M. ADT

"Will you shut the hell up, Ed! We'll find the little shit...there's no place he can hide in this airport that we don't know about. Check with Reid again; have him inspect all of the storage closets. Where are you?"

Pause.

"OK, I've just finished searching the maintenance garage; I'll meet you in the lounge in five minutes."

Snap.

Bermuda Airport Terminal Supply Closet
4:14 A.M. ADT

With faces shrouded in grief and anxiety, the four teens huddled on the cold floor of the supply closet and had no idea that Gun was stomping past the door of their hiding place at that very moment, so it was fortunate that the boys were quietly comforting the girls.

Eme's heart was in her throat, and then Reality hit her like a ton of tomatoes—they were all alone. There was no way to contact their families. Mrs. Murphy may have been an old biddy, but she didn't deserve to die; who could they now turn to for help? She succumbed to her fears and joined Kala in a pool of tearful misery.

Rafe and No were beside themselves. Evil CIA agents were one thing, but dealing with *two* wailing females was a whole new video game.

After several minutes of sobbing girls and hand-wringing guys, Eme abruptly broke away from her friend.

"H...how did it happen?"

"From what Kala was told, she died of a heart attack while arguing with the rescuers trying to release her from her seat belt," Rafe answered.

"Oh, poor Mrs. Murphy!" She shook her head sadly, then straightened up suddenly and asked, "Wait, wh...what has happened to the other kids?"

"We can only assume that they've been taken to an administration office," answered No.

"But...but how did you guys get away? Aren't th...they looking for you?" she stammered, wiping away her tears.

Significant looks passed among the other three teens. "We'd only been in the terminal for ten minutes when an airport security officer told me about my aunt," Kala began. "He was trying to round all of us up; however, since there was no way to contact our relatives with the communication towers down, he wasn't sure what to do with us."

Eme put her arm around Kala's shoulders when tears sprang to her eyes; the blonde took a great shuddering breath. "S...so he put me in charge of keeping them together until the storm ended. It was complete and utter chaos. I w...was crying, the others were crying, medics were treating the injured and consoling their friends and relatives. I had lost contact with Rafe, so I herded the kids away from the noise and confusion and told them to stay together while I went to the loo. I was on my way back to the group when Rafe and No found me." She finished, sniffed, and wiped her streaming eyes on the long sleeve of her pink cotton jacket.

No continued, "Once Rafe had revealed his identity, and his connection to you, it was clear we needed to get to you before Gun and the other guy did. Since the only places open were eateries, Rafe disabled the alarm of a clothing store, and we broke in for some sort of disguise for you and me. Then we realized that it was only a matter of time before they discovered your connection to Rafe and Kala, so we grabbed sunglasses and hats for all four of us." He pulled a crumpled tropical cloth beach hat out of his pocket, followed by a slightly bent pair of sunglasses, and handed them to Eme while Rafe and Kala donned similar disguises. "These aren't perfect, but they should help us…"

Eme had been listening intently, swiveling her head from one story-teller to another, gasping every few seconds at what they were telling her, but the incredulity of the sight before her was too much; she pulled away from Kala and burst into a combination of hiccupping sobs and giggles. "You've…got…to be…kidding! With a hurricane roaring outside, who in his or her right mind is going to be running around the airport in sunglasses and beach hats? We're going to be more conspicuous wearing these." She waved the disguise at No.

Frowns crossed the faces of the others as Eme's words sank in. She was right, and they knew it.

"The fair one is as astute as she is beautiful. We're going to stand out like lasers in Batman's cave." Kala and No frowned and followed Rafe's lead, tucking their hats and glasses away in their pockets. Eme smiled and did the same.

"OK, we're back to square one. We can come up with another plan, but first tell me what happened to the other kids," Eme prodded.

"Ah, yes," replied Rafe. "Wise Kala was surprised to find No here in Bermuda. She remembered what you had told us about him in Atlanta. Alas, she was quite confused when we told her that she couldn't return to the others, and we sequestered ourselves behind some fortuitous foliage."

"We hid behind potted palms," explained Kala at Eme's confused expression.

Eme nodded, and Rafe continued, "We began to outline the peril in which we found ourselves; however, a commotion erupted from the area where the runts were awaiting wise Kala's return and interrupted our tale. As we peeked through the fronds, we discovered the evil ones interrogating some of the distraught tykes."

"Those goons are a habit I'd like to kick—with both feet," interrupted No.

Rafe chuckled at that and continued, "Without a thought to the runts' plight, we grabbed the blonde one and headed for the nearest haven."

"We ran into the coffee shop located right behind us," explained No.

"Luckily, the barista noticed our distress and, without question, led us around the counter and out the rear portal, which is connected to the corridor from whence we emerged when we fortunately encountered fair Eme."

"Do you mean those poor kids are now in the hands of Gun?" yelped Eme.

"We don't know what happened to them or to our bags. Luckily, Rafe still has his laptop and PDA with him," replied No, and Rafe dramatically displayed his flashing wrist phone and patted his bag, which resounded with a satisfying thud. "We also have some cash, but no passports or credit cards."

Another shiver ran up Eme's spine when she realized that they didn't know about the fire that had just destroyed all of their belongings. She stuck her hand in her pocket and removed the change from her last twenty-dollar bill; two dollars and six cents lay in her clammy palm. She bent her head and shook her red curls sadly. "You need to take a deep breath; I have some very, very bad news of my own!"

She didn't think it was possible, but the three faces in front of her looked even more miserable when they learned about the fate of their luggage.

"So that was the huge explosion we heard. When the lights went out, we were hiding in the windowless food court's delivery corridor, checking the main corridor every few minutes for you to arrive; we thought lightning may have struck the terminal or the control tower, and were very thankful when the generator turned on. What are we going to do now?" Kala whispered. She dug into her pocket, producing her hat, sunglasses, and a five-dollar bill. "Rafe, I'll never doubt your rule-breaking ways again!" she whispered as she looked at him through teary eyes and patted his bag.

The other teens had no response; they continued their vigil on the floor of the cramped and dirty closet; four heads were bowed in communal misery.

A click in the lock, and a jiggle of the handle on the closet door, jarred them from their stupor and back to reality; they were on their feet in a split second, hopelessly searching for a place to hide in the tiny room. Rafe managed to turn off the light next to the door just as it burst open, revealing the hulking frame of a man silhouetted in the doorway. His facial features and demeanor were difficult to determine with the glare of the corridor lights behind him, but Rafe took no chances and clobbered the guy in the gut with a bucket of detergent he had grabbed from the floor.

With a grunt of surprise and pain, the man, clad in orange overalls, staggered backward, landing with a thud on the cement floor. No one needed prompting; they vaulted over the semiconscious airport employee and dashed toward the hangar. Not daring to take time for a backward glance, the terrified teens tore through the doorway of the deserted building.

Heads swiveled in all directions in a frantic search for an escape route. Without a word Rafe grabbed Eme's hand and pulled her toward one of the crew buses; Kala and No were right on their heels. Rafe pulled open the driver's door, and the three friends piled into the back while the brunet searched for the keys that would enable them to escape their imminent capture. When none could be found, much to her friends' horror, Eme jumped from the van.

"What are you doing, Eme?" screeched a panic-stricken Kala.

"I think I know where the keys are kept. I'll be right back," she exclaimed to their shocked faces. With that, she sprinted toward the long metal workbench by the corridor door. She was opening the cabinet over the bench, in which she remembered the van driver depositing keys an hour earlier, when the corridor door flew open, revealing Gun, Ed, and the airport employee Rafe had knocked over with the bucket.

Her friends watched in stunned disbelief as Gun grabbed the redhead around her waist. Ed tried to slap handcuffs on the struggling girl, but she reached out and grabbed Ed's wrist, digging in her long fingernails. He dropped the cuffs, yelling in pain. Gun lost his grip on her squirming body, and just as it looked as if she would make her escape, Ed recovered enough to grab her shoulders. With a mighty kick, she connected with his shins and punched him in the stomach with both hands, dislodging the key chain flash drive from his belt loop, unbeknownst to everyone but the shocked and silently cheering teenagers in the van.

Finally, Gun regained control of the girl and yelled, "Elaine Mea Venture, you're under arrest for treason and espionage—and for the possible theft of an airport vehicle." He struggled to remove the keys from Eme's clenched fist.

Eme was struggling with all of her might against the agent. "I don't...know...what you're...talking about!" she screamed, and then spat in his face.

"Don't forget assault on an airport employee," the man added as he rubbed his stomach and chin.

"Right, Reid, and a CIA agent," snarled Ed, rubbing his shins and glaring at the girl as he retrieved the cuffs from the floor.

"Yeah," growled Gun, wiping his face of the spittle and tossing the reclaimed van keys on the workbench.

"How are we going to get her out of here without being spotted?" asked Ed.

Barney Reid, the tall, rugged sixty-seven year old airport worker looked surprised at his question, and was about to ask why they needed to keep her capture a secret when Gun answered Ed's question, "Through the underground parking garage, and then we just have to locate her accomplice and find out which one of them erased the security camera footage."

Ed roughly dragged Eme toward the corridor, followed by Gun and the confused man in orange overalls. The redhead had only a second to glance longingly at the van before she and her captors disappeared behind the green door.

Stunned at the plight of their friend, No made a dive for the van door; however, Rafe's voice brought him up short, "Wait! They don't know that we've got Mr. Negative. In fact, they don't know that wise Kala and the Cyborg are working with fair Eme. We've got to let this play out and attack it from another angle."

"Are you the one who wiped that security footage, Rafe?" asked Kala.

"Do you think the Cyborg would leave such evidence behind?" he smirked and patted his computer bag. Without another word, Rafe jumped out of the van and dashed to the workbench, retrieving the set of van keys; he then stooped to pick up the flash drive that had slid behind the wheels of a huge tool cabinet. He quickly returned, dangling the keys and flash drive in front of Kala's and No's quizzical faces. "Just remember that good luck is the residue of outstanding eyesight and focus!" He laughed, secured the flash drive in his bag, jammed the keys into the ignition, and revved up the engine. With a jab at the door opener located on the visor, he threw the van's transmission into reverse and floored the accelerator; Rafe had launched them on their first leg toward freedom.

They had just cleared the hangar door and hit the tarmac when Bruno reminded them that the island was still under siege. Literally throwing caution to the wind, Rafe wheeled the van 180 degrees, jammed the transmission into first, and rushed headlong into the fray—past the returning fire crews and the burned out wreckage of the Stargate airliner that had delivered three of them to their paradise hellhole.

With hand held high, the Cyborg screamed, "Fair maid, do not despair!" And the van disappeared into the storm.

CHAPTER ELEVEN

BETTER OFF THAN A DEAD FISH

Private CIA Airport Office
Saturday, June 13, 2015
4:30 A.M. ADT

A defiant but terrified Eme hunched, handcuffed, shackled, gagged, and alone in the same unused office, and on the very couch, from which No had been liberated earlier.

As she waited for Fate's axe to fall, a myriad of *whys* swirled in her throbbing head: Mrs. Murphy's death, No's detainment, the aircraft explosion that had destroyed all of her belongings, and now this.

What had Rafe said: they were using her and No as scape-goats to cover up for the theft of some Venture: Eme program? *Preposterous!* At least No and the others had escaped. Why hadn't she provided them with her contact information? They would have no way to alert her family. In fact, her lack of a passport could be a colossal problem. That wasn't even correct—she had *no* identification. How would she prove to these men that she was a US citizen? Wait, she was being held hostage by counterintelligence agents who *knew* who she was; either way, as Rafe had so aptly put it, *I'm screwed.*

When this last thought finally sank in, the adrenaline began pumping once again, launching her into action. She had to keep her wits about her. She figured that the two goons would be gone for quite a while in search of No. A small smile played on her lips at the thought of her friends giving them the slip. Eme paused to savor that small victory before returning her attention to her desperate situation.

Her eyes scanned the tiny office for anything that would help to unlock her bonds. Seeing nothing within her reach, she lay face down on the couch and dropped her head over the side. Stretching as far as the shackles would allow, she searched the floor and felt for any loose metal staples or fasteners under the plastic covering of the couch.

"Ow!" she yelped when her fingers snagged on a bent staple. After sucking on her cut finger for a few seconds, she thought, *Maybe Fate's finally giving me a break.* Carefully she wiggled the staple free from the wooden frame. It was barely three inches long but fairly thick; she reasoned it was worth a try.

Holding the tiny piece of metal between her index finger and thumb, she twisted her wrists until the metal was next to the handcuff lock. Ever so carefully, she inserted it into the opening and almost laughed when she realized she had seen her mother perform this same operation in one of her first films, *Deliver Me From Paradise.* She shook her head and chuckled when she realized it had been filmed in Bermuda. Pushing that ironic thought from her mind, she bit her lower lip and focused on her own drama.

After several futile minutes of twisting and turning, prodding and picking, a small click in the locking mechanism brought a smile to her parched lips. Her heart seemed to stop; was it actually going to be this easy? "Don't question Fate's luck, you goof!" she mumbled. Eme grasped the cuffs and pulled the metal apart. She quickly performed the same procedure on the shackles and removed the gag. She was stunned! She was free!

She darted to the door and opened it slowly, cautiously, listening and looking for any sign of Gun or his buddy. When Eme was satisfied that no one was near, she threw it wide and dashed down the corridor in the direction of the terminal lounge, frantic to find the kids and someone who could help her.

As Eme rounded the corner, she came to a skidding halt; walking toward her, not twenty yards away, were her two new nightmares. She reversed course, hoping they hadn't seen her, and ran back toward the office, toward the exit at the other end of the corridor—the same exit door through which Gun had dragged her twenty minutes before.

Eme rounded the last corner and spotted the door, reasoning that it had to be unlocked, and made a dash for it. When she heard heavy footsteps closing in on her, she froze with her hand grasping the handle; immediately there was another hand grasping her shoulder, spinning her around; she was face to face with Ed and Gun.

"Clever little girl, aren'tcha, now?" sneered Gun, his foul breath triggering her gag reflex. Ed pinned Eme's hands behind her back, re-cuffing her. She squirmed and fought against the lanky, dark-haired agent, but her adrenalin and her energy were exhausted.

Gun shook her and was about to backhand her when Ed stopped him, "I told you we should have just chloroformed her." Gun grunted and loosened his grip on the girl. He unlocked the door that, Eme now realized, would not have been her escape route. "We won't be making this same mistake again. Let's get her out of here."

They led her down the flight of concrete steps they had used when they brought her to her office prison. Eme figured they were taking here back to the parking garage. "I'm surprised we've gotten her this far without being spotted. We should have left her down here before looking for the kid," Gun responded. "Well, we're not making that mistake again." Eme yelped as he tightened his grip on her arm.

Good, thought Eme as she grimaced with pain, *at least my friends have made their escape. But where are these goons taking me? To the same cell No occupied? If so, I hope Ed did a good job cleaning the cot.*

She didn't have long to ponder those questions; they had reached the bottom of the stairwell. Eme wondered why Gun dragged her to the right toward the blank cement wall instead of to the metal door on their left that led to the garage. A second later she had her answer. A click of a remote control device he had pulled from his pocket and the four-by-eight-foot wall slid to the left, revealing another corridor. He pushed her through the opening, followed by Ed. Another click from the remote, and the opening was once again a solid cement wall. *Where are we,* she wondered, *and how is anyone ever going to find me, let alone rescue me?* Thoughts of her GG Anne and parents filled her eyes with tears. She fought with everything she had not to give Gun and his buddy the satisfaction of seeing her cry; however, a sniffle later, and she was sobbing as if her heart would break. *So much for me acting like a grown-up,* she thought.

"Oh, the little miss is afraid of the big bad CIA agents, is she?" sneered Gun. "We thought you were made of sterner stuff, being a spy and all." The goon broke into peals of laughter.

Eme held the retort that was burning on her tongue. *What good is it to argue my case against an obvious setup,* she reasoned.

The Gun continued to laugh at Eme's discomfort for the few seconds it took to drag her down the short corridor to another security door. This one was much more sophisticated and required an iris scan for admittance. Gun stared into the tiny camera lens, activating the locking mechanism. The steel door swung inward, allowing the three of them access to an astonishing, cavernous room. A lighted world map blanketed the central wall while several rows of desks and computers filled the center space. More high tech computers and equipment were located along the right side wall. Dark hallways were located to the right and left of the gigantic map. Eme did not want to know what was down those passages but figured that was where she would be taken. Sure enough, just as the thought left her mind, Ed and Gun led her toward the hallway on the right. As she passed the command center computers, she wondered why there were no other agents present. She didn't have much time to contemplate this; two seconds later, Eme was facing her worst nightmare, two empty jail cells, one with a heavily-stained cot.

"Say hello to your new home, Missy," Ed cheerily announced. He opened the closest heavy iron-barred door, and, with his right hand, guided the redhead inside toward the damp, disgusting cot. With his left hand, he placed a foul-smelling cloth over Eme's nose and, mercifully, she knew no more.

Gun watched the scene and sneered at Eme's unconscious form. Ed joined his partner and locked the door; the two chuckled as they left the corridor, turning off the lights behind them. Gun continued to laugh as they exited the command center.

However, Eme was not left alone.

Bermuda Airport Bridge to St. George's Island
4:30 A.M. ADT

Through the curtain of rain pierced by the headlights, a solid vertical wall of concrete appeared before the van.

"Shit!" No cried.

The swing bridge was up.

Rafe slammed on the brakes and spun the wheel hard to the left; however, the road was soaked, and the tires could not grip the rain-slick asphalt. The twelve-passenger crew bus veered out of control and spun 180 degrees in a hopeless attempt to gain some traction. The aching crunch of crumpled metal joined the wild squealing of the van's rear tires, screaming for purchase. The back doors slammed into the metal barrier on the side of the bridge; it then continued to slide to the edge of the bank. The impact sent Rafe's head into his headrest, hard enough to leave his ears ringing. He took a moment to understand what he was seeing as the view from the windshield steadily rose to encompass the dark sky and the torrential downpour. *Oh dear*, he had time to think.

"We're about to fall," Kala said simply, shaking her head in a daze. She seemed to think about her words again. "Rafe, floor it!"

Rafe flattened the accelerator; however, the rear tires spun on nothing but air. He surprised even himself when he began to chuckle at their current predicament.

"Too late!" No gasped and gripped the front seatback as hard as he could, eyes wide and knuckles white.

The van fell.

Kala screamed.

No was too shocked to blink.

Rafe laughed all the way down.

Vroosh!

Hitting the water was more of a shock than hitting the barrier. Rafe bounced around in his seat, gripping the wheel hard. Kala tumbled over No and kicked each boy in the head on her way into the driver's side window. The van sank, taillights first, and then bobbed to the surface before falling forward onto all four wheels. For one brief moment, it looked as if Rafe could drive on the water, but then the vehicle listed to the right and began to take on as much of the Atlantic as possible—which wasn't much.

Rafe groaned and tried to push his door open. It wasn't easy with Kala's sole pressed against his ear, and he couldn't manage it against the insurgence of water. Instead he lowered the window.

"Evacuate! No, you've got a window—use it!"

Kala scrambled over the steering wheel and squeezed through the opening into the stormy bay. Rafe reached down under his seat and grabbed his laptop carry case, the interior of which was waterproof, as was the main core of his laptop and his wrist phone. He'd lose a few of the external drives in the side pocket of his bag, but his wrist PDA was made especially for deep sea divers. He hoped his newly-acquired flash drive would also survive—he had a feeling that Eme's life depended on it. However, if he and his other friends didn't make it to the shore soon...

Bruno had whipped the bay into a choppy mass of surging walls of water and narrow dives between valleys of encroaching sea foam. The wind whistled and howled, slinging water into Rafe's face as he struggled to slip his case strap over his head while grasping for Kala's hand and his ever-present hat; she was coughing and spluttering, swimming in circles.

The ocean was dark, and there was no fighting its power. Rafe managed to get a grip on Kala, and she on him, but there was no sign of No. The current pulled them along through the surf. An eerie glow played across the surface of the water nearby as the headlights from the van shone from beneath the water; pockets of air bubbled to the surface, but several seconds later they were in darkness; the vehicle had been claimed by the inky depths.

"Are...you, OK?" Rafe yelled.

Kala could only chatter her teeth in reply. The water was icy cold. Deathly cold.

There was still no sign of No.

The current swept Kala and Rafe across the wide expanse of the bay. The water was awash with debris from the full might of the hurricane; Bruno had tossed anything and everything into the bay—mostly heavy ferns and branches thick with foliage. Rafe and Kala were being pulled along helplessly—two more pieces of debris for the surf.

Nothing about this situation is advantageous, Rafe thought. He was kicking his legs hard to stay above the surface, but already his toes were tingling, heading toward numb. How wide was the bay? How close was the shore? *The current should eventual...*

Rafe screamed.

Something had clamped down hard on his shoulder. He spun in the water, fearing a shark, a giant squid, the Creature from the Bloody Lagoon; it was No—bedraggled and pale—but it was No.

"Went for a swim on your own, did you?" Rafe shouted with genuine relief flooding through him.

"Well, if you know a better way to maintain this masculine physique..." A flash of lightning illuminated the strand of sea-weed plastered to No's head. "What now?"

Kala swam around No to get a grip of his free hand, and the three of them held each other while they rose and fell on the whims of the tide. Thankfully, being in the bay and beyond the breakwater meant that the only waves they had to contend with were the ones whipped up by the tail end of Bruno. Those waves seemed to be propelling them toward the far shore—a dark mass against the stormy sky in the distance. There were a few lights, but merely a few, probably from buildings with generated power as it appeared the street lights were out.

It got cold fast.

The three friends shivered and shook. Rafe watched as first Kala's, then No's, lips turned bruised purple. He imagined his own looked the same. Slowly but steadily the rising swell of the bay carried them closer to the shore; the six or seven minutes it took seemed an eternity.

It was a shock, more than anything else, when Rafe felt the dead weight of his numb legs brush against something soft, yet unyielding. He realized what it was at the same time as Kala and No; then they were all clambering to stand up on the sandy ocean floor—the shore no more than a few feet away.

"That w...worked out for the b...best," Kala gasped. Her eyes squinted shut against the cold, but she managed a smile.

Rafe wondered if she was still in shock from the fall, but Kala was the first on her feet, dragging him and No up by their drenched shirts. Rafe's legs felt heavier than lead; however, they worked with some effort, pulling hard against the retreating tide. The bedraggled and weary teenagers waded to shore—three dark shadows emerging from the depths of what could have been a hellish eternity.

"Do you have your laptop?" No questioned upon reaching the sandy, and relatively dry, shore. He collapsed onto his rear, panting and shaking.

"Leave no man or woman behind," Rafe replied. His mind was stretched too thin, at the moment, to think of an appropriate Shakespearean retort.

Kala sighed. "Oh, poor Eme."

"Fair Juliet is undoubtedly warm at the moment. Her would-be rescuers will not be much good to her if they don't make it to the nearby country club and borrow an empty cottage. Arise, troops!"

No groaned, rubbing his legs to make them work. "How far is it?"

"We must be five miles south of Woop Woop! Stunning driving, by the way, Rafe."

Rafe grinned. "I knew wise Kala wouldn't let that slide..."

"Slide? Like you did, off a bloody bridge? And, no, you've not heard the last of it."

"How full of briers is this working-day world? How was the Cyborg to know that the bridge would be impassable?" He doffed his drenched plumed hat and bowed to Kala, tickling her with what was left of the once fluffy purple plume. "Next time, Maria Andretti shall drive."

Kala giggled and slapped him on the back of his head. "Gladly."

"Guys," No said. "Let's hoof it; a bit of a walk will get the blood flowing."

Rafe agreed, replaced his hat, and made to stand up; however, the sand beneath him shifted under his weight; he fell back, throwing out his hand for balance. Something squished beneath him as he hit the sand, an overpowering stench of something—something rotten—broke through the wind and the rain to reach his nostrils.

"Ugh." He nearly retched. "What villainy is this?"

"Holy-dooly, that's ghastly," Kala gasped, pulling her shirt up over her nose.

No chuckled, wafting the stink away from his face as Rafe rolled over. "You just sat in a dead fish, pal; been there a day or two, I'd say."

Rafe did retch then; his eyes stung from the smell.

"We're not walking anywhere near you," Kala said, moving away in the darkness. "Whoa, that's dreadful."

Batman wouldn't have these problems, Rafe thought. He was tempted to jump back into the ocean to wash it off, but the threat of the cold was greater than the threat of the smell. "Carry on," he said darkly. "However, under these most dire of circumstances, the Cyborg claims first shower."

Rafe led the way, as he knew the way, a shadow disappearing into the darker shadows surrounding the island. Two shadows followed a bit to his right, mindful of what clung to his back. The wind and rain whipped around the three ghostly figures—an invisible barrier now against the frothy ocean swash that had thankfully spit them ashore.

From the darkened beach to the darkened road beyond the swing bridge, Rafe's face remained grim—determined. He was angry, and perhaps a touch afraid, that the night had so far proved disastrous for both himself and his small group of friends. He would rescue fair Jul—Eme. He would rescue Eme Venture. The evil entities who had taken her had no right—none at all.

His anger trumped his fear.

The unexpected high dive off the bridge had been a mere delay. The rotten fish, however—that was just one step too far on this night of tempered tragedy. It had ensured that Rafe's determination would not wane; it had, in fact, been hardened into something swift and true—something treacherous.

A sense of true danger rippled through his mind. It was a terrific feeling, a fantastic feeling—the feeling that for once, for the first time in his life, there was something real at stake.

Onward he fared, two companions at his side—actually behind him—into a Bermuda night that had just become a whole lot more certain for the Cyborg of Cyberspace.

CHAPTER TWELVE
HOT SUDS AND COLD REALITY

CIA Secret Command Center
Saturday, June 13, 2015
5:05 A.M. ADT

"We've got a potential disaster on our hands; you do realize that!" complained Ed.

"What's he gonna do, run and phone Mommy? Tell the cops? Airport security? He's got nowhere to run—nowhere, and he can't hide forever. We're the only ones who know every hiding place in this airport, thanks to Reid and his original set of blueprints; and Reid's not talking—not anymore," Gun snickered.

"But who erased the camera feeds? Where are their accomplices? *Who* are their accomplices? And where is No Henderson? I told you to keep him in the command center!"

Gun and Ed had just finished securing Eme in her cell and were now making their way slowly up the stairs to the main terminal—Gun with a grimace, Ed now lost in thought. No more was said until they reached the final security door where they had stopped Eme's escape attempt.

Gun peeked through the safety glass and froze. He pushed Ed back against the wall behind him, placing a hand over his mouth. "Shhh! Someone's in the corridor! Maybe it's our target looking for his little girlfriend. You stay here, and I'll go check."

Ed nodded, and Gun removed his hand from his mouth, opening the door slowly. He stopped dead in his tracks when voices drifted down the corridor from the direction of one of the offices.

"I don't know, Mrs. Kettering, I remember seeing two old guys, with a young red-haired girl, walking down this hallway about an hour ago."

"OK, Jason, if you think of anything else, or see the men again, you let me know right away. Do you understand? Right away!"

"Yes, Mrs. Kettering. Do you think she's in some trouble?"

"I hope not, but we won't know until we find her, her two companions, or those men. When you finish cleaning these rooms, come to my office. The CIA and other authorities will be here as soon as the runway is cleared enough for planes to land. They'll want a complete description from you."

"Yes, Mrs. Kettering. Ten more minutes should do it."

The hum of a vacuum cleaner drowned out the retreating clicking of high heels as the young man returned to his job. A minute later: a thud, the scraping of feet, a slammed door, and an unmanned vacuum cleaner hummed to an empty office.

St. George's Club Cottage
Saturday, June 13
5:30 A.M. ADT

Kala left the two guys while they attempted to start the generator they had located in the garage of their "borrowed" cottage. She felt her way through the living room and down the dark hall toward what she believed to be the master bedroom. When she heard the generator roar to life on the patio, she heaved a satisfied sigh, flipped on the nearest light switch and froze—before her was the most gorgeous bedroom she had ever seen: magnificent pieces of intricately-woven rattan and rosewood furniture complete with an enormous four-poster bed and beautiful Persian rug occupied the space.

As she passed the bed on her way to the master bath, she trailed her fingers across the deep rose silk duvet, hoping she'd soon be sleeping beneath its luxurious warmth. With high expectations, she stuck her head through the bathroom doorway, flipped on the light, and wasn't disappointed; an immense sunken garden tub and an oversized river rock shower met her weary eyes. Decisions, decisions: a long hot soak in the tub would be heavenly, but her thoughts drifted to the plight of poor Eme, and she settled for a quick shower.

Without a warning to the boys of her intentions, she closed and locked the door, peeled off her stinking, slimy clothes, and jumped into the cold, invigorating spray of the huge rainfall shower head located in the ceiling. By the time the hot water tank kicked in, the two boys were banging on the door at the unfairness of beating them to the bathroom.

Ten minutes later, relaxed, refreshed, and more importantly, clean, Kala emerged from the steamy room, one large, fluffy pink towel wrapped around her long blonde hair and another wrapped, sarong-style, around her petite body. "OK, boys, it's all yours!" she announced to the gob smacked faces of Rafe and No.

Torn between their desire to stare at the terrycloth temptress before them or to cleanse their vile bodies, they hesitated for just one moment before cleanliness won out. As if both were shot from the same cannon, they converged on the doorway together, becoming wedged between the doorjambs. Fighting for supremacy, No won out, but he reached behind him to grab Rafe, and they both disappeared behind the door.

Kala laughed when she heard the simultaneous sounds of running tub and shower water. She shuddered as she imagined what the room would look like once the two of them were finished with it. At least she had given them a clean slate; all the muck they left behind would be theirs to clean up.

Secure in that knowledge, she explored the beautifully appointed cottage and wondered about the owners; were they Americans? They were obviously well-off; the furnishings were of very rare wood, and the tropical paintings appeared to be original oils.

Kala wandered through the three bedrooms, and a smaller bathroom, and then ambled back to the huge living room, past an ornate glass case filled with physical fitness trophies and awards. She stopped suddenly when she spotted a silver picture frame nestled in the corner of the case and leaned down to look at the handsome gray-haired couple seated beside a sparkling swimming pool; a large, mossy stone manor house was visible in the background. Assuming they were a famous American or possibly English couple, she opened the door to examine the picture more closely and nearly dropped the frame; there in the background, exiting the door of the magnificent house, was a boy, a very familiar, albeit, slightly younger boy, toting an extremely familiar computer bag—*Rafe!*

"These are Rafe's parents," she breathed. "No, wait, they're a bit too old to be his parents—could they be his grandparents?"

She studied the picture for a few more minutes, and then noticed the names engraved on the trophies: William Romero. She remembered the name of Rafe's guardian on the list of students her Aunt Mayrah had given her. *So it is Rafe's grandfather and grandmother! Why didn't he tell us? He made us believe he was breaking and entering—was bloody proud of his lock-picking skills.*

It all became clear: why he was so fixated on reaching St. George's Club, why he had hustled them relentlessly through the streets of St. George's Island to this cottage. She and No had figured it was the only place they would be able to find an empty residence due to the low vacancy rate of hurricane season. *That also explains how he located the flashlight and generator so quickly,* she thought. *Just wait until I get a hold of him! Wait until No finds out! I don't think he's ever asked Rafe for his last name, so if he notices this trophy case...*

Here's a fun thought, she mused. *I won't let on that I know.* She smirked and opened a nearby desk drawer, placing the picture carefully inside. She'd play along with Rafe to see how long it took him to come clean—a clean that wasn't the result of a few minutes under the shower.

Smiling to herself at the ruse, she made her way to the gleaming galley kitchen. *Maybe there is something in the cupboards for us to eat.*

Many minutes later, two laughing, squeaky-clean teenage boys, wrapped in matching pink fluffy towel sarongs, burst forth from a now disgusting, filthy bathroom. They emerged from the hallway, and stopped dead in their tracks at the sight before them: a dining room table filled with food, a bottle of wine uncorked and ready to pour into crystal goblets, and candles blazing on a white linen tablecloth.

"It was the best I could do under the circumstances," Kala complained while the corners of her mouth threatened to expose her delight at their faces. "Well, don't just stand there dripping on the carpet; let's bloody well eat!"

They didn't need to be told twice; the boys scrambled to the table, and the three teens, robed in identical pink towels, feasted on corn chips and salsa, caviar, and cold canned salmon (on slightly stale crackers), and then washed it all down with a bottle of Napa Valley Cabernet.

They raised their glasses in a toast: "To rescuing the fair Eme—*Quo Fata Ferunt*," Rafe proclaimed.

"What sinister declaration did you just make?" quizzed No through a mouthful of caviar and rye cracker.

"It's fitting—Bermuda's motto, 'Whither the fates carry us,'" Rafe responded with a grin.

Kala and No stared at their friend in astonishment.

"How could you possibly know Bermuda's motto, Rafe?" asked Kala after her first sip of the intoxicating wine.

"Yeah, Rafe, we just arrived here a few hours ago, and you're already speaking their language—Quote fatty, the runt!" No accused.

Rafe smirked at his friend. "Their language is our language, Mr. Sarcasm—English, and all that rot. Besides, the motto's in Latin and hangs proudly hence." He pointed to the fancy script emblazoned on an ornate plaque that was hanging above the large overstuffed sofa in the living room.

"Oh, right," was all No could say in response, and he finished his glass of Cabernet while Kala giggled at the byplay.

A half hour later, as a quieter dawn broke over Bermuda, two tipsy teens headed for bed: Kala in the master suite, No bunking on one of the twin beds in a guest room, while Rafe hunched over his laptop, the recovered (and thankfully, waterproof) flash drive protruding from a USB port, determined to discover just whither the fates would take him in his attempt to rescue Eme.

Bermuda Airport
9:30 A.M. ADT

Gorgeous tropical sunlight broke through the remnants of Bruno's clouds, blinding the work crew clearing branches and other debris from the damaged Bermuda runway. The burned-out hull of Flight 65 rested on the median after the hours of intense removal effort by the small army of workers. Time was fleeting, and the first contingent of parents, CIA, and FAA officials from Washington was due to arrive in six hours. The severity of the storm, and subsequent disaster of the Destiny crash and explosion, had left the runway dangerous for even the smallest of planes. Therefore, as soon as Bruno had given them a window of opportunity, bulldozers and paving machines had descended upon the storm-ravaged airport.

All of the passengers had been transported to nearby hotels or hospitals, except for the St. Bruno students, who remained at the airport with a nurse chaperone. The office of the airport director was relocated to a makeshift command center on the main concourse. Banks of telephones lined the cafeteria tables; nurses, airline agents, and airport administrators manned the stations. Physical access to the airport was still impossible and computer access was limited, but that didn't stop the hundreds of news agencies, from around the world, pulling any and every scheme to obtain information via telephone about the five dead, forty-two injured, and three missing passengers.

"Look, I don't care what government you represent. These phones are strictly for the relatives of the passengers..."

"Hey, Buddy, no you can't get that information unless you can prove that you're a relative..."

"Yes, Mrs. Greer, your son, Michael, is safe and sound and still asleep in one of our administration offices. I'm sorry, but I can't give out any information about Mrs. Murphy or any of the other passengers..."

"Yes, Dr. Murphy, we're so sorry for your loss; your mother's body is at the coroner's office and will be on the first available flight to Switzerland..."

"I don't care who you are, unless you're a relative, I can give you no information about the passengers. Sorry, and please don't call again...disguising your voice isn't helping you, nor are your accents."

"OK, Agent Dvorsky, we'll be expecting you..."

"Her injuries are minor, Mr. Duncan, and she's resting comfortably..."

"The runway should be open in another five hours. No, there is no other way for you to get here sooner. I'm sorry you feel that way, Governor Long, but there's nothing..."

"No, Mr. Romero, we still have not located him. Yes, we're doing everything we can with our limited resources. Yes, we'll be expecting you..."

"Mrs. Malone, please, we're doing all in our power to locate her. Yes, we'll be expecting your arrival..."

With the flurry of activity occupying the airport personnel, no one noticed the absence of either of two maintenance workers, until a scream reverberated from a corridor at the end of the long concourse. Suddenly a frantic middle-aged woman in green high-heeled shoes ran screaming toward the emergency command center.

"He's gone!" she panted as a nurse ran to meet her. The nurse grabbed the distraught airport administrator and led her to one of the waiting area seats bordering the concourse.

"He was supposed to report to me over three hours ago," she gasped and then burst into tears. "I should have checked...up on him, but with all the…commotion, oh, I'm so sorry; poor Jason; he…may have met the same fate as the Venture girl. He had information about…about…" With that she collapsed against the surprised nurse while half of the staff looked on in shock and confusion; they waited for the woman to regain her composure and give an explanation for her fears.

After a moment of sobbing, she recovered enough to point toward the corridor from which she had just emerged and squeaked, "His vacuum cleaner is still running, but he's *gone!*" She collapsed once again in a fresh round of tears.

While Mrs. Kettering was trying her best to compose herself, two security guards and a nurse ran to the corridor. The rattling of an obviously overheated vacuum led them to the empty office near the end of the hallway. Not wanting to disturb a potential crime scene by touching the plug, a gray-haired security guard hustled everyone out of the room while he located the circuit box and ended the misery of the dying machine.

CHAPTER THIRTEEN

SACRIFICIAL
LAMB...ER, BUNNY

St. George's Club Cottage
Saturday, June 13, 2015
11:35 A.M. ADT

Sunlight filtered through the sheer curtains of the master bed-room, painting the sleeping form of the amber-skinned blonde with its golden brush.

One eye blinked open, and an arm stretched out from beneath the downy, rose duvet-covered comforter; a loud yawn, and Kala fully awakened to...a massive headache. "Ooh, that'll teach me to drink red wine before bed," she moaned.

Burying her head beneath her pillow, blocking the harsh glare of the unwelcome sun, was but a momentary respite; a minute later the door burst open, and a heavy weight pounced upon her legs.

"Are you sleeping, are you sleeping, lazy girl, lazy girl? Morning birds are singing; stormy clouds are winging!" No continued to bounce on the bed in time to his rendition of "Frere Jacques" while Kala just groaned and rolled to the opposite side of the king sized four-poster—as far away from the lunatic as possible.

"Go away," she croaked, reburying her head beneath the pillow. "I have a headache," she finished in a muffled groan.

No was not swayed by her misery, and he grabbed her kicking feet, pulling Kala, covers, pillows, and all, off the bed and onto the floor. Screams of righteous indignation erupted from the squirming bundle on the Persian carpet.

"Bugger off!" shouted Kala, once her head had emerged from beneath the covers, and she'd recovered her breath. "What do you think you're doing?" She struggled to stand, but No was sitting on top of her.

"I do declare thee an enemy of the state and, hereby, take thee as my prisoner!" No swore with a Rafe-like flourish, tickling the girl lying helplessly beneath the covers.

"You deranged fool, let me up *now!*" screamed Kala. "You have a few Kangaroos loose in the top paddock, No!"

No laughed and scrambled to his feet, helping Kala off the floor. It took several attempts to get her bearings, but the blonde finally got her legs to cease wobbling, and she faced No with a snarl.

"What are you—three?" she snapped, ignoring his smirk, and proceeded to compose herself by straightening her red silk pajamas—pajamas she had borrowed, she assumed, from Rafe's grandmother's bureau drawer.

"I humbly beg the forgiveness of Your Royal Highness," No bowed, "but Rafe has been up all night studying the files on the flash drive and planning Eme's rescue! Besides," he paused, "how did Rafe just say it—oh yeah: the sun is high, Brutal Bruno has passed, and the Cyborg's plan is nigh!" He noticed Kala's perplexed expression and continued, "Well then, in my own words..."

"I get it, I get it! I'm just not a morning person!" she snarled, rubbing her temples.

"I beg your pardon." No bowed again. "But the morning has already passed with Bruno. It is now almost noon, and I've completed all the domestic chores, including the scouring of your disgusting clothes." Kala smiled at that, noticing his better-fitting clothes.

No answered her questioning stare with, "I trashed my beautiful orange monkey suit and nicked these from a drawer in the guest room...nice of our hosts to have clothes nearly my size." He turned around, wiggling his butt and flexing his ample muscles, for Kala to admire his new black jeans and light blue T-shirt. Kala thought they were probably Rafe's duds, but wasn't going to say anything—yet. She whistled at No's assets and improved appearance, then winced at the renewed pain in her head.

No smiled at her, then quickly sobered and continued in a solemn voice. "Listen, Gun and his buddy have had poor Eme in their slimy clutches for nearly eight hours. We've got to launch our rescue attempt soon, or who knows what they may do to her."

"OK, I understand. Just please, please get me some bloody aspirin!" Kala massaged her temples.

"Better than that, Kala, is my hangover cure, which is waiting on the breakfast bar," No responded with a wicked grin.

"Do I even want to know what that entails?" asked the wary girl with a snarl.

No broke into a fit of laughter at the look on his friend's face, and he dragged her into the kitchen.

Rafe was hard at work on the two computers; he had internet access once again, and the airport surveillance cameras were visible on the desktop, while a series of codes streamed on his notebook, a familiar flash drive key chain clip dangling from its USB port. His shoulder-length black hair hung limply, covering all of his face except the grim, determined set of his jaw and the thin, hard line of his lips.

When she tore her gaze away from the computer genius, confident that he would soon have Eme's rescue plan up and running, a disgusting orange concoction, in a cut crystal wine glass, was thrust under her nose. It took No's tight grip on her arm to keep her from escaping to the bathroom.

"Oh, no, No, you can't be serious! That is the most disgusting looking, bloody mess I...I've ever seen!" she stammered and smelled the contents.

Rafe left the desk and joined his friends at the breakfast bar. "Nectar of the gods," he began with a smile, which promptly turned to a grimace of pain, "it is not!" but he quickly continued, "However, it works! So drink up there, Kala; eye of newt and toe of frog await thee!"

"Honest, Kala, it'll make a new woman of you, although," No looked her up and down, smirked and wagged his eyebrows, "the old woman ain't half bad." Kala just glared at him. No, unfazed by her reaction, continued his sales pitch, indicating the empty glasses in the sink, "Look, Rafe and I drank ours, and you can plainly see how perky we are now!" Rafe matched No's cheeky grin.

"Perky? Hell, you're downright demented!" she protested. No released her arm and raised his two hands in feigned shock at her attack.

"You wound us to the core, dear lady! We wish only to assist you with your malady and cast out the demons that darken your demeanor," Rafe replied.

Rafe and No put their two heads together and batted their wounded puppy dog eyes at Kala who couldn't help but giggle at their antics. "OK," she huffed, "You win!" No happily passed her the glass. "But," she continued, eyeing No, "if I get sick, I'm aiming for you!"

"Yes, aim in Mr. Negative's direction," agreed Rafe, rushing back to the desk, pretending to shield the computers, then he sat down and turned to watch the unfolding drama.

She sniffed at the glass again, shuddered, held her nose, and downed the juice in one gulp. A smile lit her face. "Hey," she commented, smacking her lips. "Bit of all right. What's in it?"

As she drained the last drop, a quick glance passed between the two boys before Rafe turned his eyes back to the computer, and No leveled a frown at Kala. "Uh, trade secret; the recipe's been in my alcoholic family for generations!" he replied sheepishly.

"Oh, come on, like who am I going to tell?" Kala asked with a smile as her headache and queasiness began to dissipate; she waited for No's response.

Rafe smirked and turned around again to watch Kala's reaction to the recipe, when No relented. "Well, it's simple, really: frozen orange juice..." he began.

"Yeah, I figured that one out," she interrupted with a smile.

"Tomato juice..."

"Oh, of course," she nodded absently, dabbing her mouth with a napkin.

"A shot of whiskey..."

A wrinkled nose greeted this announcement.

"Frozen egg whites and yolks, and..." No did not finish his list of ingredients, because a white-faced Kala, napkin clutched to her mouth, pushed him aside in a mad dash for the bathroom.

"Was it something I said?" asked a confused No to Rafe's roar of uncontained hilarity.

"Frailty, thy name is woman," spluttered Rafe. And they laughed until tears streamed down their cheeks.

Fifteen minutes later, a showered, dressed, but still pale Kala joined the two boys who now had their sober faces glued to several live video streams on the desktop monitor, while lines of code continued to scroll on Persephone. The airport lounge in the upper left corner of the split screen captured her immediate attention; she marveled at its transformation into some sort of command and information center. Her heart beat wildly while she continued to scan the other live airport security camera feeds, until she reached the last video in the lower right hand corner, and her heart stopped; there, lying curled in a tight ball, sound asleep, in what looked like a jail cell, was a small girl with a very familiar tangle of red curly hair.

"Oh, no, poor Eme!" She exclaimed. "Here we've been having a beaut of a time: eating, drinking, and sleeping in comfort..." she started. Then she noticed the dark circles under Rafe's bloodshot eyes. "At least No and I have." Rafe's smile at his friend was more of a grimace; Kala sighed and continued, "And there she is...where is she, Rafe? How did you get that video footage?"

Rafe isolated and enlarged Eme's video.

"Our own Hacker Jacker has hijacked airport security cameras again, and it looks as if he's found CIA headquarters—probably where I was taken," answered No without taking his eyes off of Eme's sleeping form. "Wait a minute, that's my cot!" he suddenly yelled, pointing at the monitor. "They've got her in the same cell...look, that's my disgusting stain down near the end of the cot!"

"Ewwww, poor Eme!" moaned Kala.

"Well, at least she's not lying *on* the stain, and she's sleeping through the smell, so maybe Ed used a top secret, government-issued deodorizer; you know, the kind they use to cover up all the government's stinking messes!" No countered with a loud guffaw.

Rafe and Kala just smirked at their sarcastic friend and continued to stare at Eme's sleeping form.

Finally, Rafe answered Kala's question, "The Cyborg's best guess is that these cameras are not on the airport's network, which begs the question: who or what agency is responsible for this room's existence?"

Surprised and dark looks passed between No and Kala as they realized the implication of Rafe's remarks.

A few clicks of the keyboard, and the image miniaturized again; then Rafe launched into Decode Mode on Persephone.

Kala and No watched, fascinated, as encrypted data continued to scroll down the screen. With a few more clicks, the files morphed into English; Rafe bent closer to read the information.

Several more minutes of study, a few lines of code entered into his computer, and Rafe jumped to his feet, clapping his hands and knocking over his chair. "By Jove, the Cyborg's hit the mother lode!"

Not surprised at finding Kala and No on the floor behind him, he quickly reached down, lending each a hand. Once they were on their feet, No admonished him, "Next time, give a warning, pal!"

"Warnings be damned, Time waits for no one!" Rafe admonished, rubbing his hands together in glee; his face looked like Christmas morning. "Ignorance is the curse of God, Knowledge the wings wherewith we fly to Eme's rescue; the Cyborg knows how to free the crimson goddess!" He thrust his fists into the air, lowered his head, and executed an abbreviated war dance in front of the computer.

"How?" No and Kala exclaimed together, eyes wide, clearly fearful for their friend's sanity.

Rafe stopped suddenly and stared at his friends with wild eyes. "No time for explanations; suffice it to say yours truly knows all, thanks to this beauty." He pointed dramatically to the small device protruding from the USB port. "The why, the where, the when, "he paused a moment and thrust his index finger in the air, exclaiming, "...and the how! *Quo Fata Ferunt!*" he finished, his finger now pointing at the computer. "Whither the fair one goest, the Cyborg shall soon follow!"

No shook his head. "Not that fatty runt stuff again. Come on, Rafe, talk to us in English! What are we going to do to help Eme?"

Rafe calmed his rant, faced his friends and looked them squarely in the eyes. "It's not what *we're* to do, but what the Cyborg is *destined* to do!" he proclaimed, then paused for a few seconds in thought, removed the flash drive from the computer, caressed it reverently, and clipped it to the belt loop of his faded black jeans. He paused another second, then ran to the kitchen and grabbed a long-stemmed crystal goblet from the cupboard, placing it upside down on the granite breakfast bar.

"But, but, what..." No stammered at Rafe's renewed burst of activity. He and Kala watched in confusion as the handsome computer genius, wearing his freshly laundered red Hacker Hawk T-shirt and his rumpled pink-plumed Shakespeare Festival hat, pulled out the embedded 3DX laser scan pen from his notebook.

They continued to watch in silence, fascinated, as Rafe carefully adjusted the recently downloaded program. Once he had the Venture: Eme logo on the screen, he turned on the scanner and aimed the light at the stem of the inverted wine glass on the breakfast bar of the kitchen. Finally, he moved a barstool to the middle of the living room floor, in line with the two electronic devices, and retreated several feet to study the effect. Rushing back to the bar, he readjusted the glass, moving it a fraction to the left. Another glance between the scanner and the glass, another adjustment, a hair further to the right, and a slow, satisfied smile graced his face. Without a word he took a seat on the stool, folded his long legs beneath his body, and, bathed in an otherworldly light, turned to face his astonished friends.

"What's going on, Rafe?" demanded a deadly serious Kala.

"Yeah, let us in on this, this...what is it, a satanic ritual?" laughed No.

Another moment of quiet hesitation, another dimpled smirk, and Rafe jumped off the stool proclaiming, "Some experimentation is first warranted!" Kala and No shielded their eyes from the unblocked light, until Rafe switched off the scanner and scampered into the hallway and out of sight.

Kala and No watched their maniacal friend dash frantically from room to room, not knowing what to do to help him, each silently blaming his illogical bustle on lack of sleep.

Another few seconds elapsed, and Rafe bounded back into the room, sporting a huge smile and clutching a rather large stuffed blue rabbit. Placing the toy firmly on the stool, he proclaimed, "Into cyberspace with you, Horatio, my sacrificial lamb, er, bunny!" He returned to his computer. With one click, the beam of the 3DX laser scanner entered the stem of the crystal goblet. The result was spectacular; the beam fractured and intensified, illuminating the rabbit. The teens had to shade their eyes again from the glowing toy that seemed to be lit by some internal halogen bulb.

Rafe made several more clicks on the computer keyboard, and before the horrified faces of his friends, the bunny seemed to dissolve into a frosty fog. Rafe's eyes swam with tears of ecstatic discovery; a few seconds later, Horatio had completely disappeared, leaving an icy mist on the notebook's USB hologram port. The computer genius was stunned for a second, before the reality of what he had done registered. He laughed at his open-mouthed friends, threw his fist into the air once again, and leaped onto the empty bar stool with a blood-curdling scream.

"What..." began No.

"Just..." continued Kala.

"Happened?" finished Rafe with a huge grin, jumping down from the stool. He danced into the living room, patting two shocked faces as he passed.

"Yeah! That!" answered the other two in unison, their wide eyes turned to a gleeful Rafe who continued dancing around them, clapping his hands in glee, tears streaming down his flushed cheeks.

"Rafe!" they once again screamed together.

He slowed his dancing long enough to wipe his eyes and answer his friends. "Some are born great, and some have greatness thrust upon them—Horatio has gone to rescue fair Eme!" He ran to Persephone, minimized the Venture: Eme program and accessed the image of Eme's prison cell.

Kala and No looked at each other in alarm and cautiously followed him to the computer table; they peered over his shoulder to see Eme lying in the same position on the bare cot.

"Maybe you should go lie down..." No began, placing his hand on Rafe's trembling shoulder.

Rafe shook it off with a sneer and continued his frantic quest, accessing a different security camera.

Suddenly, the picture changed; banks of computers now filled the screen. He gained control of the scanning mechanism, and the camera slowly panned the room. Something familiar caught his eye, and Rafe zoomed in on a computer located at the far right corner of the cavernous room.

Two pairs of eyes nearly popped out of their heads, while another pair glistened with delight; there, resting comfortably on a chair next to the computer, was a very large stuffed blue rabbit.

CHAPTER FOURTEEN
UNTO THE BREACH

Reagan International Airport, Washington, DC
Saturday, June 13, 2015
12:15 P.M. EDT/1:15 P.M. ADT

"Let me get this straight, Agent Dvorsky, you *think* there was a foreign operative aboard Flight 65, and you got word of this when the plane was stranded in Atlanta. Why did you allow the plane to take off without a thorough investigation? Why wait to bring it down in the middle of a hurricane?"

Agent Stuart Dvorsky was pinned against the flight information desk by numerous distraught and irate relatives of the dead and disabled passengers on the doomed Destiny airliner. Many were emotionally drained, many beyond tears and anger. Others, like Mr. Romero, whose anger trumped his grief, wanted answers and a few heads to roll for the disaster.

Stuart Dvorsky had faced enraged mobs before—had dealt with terrorists before—and had always remained detached and unflappable under fire, because he knew he was on the right side of things.

This was different.

He understood the anger and resentment of these people and felt their pain. This was the fault of the Agency, pure and simple, and when he got his hands on Edward Turner and Gunter Dexter, there would be an accounting for their reckless maneuver.

"Mr. Romero, I appreciate your anger and concern, but..."

"No, you know nothing of the anger and concern of those of us who have lost our family members, Agent Dvorsky," Bill Romero seethed, fists clenched, "but rest assured, you and your agency will soon enough. What we want to know right now," he growled, "and I believe I speak for everyone here, is what are you doing to recover the missing children?" He turned his head to see many nodding theirs in agreement. "I also understand that several air-port employees have gone missing."

The CIA agent was thrown by this statement; how had this civilian learned of the missing workers? The shock must have shown on his face, because the next words from the distinguished grey-haired man cut him to the core:

"I also have my sources, Agent Dvorsky; the CIA isn't as secure as you may believe. Maybe there's more to this story than even *you* understand."

He turned on his heel, leaving a stunned and red-faced agent to field questions from a few of the other relatives. Seething, Bill Romero marched to the nearby cafe for something to calm his nerves. An older woman joined the tall, exasperated man at the counter.

"May I be so bold as to offer you a well-deserved cup of cof-fee?" she asked.

Bill turned a startled face to the lady standing next to him as she continued. "It's the least I can do for stating so eloquently what has been on all of our minds." She offered her hand. "My name is Anne Malone, and my great-granddaughter is one of the missing teenagers."

Bill Romero extended his hand to the lovely woman in front of him. He studied her for a moment. "It's not often someone surprises me, Ms. Malone, but...let me get this straight, you have a *great*-granddaughter. Excuse *my* boldness, but I find it hard to believe that you're even old enough to have a *grand*daughter," he finished.

Anne blushed but quickly recovered her composure, "Thank you for the compliment, Mr.... Romero, is it?"

"Yes, I'm sorry, please call me Bill, Ms. Malone," warmth shining from his sparkling dark eyes.

"Anne, please," she said. "So a cup of coffee, then..."

"No, please, let me buy one for you." Without giving Anne a chance to argue, he turned to the barista behind the counter. "A cup of herbal tea for me, and for the lady..." He turned back to look at Anne.

"Herbal green tea—iced, please," she added. "Thank you, Mr....uh, Bill." She smiled and blushed again.

A moment later they were seated at a small table near the back of the shop, sipping their beverages.

"So, your great-granddaughter was going to St. Bruno's Academy," Bill inquired, concern written on his tanned, chiseled face.

Anne glanced up. "Yes, it was a last-minute decision, but she was so excited at the prospect of going away for the summer. Her parents are not aware of the situation on Bermuda; I have no way of reaching them for another two days."

"Excuse me," Bill said, looking stunned. "Where could they be that would put them out of range of a cell phone?"

Anne chuckled, "They're on a remote island in the Mediterranean, shooting a movie."

"Oh, I see!" he replied, "Actors; that explains it." Anne laughed. "But that certainly puts a burden on your shoulders."

"I've been Elaine's—Eme's—guardian all her life. She's more of a daughter to me than a great-granddaughter; it is better that her parents not hear about this crisis until it's over." She took another sip of her tea and glanced at him. "We will find them, won't we, Bill. You seem to know more about this than the authorities are letting us know."

"Attention, please," interrupted the airline desk agent. "Flight 81, nonstop to Bermuda, is now boarding at Gate 10."

Bill helped Anne to her feet and grabbed both of their bags. "Anne, it's time to get some answers to our questions. Please, sit with me on the plane; I'd like to learn more about your great-grand-daughter—Eme, is it?" He paused and she nodded. "And you."

Anne smiled. "Thank you, Bill, I'd be happy to join you." She placed her hand on his arm, and together they joined the queue of anxious passengers and federal agents boarding the plane to Bermuda.

St. George's Club Cottage
3:13 P.M. ADT

"Where shall we three meet again: in thunder, lightning, or in rain?"

"Rafe, this is insanity," pleaded No. His friend was preparing to replicate the experiment that had transported the toy rabbit to Eme's dungeon a few hours before.

"Never suffer from your insanity, Mr. Negative; enjoy every minute of it!" laughed Rafe.

"No's right, Rafe; a toy is one thing, but we don't know what will happen to a digitized living, breathing person." Kala's knuckles were white from gripping the lounge chair.

"There's one way to discover the results of human Internet transport, and the Cyborg will report back with the details—when he delivers the fair, imprisoned one to the safety of our sanctuary," he said with conviction. He wagged his eyebrows at his two companions.

The three friends were lounging on the comfortable patio furniture they had dragged from the cottage garage to the covered terrace overlooking the Atlantic Ocean. Sipping soda and feasting on stale taco chips and leftover caviar from the night before, they had planned and plotted, and then argued about their proposed rescue attempt through the long, humid afternoon. Rafe had described the CIA's project, Venture: Eme, and had formulated a theory about the feasibility of their operation. Since there was no TV in the cottage, they had tapped into Internet news feeds and monitored the increased activity at the airport; however, there had been no mention of any of their disappearances, only of the stolen airport van that had plunged off the embankment near the swing bridge, with no sign of a driver or passengers.

"We did a better job of covering our tracks than I thought," No quipped.

The only news report out of Atlanta was not about No's disappearance; the mysterious disappearance of Tim Edelman, the head programmer and CEO of Amazemail, was the number one news story of the day. He had not reported to work, and his wife, Kelly, and two young sons were not at home when the clients of Mrs. Edelman's day care tried to drop off their children.

"That's got to be the inventor of the e-mail protocol—Tim Edelman is the name on the program," reasoned Kala. The other two readily agreed.

"If he's mixed up with those two goons..." No began.

"T'would be unwise for a man with a family to get involved with the two devil dudes; there's more to this unlikely story, and as it unfolds, we'll learn the truth."

Rafe's extensive investigation of the protocol, plus Horatio's successful landing, had empowered him, and now he was ready to follow the bunny's lead to CIA headquarters, but his well-intentioned friends were trying to stop him from pursuing this next logical step in rescuing Eme; they had thrown every argument and counterplan imaginable into his path.

"OK, let me get this straight," began No, "you're going to rush into heaven knows where with no ironclad way of escape?" Then a thought hit him, and he perked up. "How are you planning to digitize yourself and Eme? You won't have your notebook 3DX laser scanner with you, and you don't know if there is one embedded on their desktop computer." Confident that he had just manufactured the perfect excuse to keep Rafe from his foolhardy mission, No smirked at Kala, and they both relaxed on the patio lounge with expressions of smug superiority.

The setting sun enhanced the mischievous glint in Rafe's blue eyes. "You two *think* you know everything, but you're irritating the hell out of the one who truly knows all," was his cheeky response. "If I'm not mistaken, the Cyborg and the crimson one's return will be assisted by a very captivating piece of technological brilliance sitting next to the protocol computer."

No and Kala frowned and were about to add another protest, but Rafe sprang from his chair with catlike grace and turned in midair to face them, bloodshot eyes ablaze. "Now that all avenues of contention are exhausted, the un-caped crusader must vanquish the dark dudes and release fair Eme from her bonds. It is not in the stars to hold our destiny but in ourselves." He spun on his heels and bellowed, "Into cyberspace and beyond!" Then he marched inside to the launching stool.

Not knowing what else to add to dissuade their maniacal friend from his suicidal mission, a resigned No and Kala expelled the last of their worn-out emotions by uttering a few expletives, and followed the stoic figure into the kitchen.

Once Kala and No were positioned behind Rafe, the three teens carefully checked the live video feed of the command center on the monitor; by all indications, the coast was clear. No and Kala reluctantly assumed their well-practiced positions, and once Rafe was situated, feet tucked firmly under his hunched body, hat in his lap, Kala clicked the 3DX laser while No pushed the preset computer keys.

Rafe grinned at his two friends. "Danger glistens like laser shine, my comrades!" was his parting shot. One flash from the prism-intensified laser beam, and an unearthly glow bathed his entire body. The digitization process was instantaneous. Seconds later, all that remained on that section of the living room carpet was an empty stool grasped by two very frightened teenagers.

CHAPTER FIFTEEN

WHITHER THOU GOEST...

CIA Secret Command Center
Five minutes earlier

With no noise and no sun to disturb her drug-induced slumber, Eme didn't awaken until Ed and Gun entered her cell carrying clean clothes and a tray of food.

"Sleeping away the day, missy?" Ed threw the clothes on top of a disoriented Eme.

"She's going to be no use to us in this condition, Ed. I told you not to chloroform her," complained Gun as he tried to hand the groggy teen her tray of food.

Eme nearly spilled the hot soup, crackers, and cold drink when she shifted her feet to the cement floor. "Where...am I?" she croaked as Gun replaced the tray on the stool in front of her.

"Where you are now should not be your concern, Miss Eme Venture. It's where you're going—now that's the question, eh,

Ed? Should we tell her where she's going?" He broke into peals of evil laughter; Ed just shook his head sadly at the bewildered girl.

"I...I don't understand," Eme started, regaining some of her equilibrium. And Gun broke into new gales of demented amusement.

"Eme," Ed began, over Gun's continued merriment, "I'm afraid you're a means to an end, and it just happens that your end is necessary to achieve our end."

Gun began the explanation. "What my soft-hearted friend," he said, jabbing his thumb at the man behind him, "is trying to say is that we need you to give us an alibi. And, since there's *no* way you'd cooperate with us if we left you alive, you're going to end up *dead* when we shoot you in your escape attempt on board a stolen boat, fall overboard, and disappear forever. We 'believed' you were a foreign operative, Eme Venture—you and your friend, No Henderson, whenever we find him. You two stole the Venture: Eme protocol from its inventor, killed him, and have already sold it to a foreign government." He let out another extremely loud bark of a laugh and continued, "You are the perfect foil to cover our tracks when..."

Suddenly there was a clatter in the Command Center, and two panicked agents turned on their heels, leaving a totally bewildered Eme in their wake. With guns drawn, they ran to the end of the corridor and peered around the room at—nothing. Cautiously they entered the room, creeping slowly by each of the three banks of computers; they searched the floor and computer counters, on and under the chairs.

After a thorough sweep of the room, they noticed a broom lying on the floor next to a heavy oak door near the security entrance.

"Wasn't that too large a noise for a falling broom?" whispered Ed.

Gun motioned for his partner to stand next to the closet door while he approached it; slowly, he turned the knob and, with a mighty yank, flung it wide open to the storage room. Throwing the light switch, Gun rushed inside, followed by Ed.

The well-stocked kitchen/storage room was filled with technical equipment and a wide array of hardware, but was entirely devoid of human occupation. Taking no chances, they searched under a desk and sink, through a collection of ropes, pulleys, computers, and peripherals. They even looked under and behind a small couch. Feeling rather foolish for their paranoia, they looked at each other, grinned, and exited the room.

When a quick check of the bathroom also turned up no intruder, they holstered their guns and were about to return to Eme when Gun's cell phone rang.

"Yeah," he barked. "Oh, yes, sir, we'll be right there." He snapped the phone closed and jammed it into his pants pocket.

"They're here. Let's go before we arouse any more suspicions."

Ed turned back toward Eme's cell.

"Forget about her; she's not going anywhere," Gun snickered.

With that the two double agents headed for the security doors, completely unaware of the flashing blue eyes watching their every move.

Airport Terminal
Saturday, June 13, 2015
3:19 P.M. ADT

"They should be here any minute—poor kids!"

"Wait until the CIA starts questioning them! I hope their parents arrive before the feds!"

"Oh, you must not have heard—they're all flying in together from Washington. How would you like to be aboard that flight?"

The four airport employees continued their speculation about the devastating plane crash and disappearances and deaths of so many passengers and two airport employees. Not many had an answer, or even an educated guess, as to the cause of all the bizarre occurrences. Some Bermudan officials blamed limited airport disaster preparedness; others blamed Bruno itself. Some went so far as to call Bruno "the Devil Wind" and predicted the end of the world.

The arrival of a large contingency of paparazzi at the terminal entrance interrupted the baggage handlers' gossip session, and they rushed to the doors, ready to perform the crowd-control operation they had been assigned.

CIA Secret Command Room
3:20 P.M. ADT

The final click of the security door launched Rafe from his hiding place behind the immense wall map of the world where he had stood perched on a narrow ledge. Still holding Horatio by one long blue ear, he paused for just a second to determine Eme's location. Since he had seen Ed and Gun enter the room from the right-hand corridor, it was the first place he looked.

Sure enough, there, sound asleep on a very uncomfortable-looking, very smelly, stained cot, was the girl he had jumped into the void to rescue. He rushed through the unlocked door and knelt by her side, placing Horatio next to her.

"Fair maiden, awake; we must make haste and escape this dank place before the twisted twosome return," he whispered, taking her cold hand in his, caressing it, and bringing it to his lips.

Eme stirred and moaned, "Ohhhh...my head. Is that you, Rafe?" Her eyes fluttered open and landed on the blue rabbit. With a raspy voice, she whispered, "Oh, Rafe... you brought me Mittens; how...how sweet." One shaking hand grasped the comforting warmth of its fur. She glanced at Rafe through bleary eyes and hugged the bunny to her chest, closed her eyes, laid her head down on the disgusting cot, and fell asleep once again.

"Mittens?" Rafe shook his head and was about to correct her, but he was captivated by how sweet she looked with the blue bunny in her arms, and then reality hit. "Eme, wake up! We've got to get out of here now!" Wasting no more time on chivalry, he grabbed her hand and pulled her to a sitting position; Horatio was still clutched against her right side, but her eyes remained closed.

"G'way, Rafe," she slurred. "I have to sleeeep...come back tomor..."

She tried to lie down again, but Rafe had other ideas. He spotted the untouched tray of food on the stool next to her bed and picked up the glass of soda. "Desperate times call for desperate measures," he announced and threw the entire contents in her face.

To say the 'desperate measure' had the desired effect would have been an understatement; Eme launched herself off the cot and slammed Rafe into the bars of the cell. Horatio went flying through the open door, landing on the cement corridor floor. "What the hell!" she screamed in his face, shaking soda from her sopping wet curls.

Rafe recovered quickly and, by way of explanation, grabbed her hand and yanked her through the doorway. He stopped just long enough to once again snag Horatio by his blue ear before running to the command room with an extremely confused redhead in tow.

Dragging her to the computer in the farthest corner of the room, he dropped the bunny on the floor and pushed her down on the chair, placing his face an inch from hers. "Ask no questions, fair Eme; just do as the Cyborg instructs. Neither move nor speak." Then he whispered more softly, "Trust me." He rubbed her arms to get her attention and help her focus.

He must have had her attention; she nodded and stared in stunned disbelief while he booted up the computer and turned on the large conical 3DX laser scanner he had admired from the cottage video feed. Once he had the flash drive inserted, he entered some data and an e-mail address, and aimed the scanner at the redhead, making certain that her entire body, including every damp red curl, was illuminated by the beam. He blocked the light for one moment while he turned, caressed her wet cheek, and kissed her on the lips; he then returned to the computer and activated the scanner.

She blinked once, sucked in a shaky breath, and her eyes grew wide with fear as the bright light from the scanner intensified. Before she could let out her breath or blink again, she dissolved into ice crystals and disappeared through the holoport of the computer.

"Wow!" Rafe loudly proclaimed to the empty room. "Now, that's a laser!"

"Who's out there?"

Rafe froze.

St. George's Club Cottage
3:33 P.M. ADT

Two pairs of arms embraced her while she sat upon an unfamiliar stool in a decidedly unfamiliar room. It took her a few seconds to realize that Kala and No were attached to the arms and that she had no idea how she had been transported to this place without being aware she had left the command center.

"OK, now this is..." The rest of her words were muffled by the intense hugging she was receiving from her two immensely relieved friends.

"Oh, Eme," Kala cried, tears streaming from her bright amber eyes. "You don't know how worried we were!"

No's eyes were wet as well, but he was laughing and was soon dancing around the cottage, chanting, "It worked, it worked, it worked, it *worked!*"

The girls stayed locked in their embrace, watching the antics of the ecstatic boy.

After a few seconds, Kala began laughing through her tears while Eme watched in stunned disbelief. *What just happened, and...* "Where is Rafe?" she finally blurted.

The other two stopped and raced to the monitor to see Rafe cautiously approaching the corridor on the left side of the room.

"What is he doing?" screamed No at the monitor.

"How...?"

"Not now, Eme, Rafe is going to have to explain all of this to you; just know that you just traveled across Bermuda by e-mail," explained Kala. She, too, had her eyes glued to the live video before her.

"E-mail? What? That's not possible! Is that..." she began again, staring at the monitor and dismissing Kala's comment as a joke...for the time being.

"Yes!" Kala and No answered in unison, not moving their eyes away from the unfolding drama.

"What is he...?"

"We don't know; he was supposed to follow you, but...look, he's going down that corridor," finished No. "Quick, switch to another monitor, Kala."

Kala fiddled with the controls but could not find a camera for that part of the complex. To her astonishment, No pushed her aside to take a look, but he had no better luck.

"Sorry about that, Kala," he smiled sheepishly under her scathing glare, when he turned back to the girl.

She recovered, smiled, and responded, "That's all right, No." She hugged him. "You're just as buggered as I am." No looked as if Christmas had arrived and hugged her back—with enthusiasm.

After a few seconds, they seemed to remember that Eme was in the room and turned to see her smirking at them.

"Don't bother about me, you two; it looks like a lot's happened while I was...uh, away!" She smiled and turned to the monitor. "Hey, there he is, and there's a man with him. Look, they're headed for the monitor. Rafe's writing something on a tablet."

Kala and No turned back to the monitor, and Kala bowed to No and extended her hand silently, offering him the controls. A goofy smile lit his face; she blushed, and then he remembered his mission and zoomed in on the tablet, which read "We're coming through!"

They watched in silence as Rafe performed the well-practiced e-mail protocol operation with this strange man. There was a bright glow, and a second later the stranger appeared on the stool Eme had occupied only a few minutes before.

"Hi there!" Kala greeted the dazed man. "Who are you?"

"Let him get his bearings, Kala," Eme admonished her friend, realizing she must not have been joking about this e-mail traveling thing. "It's a very disorienting feeling."

"That's all right, Miss, I assumed the sensation would be something like that." He laughed at the stunned looks on the three faces in front of him as he rose from the stool. "I'm sorry, I should introduce myself..." His introduction was interrupted when No screamed, "He's not coming through! What the hell does he think he's doing now?"

They all gathered around the monitor again, this time to watch Rafe running around the command center with a broom in one hand and Horatio in the other. He deposited the broom on a chair next to the transport computer; then he ran to the opposite end of the room and disappeared into what looked like a closet. Several breathless seconds later, he reemerged with a tiny glass bottle, a white plastic coffeemaker, and Horatio, the first cyber traveler.

With the blue rabbit tucked under his arm, Rafe set to work; he deposited the coffeemaker and bottle on the desk, rolled a black leather computer chair out from under an auxiliary terminal, and placed it directly in front of a door, through which they'd last seen Ed and Gun leave those few short minutes before.

Since the cameras were video-only, they couldn't hear him say, "Fare thee well, Horatio," as he placed the toy on the seat facing the door, "we barely knew thee."

Four sets of eyes watched as Rafe patted the rabbit on the head and returned to the main computer terminal; he plugged the coffeemaker into the control panel and programmed the timer. He loosened the cap on the bottle, covered his nose, emptied the contents into the pot, capped the pot and the bottle, and placed the pot under the desk. Then he situated himself in front of the mainframe and, with an evil smirk, recorded several seconds of audio while his fingers flew across the keyboard.

"It looks like he's recording something!" said Kala.

"Probably his audition tape for *Bermuda's Got Crooners!*" No smirked, followed by groans from the girls.

Again Rafe was up and moving—this time closer to the transport terminal. The cyberwhiz quickly booted the computer and entered more verbal and written information. He performed this procedure on two other computers, before returning to the main transport terminal.

They watched their friend's flurry of activity for another two minutes, his plan becoming no more obvious.

"Traveling through cyberspace must have addled his brains," Kala whispered, afraid for her friend's sanity.

"Not with that short a trip," responded the man beside her.

Three heads turned in unison at his remarks. "How do you know that?" asked Eme.

He was about to answer; however, their attention was drawn back to the monitor by Kala's scream.

A heartbeat later, Rafe was sitting on the cottage stool.

Without a word, three ecstatic teenagers threw themselves at the new arrival. Rafe braced himself against the kitchen counter and laughed at his homecoming committee.

"If this were played upon a stage, I could condemn it as an improbable fiction, yet here we are, flesh once again."

Everyone laughed at Rafe's attempt to lighten the moment and lessen the actual life and death feat that three of them had just performed.

"Do you think Gun and Dumber will be able to follow you?" asked No.

"The Cyborg runs like a silent stream under the radar in the world of technology. I've left a trace of my intrusion but none of my departure." He smirked at their confusion and laughed when understanding dawned in their eyes.

"You're a bloody genius!" Kala announced.

"Not to mention brave!" the man added with a grin.

"And out of your freaking mind!" smirked No, slapping Rafe on the back.

Rafe bowed his head at Kala's and the man's pronouncements and smiled wickedly at No's snarky remark.

They stood in a small group, the Bermuda sun casting a warm glow on the scene. No one wanted to break the euphoric, yet tense moment; no one knew exactly what to say, until…"Would someone like to tell me what just happened and explain where the hell we are!" Eme stood in the middle of the room with her hands on her hips.

That broke the dam as quickly as an earthquake, and everyone began talking at once:

"Well, you see…"

"It's like this…"

"How poor are they that have not patience…"

"Maybe I can help explain…"

"Enough! One at a time; one answer to one question! First," Eme said, turning to the newcomer, "not to be rude, but who *are* you?"

Rafe jumped forward at this and extended a hand, still holding the flash drive, toward the stammering man. "Why, the world's now mine oyster, which he, with laser and flash drive, did open." He waved the device in his hand. "Meet the ingenious inventor of your namesake, Venture: Eme." With a huge grin, he doffed his ever-present, although now severely dilapidated, purple plumed cap and bowed to the red-faced man; the three teens were shocked into silence.

However, Rafe had not yet finished delivering his curveballs. "Ladies...and gentle*man*, this is Timothy Edelman. Tim, may I call you Tim?" At the man's nod, Rafe continued. "This lovely young lady shares the name of your invention: Eme Venture." He put his arm around Eme and kissed her flushed cheek.

At the man's shocked expression, Rafe explained, "Her name has perpetrated our casting into this amazing farce."

Tim paled and asked, "You're Eme and you're...you're Rafe?"

When they nodded, Tim found his way to the sofa and, with a sigh, sank wearily into its welcoming depths. The others joined him; Kala and No sat on the Persian rug; Rafe and Eme sat on the rattan settee that faced the sofa.

"If I had known then what I know now..." he began.

"I think we'd all agree with that statement," interrupted No. "I won't attend the evil agents' funerals when they're finally caught and hanged, but I'll send a thank you note, saying that I approve of it!"

"Shhh, No, let the poor man talk," Kala admonished.

"Sorry," No blushed, and his friends smiled at him as if he were an unruly puppy. They all returned their attention to the man on the sofa.

Tim continued, "I can imagine what you've been through if Gun and Ed were involved. They're ruthless, but the CIA must trust them." He paused a moment. "Or they did; if the agency ever discovers their duplicity in the airplane disaster, this whole can of worms will be blown wide open."

The teens looked around knowingly at each other.

Suddenly, Eme bounced off the settee, excused herself, and made a beeline for the guest bathroom; Kala followed, stating, "We'll be right back! Don't discuss anything important."

The guys smiled in understanding; Rafe and No respected the girls' wishes and switched the conversation to their exploits with the rogue agents.

Once Kala and Eme were in the guest bathroom, Eme relieved herself, stripped, and jumped into the shower while Kala filled her in on their escape from the terminal in the van. Eme gasped, inhaling a mouthful of shampoo lather, when Kala got to the part about their plunge off the swing bridge and impromptu swim in the bay. Then, while she towel-dried her body and hair, Eme relayed the story of her own near-escape; Kala just shook her head, eyes glistening with tears at what her friend had endured.

"I sure hate putting these grimy clothes on my nice clean bod," Eme said shaking her head at the soot and blood-stained denim outfit lying in a heap on the bathroom floor. Kala excused herself and darted to the master bedroom. After a quick search in a dresser, she grabbed some underwear, jeans, and a T-shirt, quickly returning to her friend.

"Whose are these?" Eme asked, smiling at her luck that they were her size. Kala just shrugged, and the redhead pursued it no further, just happy to have any clothes other than the ones she'd been wearing for more than two days. She hugged Kala, placed all of her filthy clothes in a plastic bag she'd found under the sink, and they returned to the living room.

"OK, now I think I can concentrate a bit better!" Everyone chuckled as Eme took her seat next to Rafe, patting him on the arm. He tousled her damp curls, grabbed her hand, and gave her a kiss on the cheek. She blushed and squeezed his hand in return. When she turned back to her grinning friends, her blush deepened. "So...so, what about the CIA's involvement in this mess?" she quickly asked, trying to refocus everyone's attention.

An expression of smug understanding passed between No and Kala as the newcomer began to speak. "I don't think they have any idea what Ed and Gun are up to," replied Tim, taking up the conversation where they had left it. "They must have given them some song and dance about my program, but from what I overheard, bringing down the plane on the island was a last minute decision."

"We can only hope the Central Intelligence agents are as intelligent as their name implies, and will see through the 'The Ed and Gun Show,'" No replied. They all nodded in agreement with No's assessment, and he continued, "They should all be in the terminal by now."

Tim smiled at that and stretched his hands toward the floor. "I have something else very important that...," he began.

However, No's remark had launched Rafe from his chair, and he sprinted across the living room to the computer. "Hold that thought for just a trice, ingenious sir." After a few seconds, the picture of the main terminal lounge filled the screen.

Curious, the others joined Rafe; they peered over his shoulder at the madhouse of passengers, paparazzi, terminal employees, and government agents who crowded the makeshift information desks lining the concourse.

A few seconds of comments from the small group in the cottage and...

"GG! There's my GG Anne!" Eme pointed to the image of her great-grandmother conversing with an older gentleman by one of the information desks. Rafe zoomed in closer.

"And she's talking to my *grandfather!*" exclaimed Rafe. "Our respite is now doomed!"

The cottage occupants turned to Rafe, shock on all of their faces at his comment.

"What exactly does that mean in bloody English?" demanded Kala.

He returned their gaze and spoke urgently. "It means that they will appear here at any moment— this humble abode belongs to my grandfather." No's jaw dropped and Kala smirked as Rafe continued, "I have no time to enlighten you further, for if I'm not mistaken, Ed and Gun will accompany them."

Realization hit them all simultaneously, and a flurry of activity ensued: Kala headed for the bedrooms, No stormed to the bathroom, Rafe loaded Tim's program onto his grandfather's computer, while Eme and Tim stood like statues, watching the pandemonium.

"I guess we should do something," ventured Eme. She looked around the living room and headed for the vacated chairs, plumping and brushing the deep rose velvet cushions; Tim got into the swing of the moment by putting dishes into the cupboards and wiping down the counters.

Five minutes later, with the cottage in pristine condition, they converged, once again, in the living room, awaiting Rafe's final orders.

"Eme, what is your great-grandmother's e-mail address?"

"Uh, e-m-e-g-g, no, g-g-e-m-e at cybersleuth dot com—or is it dot net? Wait a minute; it's in my..." Her face paled. "Oh, no, it burned up in the plane. Let me think a second." She turned and grabbed a pencil and paper off the computer desk and slowly wrote several letters while everyone watched nervously, Rafe's plan becoming clear.

Finally, Eme produced the paper with the e-mail address written carefully in large block letters, and Rafe entered it into the Venture: Eme program.

"I assume she has the Amazemail program installed..."

At her nodding, Rafe continued. "Queue up; time waits for no man—or woman," he added after a quick, sober glance at Eme and Kala.

Tim's eyes widened when he saw the makeshift laser. "Very good, Rafe, I would never have thought to use the stem of a crystal glass to intensify the beam."

The teenager gave his new hero a lopsided smile when Tim patted him on the shoulder and mounted the stool. "The Cyborg is anxious to discuss all of this when we meet again." Tim nodded, and Rafe performed the protocol operation; a blast of intense light bathed the smiling man as he disintegrated into a series of ones and zeros, finally disappearing into the holoport. Eme gasped at the empty stool.

"That was amazing—scary, but amazing!" She gaped at the knowing looks from her friends.

Kala put an arm around her shoulders and patted her arm. "We'll get used to it, Eme; I have a feeling this isn't the last time we'll be traveling like this."

No shuddered at her words, shook his head, and took Tim's place. "Give my regards to...to Broadway!" he said with a cheeky grin. Kala reached over and gave him a kiss on the cheek. No's face reddened, and he was about to jump off the stool and grab her when Rafe brought him up short.

"You can deliver those regards yourself, Mr. Negative, to Broadway and to a few other..." he began as their eyes met briefly, before Rafe scanned the smirking teenager and sent him on his digitized way.

An exceedingly nervous Kala now ascended the stool. While Rafe was busy adjusting the scanner, she bravely stated to her remaining friends and to Bermuda: "Wherever the fates may take us..." And with a click and a blaze of light, she was nothing but a frosty mist in search of a new adventure.

Eme stepped up next and sat stoically on the stool with her bag of dirty clothes on her lap, but before Rafe could activate the scanner, she suddenly asked, with a hint of panic in her voice, "Wait, who's going to send you?"

Rafe smiled and pointed to the broom standing in the corner of the kitchen. Eme frowned and then smiled in understanding. "Going to make it a clean sweep, then?" The lanky brunet laughed, leaned over, brushed her smooth cheek with the back of his fingertips, kissed her on the lips, and sent her to her great-grandmother's house.

"Over the river, through cyberspace, to Grandmother's house you..."

Rafe's song was interrupted by voices coming up the front walk. He reset the program and power timers on the desktop computer, grabbed his computer bag, mounted the stool, and flicked the switch on the scanner with the broom handle; the last things he heard, before he disappeared, were the clatter of the falling broom and the click of the lock on the front door of St. George's Club Cottage, number 34.

CHAPTER SIXTEEN

CONFLICTS AND CONSEQUENCES

Outside St. George's Club Cottage
Saturday, June 13, 2015
4:14 P.M. ADT

"OK, Ed, search the place!"

"Wait just a minute, Agent Gun!" The tall gray-haired man grabbed Ed's arm as he attempted to cross the threshold of the cottage. He glared at the surprised CIA agents before he continued. "I have allowed you access to my home, without a search warrant, because I want to find my grandson as much—no, much more than you do. I will not allow you to tear the place apart. You may come in and sit down so that we can discuss what has happened to this point and what we need to do next to locate *all* of the missing children." He glanced at a teary-eyed Anne standing beside him.

Ed and Gun smiled their trademark insincere smiles. "Of, course, Mr. Romero; we were just anxious to do our business. Let's go inside and discuss what we know," replied Gun as he stepped aside so that Anne Malone and Bill Romero could enter first. A glance and a smirk between the two agents told a different story; as soon as the door closed behind them, Ed grabbed Anne, while Gun drew his gun on an unsuspecting Bill.

"Now, you listen to me, Mr. Romero; we're the CIA, and we don't need no fancy, schmancy search warrants to do our job of protecting the United States, and its citizens, from terrorists and *kids*. We're going to search this place, and if we mess it up a bit in the process, sue us!"

Ed threw Anne roughly on the couch. Her scream startled Gun, which gave Bill the opportunity he needed to grab the gun from Gun and knock him against a bookcase with a roundhouse kick. Anne bounced off the sofa and away from a surprised Ed, just as a heavy Grecian urn atop the wobbling bookcase crashed down on Gun's head. He staggered and finally fell against a glass trophy case which shattered, dislodging many golf and physical fitness trophies, one of which succeeded in knocking the agent unconscious. Meanwhile, Bill had the gun trained on Ed who toppled onto the sofa.

"You're obviously not to be trusted. I know a little about the law, having studied it at Harvard forty years ago, and I'm certain that US citizens still have a say about unlawful search and seizure." He pulled out his cell phone and called directory assistance. "Yes, please connect me to the CI..."

"Wait!" Ed shouted, just as Gun regained consciousness. "We'll cooperate with you, just..."

"What Ed...is...trying to say..."gasped a groggy Gun, staggering to his feet and brushing the glass from his clothes, "is that we'll go get your search warrant, but you're hereby placed... under house arrest for assaulting a...a federal agent."

"As I said to your partner, while you were napping, as a US citizen, I was just protecting my property and person from an unprovoked attack. You have no grounds to arrest me, nor do I want you in my house. Leave, or I *will* call the police."

Gun shrugged, pulled a few shards of glass from his bloody hands and face, and then turned to Ed. "Guard the outside of the cottage while I get the warrant. Call me if Mr. *US Citizen* tries to leave." He turned to Bill, who still had the gun aimed at his head, and turned on his trademark smile. "You have no idea who you're dealing with, and you *will* hand me back my gun."

"Not on your life, Buster. Now get the hell out of my house." He waved the gun at the two agents and moved them toward the door, which Anne ran to open.

As they crossed the threshold, Gun turned abruptly and gave his parting shot, with no smile present, "You, both of you, are now my enemies and, as such, are enemies of the United States!" With that he turned on his heels and disappeared around the corner of the cottage while Ed stood stoically at the end of the path— just beyond the Romero property line.

Satisfied that the two agents were no longer an immediate threat, Bill slammed the door and turned to Anne. "Something's not right about those two. I have half a mind to call the CIA; however, I'm sure I've not a leg to stand on."

"But I thought you were within your rights about…"

"Oh, don't get me wrong, I'm in the right, but I'm certain that Agent Gun carries a lot of weight, not just in his gut, but within the federal agency." Anne laughed at his comment. Bill gave her a dimpled smile in return and ran his hands through his wavy grey hair. "Our kids are more important to him than he's letting on. I have a feeling they're mixed up in something regarding national security; we just have to discover what that entails before they return."

He turned to the mess made by the skirmish and shook his head. "If Amy, my deceased wife, could see this mess…" He shook his head and looked at Anne. "She took such pride in keeping this place spick-and-span. It was her favorite vacation home. Ah, well, let's get busy; I can clean up later."

As he made his way to the computer desk, he noticed the icy condensation covering the holoport. "Now, that's odd." He flipped the power strip and booted the desktop computer.

Anne quickly joined him at the desk and noticed a slip of paper with her e-mail address lying next to the extended 3DX laser scanner. "They've been here!" she nearly shouted. She continued in a whisper. "Look, this is my e-mail address; it's written in Eme's handwriting—I'd know her block lettering anywhere." She turned to Bill. "Her handwriting is so illegible—the only way anyone can read it is when she prints in caps. The main reason we got her a computer was to give her another method of writing—her parents and I were so grateful!"

Bill laughed and took the slip of paper from Anne. "They must have tried to send you a message." With a smile, he eagerly checked the Sent folder of his account and turned ghostly white. "That's impossible!" Anne grabbed his arm and gasped at the information on the screen.

Cyberspace

Rafe's vision was washed away in a blinding flash of light strong enough to eclipse the sun. For the briefest of moments, he felt as if his entire body had been squeezed through an extremely small tube, stretched, scraped, and twisted to fit into a space no wider than a pinhead.

And then there was nothing but infinity—and an immense cold.

He tried to look down at his hands and found that he couldn't; he was nothing.

Sheer size encompassed everything, and Rafe was overcome by a sensation of traveling through a space so eternally immense that he was a nonentity in comparison: a speck on the face of some previously unknown and inaccessible world, traveling at a speed so fast that distance held no meaning, not even across the long, empty fathoms through which he found himself propelled.

Space, he thought. *This is how wide space is—dark and forever: Outer space.* He was struck by a better thought: *Cyberspace—I'm in cyberspace.* The word seemed to give the vast emptiness around him greater definition: *Cyberspace—it was cold in cyberspace.*

At first it was dark, but then, in the darkness, Rafe focused on beads of light traveling just as fast as he, some even faster, streaking in all directions. He was reminded of stars—of stars painted on the dark canvas around him. It was oddly beautiful, yet he could not shake a sense of terrible foreboding.

A howling wind filled his digitized ears; the darkness stretched into long shadows, reaching away from a blazing white light that spanned the impossible horizon. Rafe groaned as an enormous weight settled on his shoulders; it was a pressure as deep as the sea and as fiercely cold. The light became a mist: a dense fog that surrounded his form. Mist roared past his eyes and ears; beneath it—beyond it—was a terrible sensation of something dreadful. He couldn't breathe.

Rafe was afraid.

The hairs on the back of his hands (hands he couldn't see, couldn't clap together) rose against the chill and the fearsome realization that he was being watched, that he wasn't alone in the mists of cyberspace. Terror clawed at Rafe's chest; the mist descended from pearly white to an awful crimson curtain.

Something lunged at him from out of the mist—a dark shape with gnashing, frightful jaws and hideous sharp teeth. He could do nothing to protect himself as it tore at his eyes.

Then Rafe was on his knees in a bright world filled with warmth and sunshine. Eme was beneath him, shivering and wide-eyed.

Rafe picked himself up quickly, feeling for the gash in his eyebrow with hands that were numb from the cold. There was nothing—no gushing blood, no horrible teeth marks. He stumbled against a table supporting a laptop PC, his head spinning, his whole body shaking. He inhaled—a deep and long breath that seemed to clear his head.

"Cyberspace," he said after a moment, his voice a dry rasp, "not for the faint of heart."

Nearby, No was staring out of the living room window at nothing; next to him was Tim, his face pale and expressionless. Silent tears rolled down Kala's cheeks, and Eme sat in quiet contemplation against the table, trying to control the shakes of her body.

Rafe felt he should say something, anything, but words seemed to travel slowly through his mind, from a tremendously long way away—Bermuda, perhaps—and he faltered.

"I see dead people!"

Rafe nearly jumped out of his skin. Across the room was a colorful bird, feathers of gold and sky blue: a macaw, if he didn't miss his guess. It squawked again, looking him right in the eye, daring him to prove him wrong.

"Well..." Eme said to end the silence. She cleared her throat. "Well, it sure beats flying in a hurricane." Then all was blissfully silent, until an annoying yellow duck delivered a message from Bermuda.

Bermuda Airport Swing Bridge
4:32 P.M. ADT

The late afternoon sun glinted off the gigantic steel crane as the airport crew bus was hoisted high above the bank of the channel. Green slime and debris clung to its mangled body; it was unceremoniously dumped onto the soggy ground with a loud clunk. Uniformed agents swarmed the carcass of the vehicle while divers continued combing the murky channel. Doors were pried open with crowbars, allowing a flood of bay water to escape.

Gun watched the operation from the blue sedan, contemplating his next move. "Where are you, Rafe Romero, No Henderson?" he growled when it was clear that no one was to be found inside the van or in the water. He continued to watch while the vehicle was hoisted onto the back of a flatbed truck and secured for its return to the hangar. Once there, it would be thoroughly searched for any evidence or clues leading to the teens' disappearance and location.

As he watched the last of the agents depart for the airport, Gun slammed his bloody hands onto the steering wheel, driving several pieces of glass even deeper into his injured right hand. "Damn it all!" he yelled. With that he shifted the car into gear and jammed his foot onto the accelerator, leaving skid marks on the street; with nagging thoughts of impending doom, he sped over the bridge and back to the airport.

GG Anne's House, Malibu
12:29 P.M. PDT/ 4:29 P.M. ADT

"What does it say?" asked No.

"Do they know what bloody well happened—that we're here?" Kala inquired.

"From whence did it come?"

"Hold on, everyone, I'm trying to figure that out!" answered Eme.

Five panicky people and one suspicious bird gathered around a laptop computer in the living room of Anne Malone's house, each person trying his or her best to read the incoming e-mail that had just been announced by her unfortunate choice of e-lerts: an annoying fluffy yellow duck that preened its feathers and quacked until someone responded to its latest missive. Eme had just lasered the bird which, to everyone's relief, closed its bill, ruffled its yellow hologram feathers, and waddled back into the holoport of the computer.

"OK, everyone, it's from GG. She's with your grandfather, Rafe, at the cottage. They want to know if we're safe, and about the strange program they found on the computer. She turned to the anxious group. "What are we going to tell them? They know there were five e-mails sent that were far too large to be possible. Tim, what should we do now? We have to let them know we're safe."

When Eme finished talking, the room became as quiet as the passage of time. Even Bogey had stilled his antics, calmed by the deadly seriousness of Eme's tone of voice.

After a few anxious moments, Tim broke the silence. "Sit down, everyone, we have to discuss this, and determine whether or not we need to get your grandparents involved. The CIA is no doubt on their way to investigate your disappearance, if they haven't already done so."

All complied with his request, except Eme who continued to read the e-mail from Rafe's grandfather. "Right, you are, Tim; listen to this: 'Agents Gun and Ed have just left the cottage to obtain a search warrant. If you're reading this, Rafe or Eme, please call us here before they put a tap on our phones. We want to help you.' And, it's signed Bill Romero." She looked to Tim again. "Should one of us return and bring them here?"

The subsequent silence was deafening, and then everyone spoke at once:

"Bloody cyberspace—never again!" Kala croaked.

"I had a relaxing trip, Tim—but *that* wasn't it," added No.

"But they'll arrest GG Anne and Rafe's grandfather..."

"Once more into the breach, dear friends, once more...!"

"Are you volunteering to go again, Rafe?" asked Tim, utterly astonished.

All talking ceased, all eyes turned to Rafe as he slowly rose from his armchair and returned to the computer.

"It is only right that I do this," he said, turning to look at the others through bloodshot eyes. "My grandfather and Eme's great-grandmother do not deserve to be struck down by the foul felons on our behalf."

"We don't have the program," No commented. Rafe responded by reaching into his laptop bag, producing the flash drive with Tim's protocol. No sighed, "Sometimes the way less traveled is *less* traveled for a reason, Rafe. I'm just saying," he added.

"Ask not, fear not, just produce a crystal wine goblet, fair Eme; the Cyborg must take the current when it serves," he winked at the redhead, smiled, and finished, "or we lose our *ventures*."

Kala and No smirked. Eme blushed and then made a mad dash for the dining room, where remnants of Anne's interrupted meal were still evident on the table. She paused for a moment when she spotted Boomer's water dish in the corner and realized that he was missing. Bogey must have read her mind, because he flew to her shoulder and rubbed his soft head against her cheek, snapping her to the conclusion that GG had probably sent him to their next-door neighbor's house until she returned.

Breathing a sigh of relief, she grabbed a goblet and ran back to the living room with Bogey digging his claws into her shoulder as if his life depended on it.

By the time she returned, the program was installed, the scanner hummed, and Rafe was perched cross-legged on the coffee table, clutching his computer bag with a grim look of determination on his face.

Eme upturned the wine glass on the desktop, and Kala adjusted the beam to reach all of Rafe's lanky torso, head, and ever-present hat. When all was ready, Eme leaned over, kissed Rafe on the cheek, and whispered in his ear, "Thank you so much, Rafe." They both blushed when their eyes met, and, with a parting salute from Bogey and one click of Tim's finger, Rafe melted into frosty mist and was gone.

"To infinity—and beyond!"

St. George's Club Cottage
4:32 P.ᙏ. ADT

"Bill, you're wearing a hole in this beautiful Persian rug!"

"I'm sorry, Anne, but I'm so worried about the implications of what's on this computer and what has become of the kids, not to mention what will become of us once the feds return with that search warrant."

He stopped his pacing long enough to embrace the woman he had only known a few hours; he was unable to wrap his head around how important she had become to him in such a short span of time. Strange, how life's tragedies could throw two complete strangers together with such ferocity; but here they were, a testament to that very thought. He glanced at Anne and marveled at how she could look so beautiful with a tear-stained face and red, runny nose. He kissed the top of her head and held her close while she silently wept for their grandchildren.

This is the way Rafe found them when he emerged from the holoport. No quacking duck or other e-lert would dare disturb the emotional scene before him. Should he clear his throat? He didn't want to be the cause of a heart attack, but time was short, and he had to get them away from Bermuda—now. Throwing caution to the winds, he coughed.

The reaction was immediate; the two people before him whirled around so quickly that Anne snagged her heel in the rug and was caught just in time by Bill before hitting the floor.

"Rafe!" his grandfather screamed, nearly dropping Anne again. Once righted, they both threw their arms around the bemused boy before breaking away. Then the questions started:

"How did...?"

"Where is...?"

"Cease and desist! We have but little time, and I have no answers, until we can depart from this place."

"But we can't. There's a CIA agent...wait a minute, how did you get past him?"

Rafe didn't answer; he prepared the laser and repositioned the wine glass while the older couple watched his actions in silent fascination. Once set, he motioned for his grandfather to sit on the stool. Bill complied and was about to ask another question when his grandson stopped him with, "Trust me, Grandfather, all will be explained in a trice."

Without another word, Rafe switched on the laser, which bathed the older man in otherworldly light. A click, and he was a mist that vanished into the holoport.

Anne started to scream, but Rafe held his hand over her mouth to keep her from alerting Ed. Once she had recovered from her shock, she turned wide, questioning eyes to the stranger before her. He merely motioned toward the now vacant stool and said, "Please, great-grandmother of the fair Eme, trust me. You will see her soon."

Anne began to protest and tried to flee from the stool; Rafe gently calmed her with his hand on her shoulder. She remained seated, but didn't take her frightened grey eyes from the teenager while she made herself as comfortable as possible upon the stool. With a flick of the switch, she too was bathed in an unearthly glow and was soon a frozen mist that disappeared into the holoport of Bill Romero's computer.

"Alone at last!" Rafe placed his hand on the computer. "What to do with this evidence of our departure?" He was about to throw caution to the wind and just repeat his first escape with the help of the broom, when his head snapped up, and he ran to his bedroom. He figured he had only a few minutes for his idea to work, and he didn't waste a second. Back to the living room he scrambled, grabbed the desktop computer, laser, broom, and wine glass, quickly returning to his bedroom.

I hope the wireless connection is strong enough.

CHAPTER SEVENTEEN
REUNIONS AND
RETRIBUTIONS

Bermuda Airport
Saturday, June 13, 2015
4:45 P.M. ADT

Hot, bloody, and hungry, an extremely disgruntled Agent Gun opened the door leading from the transportation corridor to the airport lounge. The few passengers lingering near the doorway flinched in horror at his appearance and backed away. Gun took no heed of these people, totally focused on his primary objectives: getting medical attention, grabbing a snack, obtaining a search warrant for the Romero cottage, and seeing to his prisoners.

He searched the concourse command center, still buzzing with activity, for any remaining CIA agents. Confident that all had retreated to headquarters in Hamilton or flown back to the mainland, he snarled and made his way to the first aid station. No one stopped him as he plowed through the various family members of the hurricane disaster and blustered into the now quiet triage center.

"Agent Gun, what happened to you?" asked the shocked nurse on duty.

"Never mind what, Nurse, just fix me up! I'm in the middle of something too important to discuss with you. Just do your job, and be quick about it!"

Unruffled by the rudeness of his demand, Susan Nelson, RN, did as she was commanded and removed the last shards of glass from Gun's face and hands. She then washed, stitched, and bandaged all the wounds. Gun neither flinched nor spoke during the ten-minute operation, and he left without a word to fulfill his to-do list.

Once his gut was full of pizza and beer, he made a phone call to the federal judge's office for the warrant; he informed the clerk that he'd pick it up by six o'clock, then he headed down the stairs to the command center.

"Have I got a surprise for you, missy," he mused as he glared into the iris scanner. The door opened and he stopped dead in his tracks.

GG Anne's House, Malibu
4:45 P.M. ADT/12:45 P.M. PDT

"They're *he-ere*," squawked Bogey when the hologram duck quacked and waddled through the holoport.

Many anxious souls gathered around the computer to assist their new arrivals into the relatively *real* world of Southern California.

Dazed, confused, and anxious, Anne stumbled into her familiar living room, which was now filled with strangers. After taking a deep and shaky breath, she shook her head and, once her eyes focused, she realized that she was in her precious great-granddaughter's arms. She cried with relief at the sight of her familiar red hair and sweet, albeit bruised and lacerated, face.

"Oh, Eme, dear, what has happened to your beautiful face?" she cried, caressing her cheek. "And where did you get those clothes?" she finished.

"GG, come and sit down," Eme replied, "and I'll explain everything." She led a grateful Anne to a large wingback chair near the computer desk. The others watched in silence while the two tearfully embraced. No words needed to be spoken; they all knew how the older woman felt after her terrifying journey.

The tears of the reunited family members were cut short by the quacking announcement of the next cyber traveler, Bill Romero who emerged from the misty holoport, sporting a huge smile for his welcoming committee.

"Ah, so this is where you live, Anne. Delightful," was his greeting as he gazed serenely around the beautifully furnished living room. "That was an unusual method of transport!" he finished when he noticed the gobsmacked faces of the other inhabitants of the room.

Anne rushed to his side, pulling Eme with her. "Bill, how did you manage to emerge from that hellish ride with…with nary a hair out of place?" accused Anne. "And how did you manage to arrive *after* I did? You left ahead of me!" she continued.

Bill brushed his wavy grey hair off of his forehead and answered serenely, "Meditation, my dear Anne, and I stayed a bit longer to study the mysterious cyberspace…fascinating!" He scanned the crowd still gaping at him. "Remember, meditation can see anyone through the direst of circumstances." He paused and added, "What a charming group of young people." He turned to Eme. "And you must be Eme; I've heard so much about you from your lovely GG Anne. I'm Bill Romero, Rafe's grandfather."

Eme recovered from her shock at this handsome man's composure, and shook his outstretched hand. "Yes, sir, I'm so happy
to meet you; may I introduce the rest of the people involved in
this crazy...what should I call it...cyberadventure?" She smiled at
the charming man.

The others gathered around the distinguished gentleman
and Eme's great-grandmother and waited patiently for Eme's
introductions. She turned to the person closest to her. "This is No
Henderson. He was on the first flight with me to Atlanta and was
taken prisoner by Agent Gun when he found out that he was a
friend of Eme Venture. In fact, it appears that my name started
this horrifying chain of events."

Anne and Bill stared in shock at the redhead. "Your name?
Why would your name cause him such distress that he would
take someone prisoner, let alone someone..."

"We'll get to all of that in a minute, GG. We have a lot to tell
you that you're not going to believe."

"I already find most of this an unbelievable nightmare," Anne
answered. She shook her head and hugged Eme again. Bill nodded in agreement.

"Not a nightmare," No interrupted, "A terror! That's when you
wake up screaming and realize you haven't fallen asleep, yet!"

Anne narrowed her eyes and stared thoughtfully at No while
the others nodded in agreement. "Well put, young man." She
hugged him and then turned back to her great-granddaughter.
"Please, finish your introductions, darling."

Eme then grabbed Kala's hand to lead her forward. "This is
Kala; she's from Australia, and was helping her Aunt Mayrah who
was our chaperone and St. Bruno counselor..." Eme paused and
looked sadly at Kala, "...but she died in the plane crash."

Bill and Anne both gasped, and Bill exclaimed, "Mrs. Murphy
was your aunt?" At the girl's nod, Anne shook Kala's hand solemnly then pulled her into a hug, which the girl gladly returned.

Soon everyone was joining in the hugging—No more ferociously than the others.

Completely ruffled by the show of affection and support, Kala broke away from No and responded to the crowd of people surrounding her, "Thank you, all of you. It has been a bugger of a weekend. I'm just glad that all of you are here now." She jerked her head around to the computer. "Wait, Rafe hasn't arrived yet."

Realization hit them all at once; everyone headed for the computer. It had been several minutes since Bill had emerged from the holoport, and there was no quacking duck announcing the last member of their group.

"What could have happened to him?" Kala whined.

"Gun and Ed! They must have returned and arrested him after he sent you and his grandfather, GG," moaned Eme.

Bill turned to face a now teary-eyed Eme. "Now, now, Eme, I know my grandson's tenacity and resourcefulness; he is probably setting up some elaborate scheme or trap for those two. After what they've put you all through, I wish I could be part of his plan of retribution."

"There're too many psychos and not enough horror shows," No calmly added.

Everyone laughed at No's comments, and the atmosphere in the room seemed to relax until a bucket of ice water, named Tim, splashed on the scene.

He had been quietly standing apart from the group, and now he stepped forward with his hand outstretched. "We haven't been introduced, yet, Ms. Malone, Mr. Romero. I'm Tim Edelman, the lead computer programmer with Amazemail and, I'm sorry to say, the cause of this disaster."

"Well, here's another nice mess you've gotten me into!" Bogey's words seemed to echo the feelings of the whole room.

Bill Romero shook the man's hand. He said with a frown, "Would you care to explain your part in all of this? I, for one, certainly deserve an explanation."

Tim stared the older man in the eye; then he bent down and slowly removed his left shoe and sock, along with a tightly folded piece of white paper wrapped in plastic that had been wedged between two of his toes.

Romero Cottage Secret Closet
4:45 P.M. ADT

Escaping from Bermuda, before Gun blasted his way out of the secret command room at the airport or Ed blasted his way in, was his total focus. If they figured out the protocol and entered the system...well, after what he had set up for Gun, he didn't want to think about his fate.

Rafe stopped and whirled around in the small, dark secret closet toward the computer. "Why not!" he laughed. "It can buy me time, and heaven knows the Cyborg needs lots of that to keep Eme and the others out of harm's way."

He reached into the side pocket of his ever-present computer bag and grabbed a tiny halogen flashlight that he activated and stuck between his teeth. He booted up the computer, typed in a series of codes, downloaded a program that he had stored online, waited a moment, installed it to the hard drive, and spent three more minutes programming.

With a heavy sigh, he set the timer to activate the program in thirty minutes. Satisfied that his plan was flawless, he prepared for his last launch out of paradise and into the real world, the one in which his friends, his only relative, and his new hero awaited his arrival.

One more minute, and he was but an organized series of ones and zeros, hurtling in a subzero light stream toward Malibu; an empty stool, computer, broom, and goblet the only witnesses to his departure.

Bermuda Airport Secret Command Room
4:59 P.M. ADT/12:59 P.M. PDT

"What the…" He made a move for his gun then seethed, "Damn you, Romero!" when his hand met the empty holster.

A stuffed blue rabbit with a cheesy grin sat atop a chair just inside the door. It stared at Gun, and Gun stared at it for a full two seconds before the agent's eyes narrowed; then he stepped over the threshold. "OK, Edelman, I don't know how you got out of your cell, but you're not going anywhere…get out here, now!" he shouted.

He scanned the room; *Where is he?* He stalked past the rabbit, and the security door hissed closed behind him, sealing with a quiet thud. All of the monitors were active, including the gigantic screen in front of the map of the world on the center wall.

Gun felt vulnerable without his sidearm, but the command center appeared empty. He cautiously entered the closet behind him and relaxed when he checked his gun cabinet—it was still locked and secure. Feeling foolish for his paranoia, he opened the cabinet, grabbed a handgun and some ammunition, and reentered the main room, holstering the weapon and pocketing the clips. A quick check of the cells confirmed that Edelman *and* the Venture girl were gone: another setback, promising to destroy all the work that had been put into this operation.

"Damn! How did they get out of here?" he growled as he stalked back to the chair in front of the entry door. He picked up the rabbit by its floppy ears and kicked the chair aside. With a grunt of rage, he tore the head off the toy and tossed the decapitated body aside. He needed to speak to Ed—this changed everything.

With a nasty snarl, he placed his eye in front of the scanner, and waited for the door to open. The scanner buzzed angrily; the door remained sealed. The agent swore and blinked a few times; *damn technology was so sensitive*; he placed his eye in front of the scanner to try again.

No luck—he was locked in.

"Damn! Damn! Damn!" Gun thundered, pounding his fist against the door, popping a few stitches. "I'll have to use the other..."

"Sorry to bother you, agents," a voice announced from across the room.

"What the...?" Gun spun and pulled his gun, his lip curling back in a sneer. He wasn't alone after all.

"All the world's a stage, and all the men and women merely players; they have their exits and their entrances, but it looks like you're not going to have your exit, Agent Asshole—the scanner has been deactivated."

Gun realized the voice was coming from the mainframe computer, a recorded voice amplified through the computer's main speaker system, and the airport security cameras were transmitting live scenes to all of the monitors. It wasn't Edelman; whoever it was, he sounded young and confident.

With his eye twitching, Gun walked slowly to the computer, watching the monitors, and holstering his gun, as the voice spoke again:

"You're trapped here, I'm afraid, but look around, there's plenty to see. No doubt you'll be able to watch the *real* authorities sweeping through the airport, drawing ever closer to your position." The voice laughed, and Gun's hands clenched into fists, closing around an invisible neck. "My friends and I will be gone by then—beyond your demented control. Fear not for our safety; fear only that we *don't* remain silent."

"It's one of those kids!" Gun seethed. Feeling outfoxed, he flipped on the mainframe CPU and began to type, but the keyboard was locked—frozen. He snatched it off the desk and slammed it to the floor.

"I'd advise you not to pursue us," the smug voice continued. "You have kidnapped my friend, and people have died. The Cyborg's patience has worn thin, and his anger is as razor-sharp as his wit. Follow us, gentlemen, and you will incur life-altering consequences."

Gun sank back onto the chair next to the mainframe, too tired to think clearly; he was totally unaware that the moment he had activated the computer, the timer mechanism on the coffee pot below his desk had begun brewing something quite intoxicating.

CHAPTER EIGHTEEN
WARM WELCOME

Anne Malone's Malibu Home
Saturday, June 13, 2015
5:10 P.M. ADT/1:10 P.M. PDT

"Quack, quack, quack!"

"I'm going to kill that bloody bird!" squawked the other bloody bird in a remarkable imitation of Harry Potter's uncle Vernon.

"He's here!" screamed three exuberant voices.

A second later, a trail of chilly vapor escaped the holoport of Anne's overworked laptop and reassembled into Rafael Romero's lanky frame. He had barely enough time to take one shaky breath, before it was brutally expelled by the collective hugs of his three anxious friends.

"Ooof!" Rafe lost his footing, landed with a thud on the thick beige carpet, and was buried in a barrage of laughter, hugs, and kisses.

"The Cyborg shall just return to Bermuda and try that again?" he managed to utter before he was smothered once again.

"You'll go nowhere anytime bloody soon without us," was Kala's response once they had all resurfaced, red-faced and happily sitting atop the latest cyberspace traveler.

"Get off, Mr. Negative, and if you ever bring those lips of yours near the Cyborg again, you'll be drinking your meals through a straw!"

No threw up his hands in protest. "I never admit to nor deny anything—it makes me more interesting." He wagged his eyebrows at Rafe, smirked, and bounced quickly to his feet.

Rafe growled at No's response and then continued more sweetly, "But the fair ones may stay as long as they desire!" Rafe grabbed Kala, and then made a grab for Eme, who realized that her GG Anne had witnessed her utter lack of decorum, and scrambled to her feet to see the adults in the room trying, unsuccessfully, to suppress their laughter.

All four red-faced teens were now on their feet; they turned as one to face their amused audience.

"I want some of whatever they're having!"

"Ever the opportunist, aren't you now, Bogey?" Everyone snickered at Anne's words.

"Welcome back, you brave boy," exclaimed Anne as she rushed forward to give him a gentler hug. "We are all so grateful for your quick thinking." She kissed his bright red cheek.

"Rafe, your parents would be so very proud of you—as am I. You may have saved many lives today, my boy." And his grandfather embraced him.

Tim stepped forward, still clutching the paper he had been a second away from unfolding, when Rafe made his sudden appearance.

"Rafe, you and Eme have haunted my dreams for many days." All the faces in the room turned to this humble man who had invented the program with the potential to destroy the world. Rafe and Eme blanched at his words.

"What do you mean by that, Mr....Tim?" asked a shocked Anne.

"Yes, we'd all like an answer to that question—and many more," added Bill.

Tim ran his hand through his mop of sandy-colored hair and gestured toward the large seating area of Anne's living room. "Please, all of you, come and sit down, and I'll tell you as much as I can. You, of all people, deserve the whole truth behind Venture: Eme."

"No legacy is so rich as honesty," Rafe remarked as he took Eme's hand and followed the others to the comfort of Anne's overstuffed sofa and chairs.

Once everyone was situated, Anne jumped up. "Oh, I'm so thoughtless; may I offer you something to eat or drink?"

"Now that's a capital..." began No who was sitting next to Kala on an oversized chair.

"No, No!" Rafe, Kala, and Eme shouted together. That seemed to break the tension in the room that had been as tight as a banjo string. They looked at each other and burst out laughing at No's red face.

Bill grasped her hand and responded, "Thank you, Anne, dear, but I, for one, need to know what other trials and tribulations we face before trying to eat or drink anything. In fact, if it's as serious as it sounds, none of us may have appetites for quite some time." He gave her hand a squeeze, and she nodded and blushed. They all returned their attention to the man holding the now unfolded mystery paper.

When he was sure that all were composed and focused, Tim sat up ramrod straight on the edge of the sofa cushion, retaining a death grip on the paper in his hands. "It all began June 10, an hour or so after I had put the finishing touches on my e-mail protocol, naming it Project: Amazemail."

"But it's called..." blurted No who was shushed by Kala, Eme, and Rafe. "Sorry," he whispered, and Tim continued.

"Yes, No...now that must get confusing. Is it Noah?" he asked the now chagrined No who shrugged in response to his question. Unfazed by the reaction, Tim plunged ahead with his story. "The phone rang upstairs—my lab is in the basement," he added. "Anyway, my wife, Kelly, answered the phone and yelled my name—she doesn't usually do that, so I knew something was wrong. I made it up the steps in three leaps and grabbed the phone from her trembling hand. From her reaction I thought it best to record the call." He acknowledged the wide-eyed nodding heads around him.

"The Deadly Duo!" stated an enthralled No.

"Right, you are, No! And I don't need the tape to recall the first words I ever heard Ed speak: 'We're the CIA, and we want you and your e-mail protocol!' Since the recorder had activated the speaker, Kelly was in tears. She had pulled the boys into a tight embrace and looked as if she would crumble right where she stood." Anne gasped at that. "Ed went on to tell me not to leave the house—he had it under surveillance. My first thought was to escape by means of the protocol, but I didn't want to risk Kelly and the boys," he finished in a small, shaky voice.

Bill stood up and began pacing in front of the coffee table, his mind reeling at what he had just heard. He stopped and faced the programmer. "Did you search for the surveillance equipment? Did they hack into your computer?"

"I had no idea at that point. I felt ninety-nine percent certain that they couldn't hack my files; my encryption program is my own and, if I do say so, nearly flawless...well, until Rafe, thankfully, found the only flaw and hacked it..." The teens grinned at this statement, and Tim continued, "Anyway, the CIA hadn't breached my encryption. But at the time, I wasn't sure of anything but the immediate protection of my family, so I asked what they were planning. The bastard..." He looked around at the kids to apologize for his profanity, but found them shaking their heads at him with their mouths hanging open, so he continued. "The bastard threatened my family. He told me to cooperate and meet him at the Atlanta Airport on June 11, at midnight, with my protocol and equipment, ready to fly with him to Washington."

"Washington?" chorused the four teens in surprise.

"Yes, that was the original plan, but the hurricane's arrival threw a monkey wrench into this idea, and when I finally woke up, after being chloroformed for several hours, I was in a cell in Bermuda." There were gasps from everyone.

"I was on that flight with you, then!" interjected No, his eyes wide.

Tim's eyes also widened and he stared at the boy. "You were?"

"I was kidnapped by the gruesome twosome in the Atlanta Airport, blindfolded and handcuffed—I had no idea there was anyone else on the plane ride to Bermuda!" he exclaimed.

"I'd like to hear more about what you went through later, No; in fact I want to hear more about all of your experiences, but let me finish this first." All nodded in agreement. "I'm getting ahead of my own story. I was still planning on making some sort of a daring escape with my family when I got an e-mail, a few hours later, that drastically changed everything...this e-mail from Eme and Rafe." He held up the piece of paper.

A chill colder than any trip through cyberspace enveloped the small group. Their mouths agape, all blood drained from each and every face as Tim's words reverberated in their minds like an echo off the walls of a canyon.

"But that's not possible!" Rafe had recovered first to speak for all present. "The Cyborg and the fair one just met you two hours ago."

"May I see that paper, Tim?" asked Bill in a less than steady voice.

"Certainly." Tim handed the paper to Rafe's grandfather who glanced at it and passed it to an extremely anxious Rafe. He scanned the document and nearly fainted.

"What villainy is this?" He shook the piece of paper in his hand and jumped to his feet, staring at Tim. "We had no connection to you until this day?"

"Rafe, you're...you're scaring us!" cried Eme, wringing her hands.

"Yes, Rafe, please, what does it say?" pleaded Kala, nearly falling out of her seat.

"I'm not sure what's wrong, but it's all Rafe's fault." No tried to smile, but the lack of response from the grim faces around him proved that his plan to lessen the tension in the room had failed miserably.

Anne and Bill looked at each other and then back to Tim who finally spoke. "Go ahead, Rafe, you'd better read it."

Rafe, recovering his composure, cleared his throat and read the e-mail, clearly enunciating each syllable. "All is lost! We only have time to tell you to rename your protocol, Venture: Eme. Signed: Eme/Rafe BWR BRU..." He looked up at the shocked faces around him and continued in an extremely shaky whisper, "It's from somewhere in Switzerland, time and date stamped, 11:59 p.m. CEST, September 10—2021!"

CHAPTER NINETEEN

FOREWARNED
IS FOREARMED

LAX
Saturday, June 13, 2015
5:10 P.M. ADT/1:10 P.M. PDT

If he had any idea that the son he was desperate to reach in Atlanta, was but a few miles from his taxiing airplane, this concerned father would be thrilled, until he learned how the boy had returned to California. Then this ambitious attorney's thoughts would focus, not on the money his handsome, athletic son would earn for him during his professional sports career a few years hence, but on how this information could benefit him *now*.

However, he did not have that information, nor would he see his son again for a very long time. For now, Phil Henderson was a father on a mission, one that involved his missing meal ticket and his ex-wife's tragic accident.

He let his weary body relax into the comfort of Destiny's first-class seat and worried, for a moment, about his mounting credit card bills.

Dismissing these thoughts as a silly nuisance, he recalled the previous day's frantic phone call from the dim-witted musician who had stolen his wife all those years before. That ensuing scandal had eventually robbed him of his bid for the governor's mansion in Sacramento and, ultimately, his Senate seat. His law practice had also suffered in the aftermath of the messy divorce and custody case that awarded him sole custody of their four-year-old son.

"Gov'na, you bloody well get yer pompous ass out here now!" spewed forth from his answering machine and prompted him to intercept the screened call.

"Loudon, what's got your knickers in a twist?" He laughed when he picked up the receiver.

"Norma's been in…in an accident." The jerk's sobbing almost softened his heart until he remembered the pain, plus the loss of money and prestige, the two of them had caused him.

"Put No on the phone; I want to get the details from a man, not some sniveling wuss!"

Through the following series of sniffs and sobs, the story about the near-fatal accident, and the mysterious disappearance of his son paralyzed Phil Henderson with fear. He had to find his son; Norma was no longer his concern.

When his call to the Atlanta airport, an hour before Loudon's call, had produced no word of his son or any indication that he had *not* been picked up after his flight, he assumed that his mother had fulfilled her responsibilities, retrieved their son, and taken him on a shopping expedition to atone for her transgressions.

That fantasy was put to rest by the drugged-out Brit's pathetic wailing; the repeated calls to his son's cell phone had gone to voice mail.

It had taken him a full day to clear his calendar, the dinner with his potential new clients the night before, notwithstanding (if he expected to land their multimillion-dollar account for his law firm), but after that, he was on the trail of his precious missing son. He closed his eyes and spun his new fantasy: he was only five hours away from solving this mystery. After all, he had scored the highest grade in his Yale law forensics class; his mind was like a steel trap. He could picture the headlines in all the papers, could envision the various rounds of talk shows—his voluptuous new wife on his arm, his handsome, adoring son by his side.

A book! He could write a book, followed by a movie; he would portray himself—Ronald Reagan had been an actor. Once he was a little too old for the movie business, Governor Henderson and then President Henderson. He smiled; then he grinned and patted the hand of his beautiful companion.

Hang on, No, your faithful and loving dad is on his way!

Anne's Malibu Home
5:35 P.M. ADT/1:35 P.M. PDT

"What we've got here is a failure to communicate!" Bogey broke the silence that had permeated the room after Rafe's revelation.

As if awakening from a nightmare, Eme shook her head and declared, "That's ridiculous!"

"The Cyborg agrees with fair Eme, and yet here it is, date stamped and coded with the Swiss domain code, CH—Confederation Helvetica."

"How do you know all this stuff, Rafe? How is it that you know everything?" asked No in awe.

Rafe grimaced. "Alas, the Cyborg knows not the meaning of the numbers following the code, Mr. Negative, but he will in a trice." Rafe made a mad dash for the computer, which snapped everyone into focus.

All eyes were trained on the teenage computer whiz in his quest to obtain some answers to this puzzle. An e-mail from the future—absurd; however, how could Tim possibly know Eme and Rafe's connection to each other and...

"The Cyborg is slipping...CH 3175—it's from Brienz, Switzerland." And the dimpled smile that followed seemed to add to everyone's confusion.

"He's smiling; now *that* scares me!" No's comment just about summed it up.

"Out with it, Rafe!" demanded Kala.

"Yes, my boy, you're killing us with suspense," added his grandfather, and all heads nodded in agreement.

"St. Bruno's Academy!" was Rafe's response, and everyone began talking at once.

"Oh, my, that's just too bloody...

"It can't be possible!"

"Is this that hidden camera show?"

"Ed and Gun are behind this hoax!"

"Quiet, please, everyone; I have something to say!"

All eyes turned to the person who had thrown them into this Amazemail farce.

"First of all," Tim began, "I researched this e-mail thoroughly—well, as thoroughly as my cyber skills would allow, given the time element. Rafe is correct, it is from Switzerland, and it is authentic." He paused for the gasps and comments to abate and continued, "Furthermore, when I received this e-mail, as best as I can calculate, Gun didn't know that Rafe and Eme existed, let alone their connection to one another or to Switzerland."

The logic behind this last statement slammed the last of their doubts and left them all speechless, all except Bogey...

"Of all the gin joints in town, she walks into mine!" Bogey was right; Tim had just put the final nail in their coffin of horrors.

"What does this mean?" asked Kala.

"Better questions, perhaps: Why Eme and Rafe? Why the warning about Bruno? I assume that's what the BWR BRU indicates," responded No. "Is it the hurricane or the school? Or," he paused and searched the faces in front of him before adding with a nervous smile, "or both?"

Rafe rose from the computer and joined the somber group.

Anne had been very quiet during this discussion; she suddenly jumped out of her chair, startling everyone. "I don't know how any of you can think; when was the last time you ate?" Without waiting for an answer, she headed for the kitchen, Bill on her heels.

"As God is my witness, I'll never be hungry again!"

"Very funny, Bogey. That's my GG Anne; food is the way to solve all problems!" Eme rose from her chair and was about to leave for the kitchen when Kala responded.

"About that: I think these past few days of stress trimmed a few pounds of fat off my bod." As she stood, she ran her hands down her sides to No's appreciative whistles.

"I'm mellllting, mellllting!" sang Bogey, and everyone laughed at the timely comment.

"Eme, where did you get that bird?" asked No.

She chuckled. "That's a very long, funny, but bittersweet story."

"Something of an amusing nature would be most welcome, fair Eme; please enlighten us," Rafe responded.

"How about over lunch; I should help GG right now."

"I'll come with you," said Kala. They headed toward the kitchen.

The three remaining cyber travelers looked at each other, unsure of what to say next. After several more seconds of silence, Rafe asked, "Ingenious sir, what has become of your family?"

A smile lit up Tim's face when he answered, "They are in a place no one will ever find them. They are safe, at least for a few more days," he added at the concern on their faces. He then frowned. "However, I cannot risk contact with them until Ed and Gun are truly gone—locked up or," he smiled again, "dead!"

No nodded and Rafe looked thoughtful. "Your wish may be granted if the unscrupulous ones dare to follow us."

Delight lit No's face. "Why, Rafe, you brute, what did you do to them, pray tell?" he smirked. "We want all the gory details, right down to whose e-mail trash folder their parts are buried in." And he rubbed his hands together gleefully.

"It's not what the Master of Cybermatter did to them; it's what they'll do to themselves if they discover and use the protocol," Rafe responded with a smirk of his own.

Eager to hear his elaborate story, the other two leaned toward Rafe, and they were not disappointed with his tale.

Five minutes later, the three relaxed on the sofa, sipping the coffee Kala and Eme had brought them.

"Join Rafe's Army; meet interesting people—mutate them. I wish I could be there when they emerge with their arms sprouting from their eye sockets and their eyes stuck to their gonads—gives a whole new meaning to the term voyeurism," No demonstrated as the two others put down their cups and roared at his antics.

"So, ingenious sir, how does it really work?" Rafe asked once he recovered from the "No Show."

Tim rubbed the rough stubble on his cheeks, smiled, and then clapped Rafe on the shoulder. "You filled in the blanks, my boy; why don't you tell me?"

Rafe shook his head with a laugh. "All the Cyborg did was to flip a switch, really. I've no idea how your amazing protocol does what it does—only that it *does* do it."

"You weren't afraid to use it, were you?"

"Afraid? No, awed and excited," he answered with a grin. And that was the truth. Cyber travel, jumping through the invisible networks, was the greatest rush of his life.

"It's a little hard to explain in layman's terms, Rafe." Tim shrugged. "But you're a bright kid; once we're able to return to our normal lives, you can come to work for me at Amazemail." He took a sip of his coffee and smiled at the teen.

"How about a job for me, too, Tim? I'm great at research; it's what I do when I don't know what I'm doing."

"Which is most of the time, Mr. Sarcasm," added Rafe. He then responded to Tim after rubbing the arm No had just punched, "Testing technology that is impossible and should never exist would be thrilling." Rafe grinned at Tim and smirked at No.

"Something like that, but here..." Tim put down his cup and picked up a pen from the desk, sketching a rough outline of the laser scanner onto a page. "This is what makes teleportation, for lack of a better name for the process, possible."

No and Rafe studied the diagram. "The holoport 3DX laser scanners; there isn't a computer out there without one," Rafe exclaimed. No raised one eyebrow.

Tim rose from the couch and paced the floor for a few seconds, gathering his thoughts. He stopped and stared at the boys. "Nanotech is the future, boys. My protocol modifies the billions of nanobots in these scanners, rewriting what they're supposed to do. Any 3DX laser scanner and holoport shipped out of computer factories in the last eighteen years is capable of harnessing the protocol."

The teens were on the edge of their seats, stunned, as the realization of that statement registered. But then Tim delivered the knock-out punch: "Also, there isn't a *spam filter* that is capable of blocking any protocol e-mail that is running Amazemail; the program will activate a dormant computer and deliver the message, person, or object through the holoport in a matter of seconds—those were the first modifications I made in the code once I had a viable program."

Rafe let out a soft whistle at that comment and thought about the possibilities it presented: all of the computers worldwide had just become a conduit for cyber travel, unbeknownst to their users. The world had just shrunk a few sizes; travel virtually anywhere was possible with the click of a few buttons. It was a little frightening, he supposed. What safeguards were in place? People who wanted to do harm, like Ed and Gun, had the world at their fingertips.

No must have had the same thoughts. He sank back into the sofa, arms over his head, and let out a deep breath but kept any comments, sarcastic or otherwise, to himself.

Tim sighed and sat down again. "You're beginning to see the trouble this can cause, aren't you?"

The boys nodded. "Yes; however, what is done cannot be undone," Rafe proclaimed.

"Too true. Well...I'm to blame, I suppose: too damn smart for my own good...and too damn dumb to know better. But I thought it was our new Manifest Destiny—the last frontier—and who knows what that entails! A quote from T.E. Lawrence has been playing through my mind day and night since I was kidnapped: '*All men dream, but not equally. Those who dream by night in the dusty recesses of their minds, wake in the day to find that it was vanity: but the dreamers of the day are dangerous men, for they may act on their dreams with open eyes, to make them possible.*'"

An awkward silence stretched among the three. Rafe understood the impossible burden that was now placed upon the shoulders of this brilliant man. But, he wanted to know more, wanted to know the sheer mechanics of something that could, very easily, become a weapon of mass destruction. If this technology was a permanent part of their future, he wanted to be able to understand the risk.

No was the first to break the silence, "You're being way too hard on yourself, Tim; someone, someday, would have come up with your invention—you just escalated the timeline...oh, by a billion years or so."

The laughter that followed No's remark seemed to break the awkwardness and put them back on course.

"So, how's it work then?" asked No.

Tim relaxed a bit and smiled at the eager faces before him. His answer astonished Rafe and No by its relative simplicity. "I developed Amazemail my first year as a student at St. Bruno's, twenty years ago, summer of 1995; I was sixteen. It took me another year of development to perfect it. The following summer, when I designed the laser scanner and the hologram e-lert, the possibility of reversing the process occurred to me—what comes out..."

"...might go in," finished Rafe, his eyes wide in astonishment. "Amazing! I can see why you named it *Amazemail!*"

Tim chuckled, "It was a simple concept, but, it took me several years after developing the holoports just to get my head around the physics involved in this technology; the premise alone left me weeping most nights. I can't explain it to you in five minutes."

"Just an overview, then; something that shows us how it works," continued No to Rafe's nodding encouragement.

Tim nodded. "An overview..."

"How does the laser scanner make us disappear? Where do we really disappear to? How do we come out the other end in one piece?" he asked.

Tim paled, his eyes cast with anxiety, and he turned to the brunet. "Until you did, Rafe, no one—no human—had come out the other end in one piece. You were the first successful human trial. Congratulations," he finished with a cheeky grin.

No's eyes were as large as silver dollars, and both boys paled at that pronouncement. "Living on Earth used to be scary and expensive; now it's still scary, but Rafe, you've made it possible for *free* trips through cyberspace."

Rafe and Tim laughed at the lanky blond, but Rafe didn't like to think too much about the consequences of being an unsuccessful trial. "Horatio successfully traveled through in one piece—why wouldn't the Cyborg?"

Tim coughed then chuckled. He stared at Rafe for a second, and clamped a hand on his shoulder. "You're a bit more complex than a stuffed toy, Rafe. Your body is full of alternating electrical signals, blood flows through your veins, the central nervous system; your brain is constantly active...and you have a soul."

"A soul makes a difference?" asked No, too much in awe to come up with a sarcastic reply.

"My protocol preserves the object intact, so to speak. It ensures continuity of existence." Tim shrugged. "Otherwise it would be like sending a fax, you see; you go in one end, but a copy comes out the other end—identical right down to the hairs on the back of your hand, but still a copy of the original. Can you imagine the religious and moral outrage of a teleportation device that destroys the original and spits clones out the other end? We'd be hanged."

Rafe agreed—it was another terrifying thought, however he managed to find some comedy in the drama: "Egad, copies of No! The world's barely ready for one!" He held up his index finger at No's frown. "However, two negatives do equal a positive—perhaps there is hope!" He dodged out of the way of No's incoming punch.

Tim smiled. "In theory, the protocol even allows for a mechanism similar to time travel—through a process of displacement."

"Time travel, like the message from the future Cyborg and the fair one?"

"Aha! Time travel! That's what happened to Rafe!" interrupted No. "Light travels faster than sound; that's why Rafe appears bright, until he speaks."

And Rafe's punch connected.

Tim continued, "Yes, but the processing power required, and the backlash, would be devastating. I can't imagine what was involved to send that message from the future; the consequences must have been cataclysmic. And, we're not even talking *human* time travel, but transit of *stable* information."

No opened his mouth to make another comment, but with Rafe's raised fist and glare, he merely smirked at his friend instead.

Tim smiled at the teenagers' byplay and continued, "Time travel is possible, Rafe, but at a great cost."

Rafe was astonished and intrigued by the idea. He tapped his foot eagerly against the plush carpet. "Though this be madness, yet there is method in't; science fiction is truth?"

"Again, theoretically, it's never been done. But the protocol works, and the protocol teleportation is the basis for it all." Tim sipped his coffee. "The next five, ten years are going to be interesting."

Rafe thought so, too. He was beginning to get a glimpse of a much bigger picture, one without a border. He felt a new respect for Tim Edelman, the man with the mind that designed it all. He looked at him, smiled, and made a slight change to his new mantra, "Why, then the *universe* is mine oyster, which I will, with 3DX laser scanner and password, open." No laughed, but Tim looked pensive. He rose from the sofa and motioned to the boys to follow. Sitting down at Anne's computer, he inserted his flash drive into the USB port and typed in a password.

"Here it is, boys, Virtual World one point zero." The screen ran with script after script of 1's and 0's—so fast it hurt Rafe's eyes to watch. It was impressive code—he understood the pride in Tim's voice.

Suddenly a burst of static washed away the code, and the screen went black.

"Wh...what...?" stammered Tim, startled by the interruption in his demonstration.

Bright flashing red words appeared on the black screen: *Burst Received: Unknown Nexus Open...*

Rafe took a moment to process them. "What does that mean?" he asked, bemused.

"That's...not...possible," Tim said carefully—too carefully. He turned suddenly to the teen standing behind him, "Rafe, unplug the modem—now!"

Rafe moved toward the modem just as smoke began to pour out of the holoport—real smoke, but cold, very cold. Rafe froze, fascinated by the unexpected occurrence. The smoke thickened and darkened, solidifying into an arm—skeletal thin with long, clawed fingers.

Tim tried to keep Rafe from approaching the computer, but he seemed paralyzed, or hypnotized, by what was in front of him. The claw reared forth from the holoport and slashed at Rafe's throat, his face—warm blood trickled into his mouth a moment before the shock let him feel the pain.

Tim dove for the modem's power plug.

Once the current was cut, the claw and its smoke dissipated as quickly as they had appeared.

Shock also rendered No speechless and rooted him to the spot; Tim reached for a napkin on the coffee table and handed it to Rafe who had a smile on his face and a haunted look in his eyes.

"Are you OK, Rafe? Say something!" exclaimed an anxious Tim as he placed a hand on the teenager's shoulder.

"Brilliant, utterly brilliant!" was all Rafe uttered as he dabbed the paper napkin at the nasty gash on his cheek.

No finally recovered from his shock and rushed to his friend, guiding him to the sofa, while Tim carefully removed his flash drive and joined the two boys.

"What just happened, Tim?" No asked while he examined Rafe's smiling though bloodied face.

"B.R.U.N.O."

That wiped the smile off of Rafe's face, and both boys nearly jumped out of their skins.

"You jest, dear sir!"

"No, I'm afraid not…Burst Received: Unknown Nexus Open—B.R.U.N.O., for short."

No's mouth gaped like the grisly opening to Hell; Rafe recovered first. "How is it possible that this name hounds us once again? We're haunted by its reoccurrence in this farce."

No nodded and quipped, "Just a crazy coincidence?" Tim shrugged.

"The Cyborg thinks not! Something that the beautiful blonde one mentioned at the Atlanta Airport is also perplexing; someone changed the name of the hurricane to Bruno, when its predetermined name was Bill."

That brought Tim to his feet; in two long strides he reached the computer table where Rafe had stashed his laptop, plugged in the modem, and quickly brought up the NOAA Website, scanning for projected hurricane names.

No and Rafe peered over his shoulder.

What they saw was mind-bending—the name of the hurricane had, indeed, been switched from Bill to Bruno. There was a footnote blaming the name change on a clerical error that wasn't caught before it was released to the media.

Tim turned to the boys and stated emphatically, "It's a name that threw us all together: Eme Venture; and now it's a name that's leading us all to—where? St. Bruno's? Rafe, I think your future self is still guiding us, and I think we need to keep this to ourselves until we all have time to sit down and study the ramifications of this new revelation."

The boys nodded their heads in agreement, and they all returned to their seats, remaining lost in silent thought for a minute, before Tim stood again and started pacing. He suddenly stopped and turned to the expectant teens.

"What do either of you understand about wormholes?"

"Oh, now you're talking *my* language." No brightened. "That was one of my favorite video games, *The Worms That Ate Walla Walla!*" His smile faded at the blank faces before him, and he continued, nodding and gesturing with his hands for understanding. "You know, you tunnel through the wormholes with your Worm Gun to catch the nasty buggers before they swallow all of Washington State!" At the shaking of their heads, No gave it up as a bad job and snarled, "That's the trouble with you math types, no creativity."

Rafe turned to Tim, gesturing toward No, and tried to answer his question about wormholes. "Only enough to understand why Mr. Negative is..." he began; however, a headlock stopped him from finishing.

Tim laughed, reclaimed his seat, and then he waited patiently until the two completed their shenanigans before he continued. "You were the first person to travel through one." That got the boys' attention. "Wormholes are the trick to this cyber travel. The 3DX scanners, or more accurately, the nanomachines, create millions and millions of tiny wormholes—the white mist is a by-product of the process—and suck you into the computer."

Rafe quirked an eyebrow and responded, "It's not really the computers, then?"

"Smart lad. No, it's not. More like the wireless networks along certain wavelengths...I even wonder if it breaches dimensions. This is why there have been no human trials, you see. The worry is not if you'll come out the other end, but where you'll end up if you don't. Ed and Gun sacrificed a live crab that they purchased at a local fish market; it ended up in their Internet mail Trash Folder..."

"Whoa!" cried No.

"How is that even possible?" exclaimed Rafe.

Tim chuckled, "I didn't tell them that the receiving e-mail client needed to be a Post Office Protocol, Amazemail account. From its inception, all of our clients' Amazemail programs were designed to accept any mail that would eventually use the *Project* Amazemail program. I thought that I'd have the Project Amaz...er, Venture: Eme program, perfected in a year from my company's launch. And here we are, fifteen years later..."

"Do you think that claw thing was the missing crab?" asked No.

Tim didn't have the opportunity to respond, and two very pale faces met Eme and Kala when they entered the living room to call them to lunch. The rest of Tim's story was put on hold for the next hour, as was all mention of protocols and anything to do with Ed, Gun, Bruno, and Switzerland, at Anne's request.

After Rafe blamed his facial laceration on a "computer error," seven people had the opportunity to get to know one another over a most excellent lunch of poached salmon, German potato salad, sparkling cider, and chocolate fudge sundaes. "Sorry, it's all I have!" was met with cheers and rave reviews from Anne's uninvited guests.

"I'm totally in love with Bogey, Eme," Kala said. "Please, tell us how you trained him to be so clever and to be..."

"...so appreciative of Kala's loveliness," interrupted No, wagging his eyebrows to the guffaws at his cheeky comment and Kala's red face.

Once the laughter had subsided, Anne began relating the poignant story to her attentive audience:

"Bogey was a present to a dear friend on his sixty-fifth birthday. Toni, my granddaughter, and I met Bertie Bernard when we moved to New York, and he became Toni's theatrical agent."

"Benjamin Bertie Bernard, the stuntman?" Kala asked with wide eyes.

"Yes, Kala, do you know his work?"

"She knows everything, Mrs. Malone; it's probably in her trivia books, so why don't you tell the story, Miss Smarty Pants?" No chided.

"Ow! Hey, you're supposed to love your enemies—that's what really pisses them off." No rubbed his shin where Kala had kicked him. He then made kissing noises at Kala who stuck out her tongue, much to the amusement of all the lunch guests.

"Fuh-get about it!" squawked Bogey to more laughter.

"That's right, Bogey, you tell him!" laughed Kala.

Once the laughter had subsided, Anne continued, "Yes, Bertie had been a Hollywood stuntman, until he fell from his horse while making a movie. He was in a wheelchair the last twenty-five years of his life. Since he could no longer work in the movie industry, he moved to New York to become a Broadway theatrical agent. However, he still loved the movies; when we gave him Bogey, he named him after Humphrey Bogart and taught him many movie one-liners, and I taught him the trigger words and actions for each one." Many nodded and smiled at that. "When Eme's parents married and their soap opera careers ended, their movie careers blossomed; we moved back to California so that they could be closer to their movie studio. Bertie came with us and lived here until last year; he...died during his eightieth birthday party." Anne stopped for a moment to wipe her eyes; Bill rubbed her arm, and she continued quickly. "He...he loved a grand exit; one of his favorite movie lines was..." She pointed to Bogey; he ruffled his feathers and responded, "Frankly, my dear, I don't give a damn!"

The room was silent, in awe of the amazing bird. Then, one by one, they stood and applauded Bogey; he pranced across his perch, bowing and squawking his appreciation.

With spirits lifted, and the kitchen table cleared, they once again returned to the living room to discuss their next move.

"OK, let's get down to the business at hand!" Bill began as all took their seats.

"It's showtime!"

"That's right, Bogey, it's time to show Ed and Gun, and the CIA, that we're not going to be pushed around!" responded Kala who was sitting on the floor next to No.

"We're mad as hell, and we're not going to take it anymore!" quipped Bogey to more laughter and nodding heads.

"Don't forget the FAA, Mr. Romero," reminded No.

"And the FCC," added Tim. "They're bound to know about the CIA's involvement with my disappearance and the Amazemail or Venture: Eme protocol—I'm not certain that Ed and Gun told them about the name change."

"We're nearly killed in a plane crash, kidnapped and chased by mad men, made enemies of the United States, and now you tell me things are going to get a lot worse?"

"No, that's exactly what I'm telling you," answered Tim.

Anne then asked the question on everyone's minds. "Who can we trust?"

Bill put his hand on hers. "We have only ourselves at this juncture; we have to stay together and keep a low profile."

The group sat quietly, each lost in thought, and then the telephone rang.

"ET, phone home!"

"Don't answer it, Anne!" yelled Tim as she started to rise from her chair.

Bill pulled her down again and said, "Tim's right, Anne. We can't let anyone know we're here."

She began to protest then realized the wisdom in their words.

"Someone's going to realize we're here sooner or later; Marigold Bloom, my nosy but sweet neighbor, has Boomer, Eme's dog; she's bound to wonder what has happened to me."

Eme responded, "Poor Boomerman. Maybe I..." Eme started to rise, but Rafe grabbed her hand.

"No, Eme," Bill replied, rising from the sofa. He walked over to where Eme and Rafe were seated at the computer and put his hand gently on Eme's shoulder "No one can know we're here. I agree with Tim; it's not going to be long before we're reported missing, and the FBI will get involved. If they find out we're off the island, there will be chaos."

"Can you imagine the bloody media getting a hold of this?" Kala added.

"Not to mention foreign governments—who knows what country or countries are in cahoots with Ed and Gun!" added Anne.

"Sending e-mails from a train wreck, wish you were here."

No's sarcasm lifted the tension, for a minute, until Rafe brought them back to reality with the latest news bulletin from his computer:

"FBI and FAA agents are on route to Bermuda to join the FCC and CIA; the mystery behind the Hurricane Bruno air disaster deepens."

"Lions and tigers and bears, oh my!"

And the air left the room.

CIA Headquarters, Hamilton, Bermuda
6:40 P.M. ADT

"What do you mean you don't know what happened to him? When was the last time you talked to him, Agent Turner?"

"Five thirty, sir. He was just finishing up some business at the airport before he picked up the warrant at six o'clock. I've been trying his phone for the last fifteen minutes; I figured something was wrong when my calls continued to go to voice mail."

"So you've abandoned your post in front of the Romero cottage to come here. Haven't we taught you anything in the past twenty years, Agent? You stay where you're assigned, do you understand, or we'll assign you to guard the latrines at Attica!" Spittle flew as Agent Stuart Dvorsky slammed his hands on the large mahogany desk in his elaborate new office.

"Yes, sir," Ed whispered. He turned to leave the office.

"And just where do you think you're going now?" roared Dvorsky. "Get back here! Sit down!"

Ed complied and quietly took the seat indicated by his boss while the older man jabbed a button on the intercom. "Mandy, get the federal magistrate; then call the FAA once I've finished with the judge." He returned to Ed. "Now, you listen to me; we have a situation on our hands that is ready to blow up in our faces. I can't explain away Gun's and your involvement in this airplane fiasco. With so many lives lost, there's a full FAA investigation underway, and heads are going to roll; mine is not going to be one of them."

"What do you mean, sir? Do you want our resignations?"

"No, not exactly; I want you and Gun to admit that you were mistaken about terrorists on board and take full responsibility for your actions. Then I want you both to take whatever punishment is dished out by the US courts. It may mean federal prison, or, because of Gun's stellar record with the agency, it may mean probation."

Ed had sat quietly during this pronouncement, but his face drained of all color. Prison; no way—he had heard stories, seen pictures of what they did to government agents who had gone bad. He'd rather die by his own hand than those of the sadistic thugs housed in those institutions.

"But...but sir isn't there any other alternative? Can't you explain that there really were terrorists on board, that we probably saved the lives of everyone in Europe by our actions? We'd be heroes instead of criminals."

Dvorsky jumped out of his chair and leaned over his desk, murder in his eyes, as he glared at the agent in front of him. "You didn't *hear* me, Agent, the Federal Aviation Administration is involved; they're going over the manifest and flight recorder as we speak." He jumped out of his seat, slamming his chair into the bookcase behind him, and started pacing in a tight circle in front of his desk. "You and I know there were no terrorists on board." He paused and glared again at Ed, just inches from his face. "That jetliner was ordered down in a hurricane—for *no good reason!*" Dvorsky's voice rose with each word, followed by more spittle, until Ed was cowering in his seat in front of the red-faced man.

After a few seconds of blissful silence, the lead agent calmed his blood pressure, retrieved his chair, and continued in a quieter voice. "Look, I'm not insensitive to your plight, but it is *your* plight and *your* consequence for *your* ridiculous course of action. I still don't understand how you could have thought that a mere teenage girl could be involved in some terrorist plot to steal classified material. What proof did you have, other than the fact that she was headed to St. Bruno's and her name had something to do with e-mail...what was it, Eme?"

"Sir, with all due respect, you know what we believe is going on over there!"

"*But! You! Had! No! Proof!*" Each of these words was punctuated by the pounding fist on his gleaming mahogany desktop.

"We need ironclad proof before we can charge into a school and arrest people."

"We're still working on it, and we have almost…"

"*Almost?* Almost doesn't cut it, Agent! Now, this whole story, and all our undercover work, is going to be blown wide-open when the FAA is finished with us; the FCC will be the next to chime in, once they learn that their precious Internet is involved, if we don't nip this in the bud right here in Bermuda. No one else must know what we've—what *you've* been investigating."

He calmed a bit, leaned forward on his elbows, and glared at Ed. "What happened to Tim Edelman? He's been reported missing." Ed's face paled. Dvorsky threw up his hands. "Don't tell me that you're mixed up in that, *too!*"

Ed bowed his head, damning Gun under his breath for getting him involved in his rogue activities. "Uh, no, sir; we have no idea what happened to Mr. Edelman. I think I heard a rumor about an extramarital affair, and a possible…"

"Don't BS me, Turner; Gun's signature is all over this!" he yelled. "Oh, never mind, we'll get to the bottom of all of it once the FAA arrives." Dvorsky placed his notes in the desk drawer and returned his attention to his cowering agent. "Now go find your partner and bring him back here at once! I'll get the search warrant and take care of the Romero cottage myself; although I doubt there is anything to be found."

He looked up and stopped Ed in his tracks with his next remark. "By the way, Mr. Romero's lawyer, er, *team* of lawyers is already playing merry hell with Washington over this whole mess. Now get out of here, and don't come back without Gun!" He finished by slamming down his hand once more in concert with Ed's slammed door. Mandy was patching through the call to the federal magistrate as Ed made his hasty retreat past her desk. She smiled at him; a grimace of extreme pain was all he could muster in return.

He was outside in ten seconds flat; the warmth of the descending tropical sun would not, could not penetrate the state of icy shock that had invaded his body. He trembled. *Prison.* He shook his head to dispel the word from his mind. *Prison.* The word was tattooed on his brain. He had to find Gun.

Ten minutes later, he had parked his car in the airport maintenance garage and was rushing down the fateful corridor where this had all turned so terribly wrong. He passed the closet where the two maintenance men had been stashed, wondering if their bodies had been discovered, yet—just another nail in his coffin once the Bureau began their investigation.

Gun. Damn you, Gun.

He didn't notice a single person, nor acknowledge the greeting of the lovely woman behind the welcome desk as he urgently scanned the passenger lounge and concourse for Gun on his way to their secret command center; nor did he notice the FAA agent, who had recognized him, until it was too late.

"Ed, hey, long time! I didn't know you were assigned to this disaster," the man called from across the room.

Ed stopped in his tracks, and he could no longer contain the cold shakes; he turned to face his longtime college buddy who was rapidly closing the distance between them.

The trembling agent lowered his face when the man reached his side. "What's the matter, Ed? You look ill. Come over here and sit down."

Joe Falcone grabbed Ed by the arm and guided him toward the nearest bank of lounge chairs, lowering him gently into the seat. This act of warmth and human compassion was all it took to drive Ed over the last precipice of sanity. Bathed in sweat and shaking uncontrollably, he collapsed, thankful for the solid support of the hard plastic seat and the firm grip of his friend's hand. It was Ed Turner's last sensation before succumbing to his fear.

One cold heart ceased beating on the warm island of Bermuda.

CIA Office of Agent Dvorsky
7:10 P.M. ADT

"He seems to be resting as comfortably as can be expected, under the circumstances, Agent Dvorsky. Something really spooked him; he was cold, clammy, and shaking like a leaf before he collapsed."

"It was a good thing you were there, Agent Falcone. I have no idea what could have caused him such distress. He had just left my office and seemed to be in fairly good spirits; he must have had a heart defect that his last physical failed to catch," the lead agent lied smoothly. He sipped his diet soda to hide his smirk. Ed's demise would leave only one other agent to eliminate and ultimately blame for this entire disaster; the agency's hands would remain clean.

"I don't think that's the case. You must not have heard the good news," he added enthusiastically. "The doctors expect Ed to make a full recovery, once he's had some time to rest, and his heart returns to its normal rhythm."

"Oh?" Dvorsky nearly choked on his drink, and after a brief coughing fit, he tried his best to recover. "That's...unexpected, but...but wonderful news. It wasn't a heart attack, then," he said as he leaned over to retrieve a box of tissues from his bottom desk drawer and hide his disappointment. Once upright again, he held a tissue to his grimacing mouth but failed to suppress the disappointment in his eyes.

The FAA official started to get up to assist Dvorsky but was waved off. A bit puzzled by the reaction of Ed's boss, he continued, "Uh, no, it wasn't a heart attack. The doctor said it was an irregular heartbeat brought on by severe stress." He paused and frowned at the older man. "However, you say he was in good spirits when he left your office a few minutes before he collapsed? How can that be possible, Agent Dvorsky? Something doesn't add up, here. Ed is a very good friend of mine from college; I'm more than a little concerned about his and his partner's obvious involvement in the Destiny crash. Now, why don't you start from the beginning and tell me everything you can about Agent..." He checked the notebook on his lap and looked up again at the pale face before him. "Yes, Agent Gunter Dexter," he read, "and this computer program, Project Amazemail. What exactly is that?"

Dvorsky sagged a little lower in his large leather chair. How was he going to get out of this? What fates were at work that sent a friend of Ed's to investigate this mess? *Why didn't I retire when my wife suggested it last year?* He buried his head in his hands and gathered his thoughts for the inevitable: the truth about the agency's involvement in the crash of Flight 65.

Damn you, Gun! Damn you, Ed! And, damn you, Bruno, wherever you are now!

CHAPTER TWENTY
FUGITIVES

Anne's Malibu Home
Saturday, June 13, 2015
7:10 P.M. ADT/3:10 P.M. PDT

"No, GG, it's too dangerous!"

Bermuda's "missing persons" were sitting in Anne's Malibu living room discussing their options concerning the FBI investigation into Anne and Bill's disappearance from the cottage.

"Sweetheart, we've got our story straight. Once Bill and I return from Bermuda..." Bill was holding her hand and nodding his agreement.

"But what if..."

Rafe suddenly grabbed the sides of his head. "Oh, no! Return to Bermuda via the protocol is impossible!"

"What are you talking about, Rafe; we have to go back before the FBI investigates," his grandfather countered.

"The computer is booby-trapped!" was all he answered as he leaned back against the legs of the computer chair where Eme was seated; everyone in the room froze. Eme rubbed his shoulders. "The Cyborg had a most regrettable lapse of memory!"

Tim stopped pacing the floor and came to Rafe's rescue. "That's right; Rafe told us before lunch that he had installed a netbot on the computer at your cottage so that when, or if, Ed and Gun entered the protocol, they would be infected and killed, or at least maimed."

"Wow, way to go, Rafe!" was Kala's response from the window seat she shared with No.

"Rafe, you may have won the battle, but lost us the war!" his grandfather admonished solemnly.

"Gentlemen, you can't fight in here, this is a war room!"

"Quiet, Bogey, this is serious," scolded Anne, and Bogey hid his head under his wing.

Everyone smiled; No and Kala couldn't keep from laughing, which only increased when Bogey peeked at them from beneath his feathers. When he was sure he had everyone's attention again, he danced back and forth on his perch by the large bay window seat, whistling, squawking, and flapping his colorful wings, "I am Spartacus, I am Spartacus!"

No one could resist the charming bird, but twenty seconds later, after Kala had petted his head and calmed him down, Bill made a startling proposal: "Let's go to Switzerland!"

That sobered everyone.

"Bloody brilliant, Grandfather!"

All faces turned to Rafe for enlightenment, but Bill continued his proposal while Rafe wrote an e-mail address on a piece of Anne's blue personalized stationery. "I know of a chalet near my fitness center in Bern. It was my late wife's parents' home, and it might buy us some time."

"What about neighbors? Is there a caretaker?" asked Tim, taking a seat next to Bill.

All eyes were focused on Bill, and a collective sigh of relief was expelled when he answered, "No neighbors; it's in the mountains west of Brienz, and, it has twelve bedrooms and bathrooms; it was an inn during the early sixties when Amy's parents were newly married. When my father-in-law was paralyzed in a skiing accident, they had to give up their business. Before they passed, Amy wanted her parent's caretakers to have it, so we had the property transfer written into their will. They are a lovely couple, in their seventies now, no longer take in lodgers, and only live in two rooms of the big old house. Since my business requires frequent trips to Brienz, I stay with Helga and Franz. Anyway, it's the reason that I chose Switzerland for Rafe's summer program."

"It's not titled in your name?" Bill shook his head, and Tim clapped his hands together and remarked, "That's excellent; no one will think to trace you there!"

Excited voices filled the room.

"That's true! No one at the center knows where I stay when I'm in Europe," answered Bill with a dimpled grin.

"The Amazemail program was installed on a new computer two years ago and awaits our arrival," added Rafe with a grin that matched his grandfather's; he handed him the paper with the e-mail address.

Tim laughed and asked with hope in his eyes, "I could retrieve my family?"

"Of course, my dear man; there is no reason that you cannot reunite. You'll all be much safer there, I'm certain."

"Slow down, just a minute. What about the computer that's left here; how will we cover our tracks?" asked No with a concerned frown.

"And what about Boomer?" cried Eme, jumping up from her seat with tears in her eyes.

"Houston, we have a problem!"

"We can't leave Bogey behind!" demanded Kala who was stroking the macaw's feathers as Eme joined her and No on the window seat.

"Mrs. Robinson, you're trying to seduce me!"

That last line was too much; everyone roared with laughter at Bogey's remark and Kala's red face.

"OK, back to the business at hand," reminded Tim, rising from the sofa to take Eme's seat at Anne's computer. "First of all, I have a timer programmed into the protocol that will delete the entire program from the computer. No half-baked government agent will ever find the bits and bytes once they're sprinkled throughout the hard drive."

"Ingenious!" Rafe whispered.

"I, for one, think this is our best option," agreed Bill. "As far as Boomer and Bogey are concerned, Bogey can travel with us, and maybe we can dognap Boomer before we go." Eme and Kala clapped their hands at this remark.

"Help me! Help meeeeeeeee!" squawked an agitated Bogey.

No and Rafe shared a conspiratorial look and pulled Eme aside.

"Where does this Mrs. Bloom live?" asked No.

The adults grinned at the teenagers.

"It looks as if preparations are underway for departure." Anne smiled. "So if you'll excuse me, I'll just grab a few things and be right back." She and Bill rose from the sofa.

"Pack lightly, Anne. I have many of Amy's belongings put away there, and I know she would be so pleased that you were making use of them."

A tear glistened in Anne's eye at Bill's declaration. She grabbed his arm and squeezed it before she disappeared up the stairs to her room. The others watched her departure for a moment; then they broke into action.

"Man the torpedoes, full speed ahead!" was Bogey's battle cry.

Kala and Eme giggled and they gathered up Bogey's and Boomer's food and toys, putting them in a bag. They then straightened the kitchen and living room, started the dishwasher, and wiped clean any surfaces they might have touched.

Meanwhile, Rafe and No managed to pry a fence board loose between Anne's and Mrs. Bloom's side yards; Rafe had Eme's blood-stained cotton jacket, assuming her scent would entice her pet; they positioned themselves to intercept him when he made his next appearance in the backyard, hoping that Boomer was eating and drinking up a storm inside somewhere.

Bill and Tim set up Anne's computer; they aligned the scanner and set the timers on each peripheral and the e-mail program and copied the e-mail address, finally tucking the blue piece of stationery into the side pocket of Rafe's computer bag, to keep it from being discovered, in case of an investigation.

After ten minutes, everyone, except No and Rafe, had accomplished their tasks and were standing near the launch site. Tim was expending his nervous energy by periodically checking Rafe's computer for any new announcements from Bermuda when he came upon a live feed news report from the island. He sucked in his breath and turned to face the concerned group just as two excited boys rounded the corner to the living room, Boomer clutched in Rafe's firm grip. One look at Tim, and the smiles slid off their faces.

Boomer escaped Rafe's grasp and bounded to Eme, licking her face when she stooped to scoop him into her arms. Ignoring their reunion, all eyes were now on the computer screen; Tim moved out of the way to afford them better access.

The live feed began with a panoramic view of the golf club, bathed in the light of the setting Bermuda sun; then it zoomed in on the activity around the cottages lining the edges of the picturesque golf course.

"It's our cottage," Bill said simply.

"Are those Central Intelligence agents?"

"Well, I don't think the CIA on their backs stands for Cute, Interesting Aliens, Kala!"

"Oh, ha, ha, No. This is serious! They could find the computer."

"No chance of that, fair Kala; they won't be searching for the Cyborg's hidden domain. That big surprise awaits the traitorous ones to discover when they follow the e-mail trail left by yours truly," he smirked.

"Shhh!" came from a few people, now glued to the computer screen, followed by gasps at the images before them.

"We now switch to a video that was shot earlier today at the airport; Lisa, over to you."

A pretty blonde wearing a colorful tropical print dress was standing on the airport concourse. "Thank you, Rick. Yes, earlier today, I had the opportunity to speak to one of the last people to see these three teenagers, who are wanted for questioning in two murders, the theft of an airport van, and who are now, presumably, on the run."

"Murders?" questioned Tim, and the mouths of all present gaped in shock.

Pictures of three teenagers were flashed on the screen.

"That's us!" shouted Kala, pointing at the monitor.

"They must have procured that picture from the Cyborg's one and only yearbook," remarked Rafe.

"Look, they only have a sketch of No—pretty good likeness!" Kala snorted.

He turned an angry stare at the blonde. "I resent that remark—that looks like a monkey with a crew cut."

"I rest my case!" she replied, polishing her nails on her shirt. No elbowed her in the ribs.

"Hey, where's my picture?" replied Eme.

"Listen, they're interviewing someone," Bill remarked.

A teenage girl appeared beside the reporter in front of the airport coffee shop; Lisa introduced her to the audience. "This is Christy Grinch..."

"Gritch!" corrected the barista.

Kala jumped in surprise and pointed her finger at the screen again! "It's that nice barista!"

"Shhh!" said everyone, and they returned to the video.

The reporter turned to the young brunette. "I'm so sorry— Christy *Gritch*." She turned back to the camera with a smile. "Christy is the barista at the coffee shop behind me; she saw three of these teenagers, Kala Weston, Rafael Romero, and a mystery boy, who we hope someone will recognize from this artist sketch, just before they allegedly killed longtime airport maintenance worker Barney Reid and his young assistant, Jason Hubbard..."

"Killed?" several voices shouted together.

"Shhh, listen," said Bill.

"...stole an airport van and disappeared. What do you remember, Miss Gritch?"

"We didn't..." began Eme.

"Well, there were these three kids...those kids," she pointed to Rafe, Kala, and No's pictures displayed on a poster held up by the reporter. "They were hiding behind those ferns and were watching these two men..." She pointed to a second poster of Ed and Gun. "Those men," she jabbed her finger at the poster again, "were interrogating the other kids." "I sure hope they got away and are somewhere safe. They seemed so polite and—and scared. They couldn't have kill—"

Lisa cut her off and returned to the camera. "Thank you, Miss Gritch."

The prerecorded video ended, and the newscaster switched back to a live shot of Lisa on the airport tarmac; the setting sun glinted on a jetliner that was loading passengers behind her.

"Before we return to the St. George's Club cottage, I have one other witness who knows two of these missing teenagers." She turned to her left, and the camera panned to...

"Michael!" Three voices rang out together.

"This is Michael Greer who was also traveling with Mrs. Murphy to St. Bruno's Academy in Switzerland. Michael, what do you remember about the last time you saw your friends, Kala and Rafael?"

The camera panned to an extremely nervous young boy with a shock of sandy hair. "I—I—I don't know," he stammered.

"Poor Michael! That must be his mother and father next to him. It looks like they're about to board the plane." The others nodded their agreement with Eme.

The reporter tried again. "Were they scared? Did they say anything that would indicate that they were frightened? Did they ask you or the other students to go with them?"

"I—I—I..."

The man next to him stepped in front of Michael. "I'm afraid he's still in a bit of shock by this whole fiasco, Miss. If he doesn't want to..."

Michael peeked from behind his father. "No, Dad, I want to help find them. I just don't know what to say. I like them all." He turned to the camera and, with tears in his eyes, pleaded, "Please, Eme, Rafe, Kala! Please be OK, and if you're listening, please c—call...I hope I see you all when I get to Switzerland."

He broke down crying and was pulled into a hug by both of his parents.

The family was visible in the background boarding the Destiny jetliner as Lisa finished her live report.

"There you have it, folks—out of the mouth of babes. Eme, referred to by Michael, is Elaine Venture, the daughter of Mark Tomei Venture and Toni Malone. She was also bound for Switzerland and is the fourth teenager reported missing. However, the authorities are not sure if she was with the other three teens when they disappeared. Please let us know that you're all OK, Eme, Rafe, Kala, and Mr. John Doe. Back to you, Rick."

"Ah, poor kid, but he's still going to Switzerland—I wonder why his parents are allowing it, after all he's been through," commented No.

Kala was smirking at No. "Hey, No, can we call you John Doe, or better yet, No Doe?"

"Shut it, Kala!" No frowned. "Whoever said love lasts forever was high on drugs."

Kala gave him a kiss on the check, and he gave her a lopsided grin, grasping her hand. A few snickers emanated from the group as the screen returned to the live feed in front of the cottage. Many civilian onlookers were craning their necks to get a better look at the forensic activity while some children and teens waved hands at the camera. Rick was standing next to a somber, heavyset man who was swiping at the few wisps of grey hair still clinging to his sunburned head.

"Folks, this is the lead CIA agent, Stuart Dvorsky who has been investigating the teenagers' disappearance." The camera panned to the balding agent, and Rick added, "What have you to report?"

"We've been searching this cottage that belongs to Rafe Romero's grandfather, William Romero of Yonkers, New York. He and Ms. Anne Malone, Elaine Venture's great-grandmother, were last seen here a few hours ago, searching for the teenagers, and now have also gone missing. We fear foul play and want to question Agent Gunter Dexter in regard to their disappearance."

"Are you saying that you think Agent Dexter is responsible for these missing people?"

The camera zoomed in on the agent's angry face. "No, I'm not saying that," he retorted. "We haven't seen Agent Dexter for the past few hours, and he may have uncovered more information since he was the agent responsible for ordering the plane to land yesterday morning."

"You're saying that he did this on his own authority without the agency OK?"

Dvorsky grimaced, "Yes, that is exactly what I'm saying."

Silence.

The stunned reporter finally gathered his wits about him, turned to the camera, and declared, "That's a scoop, ladies and gentleman; Agent Gunter Dexter is under investigation for causing..."

The agent's eyes widened, and it looked as if he was about to grab the microphone out of the reporter's hand, when he shouted, "Wait a minute! He didn't cause the accident; he merely made a decision without the proper authority. We are currently tracking the cell phones of all the missing persons and should have answers..."

But the small audience of missing persons didn't wait to hear any more from Bermuda.

"Why didn't I think of this sooner?" Tim snapped as Anne's and Bill's cell phones appeared on the computer desk with a thud, while Rafe covered his wrist with a sigh and a frown.

"At least that's one thing I'm glad burned up in the plane," Eme stated in a shaky voice. No and Kala nodded in agreement.

"Should we flush them down the toilet?" asked Anne, with fear in her eyes.

"No, they need to be far away from here, preferably in Bermuda." Bill answered, putting an arm around the frightened woman.

Rafe gave one more sigh and leaped to his feet, grabbed the phones, and headed for the stool. "The Cyborg sadly missed the opportunity to bid a proper farewell to the evil ones, although my imminent presence may not be acknowledged." He smirked. "Crank up the program, ingenious one, Cyber Santa has parting gifts to deliver."

A shake of his head silenced any forthcoming protests; a moment later, Rafe was on his second digitized trip to Bermuda.

CHAPTER TWENTY-ONE
FUN ON THE RUN

Bermuda Airport Underground Garage
Saturday, June 13, 2015
7:40 P.M. ADT

Ed Turner was many things—stupid, he believed, was not one of them. Greed had led him to betray his government and join Gun in a dangerous game of *Spy and Sell* with foreign terrorists. Fear had caused him to be hospitalized briefly. Self-preservation impelled him now; ignoring the protests of his care-givers, he had released himself from the hospital, desperate to find Gun and formulate an escape plan from Bermuda.

He left the underground garage through the stairwell door opposite the underground command center entrance. Activating his remote control, the wall slid aside; he advanced to the iris scanner; however, after several attempts, he realized that some-one had been tampering with the code. Banging on the door brought no results. *Panic! Had Gun reprogrammed it? Had the Agency discovered their lair?*

Tired, fearful, and frustrated, he slid down the wall and sat on the cold cement floor.

A religious man was also something Ed Turner was *not*, but desperate times...and he crawled to a kneeling position to make one final plea.

Five seconds later...*Has God heard me?*

The door slid slowly open to reveal... *No, a merciful God would not punish me this way.*

Inside the Command Center
FIVE MINUTES EARLIER

Gun didn't witness the surreal appearance of Rafe's vaporized form as it reorganized in front of the protocol computer.

"Tsk, tsk, napping on the job, Evil Agent? Hmmm, my special brew must not have contained enough *caffeine*," he chuckled as he made his way to the mainframe computer where he unplugged the now-empty coffee pot. Gun was sprawled on the keyboard with his hands grasping the main monitor; his right foot was bent at an odd angle under the casters of the pedestal seat support; his knees nearly touched the floor.

"Well, now that appears very uncomfortable, Agent Asshole; let the Cyborg improve your lie." He kicked the severely listing chair out from underneath Gun, sending him to the floor, but not before clipping his chin on the edge of the desk.

"I foresee a painful trip to the dentist," Rafe snickered. "Couldn't happen to a nicer guy," he proclaimed while he surveyed the blood dribbling from the man's mouth. Gun was spread eagle on the cement floor with his jacket thrown open; Rafe noticed his gun holster. "Hmm, the last time I checked the Constitution, Second Amendment rights did *not* extend to baboons," he chuckled as he grabbed the weapon, tucking it into his own pocket; then he snapped his fingers, and shook his head sadly, "Forsooth, my kingdom for a camera!" He held up his arm in sudden realization. "What have we here? Ah, modern technology is a marvelous thing!" And he quickly snapped several pictures of the scene with his wrist phone, spoke Anne's email address, and sent them on to her computer, laughing at the imagined reactions from his friends in Malibu.

A loud banging on the entry door alerted Rafe to his task at hand; he hastily stashed the two cell phones plus his wrist phone in a drawer in the supply closet. Noticing the partially open door of the gun safe below the drawer, he knelt and discovered several more guns. He shook his head and whispered, "So much for sanity background checks!" before stashing them all in a canvas bag that he found on the counter. A further search in a wall cabinet revealed the bottle of chloroform he needed for his next operation. He held his breath, poured the potent liquid onto a cloth, and quickly left the closet.

Positioning himself next to the entry door, he stared into the reprogrammed iris scanner and the door slid open to reveal a surprised Agent Turner. The sight of the kneeling man astonished and delighted Rafe; he lunged forward and covered the nose and mouth of the stunned agent. Before Ed had time to do more than blink, he was out cold.

Rafe dragged Ed into the room, laying him next to his partner. "You won't need this either, Mr. Ed," and he removed the man's gun from its holster, adding it to his growing collection in the canvas bag; then he stood quietly, smiling down at the peaceful scene. After grinning at his handiwork for a few more seconds, he took a few more photos, slung the bag over his shoulder, closed the security exit door, and sprinted to the computer. He grabbed his trusty broom, activated the dispatch timer, clicked the scanner with the broom handle, took one last look at the command center, and decomposed into a vapor of icy crystals.

CIA Headquarters, Hamilton, Bermuda
7:40 P.M. ADT/3:40 P.M. PDT

"Agent Falcone, we've just picked up signals of the missing person's cell phones here on the island," the tall brunet twenty-year-old agent reported. "We thought the signals were coming from California, but there must have been some sort of glitch in the tracking device. Anyway, three of them are somewhere at the airport, the others must have been destroyed in the airliner crash."

"OK, get some agents over there and search the place again. We've got to find them. Tear the place apart if you have to. As soon as you have a lead on *any* of the missing people, call me!"

"Yes, sir!"

Joe Falcone watched the eager young agent sprint from his temporary office and wished he could feel as enthusiastic about this case. One of his best friends from college was now missing, and from the evidence mounting on his desk, he was probably working with Gunter Dexter, selling vital telecommunications programs to foreign agencies or governments, or worse—terrorist organizations. Just what programs they were dealing, the FCC, with the full cooperation of Amazemail, had yet to uncover; however, everyone assumed they were of a computer-jamming or information-hacking nature. The disappearance of Amazemail CEO, Tim Edelman and his family just deepened the mystery. All the agencies agreed (which was a first) that if Ed and Gun had succeeded, national security was severely compromised.

Fortunately, there was no way either of them could leave the island without being detected. That was the FAA's mission, and he was on top of it.

The fate of the missing teenagers and their relatives was also particularly disturbing; they, too, seemed to have vanished. He was glad his department wasn't involved in that case; let the CIA and FBI share the headaches and the responsibility for those tragedies.

Anne's Malibu Home
7:50 P.M. ADT/3:50 P.M. PDT

Cheers from his fellow fugitives and Bogey's "Here's Johnny" greeted Rafe's reappearance in Anne's living room.

Kala and Eme threw their arms around him, but No held his exuberance in check. Rafe smirked at him, and No wagged his eyebrows in return. Everyone else stood nearby and laughed at the byplay.

"Excellent photos, Rafe, but we watched the whole thing live via the surveillance cameras on Persephone and Anne's computer," laughed Bill. Rafe joined in the laughter after his initial surprised reaction to his grandfather's remark.

"Yeah, you're some mean dude, Rafe!" crowed No."

"It was no more than they bloody well deserved," replied Kala.

"I'll second that!" Eme agreed with a grin.

"It looks as if we're done with those two," Anne added. "Maybe now we can relax and..."

"Drat! The Cyborg forgot." Rafe made a mad dash for his computer. "Maybe it's not too late...they're still out cold."

"Now what's put a knot in his knickers? They're out cold in a room no one knows about," mused No.

Tim immediately followed Rafe to Anne's laptop. "Did you forget to program the self-destruct button on the protocol, Rafe?"

"I didn't want to do that because of the surprise the Master of Cybermatter had waiting for them at the cottage, but they now have *Anne's* e-mail address, and..."

"Gun's coming around, Rafe!" screamed Eme who was still glued to Rafe's laptop.

"Oh, no; what does that mean?" asked Anne, standing behind Eme.

Five anxious faces turned to Tim and Rafe who were busy downloading a program onto Anne's computer.

Rafe turned toward the group. "It means it's time to move. Queue up with whatever you're taking!"

Nothing more needed to be said as they complied and gathered together behind the launching stool in front of Rafe's computer. While Rafe rechecked the chalet's address for each cybertraveler's e-mail and finished programming his computer, Tim prepared the scanner. He took one last look at the two disoriented agents on Persephone's screen; Gun was wiping blood from his mouth and spitting out pieces of broken teeth and blood at the monitor. A few minutes later, after Gun roughly roused his partner, they were staggering toward the computer through which Rafe had so recently vanished.

"It won't be long until they figure it out, Rafe," Tim yelled.

Satisfied that he had the netbot programmed into Anne's computer, he took a sad look at Persephone. "It looks like you're the sacrificial lamb." He patted his beloved friend and quickly sobered. "However, blood is thicker than silicon. Grandfather, you go first, then GG Anne, Kala with Bogey, No with Boomer, Eme..."

"No, I'll stay until you're ready to leave," Eme responded, taking his arm.

Rafe smiled at her. "OK. Tim, you follow No and make sure they're all safe and secure. Juliet and the Cyborg will bring up the rear."

"Come with me to the Casbah!" squawked Bogey as Kala took him from Eme's shoulder and joined the queue of cyber travelers.

Boomer licked No on the nose when he picked him up from his favorite chair. "I'll take the guns, too, Rafe," and he grabbed the canvas bag, slinging it over his shoulder.

Rafe nodded and handed him the one that was still in his pocket. All were silent as one by one Tim scanned them and sent them into cyberspace. With a cheery wave, he finally took his seat on the now vacant stool, and a few seconds later, only Eme and Rafe remained in Anne's large living room.

Eme was busy wiping the last of their prints when Rafe grabbed his computer bag. "OK, fair Juliet, it's..."

Quark...cruck...queek... A hideous, sickly yellow hologram creature, two feet high, had emerged from the holoport of Anne's computer, followed by a screech from Eme and a few expletives from Rafe.

"Too late, as Bogey would have said, they're *he-ere!*"

Brienz, Switzerland
June 14, 2015
12:00 A.M. CEST/ 4:00 P.M. PDT

"Ahoooo! Ahoooooo!" Boomer was in No's arms, shaking his head and moaning in agony. Kala joined No and massaged the dog's back, while they cooed words of comfort to the frightened pooch, without success; Boomer continued his wailing.

"Shh! Keep him quiet, No! Franz and Helga..."

Too late; a table lamp flashed to life, and all four people stared at the end of a gun, held by a scowling pajama-clad man in his seventies.

"Mr. Bill, is that you?" he growled when Bill waved at him.

"Yes, Franz, it's Bill and a few friends. We're sorry to break in this way, but we had no time to call ahead."

The others nodded in agreement with that statement while Franz lowered his weapon; he was joined by a small, smiling woman, wearing a yellow flannel nightgown and slippers.

Boomer recovered enough to jump out of No's arms and make a beeline for the woman who hesitated for a moment before stooping down to pet him. This seemed to relax everyone, and Bill rushed to shake Franz's hand when a cry made everyone turn toward Kala. "He's gone, Bogey's gone! He didn't come through with me!" She collapsed in tears on the desk chair.

No one knew what to do. No and Anne ran to Kala. Tim stopped in midstride toward their stunned hosts; Bill just threw up his hands in frustration.

"Poor B...Bogey, oh, I'm s...so sorry." She sobbed harder than ever.

No and Anne hugged the distraught girl; however, she could not be consoled. Tim and Bill escorted the older couple to the sofa of the charming living room and tried to explain the reason for their abrupt appearance, but Kala's wailing spurred Helga into action. Ever the consummate hostess, Helga paused, turned, and headed for the kitchen. "I'll just put on some tea."

Anne left Kala and followed. "I'll come and help."

Bill and Tim joined Franz on the sofa and watched Kala and No for a few seconds; then Bill broke their silent vigil. "Is it all right if we stay with you for a while? I'm not sure exactly how long."

"Well, of course," came the immediate response. "This is your home as well as ours, Bill. What seems to be missing that is breaking that poor girl's heart?"

Bill and Tim looked at each other for a few seconds, each wondering how to answer that, when Tim jumped to the computer. "They're not following!"

That statement stopped Kala's wailing, and she and No joined Tim and Bill next to the computer.

Kala dissolved into tears again as Anne ran in from the kitchen. "Bill, what could have happened to them?" she asked. She again threw her arms around a distraught Kala.

Tim was busy writing an e-mail, but he stopped and turned around to the many anxious faces. "I can't send this. If Ed and Gun have tracked Rafe..."

"You're right, Tim; however, as I said before, if they have made it to Anne's, my grandson will be able to handle them."

"But if they've contracted a virus through the protocol..." Tim began.

"What does that mean? I thought the virus would kill them," No queried.

"We have no way of knowing what a virus will do to humans in the protocol, No. I've never experimented with netbots on humans, but I'll bet the result won't be pretty," the man grimaced.

"We need a Bogeyism right now," said No, and then bit his tongue when Kala collapsed in his arms in agony. The others in the room were lost in thoughts about Eme, Rafe, Bogey, and what might have become of the double agents.

CHAPTER TWENTY-TWO
MALIBU MAYHEM

Morbid fascination overcame raw fear and rooted them to the spot as they faced the holoport of Anne's computer. Slowly the frosty mist cleared, revealing first one and then two creatures, clothed in nothing but shreds of what once were blue polyester suits, and whose heads nearly brushed Anne's eight-foot living room ceiling; green slime oozed from open wounds on their mottled red skin; unearthly groans emanated from their grotesque, swollen lips. Without waiting long enough to allow their brains to register any more of what they were witnessing, Rafe pushed Eme with enough force to galvanize her into action. The few seconds it took for Gun and Ed to become oriented gave Rafe enough time to grab Persephone and yell, "Where to?"

Eme was already halfway to the kitchen. "My house!"

The destructive noises in the living room didn't distract him, and he dashed after the redhead, through the kitchen, through the French doors, and into the rose-filled garden outside.

Eme ran to her left, down the garden path, and executed a less than perfect Western roll over the low wooden gate between the towering hedges that separated Anne's house from her parents' neighboring estate. Rafe followed suit, snagging and ripping the open pocket of his computer bag on the gate. He wished he had time to smell the flowers, or sit beside the beautiful pool, rather than running for his life from the hideous creatures he had helped to create. Instead, he caught his breath, checked to make sure nothing important had fallen from his bag, gave up trying to refasten the pocket, and charged after his terrified friend, hoping she had a plan for escape.

Through the poolside furniture and over the vast expanse of well-manicured lawn, Eme led him to the rear of what Rafe suspected was an immense garage. Without stopping, she reached behind a wooden planter containing a seven-foot-tall red camellia, grabbed a key hidden between two of the wooden planks, and unlocked the large blue door, flinging it open with such force that it shattered two of the three small glass panes near the top. She disabled the alarm and dashed to the front of the garage.

Pausing only a second to brush off the fragments of broken glass, Rafe stuffed Persephone into his bag, threw it over his shoulder and hurtled into the huge garage after Eme. He slammed and locked the door, not realizing that a piece of stationery had escaped the torn pocket of his bag and was now impaled on a branch of the red camellia.

"Wipe your prints, Rafe, just in case," Eme yelled over her shoulder as she continued her sprint toward the front of the building. Rafe complied, wondering about the futility of the action since his prints were all over Anne's house. He shrugged, then turned, and stopped dead in his tracks at the sight before him: not one car, but a small flotilla of perfectly restored vintage masterpieces occupied the cavernous space. *If I died right here...*

Eme gave him no more than a moment to dream of his divine demise before she returned to his side and dragged him to the most glorious lime-green chopper he'd ever seen. As he was admiring the forty-five-degree rake of its chrome forty-inch front and 2400cc chrome engine, Eme was dragging him, once again, to what was partially hidden on the other side of the magnificent motorcycle: a hideous shocking pink scooter, sporting a pink polka dot bow. With one last covetous glance at the fantasy behind him, he sighed and turned back to his reality.

"What a pity to make our escape on..." he began with a disappointed sneer. Then he turned, pointed, and added hopefully, "Look, the key is..."

"Hey, this is Maud," she patted the black leather seat and removed the temporary paper license and the bow on the handlebars, dropping them on the garage floor, "my fifteenth birthday present from GG Anne; besides, my dad would kill me if I took his precious custom-made chopper, which is neither registered nor licensed for street use, by the way—oh, wait a minute." Eme left Rafe glaring at the moped while she snatched up the bow and license and dashed to a long shelf stacked with cardboard boxes in the rear corner of the garage. After a few seconds of scavenging through one of the massive boxes, she returned wearing a curly black wig and carrying another with flowing blonde extensions.

He sneered at the brunette, "Juliet can*not* be seri..."

She cut off Rafe's retort with, "No one can know we're here, Rafe, put it on, and let's go!"

Skipping the futile argument, Rafe threw on the wig, tightened the elastic band around his head for the upcoming *hair-raising* ride, and grimaced.

With a jab at the garage door opener, Eme hopped on the scooter, keyed the ignition, and they were on the driveway just as the back door caved under the force of the two twisted cyberdemons. *So much for taking the time to lock up,* Rafe thought as he watched his newly-created nightmares slam into a vintage black roadster.

Rafe groaned, "Not the roadster!" shook his head, tucked his computer bag into his waistband, slipped his arms around Eme's tiny waist, and they shot off the mark, skidding onto the winding drive toward the estate's main gate. The engine whirred up to speed, and the tires bit the asphalt hard as if sensing their urgency.

There was a deafening roar of a ferocious engine behind them, and Rafe glanced over his shoulder in time to see two tall, thin creatures burst out of the garage on Mark Tomei's prized lime-green chopper.

"Oh...shit, your GG Anne's house is on fire, and we're about to get burned by the devils behind us riding your dad's chopper—drive, Eme—must drive fast *now!*"

"What!" Eme tried to catch a glimpse of her great-grandmother's house, lost control of the scooter, and skidded into the rose bushes bordering the drive. They both cringed as they lay in the middle of the thorny shrubs, thinking their nightmare was soon to come to a bloody end, when there was a loud crunch from a hundred yards behind them. They both turned and caught a glimpse of the taillight on the green chopper which had crashed into the back of a giant oak.

They didn't take time to revel in their good fortune; Rafe helped Eme right the moped, and they moved it back onto the drive. Once on the scooter, Eme struggled to get the engine started again. "Agent Gun's pissed, Eme, get this...this thing started and just floor it!" Eme complied, the engine purred to life; they slowly picked up speed, and Rafe finally tore his eyes away from the sight behind them to behold the sight before them—a *closed* iron gate. "The remote, Eme, the remote!" he screamed.

Eme finally remembered the device on her handlebars and jabbed at the button; the two teens and the scooter barely squeezed through the slowly opening gateway. Once they hit the roadway, they spun into a sharp, wavering turn that nearly sent Rafe reeling. The two teens righted the moped once again, Eme hit the button to close the gate, which also closed the garage door, and they took off down the winding road toward the coast.

There was a scream and a roar that eclipsed the sound of the moped's mini engine and drowned out the daily sounds of Malibu, launching all the birds in the trees toward the sky. It was the sound of a wounded animal, of something that had been hurt and violated on a primal level; however, it was also the sound of something that had never existed before—that should never have existed at all.

Ed and Gun, or what had become of Ed and Gun, had skidded down the driveway and barely made it through the slowly closing gateway, howling their outrage, and stirring up dust as they temporarily lost control of the powerful bike. The impact of the motorcycle smashing into the cars parked on the street crushed the fenders and sides of the cars, but did little to dampen the enthusiasm of the Cyberdemon's urge to catch and destroy their prey. They had righted the chopper and were once again in pursuit.

"*Faster!*" Rafe yelled in her ear, and he chanced another glance behind him as Eme took the shoulder of the road and dodged throughout the sporadic traffic. What he saw sent his stomach plummeting and his heart soar into his throat. Over seven feet tall, thin and leathery, the two traitorous agents were no longer human, not even close. About two hundred feet behind and accelerating hard, they were close enough for Rafe to lock eyes with one the ex-agents: two hollow black spheres that seemed devoid of life. He sensed some alien presence zero in on his mind, sensed an intense and animalistic hatred directed toward him; he knew they were in trouble.

The Netbot Brothers, for lack of a better name for the twin horror show, screeched as one and continued to pursue the tiny moped. Rafe's eyes bulged as the two creatures used their long skeletal legs to balance themselves by dragging them along the street. He blinked, thinking he'd missed something, but then it happened again. Ed and Gun pushed themselves off parked cars or anything they drove too near or that got in their way. It looked like a bumper car ride at the carnival, but it was effective—it kept them upright and on course. Rafe only hoped they continued this practice, as it slowed them down enough to keep him and Eme in the lead. He shivered at the thought of them ever becoming expert riders.

Between his arms, Rafe felt Eme tense and spun around to see a set of traffic lights, a block ahead, changing from yellow to red. The brake lights on half a dozen cars in front blinked on; their occupants were oblivious to the nightmare tearing down the street behind them.

He reached in front of her and beeped the moped's horn.

"What are you doing?" she shrieked.

"A careful driver is one who honks when running a red light," Rafe joked, his lips brushing Eme's ear. He was holding her tight, holding on for life and for limb.

"It...it's a blind corner!" Eme squealed.

Rafe squeezed her gently. "Trust to fate, fair Juliet," he said. "Because if you don't, *Gun's gonna eat us!*"

Eme hesitated...but only for a heartbeat. Trusting to fate, to chance, to sheer dumb luck, and to the fear she felt in the fingers gripping her waist, she ran the red light as fast as the whirring engine could carry them over the line. Blaring horns from the left blasted their indignation at the lawbreakers as they flew across the path of the oncoming traffic.

Rafe made a strangled, gargling sound when Eme swerved in front of a hybrid and into the next lane in front of a massive Hamburg Beer truck; its tires screeched—like the screams of the savage beasts not far behind. He could taste the gas and feel the heat of the engine sweep across his face.

The tiny moped cleared the traffic and, by the grace of fate and luck alone, hurtled toward the coast and downtown Los Angeles.

"That was close," Rafe breathed in Eme's ear, feeling the urge to laugh and vomit all at once.

Metal crumpled behind them. Once more Rafe chanced a look over his shoulder and saw the truck crash into the side of a bank building in an attempt to avoid hitting the speeding motorcycle behind them. Pallets of green bottles were hurled aside and shattered upon the asphalt, sending the traffic into spasms of squealing brakes and dented fenders. "Not the beer!" Rafe cried. The two infected agents just kept coming, spurred on by something, Rafe was sure, that had come from cyberspace along with his virus. *But what*, he wondered, and then, as an afterthought: *what have I done?*

Bailee Sue's Malibu Home
4:10 P.M. PDT

"Any luck?"

"No, I get the same nasty woman every time, and no matter how I change my accent or voice, she knows it's me! 'I don't care who you are, unless you're a relative, I can give you no information about the passengers!'" she mimicked in a squeaky voice with her hands on her hips. "Miserable old…!"

"Same here. It must be the response they're required to give anyone who can't prove they're a family member. What are we going to do?"

"How about the CIA, FAA, or the FBI?"

"Great idea, Shae! How about the president, while you're at it!"

The heat of the blazing California summer sun did nothing to warm the spirits of Shaelyn McBain and Bailee Sue Gardner, Eme's two best friends; they sat in glum silence by the pool of Bailee's Malibu home; each had a Cypad on her lap and a frown on her face. They had tried every angle they could think of to get information about their friend's disappearance, with no luck.

"Have you tried GG's number lately?" asked Shae, a petite blonde, brown eyed, eighteen year-old.

"Yeah, the last call went to voicemail, just like the five before... I'm sure she's flown to Bermuda," replied Bailee, an athletic, statuesque, seventeen year-old with bright blue eyes and medium length wavy brown hair.

The two girls had been friends since preschool, but had widened their friendship circle to include Eme when she enrolled in their upper level home school academy classes three years earlier. Even though Eme was more of a geek than they—into the mechanics of the computer rather than the social aspects of the technology—they found her funny and sweet and enjoyed spending time with her. In fact, Shae and Bailee were considering adding computer programming to their senior course load, to better understand their friend and their own computers, and were anxious to see Eme's reaction when they sprang their plans on her in the fall.

"Who's taking care of Boomer? Her nutty neighbor, Mrs. Bloom?" at Bailee's nodding, Shae perked up. "What's her number? I'll bet she's got some information."

After a quick search, Bailee had the woman's number and entered it on her phone. A few seconds later, "Hello, Mrs. Bloom, I'm Bailee Sue Gardner. Do you remember? I'm a friend of Eme's."

Pause

"Yes, it's nice to talk to you again, too. I…"

Pause

"Yes, I know she's missing, that's why…yes, I…"

Pause

"Yes, that's the reason that I called…*MRS. BLOOM!*"

Pause

"I'm so sorry to be rude, but this is an emergency!"

Pause

"Yes, I should have told you that in the beginning, but I…"

Pause

"OK, I want to know if you're taking care of Boom…Mrs. Bloom? *Mrs. Bloom, what's the mat…?*"

Bailee jumped to her feet and yelled at Shae, "She started screaming and hung up on me! Let's go!"

Pacific Coast Highway, Malibu
4:15 P.M. PDT

"Where are we going?" Eme yelled over the ominous sounds behind them, weaving through traffic on the double-lane highway. "Are they still chasing us?"

"Head into the city!" Rafe yelled. "One of my grandfather's fitness clubs is along Wilshire Boulevard. I've been there before."

"And when we get there? shrieked Eme."

"Plan B."

Eme paused, almost dreading the answer. "What…what's Plan B?"

"I'll let you know as soon as I do." Rafe hollered.

"Oh, great!" Eme cried. "Think fast, Romeo!"

"Right! It'll involve a lot of hiding from ravenous monsters!" Rafe growled in her ear.

"Good plan!" Eme laughed.

"One of many you can credit to the Cyborg."

Something exploded at their backs with an ear-splitting boom; a wave of tremendous heat washed over the tiny moped and its riders. Pieces of flying metal and burning rubber whizzed past their heads; Rafe literally froze with fear; a brief image of a long, jagged piece of engine impaling him to Eme, like a human kebab, flashed through his mind.

"What was...?"

Rafe just gripped Eme all the harder as they rounded a curve in the road amidst braking traffic. Frozen bystanders gazed up the road in silent horror and fascination at the motorized scream-ing demons chasing the two speeding teens.

"Run, damn it!" Rafe shrieked at the crowds as they skidded down the road. "This isn't a movie—those things are *real!*"

"That's Topanga Beach!" Eme howled over her shoulder. "We can follow the highway down to Palisades and onto Wilshire. How far down is the fitness club?"

"A few miles—opposite the La Brea Tar Pits!"

"That's five minutes if we're running red lights; we have to lose them before then."

Rafe looked back, yet again. Ed and Gun were lost behind the curve of the hill they had just descended, but the sound of screams and crunching metal, shattered glass and worse, car-ried well from above; the chase was still on.

"Faster, Eme, faster, faster..."

"It'd go faster if you got off and walked," Eme snapped, con-centrating on the road. "Otherwise, fifty-five is as good as we'll get."

"Sorry."

"Shut up and hang on, Shakespeare!"

Eme's Malibu Neighborhood
June 13, 2015
4:15 P.M. PDT

Bailee and Shae could see and smell the smoke and hear the sirens from two blocks away when they hit the street running toward Mrs. Bloom's house.

"I hope...it's not Eme's...house," panted Shae as they rounded the corner and stopped dead in their tracks at the sight at the end of the cul-de-sac...Anne Malone's lovely home was fully engulfed in flames. *"Bogey!"* she screamed, and they raced toward the fire.

"Oh, no! Poor Bogey! cried Bailee, "I...love that bird! Poor Eme!"

"Maybe Boomer...*and* Bogey are at...Mrs. Bloom's!" huffed Shae.

Bailee nodded and flashed a weak smile at her friend as they stopped on the sidewalk in front of Mrs. Bloom's stately colonial house. Many neighbors were gathered up and down the street of elegant homes, watching in disbelief at the horrific fire. Suddenly, a distraught, gray-haired lady in blue jeans and purple T-shirt appeared from the side yard of her home, frantically gesturing to a fire firefighter. As they drew closer they heard...

"...and he's a white Lhasapoo with beige ears! His name is Boomer!"

"We'll keep an eye out for him, Mrs. Bloom, but so far we haven't found a bird. I'm afraid we may have been too late."

The firefighter continued, but Mrs. Bloom wasn't listening; she had her face in her hands. The girls ran to her side, as did two of her neighbors. All wanted to give her some comfort, no one knew just what to say.

The firefighter patted her on the shoulder and returned to the fire, while the teens and two adults moved in closer. A stout, balding man put his arm around her shoulder and then pulled her into a hug. Mrs. Bloom cried on his shoulder for a few seconds, before she lifted her head and spotted the teens. She broke away from her neighbor and rushed forward to grab Bailee's and Shae's hands.

"Girls! Oh, oh…girls, I'm so glad t…to see you. You…you have to help me f…find Boomer," she sobbed. "He must have escaped t…to Anne's yard when I…I put him outside a short while ago." The girls gave her a thumbs-up, nodded, and took off for the Bloom backyard.

Once they found the loose board, they pulled it free of the fence and squeezed through to Anne's yard. "Shhhh, we'll get booted out of here if the firefighters see us; turn off your phone," Shae whispered. Bailee nodded. They switched off their phones, pocketed them, and crept behind the trees and bushes toward Anne's rear property line. Since there was a hundred-foot vertical drop to the road below, they stayed on Anne's side of the fence and inched their way between the fence and the hedge toward the Venture estate, stopping every few yards to softly call for Bogey and Boomer.

By the time they reached Eme's property line, they were scratched, bloody, and their clothes were torn. "This is the shirt Eme gave me for Christmas," Bailee snarled, as she examined her shredded pink T-shirt.

"My brother's not going to appreciate me ruining his Flash Bang shirt, either," Shae responded, running her hands down the front of the ripped, flaming red and gold sweatshirt. "I'm going to have to ditch it before I go home and then plead innocent when he finds it missing."

"Yeah, throw it over the cliff and go home in your bra, that'll be interesting," her friend responded with a smirk.

Shae laughed. "Well, maybe I can borrow a shirt from Eme... she keeps a few changes of clothes in the pool house, and it's usually unlocked."

Bailee's eyes lit up. "Hey, maybe Boomer and Bogey went home and are hiding somewhere in their yard!" Shae nodded and smiled.

The firefighters were having a difficult time trying to save Anne's house, with the steady summer coastal wind fanning the flames, and were putting most of their efforts into containing the blaze, keeping it from spreading to the neighboring woods and homes. Several members of the crew were investigating the perimeter of her once-stately residence. The girls looked sadly at the scene from behind a Japanese maple tree, heaved a sigh, and disappeared over the low back gate.

Highway 101, Malibu
4:18 P.M. PDT

The world seemed calm—far too calm. Seagulls lazily circled the beach full of late afternoon summer sunbathers, all totally unaware of the reality that would soon be theirs.

Rafe kept a sharp watch over his shoulder every few seconds for signs of pursuit. After half a minute, there was still no sign of Ed or Gun as they raced between the heavy traffic; they were caught between the tall hills on the left and a drop into the foamy Pacific on the right.

"I think we lost them..." Rafe said, tempting fate and bracing himself for a sudden reappearance of their monstrous hunters.

Eme didn't slow down; she was riding now on the shoulder of the highway, in the shadows of the large trees and beach homes, running the length of the coast.

Lights flashed to life behind them, and the alarm of an emergency siren cut across the drone of traffic. In the handlebar mirrors of the pink scooter, Rafe saw a police cruiser pull into the lane behind them, commanding them to pull over.

"Of all the..." he muttered.

Eme began to slow, easing her grip on the accelerator; they had been doing about twenty over the limit for this particular stretch of highway.

"Don't stop!" Rafe screamed in a panic about Eme's intentions.

"They're police, Rafe, the good guys; they'll have guns!"

A joint screech broke the wailing of the police sirens, and from behind, cruising full speed and not braking, the creatures slammed into the back of the speeding police vehicle, causing it to swerve onto the median, where it crashed into a yield sign—yielding the Netbots a free pass to continue their pursuit of the frightened teens.

Eme needed no more convincing, and she gunned the engine once again as behind them cars swerved to avoid the flying parts of the disabled cruiser. Ed and Gun shot forward on the crumpled, partially destroyed bike, unwavering in their assault upon the moped and its riders. Rafe marveled at the pounding the chopper's extended forty-inch front tubing was taking—why it wasn't bent into a pretzel was beyond miraculous. *I wonder if it's some new metal...I'll have to ask Eme's fath...* "Ahhhh!" Eme swerved to miss a squirrel and nearly lost Rafe in the process.

"You still with me, Rafe?" she yelled.

He righted himself and readjusted his computer. "Yes, but just barely." He squeezed her more tightly, she giggled in return.

A fresh attack had begun with the onslaught of the heavy highway traffic crashing into, and being crashed into, by Ed and Gun. Over his shoulder Rafe watched cars sideswipe and bounce off one another as they tried to avoid the two skeleton-thin creatures who were careening in, out, around, and through the madness.

"Wilshire's coming up!" Eme cried. "The light's green!" she screamed with obvious relief.

"Right, there'll be a golf course, yeah? All this traffic's slowing them down."

It was midafternoon, and already the roads of downtown were gearing up for the rush hour drive home. If it weren't for the fact that a moped could slip between cars stopped at intersections, Eme and Rafe wouldn't have made it this far, but Ed and Gun also had that advantage.

"Red light!" yelled Rafe.

Eme leaned forward, beeped the horn, and didn't touch the brakes. Rafe felt her tense once again beneath his hands and closed his eyes as they sped through the intersection. He more than half expected a slam-bang impact, then pain and darkness, but the wind kept blowing in his face, and the moped kept vibrating beneath them. Angry horns followed in their wake, quickly drowned out by more shattering glass and crushed metal.

"Where'd you learn to drive so well?" Rafe hollered as his heart resumed its beat.

"My dad—that chopper—at performance tracks," Eme babbled, clearly shook up. "Wasn't about to let you steer, though—didn't you drive off a bridge into an ocean the last time you drove?"

"The Cyborg..." Rafe caught his tongue and gave his response some thought. "Good point."

The chaos and destruction from behind echoed from the cement underpasses of the highway, and Rafe stopped craning his neck to see what was happening; the pictures in his head were horrific enough. Whatever Ed and Gun had become, they seemed as indestructible as their bike. It was only the constant stream of traffic that slowed them down and kept the Bot Brothers from pouncing on the electric pink moped.

The road curved up and around and through downtown, cutting over a golf course. The squeals of brakes and crunch of wrecked cars faded into the distance.

"There!" Rafe cried as they drew level along the La Brea Tar Pits. "Across the road—duck in quick before they catch up."

Now, well-adjusted to the fierce sound of blaring horns and angry tires squealing under harsh braking, Eme cut across the lanes of traffic, bumped up and over the curb, and steered the pink moped into the parking lot of the fitness club on Wilshire. She gunned the engine a final time and came to a shuddering halt in front of the revolving glass doors. *La Brea Fitness & Swim Center* was written in bold red letters six feet high across the front of the two-story white granite building.

"Drive inside," Rafe urged. "I don't know how many brain cells are left in what's chasing us, but they might still be clever enough to spot this shiny pink moped in the car park and put two and two together."

"Are you serious?"

"The Cyborg would rather be arguing with a pissed-off security guard than an infuriated cybermonster. In you go, Juliet!"

Eme took a deep breath and accelerated onto the sidewalk outside of the gym, startling a few of its patrons, and squeezed into the gap in the revolving door. The tires squeaked against the glass, and they almost didn't fit, but the doors soon spat them into the air-conditioned lobby. A rush of fresh, crisp air and the smell of chlorine fought with the heat of the sun and the sweat coating their faces.

"Excuse me!" a voice cried in outrage from behind the reception desk.

Rafe leaped off the scooter, his legs aching from the bumpy ride. "Hi..." He spied her name badge pinned to a black sports bra. "Janette, is it? Hi, Janette, we'd like a membership."

"I...what? You can't bring that bike in here!"

"Dreadfully sorry, but my name is...," he began.

From outside, the roar of a 2400 cc chopper engine, screeching brakes, and startled screams permeated the outer shell of the fitness club. Feeling the hairs on the back of his neck rise, Rafe spun around to see the nightmare that had chased them all the miles from the hills of Malibu bounding across the parking lot, heading straight for the glass front of the fitness club.

"They're not fooled!" Eme screamed.

"Come on!" Rafe yelled, reaching for Eme's hand and pulling her from the moped. *How the hell did they find us?* "Everyone, *run!*"

Eme's Back Yard
4:26 P.M. PDT

"Duck, Shae! Quick, before they see you!" Bailee called from beneath the branches of a flowering plum tree.

Shae dove under the nearest shrub, a gorgeous pink pearl rhododendron, allowing her racing heart to calm while the helicopter passed beyond the treetops and roofline of the Venture home. "That's the fourth one! What's going on?"

"I'm sure they're covering the fire, but why so many?" Bailee answered as she reemerged from behind a flowering cherry tree and joined Shae who was still on her knees in front of the rhododendron.

"Well, she is the grandmother of a famous movie star, so I guess it makes sense." Shae answered with a shrug.

Bailee and Shae had spent the last few minutes covering the back side of the Venture estate, calling for Eme's pets with no luck. They had worked their way toward the house, checking in, under, and behind every tree, shrub, and flower. Anne's house was now a smoldering pile of ashes, and the news helicopters had converged on the scene like a pack of swarming vultures over the carcass of a long-dead animal, making the girls' search difficult.

"Bogey and Boomer must be terrified of the noise; we're never going to get them to come out of hiding," moaned Bailee.

"We've got to get to the house," replied Shae, "they're probably hunkered down closer to the safety of their home."

Just then two of the helicopters made another pass over the Venture property. The teens hid under the limbs of a giant oak. "How are we going to get there?" asked Shae.

"Back to the hedges!" Bailee grimaced, Shae nodded, and they took off at a run as soon as the last chopper disappeared.

The girls plowed into the seven-foot tall privet hedge. "Ow! Why couldn't they have planted something with less-lethal foliage?" Bailee complained as she pulled her arms and head into her shirt.

Shae laughed at her friend, "Good thinking, Girl! We should have thought of this before," and she followed Bailee's lead. The two "headless and armless" teens worked their way toward the house, calling for Bogey and Boomer as they went.

Once they reached the pool house, their arms and legs reemerged from their protective covering, and they scampered around the corner of the small white stucco building to the rear entrance of the huge garage, and stopped in horror.

"What the...!" Bailee began and automatically reached into her pocket for her phone.

"Wait!" shouted Shae as she approached the smashed door.

"Are you crazy!" Bailee cried as she grabbed her friend by the shirt and tried to pull her away from the opening.

Just then another helicopter made a pass, and the fear of being seen trumped the fear of what was behind the broken door; the two girls threw their fates to the wind and dashed into the garage.

Malibu Fitness Club
4:25 P.M. PDT

Rafe frantically pulled Eme through a pair of white swinging doors, with frosted porthole windows, into a cavernous room full of people. Club members were running on treadmills, lifting weights, using the rowing machines, and stretching against the bars along the walls; no one had a clue that their fitness club was about to undergo unwarranted renovation.

"Gym's closed!" Rafe hollered. "Everyone, get out the back door!"

The whole building shook, and Rafe imagined all the plate glass windows shattering as one out front as Ed and Gun let themselves in. He had to find somewhere to hide—fast. This room was too open; there was too much heavy equipment that the creatures chasing them might easily cast aside or use as weapons.

They ducked through the weight machines, dodging hysterical, sweaty, fleeing bodies and into the changing rooms which, Rafe recalled, led to the Olympic-size swimming pool. Fresh screams arose from the fitness floor behind them when they entered the pool room. The swimmers curiously gazed at the wall, frowning at the muffled chaos emanating from the other side.

Suddenly, heavy crashes and tremendous bangs shook the slippery floor. Ed and Gun were making short work of all the exercise machinery in their way. Rafe skidded and would have ended up in the pool had Eme not yanked him back.

"This was a bad idea," she said. "Plan C, Rafe."

"What's Plan C?" he asked.

"Run! Get the moped back, or a car, or a shuttle into orbit; then we'll wait for the cops or the army to take your monsters down!"

Rafe winced. *My monsters...* "All right, we'll double back to the moped." He pointed to his right. "This way through the showers."

"You really know where you're going?" Eme screeched.

Rafe hollered with authority, "I grew up in these places all over the world; they're basically the same design."

They ran through the showers, and Eme blushed as several naked men blinked at her from under the spray. Not waiting around to discuss modesty, Rafe pulled her past the frosted glass door and into a deserted part of the complex, complete with squash walls and a basketball court.

"Do you hear that?" asked Rafe. "There are screams but no sounds of destruction." He came to a stop in the middle of the court next to a rack of basketballs. "Why aren't things being destroyed?"

Eme took a moment to catch her breath. She put her hands on her knees to stop them from shaking. "Maybe they fell into the pool," she managed with a half-smile and a hint of hope in her blue eyes.

Rafe snorted, "Yeah...come on, we can cut back through here to the moped."

Moving slower now, carefully, Rafe and Eme listened intently for the sounds of pursuit; however, there was nothing but the sound of Dooby Wilhelm's voice blaring from the club's speakers.

"Hollyweird is falling down, so stay right here in your home-town," Dooby sang. "Don't return to the lights of the Hollyweird Strip—take this advice and save the trip."

Rafe felt sure that Ed and Gun had not given up; although the screams had faded, as the fitness club emptied, they were not alone in the gym, not at all. They were still being hunted.

After the horrendously destructive chase through the Malibu Hills, the subtle creeping of Ed and Gun through the fitness club was insidious and heart-stopping. Where were they? Why were they waiting? Rafe felt as if he'd led them both into a trap.

"Well, baby, baby, if you don't heed my warning, I wish you well..."

There were no dead bodies back in the main area of the club, but there was a ton of twisted equipment littering the floor.

A few screams and approaching police sirens from outside permeated the otherwise silent room. Rafe glanced at Eme, weighing their options. The moped was just beyond the swinging white doors across the floor, but where were their pursuers?

"On three," he whispered, "we'll make a run for it. I think they're behind us in the pool area! One, two, thr..."

The mirrored wall with the stretching bars, directly across from Eme and Rafe, exploded in a plume of plaster and shattered glass, and the wicked screech of the two dreadful ex-CIA agents filled the silent gym, drowning out the police bullhorns asking for everyone inside to throw down their weapons and come outside.

Rafe froze as Ed and Gun leaped into the fitness hall, less than two hundred feet away; the bright pink and once shiny moped crumpled in one of their hands. Their eyes met. Once more that alien presence settled on his mind, leaving him terrified. Eme screamed at his side, gripping his arm like a vice. Rafe instinctively took a step in front of her, shielding her from his mistake—a mistake that took dreadful, certain steps toward him, snarling with hate. *My monsters.*

"Even if Hollyweird needs you, baby, don't end up in your own little hell!"

Rafe moved, and Eme moved with him, across the wall and away from the twin fiends that had cut a swath of utter destruction in their hunt. A distant part of Rafe's mind realized that they had been tracked by means other than sight—smell, perhaps, or some alien sense these once human creatures possessed—maybe from their scent left behind on the seat of the scooter.

"Rafe..." Eme whispered.

"Alas, fair Juliet..." Rafe began, but his voice faded to a desperate croak; he was more terrified than he had ever been in his entire life.

Ed and Gun advanced slowly, carefully, knowing they had their prey trapped and dead to rights. Almost mirror images of one another, the two creatures circled the floor, holding their only means of transportation mockingly toward them.

Not that we could outrun them, Rafe thought.

"What do we do?"

The Dooby Wilhelm song had ended, and Simone Garsone's "Rescue Me" filled the silence with crackling sound through a smashed speaker:

"...*life's a broken token on the subway of love, so take my hand and pray...*"

Rafe just shook his head. He was out of options. He felt as if he was falling off the bridge in the middle of a hurricane again—an illustrious beginning to his Bermuda rescue plan—a plan that had led him here, now, about to be gutted in his grandfather's fitness club in downtown L.A.—wearing a blonde wig. That was an absurd, outlandish thought. He began to chuckle.

"I drove right off the damn bridge," he muttered, laughing all the more. Eme looked at him as if he'd gone insane. "*Vroom... splash!*"

"You've lost it!" she squeaked, caught between staring at her babbling friend and the advancing monsters.

"Hell is empty and all the devils are here," Rafe told Eme in a fierce whisper. Then he cried, "Hey, Gun! Fancy a cup of *coffee?*"

The two twisted creatures paused and glanced at each other. They screeched as one and used the crushed moped to batter aside basketball racks and other sports paraphernalia, and in a heartbeat, erased the distance between them and the horrified teens, just as the first canister of tear gas crashed onto the gym floor one hundred feet away.

The Venture Garage
4:29 P.Π. PDT

"That was close!" panted Bailee. She and Shae were crouched behind the customized-by-Netbot roadster, staring out of the doorway, while Toni Malone and Mark Venture peered down at them from twenty movie posters plastered to the walls and ceiling of the cavernous garage.

"Something's not right!" Shae murmured and walked back to the door.

Bailee looked at her incredulously. "What was your first clue, Shae!"

The blonde turned around to face her friend and sneered with her hands on her hips, "OK, I know there's been a break-in, Bailee, but where are the cops? Why didn't the alarm alert them?"

The brunette joined the blonde at the door. "Good question," her friend agreed while Shae walked back through the doorway to the camellia bush outside. She removed the fluttering paper that was still skewered on one of the branches.

"Someone's been here who knows the alarm code," stated Shae. She turned and stared at the remains of the door, "and I'll bet someone else was chasing him or her," she finished, looking at her friend. She waved the paper at Bailee's confusion. "And, the predator or the prey left this as a clue. It's an email address written on GG Anne's stationery."

Comprehension dawned on Bailee's face and she sucked in her breath. "I can see why you want to major in criminology, Shae, you're quick!" she nudged the blonde's shoulder. "You're probably wrong, but it sure makes a good story...so when you wash out as a detective, you can become a mystery writer!" she smirked at Shae who was busy studying the paper and not listening to Bailee's babbling. The brunette just shrugged and, once again, removed her phone from the ripped pocket of her jeans...

The Malibu Fitness Club
4:29 P.M. PDT

Rafe's laughter caught in his throat as a wave of fiercely rancid air washed over him from the skeletal creatures that stood stock still ten feet in front of them. He stared at the hideous boils oozing green slime down their grotesque faces, saw them about to tear his throat out with their skeletal long hands, and acted purely on instinct—he stuck out his tongue, blew raspberries, and yanked Eme to the right toward the now vacant swimming pool area. Startled, the two former human agents of the CIA howled together with raw anger and bounded after them.

They were barely through the door when the two terrified teens launched themselves through the air and into the deep end of the warm Olympic-size pool. Rafe blew out all the air in his lungs, grabbed Eme's hand, keeping them both underwater, and watched to see if the Netbots would follow. It took a second for the goons to make their move; with bloodcurdling screams, they dive-bombed the wide-eyed teens who barely managed to avoid their monstrous bodies. The tidal wave caused by the monsters' cannonballs propelled the teens far from their pursuers. Rafe was convinced that once they'd regained the surface, he and Eme had set a new freestyle record to the shallow end. Neither of them could believe that they weren't bloody pulps at the bottom of the pool.

Scrambling out of the water, they expected to be grabbed from behind at any second, but only loud gurgling and sputtering ensued. The teens turned slowly, mouths open, to see the creatures flailing their arms; the dark orbs that were once two pairs of brown eyes were now wide and fearful.

Eme recovered first and smirked. "What's the matter boys, Mommy and Daddy wouldn't pay for swimming lessons?" jeered the delighted teen. She roared with laughter at the two floundering buffoons while Rafe raced to the wall and grabbed a life preserver. A horror-struck Eme screamed, "No, Rafe, are you crazy?"

"Ahhh...phh...phhh!" spluttered the thrashing thugs, casting what looked like hopeful eyes toward their potential savior.

"Ohhh...so sorry, boys," taunted Rafe, holding up and pointing at the life preserver. "You didn't think this little beauty was for *you*, now, did you?" He kissed and caressed the white Styrofoam buoy, batting his eyes at the struggling agents. "It's the Cyborg's only souvenir of this lovely pool party, because, more's the shame, I have forgotten my camera—again." He snapped his fingers. "Sorry to leave all the fun, but we've..." Rafe didn't have a chance to finish his parting soliloquy, because Eme had grabbed his soaking wet shirt and was pulling him toward the exit like a frightened mule. The boy, the girl, and the life preserver exited the room without a backward glance—into the tear gas–filled lobby.

A fresh wave of screams emanated from the pool room as Rafe and Eme covered their mouths and noses and, with tears streaming through half-closed eyes, they ran. They only stopped to breathe when they were behind the doors of the lounge at the end of the hall.

After a few seconds, Rafe wiped his eyes, straightened, and declared with fist raised high, "It's off to Switzerland, my fair maid—follow me!"

Eme also wiped her eyes then curtsied. "Lead on, my handsome prince; after that awesome display of quick thinking, I'd follow you anywhere!"

Rafe, wet blonde wig hanging sideways off his head, turned around for a second to smirk at the redhead in the dripping brunette wig. They sprinted to the juice bar, where Rafe grabbed a crystal goblet, before leading the way up the wooden stairs.

The door of the main office was wide-open, obviously left that way by the hasty retreat of the manager and staff. Rafe could hear police swarming in the parking lot, with still more sirens approaching the party, and knew they had little time; in fact, the current bullhorn message was giving them just one more minute to "Exit the building, hands raised!"

He pulled his computer bag from his jeans, unclipped the flash drive, and entered the protocol on the office computer; he then set the self-destruct mechanism timer that would destroy the program and all video records from surveillance cameras. Finally, he deployed and rearranged the laser scanner and juice goblet.

"My fair maiden will do the honors of preceding the Cyborg, once more, into the breach and beyond." Eme did as she was instructed and sat cross-legged on the edge of the desk while Rafe adjusted the scanner beam. With a lingering kiss on her lips, then a click of the computer, the scanner flashed, and Eme dissolved into smiling frosty mist and disappeared.

With a sigh of relief that at least he had succeeded in sending Eme safely to their friends and relatives, Rafe peeked out of the office door, wondering if the impossible monsters that had emerged from the depths of cyberspace were still treading water; he couldn't hear screaming amid the sirens. Was it possible—had they drowned? *What a pity.* He wondered if the virus was responsible for their inability to swim; surely they had to have acquired this skill as part of their federal agent training. *If they're still alive and the police get to them before they drown or make their escape...*

However, Rafe believed he had not seen the last of Ed and Gun; for the first time in his life, he was overwhelmed by regret and all-consuming guilt. The guilt, like a lead vest, festered and settled over Rafe's shoulders. People would be hurt, and possibly die, because of his virus program. He'd made a momentous, horrifying mistake.

He wiped their prints from the goblet and computer, and looked down to blink away tears as he made a stab at the send button with a long rubber-tipped wooden pointer he had found hanging from the white board. The bullhorn outside counted down the last seconds as music warbled from the cracked speakers of his grandfather's fitness club: The Harley Five's farewell serenade, "Windows of Pain."

"The window shatters from the force of my love…"

The police stormed through what was left of the fitness club entrance.

"Can you see the light fall? All around—there is no sound—except the echo of my call."

Gunshots rang throughout the downstairs.

"Why do you weep, my child? Why weep—if not for youth; don't you know, you've no hope—you cannot flee the truth?"

A frosty mist coated the holoport of the office computer.

"There's nothing left but truth."

CHAPTER TWENTY-THREE
REUNIONS AND REVELATIONS

The Venture Garage
4:35 P.M. PDT

"Now do you understand?" Shae asked after stopping her friend from calling 911, again, by outlining her theory of the break-in.

"OK, for now, but you do know how many laws we're breaking, Sherlock. Plus, GG Anne or one of Eme's family members might be in trouble," Bailee answered.

"Look, Eme and her family aren't even in the country, but maybe they sent someone to get something from the house. I don't know, but stick with me, Watson. Let's snoop around a bit first before we call it in. I also need to figure out the location of this e-mail address and find out why it's on GG's stationery. I'm not sure, but I'll bet it's a Chinese e-mail address—see, it has a CH suffix."

Another helicopter pass chased them inside once again. Bailee looked around for any signs of Boomer or Bogey, while Shae switched on all the lights. Suddenly, Shae yelped when she noticed the green slime on the nearly destroyed antique roadster. "Hey, this is the same stuff that's on the door," she commented while removing some of the substance with her shirt.

"Yuck! Why did you do that, Shae? Use a rag!" Bailee commented with a wrinkled nose.

"What do you think this is now!" the blonde responded, indicating her shirt.

"Yes, but you're still wearing it."

"Right!" Shae responded with a smirk, "That way I won't lose the evidence!"

Bailee just shook her head and muttered something about blondes under her breath.

The girls continued to call for Boomer and Bogey as they searched the rear of the garage for anything that looked out of place, when Bailee spotted a costume box on a wooden shelf, and rushed forward. "Look, Shae, Eme's mom would never let anyone mess up her prop boxes!" She pointed to the carelessly replaced lid of the box labeled 'WIGS' with a blonde extension snagged on its torn corner.

Shae joined her. "I don't know; Eme told me that these are old props her mom had given her for dress up when she was around six or seven; she really hoped that Eme would get interested in acting. Ha, as if!" Both girls chuckled at that.

"Yes, but why would anyone get into these boxes and leave them this way...Eme wouldn't have thought to take a wig to Switzerland at the last minute, would she, unless she wanted a disguise!" Bailee conjectured.

Shae was pensive, as she searched through the box, but then shrugged, "No, that's not her style. And she showed us the dark glasses her parents were making her wear on the flight. Plus, we helped her pack, and there's no green slime anywhere near here. I think we need to keep looking."

They continued their search and finally made it to the front of the garage, then stopped when they rounded the corner of a monster red dune buggy. They gawked and rushed to Maud's empty parking spot.

"This makes no sense! Who could have, would have, taken it?" asked Shae, circling the empty space.

"Maybe her mom packed it for her!" Bailee offered with a smirk. They both giggled at the memory of Eme's mom trying to figure out how to pack skis for Eme, and then Shae frowned. "Wait! Where's the chopper?" She jumped back from the space reserved for Mark's motorcycle. "It was parked right here, next to the scooter!"

Bailee's eyes widened in comprehension then she barked, "Now, we call the cops!" She reached in her pocket, again, but Shae grabbed her hand. Bailee gave her a sharp look. "Shae, we're really messing up a crime scene, here!"

"We need to wait...give it a few more hours," she cajoled, "and if we haven't figured out this e-mail and put the other clues together, we call the cops." Bailee looked dubious, so Shae continued, "Who's going to know? The gardener and cleaning lady won't be here until Eme's folks come home, and they're not due back for another day or two, so quit worrying. I really think Eme's disappearance, this mess, and GG's house burning down are all related somehow. Let's go home and see if there are any news bulletins from Bermuda."

Bailee frowned and sat down on the chrome bumper of a 1934 yellow convertible, "How do we get out of here without being spotted, Sherlock?"

"Oh, that's a good point, Watson!" Shae responded as she joined her on the bumper.

"And, it's dinner time; our moms don't know where we are," added Bailee.

Shae brightened and turned to her friend, "You call your mom and tell her you're having dinner with me, and I'll do the same." At Bailee's frown, she continued, "It's not a lie; we're together."

"Yeah, but what about the dinner part?" Bailee whined as she stood to face Shae.

Shae smirked. "I'll bet there's still some carrot cake left from Eme's party!" She wagged her eyebrows.

"Ha, I'll bet GG Anne took it home, since they were going to be gone!" the brunette retorted.

"Ha, yourself, I saw how Eme's dad was enjoying it the other night," Shae countered as she stood next to the brunette, "and I'll further bet that he didn't let one single piece of it leave this house—it's probably in the freezer!" Shae turned and headed for the door that led into the house, turning back with a smug grin.

Bailee looked skeptical, but shrugged at her friend's confident, smiling face, and followed her into the house, grimacing at the memory of the extra miles she'd had to jog the morning after her last visit with the delicious carrot cake.

The Swiss Inn
Sunday, June 14, 2015
1:35 A.M. CEST/4:35 P.M. PDT

After many pots of tea and platters of homemade scones and jam, the events of the previous days were relayed to their incredulous hosts. Anne and No took turns comforting Kala when Bogey, Rafe, or Eme were mentioned. Needless to say, by the end of the story, her eyes were red and swollen. Helga led the distraught girl to a bathroom to wash her face. When they returned to the living room, several minutes later, Kala, still sniffling, had a terrycloth ice bag pressed to her eyes.

Bill rose when they entered the room. "Helga, I'm so sorry to inconvenience you this way, but as you can see, we're really in trouble and have nowhere else to go," he apologized.

"Nonsense, Bill, you know you're always welcome here." She answered with a kind smile and took a seat next to Kala and No on the overstuffed green and yellow chintz sofa.

"I've never heard a tale quite like the one you've just spun. Traveling by e-mail! Simply amazing! Sure beats waiting in security lines at the airport!" continued Franz from the green wing-back chair, shaking his head.

"I miss the peanuts!" snorted No.

"Bogey…" *Sniff* "lov…loved peanuts." And Kala was sobbing on his shoulder again.

Anne sat down next to the teen and rubbed her back. "Oh, my dear, we don't know that anything bad has happened to him," she murmured. Boomer barked at their feet. Anne laughed and straightened so that the dog could jump onto Kala's lap, which he did then licked the tears from her face.

The girl's sobbing continued unabated in the silent room for the next few minutes, only to be interrupted by a chirping noise from the computer.

No jumped up and screamed, "They're here!" The mad scramble that ensued to reach the computer sent Boomer, Bill and Anne to the floor in a tangle of arms, legs—and tail.

"This is getting to be a habit!" Anne blushed.

"I'm not complaining!" countered Bill with a lopsided smile, making Anne's blush deepen.

"Woof!" intoned Boomer, and he licked each of them in the face as they laughed and ruffled his ears.

Franz and Helga stopped to help them up; however, No and Kala nearly burst with glee as they hugged each other in front of the computer. Several seconds later, the little bluebird e-lert disappeared into the holoport and Eme emerged, dripping wet and shivering. By the time she got her bearings, Rafe had joined her, and Boomer was running around them, yipping for her attention.

It was all No and Kala could do not to tackle the newcomers before they completely materialized and were steadfast on the floor.

"Eme!" screamed Kala. She seized the disoriented, dripping girl in a bone-crushing hug. "What..."

"N...not n...ow, Kala. I'll explain after a sh...shower," Eme chattered as she bent to pet her anxious dog. Kala could only nod in understanding before a screech came from behind her.

"Cease and desist!" warned Rafe to a giddy No. He grinned and stretched his arms toward the soaked cyberwhiz.

"Aw, not even for old time's sake?" whined No with a crooked smile. "You can thank your lucky stars that everything I wish for will never come true!" And he wagged his eyebrows at the Cyborg.

The adults were now gathered around the new arrivals, laughing at the disgusted look on Rafe's face and the water dripping from his clothes and long black hair.

Finally, Anne rushed forward but stopped short of embracing either of them. She was joined by Bill and Tim, and the seven of them converged in a group around the new arrivals, accompanied by Boomer's yips. Franz stood off to the side, grinning at the reunion, while Helga made a mad dash to the kitchen for more tea, scones, and some towels. By the time she returned, Kala and Eme were in tears, as No retold the story of the missing Bogey.

"Kala, it...it wasn't your fault; I know he...he'll show up," Eme gasped as Anne hugged the distraught blonde." Rafe held Eme, No patted her back.

Not wanting to interrupt the tableau, the other adults stood off to the side and watched in silence.

Finally Eme broke away and asked to the room at large, "M...may we please get dried off b...before we explain wh... what happened after you left?"

Helga stepped forward with the towels and wrapped them around the shivering teens. "Of, course, Rafe and...Eme, is it...I'm Helga. Follow me and we'll see if some of my and Franz's clothes will fit you."

"Thank you ever so much, H...Helga."

"The lovely Helga is always most gracious," Rafe added and winked to the amusement of their hostess, who patted him affectionately on the cheek.

With a quick wave to their friends and relatives, Eme and Rafe disappeared down the hallway to well-deserved hot showers.

After breathing a sigh of relief, Tim approached Bill who had found a place on the sofa next to Anne. "I've been meaning to ask you, Bill; I'd like to retrieve my wife and children. Do you think Franz and Helga would play host to three more people?"

Before Bill could answer, Franz interrupted from the doorway, "You have a family somewhere in hiding?"

"Yes, I do. I needed to get them away from Ed and Gun before they were kidnapped or worse. I moved them into the safe room at our home, and out of harm's way, before I was taken to Bermuda. They're probably scared to death; they haven't heard from me in days."

"Please, Mr. Tim, go...go bring them here. They will be happy to be reunited with you."

Tim grinned and nodded at the smiling adults. "I'll go right now." He moved quickly toward Rafe's bag and retrieved Persephone.

No scrambled to the china hutch in the dining room and returned with a crystal goblet, while Bill brought a stool from the kitchen. Once Tim had the coordinates set, it was barely a minute before he was a frosty mist on Persephone's holoport.

"Amazing! Simply amazing!" was all the wide-eyed Swiss man could say.

It was several seconds before anyone could tear their eyes away from the empty stool.

"Well, now, I must make some preparations for so many guests," Franz said, clapping his hands like a kid expecting a new toy. "This house will soon be filled with much happy noise!" He turned toward the hallway, Anne and Kala following close behind.

Before he disappeared, Bill called after him, "We need more food, too, Franz. I'll go to the market at first light."

"No, Mr. Bill, you should stay out of sight," replied the older man, turning back toward the living room. "I'll go to the market tomorrow. Hans knows me and won't ask questions when I tell him that we have guests." Bill sat thoughtfully for a moment, and then nodded his agreement. "For now, how about whipping up one of your healthy breakfasts? We have all the ingredients in stock, and I will make a list of the supplies we'll need. I also noticed that not one of you has extra clothes."

"Now that's going to be a problem for the teens. I still have some of Amy's and my things in storage. But, we can discuss that over breakfast." Bill headed for the kitchen, while Franz led Kala and No to the bedrooms. Once Franz had handed them off to Helga who was exiting Eme's room, he turned and ambled down the hall to join Bill in the kitchen.

"Kala can share this room with Eme, yes?" Helga asked, holding the door open to the girl. Kala nodded. "You'll find some clothes on the bed, dear." She gave Kala a hug as the girl passed her on the threshold.

Kala smiled through her tears and kissed Helga on the cheek. "I'm s...so sorry to be such a bugger of a house guest, Helga," she sniffed. Th...thank you so much for being so very kind. You remind me of my...my grandmother." And she broke down crying again as she quietly closed the door behind her.

No and Helga stared at the closed door for a few seconds, and then Helga shook her head sadly and opened the door across the hall for No.

"You can share this room with Rafe, No, yes?" she asked with a small smile.

No stuck his head through the doorway and heard the shower running. He turned back to his hostess with a smile. "Thanks, Helga, this is great."

Helga patted him on the arm before returning to the kitchen.

Nice room, No thought as he made his way toward the twin bed next to the left wall. He looked around the light and airy wallpapered room and decided to get a bit of fresh air. He walked to the window seat where he sat on the soft yellow and green chintz cushion and opened the multi-paned window. Breathing in the unfamiliar scent of the pine trees and squinting into the dark, cool night, the cold reality of their situation hit him: they were in Switzerland and on the run from the government— the *US* government. *I wish I could call my parents. Ha, my dad is probably playing holy hell with my mother for 'losing' me.* He grinned at the thought of how that interaction might have gone down. *If anyone had told me last week...*

After several minutes of contemplation, he shook his head to clear these thoughts and turned away from the window to check out the clothes Helga had left for him. *The jeans are a little short, but adequate for now...* He stopped in mid thought and cocked his head. *Wait, why is Rafe taking so long in the shower?* He tossed the pants on the bed and headed for the bathroom. Peeking around the corner, he almost laughed out loud at the sight before him; there sitting on the shower seat, under a heavy stream of steaming water, was Rafe—sound asleep. *Poor guy was up all night; I'm surprised he didn't fall asleep somewhere in Cyberspace.* His first impulse was to turn off the hot water and shock him awake...*but even I can't be that cruel.* Several seconds of thought later...*Who am I kidding?* And he acted on that first impulse with the expected result.

Thankfully, Rafe's screams weren't heard by any of the adults, but they did bring Eme and Kala on the run from across the hall; the girls were through the door and into the bathroom before Rafe had a chance to turn off the water. No had the decency to hold up a towel just in time to spare his friend any further embarrassment.

"Mean people rule!" he laughed.

Rafe shivered, turned a murderous glare on No, and reached through the shower door to grab the towel, wrapping it around his waist. Eme and Kala looked from one face, red with anger, to the other, red with triumph, clearly puzzled by the scene.

"Be careful whose toes you step on today, No..." Rafe seethed through gritted teeth as he stepped out of the shower and bumped No's shoulder, "...because they might be connected to the foot that kicks your ass tomorrow," he finished while he stalked past the girls and into the bedroom.

"Oh, get over it, Shakespeare, enjoy life; there's plenty of time to be dead, and the way we're headed, and with the enemies we're collecting..." No shot back, clearly enjoying his moment.

"Is this a kids' party, or do we need lethal weapons to play?" Eme smirked, finally catching on to what prompted the animosity between the two boys. She nudged the open-mouthed Kala and pointed to the shower faucets.

"Oh...I see." She turned to face No with a scowl. "Are you always this nasty, No, or are you just making a special effort today," sneered Kala while Eme left to join Rafe who had just pulled on a pair of jeans. She sat on his bed and watched him as he sat down beside her and buttoned a blue plaid shirt.

Kala and No continued their bickering while Eme tried rubbing some warmth into Rafe's freezing cold hands. "How did he manage to turn off the hot water without getting caught—I assume that's what happened?" she asked.

Rafe gave her a lopsided smile and shivered even harder, but not from the effects of the cold dousing he'd just received. He gazed silently at the girl sitting next to him, the girl he had rescued, the first girl to ever have his heart. Eme's heart fluttered while he searched her face for a clue as to his next move. Her smile faltered, they both gasped. His hand flew to her damp curls while her hand reached out to his sopping wet hair. "Eme, what has happened to your hair?"

"Mine? I was just about to ask you the same ques..."

They jumped from the bed and ran to the bathroom mirror, interrupting No and Kala's squabble and nearly knocking them into the bathtub.

"What the bloody...?"

"Honk next time, will ya!"

Eme and Rafe ignored the grumbling behind them and focused on their reflections. "You're right, Rafe...it's shorter." She glanced at Rafe's reflection while he examined the length of his own hair.

"The Cyborg has lost at least two inches? What cruel villainy is this!" he exclaimed, running his fingers through his wet black hair.

Kala and No recovered their equilibrium and approached the mirror, looking first at the object of their distress, and then checking their own hair. "Nothing seems different with my hair, but you both seem to have lost some length in yours," remarked Kala. "However...hmmm, I do seem to have lost a few more pounds," she added, turning slowly as she checked all sides of her body in the mirror.

Meanwhile, No was standing next to Rafe, examining his hair and body. "Nothing's changed on this handsome head!" And then he gasped, "What the..." while staring at his friend's reflection. "I'm not much taller than Rafe! I was at least two inches taller before—what's going on?

No one spoke while they continued to stare in confusion at each other's reflections in the mirror.

Suddenly, Rafe announced what was on all their minds: "Cyberspace."

"We've lost our wigs, too, Rafe," Eme directed to the brunet. "Long story," she added at No's questioning stare.

"Bugger this, I want to go home!" moaned Kala with tears in her eyes; she fled from the room, leaving the others to look after her in understanding.

"What are we going to do?" Eme asked the boys with wide eyes.

"What's done is done, we'll just tell Tim and my grandfather; they should have some idea about what we've discovered," Rafe responded checking his reflection again.

"What if this isn't permanent?" No asked as he stood on tiptoes, continuing to measure his height against Rafe's in the mirror.

Eme looked thoughtful, but Rafe looked horrified. "The Cyborg is slipping!" He stepped away from the mirror. "Mr. Negative may have a point..."

No also turned from the mirror, clamped a hand down on Rafe's shoulder, and smirked. "Yep, I'm not just another handsome dude; I'm multi-talented: I can think and piss you off at the same time."

Eme chuckled at his comment, but Rafe wasn't paying attention; he paced in front of his two friends and continued with his interrupted sentence: "...which begs the question: can a computer virus in a human be reversed?"

No and Eme stopped smiling. "What's that got to do with our missing body parts?" asked No as

Eme returned to the mirror to inspect her reflection more carefully.

She turned back to her friends, "We didn't contract a virus in Cyberspace, did we?"

Rafe faced them, shook his head slowly, and answered with a shudder, "If they didn't drown, it means that we may not have seen the last of the Bot Brothers."

The implications of his comment left No and Eme wide-eyed and speechless.

Meanwhile, in the kitchen, Franz was completing his inventory of the pantry, and Bill had put the finishing touches on his famous egg white omelets with mozzarella and salsa. He sat on the island stool and watched Franz finish his grocery list. "We can't get all the supplies in town, Franz, but maybe a quick trip to..."

"Australia?"

Eme's House
6:35 P.M. PDT/3:35 P.M. CEST

"Stop sniveling, Bailee, that wasn't Eme, period! Besides, no bodies have been found."

"But...but we don't know that *wasn't* Eme on the scooter! Who else could have taken it?"

Shae sighed and continued searching for the latest news stories. "Listen to this report from the KMALA reporter."

"...aliens, is my guess, since all the surveillance cameras along this route, checked so far, have experienced interference before and after they passed."

"Aliens? Ridiculous!" Bailee huffed and wiped her tears.

"I don't know, Bailee, all the other clues fit, and look at this slime!" Shae pointed to her shirt.

Bailee crossed her arms and sneered, "I've been looking at it for the past two hours. But it doesn't mean aliens left it!"

The girls had spent nearly two hours poring over all the latest bulletins of the Malibu chase. The Venture's kitchen table was covered with plates of leftovers from Eme's party: carrot cake, chips and dip, and bottles of soda, all but forgotten once the news of the horrific events had been uncovered on their phones.

Several sheets of paper from Eme's printer were also scattered on the table, filled with notes and charts of information they had gleaned from the various news bulletins and from clues they'd discovered in the garage.

They were certain that the two people on the scooter were wearing wigs. They didn't agree on what kind of creatures had taken the motorcycle, but they were positive they had left the green slime, because they had found more of it on the floor where the chopper had been parked.

Both girls had been positive that the moped riders knew the security code, but now, since they'd learned the creatures had disrupted the surveillance cameras, they thought that maybe they had the capability to cancel alarm systems, which was Shae's final clue that they were from another planet.

No one had yet reported the identity of the moped's owner; only that neither vehicle had a license. The girls' further investigation of the garage had uncovered Eme's temporary permit, along with the moped's bow, behind the box of wigs. They had this evidence stuffed in their pockets, just in case, although neither of them thought it would make any difference in an investigation. And, they had learned that the email address Shae thought was from China was actually located in Switzerland.

"This makes sense, Bailee. We know it's not the school's address, from what we read on their website, but it may be a private address of the principal or an instructor that GG Anne had written down on the paper, and had somehow got stuck on that bush," reasoned Shae. "The main thing we have to remember is that Eme is not in this country, so she's still out there, somewhere in Bermuda, and I'll bet she's with GG Anne."

Bailee was quiet for a moment, smiled weakly at her friend, and then yawned and stretched. "You're probably right, Sherlock, so we'd better clean up and get home. It's dark enough; besides, all the fire investigators and helicopters have cleared out."

"Good idea. I want to do some more research on my computer about Switzerland before I send this email. Plus, we have to get out of here before the cops figure out that the moped belongs to Eme."

"Yeah, it would be just like Cynthia to call them to put in her two cents worth about Eme getting one just like it for her birthday." Shae smirked and nodded her agreement.

"I wonder if we should get our parents involved," Bailee remarked.

Shae stopped and stared at her friend. "Are you mad! We'd be in so much trouble for what we've been doing without telling them. We're in this alone, Watson!" She patted her friend on the back. Bailee looked sick at that, but shrugged and gave her friend a lopsided grin.

They cleaned up their mess and were headed for the front door, when the wail of sirens could be heard coming up the Venture drive. "They're here!" the girls chorused.

They changed direction, doused the lights, slipped into the garage, and then flew past the shattered door into the cool Malibu evening. By the time they cleared the garden gate, they heard more sirens approaching the cul-de-sac. The girls ran past the yellow tape surrounding the ruins of Anne's house, squeezed through Mrs. Bloom's fence, and scampered through her side yard, reemerging on her driveway just as the last police car pulled in front of Anne Malone's property.

Their fear of being made suspects outweighed their desire to watch the investigation. Once the officers exited their cars and walked to the rear of the property, Shaelyn McBain and Bailee Sue Gardner intended to beat a hasty retreat toward home, until a familiar male voice called their names, stopping them dead in their tracks.

The Swiss Inn
3:35 A.M. CEST/ 6:35 P.M. PDT

Neither man had noticed Kala enter the kitchen. She stood quietly, tears still glistening in her brown eyes.

"I'm sorry to intrude, but with everything that has happened… I miss my home." Tears spilled down her cheeks. She covered her face with her hands and began to sob. Bill rushed to her and wrapped his arms around her shoulders. After a few seconds he pulled away and searched her tear-stained face.

"Kala, you're from what part of Australia? I have a fitness club in Perth."

Kala wiped her eyes, blinked at the man, and managed a smile, "I…I know, that's why I thought that…that maybe…"

Surprised, he asked, "You know about my club?" She nodded. "Hmmm, that's not a bad idea. Where are you from, exactly?"

Before Kala could answer, No, Rafe, and Eme burst through the doorway, looking much more presentable in clean clothes and freshly shampooed hair. "Grandfather, our hair…" Rafe began, stopping short when they noticed the serious conversation taking place between Kala and his grandfather. No elbowed him in the ribs, and Rafe swallowed the rest of his report.

Kala smiled faintly at her friends' interruption; then she continued with hope in her eyes, "Geraldton—it's just north of Perth. My aunt's a nurse in a hospital there. But I was born in Sydney. When my parents died two years ago, I was taken in by my aunt and uncle in Perth. They were regulars at your club." She lowered her head. "Until they divorced, and my aunt moved north to live near my grandparents."

Bill paused to think about this new revelation while Franz continued to set the table.

"So your uncle still lives in Perth?" Kala nodded. "How is your relationship with your uncle?"

Startled by the question, Kala blinked rapidly at the man and shrugged. "Fine, I guess, why?"

Bill thought a second and asked, "Is he trustworthy? Does he have your best interests at heart?"

Surprised at the question, she answered, "Well, he's a minister at the Unitarian church and lives with a minister from the Salvation Army." She lowered her head again. "They met at your fitness club," she finished in a whisper.

After a few seconds, Bill broke into peals of laughter, which brought everyone else on the run. Eme, No, and Rafe were startled by the outburst, and Kala jerked up her head and stared at the man as if he'd lost his mind.

"I apologize, Kala," he hugged her again. "I'm not laughing at you, just that you may have solved a very sticky problem for all of us!" He turned to all of the surprised members of the house who were now standing in the kitchen. "We need to have a family meeting. Please follow me." He closed the door on the warming oven full of their breakfast and turned toward the living room with an extremely curious and enthusiastic group in tow.

Eme walked at Kala's side. "Did he call us family?" she whispered.

"Does this make you my brother, Rafe?" asked No with a smirk, smacking Rafe on the back.

"Better that than the alternative, Mr. Negative!" Rafe answered followed by a swift punch to No's shoulder.

"And what do you mean by that?" asked Eme, walking behind the boys.

"Ignore their stupid insinuations, Eme," responded Kala with a frown.

The last of the "teenage family" had just settled on the sofa when...

"Chirp, chirp, chirp!"

Startled, and alarmed, Bill jumped up from the settee, grabbed Franz's rifle from the corner of the living room, and sprinted to the computer, yelling, "Everyone, run—it's too soon for Tim to return!"

The teenagers ducked behind the sofa while the adults stood stock-still, too shocked to move. They all watched in horrified fascination as a frosty mist drifted from the holoport and reassembled on the desk.

St. Bruno's Academy
3:38 A.M. CEST

Chaos reigned in the basement of the old manor house. Computer workstations occupied most of the floor space. Servants and men in combat uniforms scurried in and out of the many rooms that opened off the enormous main room, carrying suitcases...and weapons. On a tall wooden stool, in a dark corner, sat a young woman, alone and weeping.

"Not that, you imbecile," growled a tall blond man in his thirties. "Pack lightweight guns; we have enough grenades and putty. Remember, we must travel nearly two thousand miles on one tank of gas."

Without a word, the smaller and younger man with short, curly brown hair complied and restocked the massive gun wall with the newly manufactured ARX59. Turning on his heel, he returned to the small arms cases across the room, sneering as he selected several semi-automatic *mouse guns*. "What kind of a war is waged without *real* weapons?" he sneered, and jammed the guns and ammunition into his green bag.

The distraught brunette woman dried her eyes and joined the tall man in the glassed-in office. She threw her arms around his neck and nuzzled his shoulder while he massaged her back and kissed the top of her head.

"Don't worry, my darling, we'll take care of everything and return in time for the funeral."

"Be careful," she whispered.

He turned and joined the others as they carried their baggage up the stairs and out of sight, leaving the woman, distressed and alone, in the gigantic underground room.

Minutes later a helicopter, emblazoned with the CIA insignia and registration ID, rose from the grounds of the academy and soared over a beautiful and brightly lit inn, nestled in the hills of the Brienz Mountains, on the first leg of its long journey.

The Swiss Inn
3:45 A.M. CEST

"Toto, we're not in Kansas anymore!" A familiar squawk emanated from the materialized form of a familiar bird.

"*Bogey!*" several voices shouted at once, and the teens rushed to the computer. Bill stowed the rifle and wiped the perspiration from his forehead with an audible "Whew!"

Kala knelt, crying in front of the groggy bird. "I'm so sorry...B...Bogey, I thought we...we'd lost you." No was there by her side once again, hugging her and grinning like a madman at the bird while Boomer barked, chased his tail, then jumped up on the computer chair, panting.

Eme's eyes glistened with tears of relief; she knelt beside Kala, smiled and tried to smooth the bird's ruffled feathers. "Bogey, where have you been?" she cooed at him through her tears. "We were so worried about you."

"Where's the rest of me?" he answered. Then he shook his feathers and flew away from his welcoming committee to perch on the lower ledge of the framed dining room mirror; he shook his body and fanned his tail feathers, squawking at his reflection.

Concerned, Bill and Anne, followed by the teens, cautiously approached the distraught bird.

"There, there, Bogey, you're all there; nothing's missing," whispered Anne. "You're safe now." She held out her hand and coaxed him onto her shoulder. He continued to ruffle his feathers and squawk, "Where's the rest of me? Where's the rest of me?"

Anne gently placed him on her shoulder and walked slowly to the sofa, where Eme and Kala stroked his trembling body. Helga brought some water in a small dish and offered it to the frightened bird. Slowly Bogey staggered down Anne's arm toward the dish, keeping a wary eye on the strange woman. After taking several seconds to decide it was safe, he gulped the cool water as if he'd been stranded for weeks in the desert. Audible sighs from the concerned crowd startled him and, once again, he flew erratically to the mirror, repeating his mantra, "Where's the rest of me?"

Bill stopped Anne from rushing to him. "Let him be for a moment, Anne. He's probably terrified from the trip through cyberspace. He needs to realize that he's safe now and among people who love him." Just then, Kala and Eme returned to the living room with a bowl full of peanuts.

"This'll bring him around," said Eme, and the two girls tiptoed toward the colorful macaw. Suddenly Eme gasped and rushed the rest of the way to the mirror. Carefully she grasped the excited bird between her two hands and brought him back into the living room.

"GG, he's right; look at his tail feathers!"

While Bogey squawked in alarm, Anne examined the bird's disheveled feathers. "Oh, my, his tail and wing feathers—they're not as full as they should be!"

The four teens looked from one to another and nodded in understanding.

Bogey started to calm down as Anne continued to examine his body. "It's a hard world for little things!" he squawked. Anne placed him on the arm of the sofa.

The girls slowly approached him. "Poor Bogey! They'll grow back, don't you worry," Kala cooed, smoothing his feathers. "Have a peanut. Protein's good for repairing your body's cells." She opened her handful of peanuts. Bogey looked at her with a gimlet eye and grabbed one of the offered nuts.

"Kiss my hot lips!" he squawked at Kala, spraying peanut fragments in her face.

"You don't have lips, Bogey!" Kala chuckled, brushing away the peanut fragments.

Afraid to laugh out loud for fear of frightening him again, several hands covered several mouths, keeping the hysteria in check.

Bogey continued to eat his peanuts and make kissing noises at Kala, keeping everyone thoroughly amused, until Bill appeared in the doorway and called them to eat.

"Please, everyone just eat, and save the stories of Ed, Gun, and Cyberspace so that we can digest our food."

No one argued with Bill's edict. They filed into the kitchen, Bogey now clinging to Kala's shoulder, and they thoroughly enjoyed the meal while discussing the history of the Swiss province.

After a pleasant break from the chaos that had been their lives the previous few days, they returned to the living room where Rafe accessed the computer, anxious for news of their close call with Ed and Gun.

"All's well that ends well!" he stated to the screen. He turned to face the room. "Hopefully, the Neanderthals' fates are sealed in the tar pits, along with California's dinosaurs."

Once again the occupants of the chalet rushed to the computer, this time to watch a helicopter newscast of the events that had delayed Eme and Rafe's arrival in Switzerland. Stunned silence from the group greeted the horrific scene unfolding before them as the beleaguered reporter explained the terrifying events on the ground through a split screen—live feed and video footage.

Video Date and Time stamped:
June 13, 2015; 4:29 p.m. PDT

"No, folks, our calls to the police and other agencies have confirmed that this is not a movie. We haven't any idea who or what these things are in the video shot earlier—aliens is my guess as all the surveillance cameras along this route, checked so far, have experienced interference before and after they passed. Our videos shot high above the scene are the only known visual record of the creatures and their prey. Law enforcement is asking anyone with photos or videos of the chase to please call them with their information. What I know for certain is that these two creatures wreaked havoc down Highway 101 from Malibu to the La Brea Tar Pits on an unlicensed metallic green chopper."

The live cameras scanned the highway that was still littered with wrecked cars, trucks, and emergency vehicles. It then panned up to Wilshire Boulevard and zoomed in on a shattered two story building. "The La Brea Fitness Club and Spa, along with Mrs. Anne Malone's house in Malibu, were the only buildings, we know of, that the creatures entered and damaged. Sadly, the fitness club surveillance records were also destroyed, and the home of Mrs. Malone, as you can see, has been demolished." The cameras focused solely on the live shot of a smoldering pile of ash that was swarming with firefighters and surrounded by curious neighbors standing outside of the yellow tape perimeter.

Eme had her arm around her shocked, but amazingly dry-eyed, great-grandmother. "We can only hope that detectives can unravel clues from the eyewitnesses who were in the club when the creatures entered, chasing two unidentified teenagers on a pink motor scooter. So far no one questioned has agreed on what the teenagers looked like. Our copter was ordered to leave the area once the SWAT team arrived, so we have no video of them after that, and no one has a clue as to their fate once the creatures exited the club, battering police with the lime green chopper and pink motor scooter. Reports say that bullets bounced off, or were absorbed by their bodies as they fled across the street. They allegedly battered a fifty-year-old gardener with the wrecked pink motor scooter, and then stole his pick-up truck from the employee parking lot of the La Brea Tar Pits, after throwing the scooter and motorcycle into the bed of the truck. The wounded police officers were treated on the scene and later transported to hospitals, and are expected to make full recoveries; however, the older gentleman, whose name is being withheld, is in serious condition. There is an all-points bulletin out for this truck..." A photo of the old, battered green pick-up and its license plate number, shot earlier in the day by the parking lot surveillance camera, were flashed on the screen.

"Oh, the poor man!"

"Those dirty, rotten..."

"Shhh!"

The announcer continued, "What we know for certain is that twenty-seven people have been injured, including the six police officers." The pictures and names of the officers flashed onto the screen. "Many of the injured have been admitted to hospitals in the area. The two scooter teens are missing and presumed dead. Until I have more information, folks, we're going to have to add this to all of the other strange and unexplained occurrences of this wild week. This is your KMALA news reporter, high in the sky over Malibu, signing off."

Several more newscasts were up for view, but Rafe saved them for later so that he and Eme could give their blow-by-blow account of the Malibu Hullabaloo. All were enthralled with the horrific escape from Ed and Gun, but they were completely baffled by their shortened hair, and the loss of their wigs. "We'll have to wait and discuss this with Tim when he arrives," Bill concluded, and everyone agreed.

Even though no one blamed Rafe for the destruction and injuries caused by the rampaging agents, Rafe blamed himself. He had returned to the computer to gather more information from Malibu or Bermuda when a clip from Atlanta caught his attention. Just as the video began, Bill stopped him.

"Save that with the rest of the news clips, Rafe; we have to get some things settled before we make any other plans."

Rafe complied and rejoined his grandfather and the others at the large dining room table.

Bill continued, "First, it's obvious that we can't return to our homes. The authorities are never going to believe our version of the last few days; they may place us under arrest, and we'd have to endure hours or days of interrogation and constant surveillance."

"But what if we go to the CIA and tell them about the secret room under the Bermuda airport?" asked Kala.

"Yeah," agreed No, "why wouldn't they believe us?"

Bill answered solemnly, "You've forgotten about Tim's protocol and the message from the future Eme and Rafe. How are we going to explain that? How do we know who to trust? This protocol is too much of a security risk to the United States, and to the world, to trust to anyone; it could get into the wrong hands and end up as it did in the other reality. Also, I am really concerned about what Tim told me about the BRUNO message that popped up on his computer at Anne's house and the hurricane name-change."

Many faces sagged in understanding, and all the heads nodded in resignation.

"Then what are we to do? Will I ever see my parents again?" asked Eme. No and Kala nodded with questioning eyes.

Anne put an arm around her great-granddaughter's shoulder.

Bill replied, "Give it some time, kids, and we'll find a way to bring them here or at least get word to them. Since Eme's parents are still in a remote location, they don't know anything about all the chaos centered around you and Anne, yet. As far as No and Kala are concerned, I'll have to discuss that with you later ok?"

Everyone brightened at that, and Bill unrolled his plan:

"Undercover work—that's our next move; each of you must make a list of clothing and other personal items you absolutely need—include sizes." They all listened quietly for Rafe's grandfather to continue. "Next, as soon as Tim and his family return, he, Kala, and I will travel to my club in Australia…let's see, it's—what time is it in Perth, Rafe?"

Startled, Rafe quickly scanned the world clock converter on the computer. "It's now five-thirty a.m. here and one-thirty p.m. in Perth, Grandfather."

"Thanks, Rafe. That means in exactly…" He stopped for a second and looked at his watch. "Eleven hours, after we've rested and nourished our bodies, we will be visiting your uncle, Kala."

Kala's eyes had been wide at the announcement that she would be traveling to Perth, but now they were as large as saucers. "Wh-what? Are you kidding me? Can Eme come, too?" Eme and Kala jumped up and down in anticipation of the answer.

Bill shook his head sadly. "Sorry, girls, but this is going to be risky. We don't want to be seen. I'm taking Tim because he knows this protocol better than I do." He glanced at his grandson who had his finger in the air and was about to protest. "I know, Rafe, but I have a job for you to do while we're gone. So Kala, are you game? We really need someone we can trust, and your uncle sounds like the right person." Everyone now turned toward the teenager, anticipating her reply.

"Yes, he is, but don't you want to contact him first?"

At the confused looks on the faces before him, he added, "No, I don't think that's wise. I'd rather meet him face to face to determine how much I should tell him, even though they are Unitarian and Salvation Army ministers." He waited for this information to register. Once everyone was smiling and nodding or mouthing "Ohhhh," he continued. "With a huge donation to their organizations, I'm hoping that they will be happy to allow us a little midnight shopping spree for the things you all need."

"Brilliant, Mr. Bill!" replied Franz.

"Shylock had nothing on you, Grandfather, you sly dog!"

Anne put her arm around Bill's waist and leaned in to kiss him on the cheek.

"Make him an offer he can't refuse!" squawked Bogey from Kala's shoulder.

While everyone laughed with relief, no one noticed the bluebird announcing incoming mail.

Cybersleuth Office, Downtown Los Angeles
8:05 P.M. PDT/5:05 P.M. CEST

Twenty-eight year old, Kevin Burke, a rugged brunet with light brown eyes and his younger brother, Jim, a tall, thin brunet with eyes that were carbon copies of his older brother's, were software designers and co-owners of Cybersleuth, Inc. They had known Anne Malone all their lives; she had been their grandmother, Julie's, best friend and confident. After Julie's death, five years earlier, Anne had gone out of her way to help them with the pain of their loss by poring over photo albums and yearbooks with them at her house while relating many poignant and funny stories of their grandmother's life during and after college.

They had always felt a special connection to the sweet older woman, and that feeling only grew when they became mentors to Eme. Now, Anne and Eme were missing, Anne's house was destroyed, and the brothers were devastated, not only because they loved the teen and her great-grandmother, but because it was their fault.

For a half hour, they had sat in their red extended cab pick-up across the cul-de-sac from Anne's property, discussing their options in regard to discovering the whereabouts of their two friends, and making plans to fly to Bermuda in hopes of helping with the search, when the police arrived. Seconds later, they noticed Eme's friends, Bailee and Shaelyn, darting from behind Mrs. Bloom's house like scared rabbits. When Kevin called out to them, the girls nearly jumped out of their shoes.

At first, the brothers were suspicious of the girls' demeanor; but then they were stunned when the girls shared a look with raised eyebrows, nodded at an unspoken decision, and hurried across the cul-de-sac toward their truck. The teens were agitated and out of breath when they climbed into the cab's back seat, as if they were ready to unburden themselves of some deep, dark secret. With more police cars arriving in the cul-de-sac, Shae urged Kevin to drive to the nearest park a few blocks away. They quickly complied and were rewarded with the girls' story.

Now, an hour later, the four co-conspirators were sitting in the tiny Cybersleuth office, in downtown Los Angeles, discussing all of the ramifications associated with the creatures, Eme's moped, and their plans to solve the mysterious e-mail address.

"One thing is still bothering me..." Jim began, poring over the girls' notes spread out on his work table.

"Only one?" interrupted his brother who was standing across from him. The girls looked at each other and smiled, remembering a similar conversation hours before.

"OK, more than one," he sneered at Kevin, "but the most important issue is why Anne's and Eme's houses? Is it because someone knew they were gone and broke in? Or, is it because someone got word from them to retrieve something from the house? It doesn't make any sense. Why wouldn't they call for help and get the police involved if they were in trouble?"

As they pondered Jim's question, Shae picked up Eme's temporary moped license from the table. "This was behind the box of wigs. Why bother taking it off the scooter, and why take the time to search for disguises if you're being chased by aliens...if that's what they were?"

"Another good question; and what happened to Boomer and Bogey? There's been no news about them being found...it's like they have just disappeared like Anne, Eme, and all the rest of the people on Bermuda and Atlanta," continued Kevin.

"Atlanta?" chorused Shae and Bailee.

The brothers looked in surprise at the teens. "You didn't hear about Tim Edelman and his family disappearing from their home in Atlanta?" asked Jim. " It was at the same time the hurricane hit." The girls shook their heads and raised their eyebrows in surprise. "Well, we were very curious about it; Tim is a good friend of ours from our days at St. Bruno's Academy."

"Wait a minute! This guy is connected to St. Bruno's!" shouted Shae.

The implications of the coincidence were too great for any of them to deny, but what did it mean and how were they going to discover the connection with no one around to give them any clues?

Shae shook her head, picked up the piece of blue stationery, and sat down at Kevin's computer.

Somewhere over Arizona
(Aboard a stolen plane)
9:55 P.M. CDT (CENTRAL DAYLIGHT TIME)

"You're looking more and more like your old, ugly self, Ed!"

The CIA agent examined his hands and tattered clothes, then looked at the pilot, "So are you, Gun; I think whatever happened to us is finally wearing off. At least I feel better. But you'll never get me to enter that protocol again."

Gun smirked. "We'll see about that!"

Ed frowned, shuddered, and then asked, "How are you planning to refuel, by the way?"

"I have a friend, a retired agent, in Texas; he allows me access to his private airfield. Then we'll stop at my ranch in Atlanta, outfit this little beauty with CIA insignia, grab some clothes and provisions, and it's on to Bermuda."

"You forgot about the reprogrammed iris scanner, the FAA, Dvorsky…"

Gun smirked and answered, "Ed, have I taught you nothing? I *always* have a backup plan!"

The Swiss Inn
4:55 A.M. CEST/7:55 P.M. PDT

The "Where am I?" was so faint that it went unnoticed; the unmistakable sound of someone about to vomit galvanized Helga into action. She whirled around just in time to catch the small boy, still clutching his stuffed fiddler crab, before he fainted. He dropped his toy as she scooped him into her arms and rushed him into the guest bathroom, just as the next child materialized from the holoport.

Anne was prepared for this older boy; she picked him up and followed Helga to the nearest bathroom. The girls staged themselves on either side of the holoport, and when the next member of Tim's family arrived, they helped her to the sofa. Tim rapidly followed, holding two rather large suitcases, which unbalanced him, and he landed in Bill's arms.

"Whoa! Transporting while carrying heavy objects is not as easy as I thought it would be; I must work on that landing!" He looked around the room fearfully. "Where are the boys?"

"Anne and Helga whisked them away to the bathroom; they were a little green," answered Bill.

"Poor kids; this has really been difficult for them to understand," Tim replied with a sigh, sitting on top of one of the bags.

"Oh, I can't imagine why!" No grinned, and he grabbed Tim's bags out from underneath him.

"Gee, thanks, No!" Tim laughed as he staggered toward the sofa. No smirked and left the room.

Rafe rushed to the inn's computer. "OK, everyone is here, so the Cyborg is signing out of Amazemail for the night and unplugging the computer...just in case!" he smirked at all the nodding heads.

"Good plan," Tim agreed from the sofa.

Tim's wife tried to rise, but fell back to the sofa, sitting on her husband's lap. He laughed, "Everyone, this is my wife, Kelly. Kelly, this is..."

Kala had just handed the pretty brunette a cup of tea. She repositioned herself next to Tim and thanked Kala, staring at her husband through bleary eyes. "Honey, my body has just traveled several hundred miles in a few seconds, and my mind is still somewhere over the Atlantic; please, I need a moment—go find the boys!"

He chuckled, kissed her on the cheek, and rose to search for his sons.

Eme joined her on the sofa and stroked the woman's right arm. "We know exactly how you feel; it takes a few minutes, but you'll be fine. I'm Eme, and this is Kala." Kala took Tim's seat.

Kelly waved a trembling hand at the girls and continued to drink her tea.

After several minutes, the silence was broken by the excited cries of the two youngest members of the growing Swiss family. They dragged their father into the living room, followed by the two older women.

"Let's do it again, Daddy!"

"Yes, that was so much fun!"

"Ah, the resilience and exuberance of children!" Franz chuckled.

Everyone laughed, and Kala and Eme moved so that Tim could settle the boys on either side of their mother.

"OK, boys, we'll do it again, just not right now." He paused at the disappointed looks on their faces. "You remember what your mother and I told you...we want you on your best behavior while we're guests here." He then turned to the smiling group standing before him. "You've met Mrs. Malone..."

"They can call me GG, Tim—makes it much easier to remember."

He smiled at her and continued. "You've met GG Anne and..." He pointed to Helga.

"Just Helga to everybody, please."

"And I'm Franz." The boys were smiling, getting into this fun naming game.

"Bill here!" He waved to the boys.

Just then Rafe jumped out from behind Franz and waved. "I'm the Cyborg!"

This set the two boys to giggling, which intensified when Rafe pulled No from behind Anne. He began to doff his hat when he remembered it had been lost on one of his trips through cyberspace, so he bowed to the red-faced No. "Introducing Mr. Negative! Just call him No!"

The oldest boy paused his giggling and answered, "If he's No, are you Yes?"

That got everyone laughing at the gob smacked look on Rafe's face. He finally composed himself to answer, "Why, yes— Yes, it is!"

No couldn't resist; he put his arm around Rafe's waist, leaned his head on his shoulder, and batted his eyes. "They say opposites attract!"

Rafe finally woke up to what was happening and shrugged out of No's embrace, which had everyone in hysterics.

Tim recovered enough to finish the introductions. He sat down on the arm of the sofa closest to the giggling, youngest boy. "This is Camden."

"I'm five!" he announced.

The older boy got into the game, stood up, bowed, and proclaimed, "You can call me Maybe, and I'm seven!" He bowed again at all the laughter, while his little brother jabbed him in the stomach.

"You're not Maybe, you're Owen."

"You're both too cute," Eme chuckled, which made Owen beam and Camden hide his face behind his mother.

Camden finally peeked out and put his hand in Kala's. "You're pretty," he said, looking up at the blonde's surprised face.

While everyone was focused on Kala, Owen took his seat again, next to Eme, and grabbed her hand, grinning.

"Wait a minute, you little interlopers, those are our girls," No laughed.

"Too late, boys, you had your chance—now you have each other." Kala and Eme smirked, and the two girls, still holding the younger boys' hands, leaned back into the sofa, laughing at Rafe's and No's shocked faces.

Rafe looked at No and proclaimed, "Methinks we have protested too much, Mr. Negative!" And they plopped down on the floor in front of the sofa, hanging their heads in mock sorrow. Eme and Kala roared with laughter.

A wild squawking from Bogey sobered everyone and brought them to their feet. Camden spotted what the bird was doing and made a mad dash across the floor toward the stuffed toy he had dropped when he arrived; Bogey was in the process of pecking it to pieces.

"Demon's wind! Demon's wind!" the bird squawked as he tore the eyes off the fiddler crab.

Camden screamed, stamping his foot at the wild bird. "Stop it! Stop it, that's my Freddy!" He might have kicked poor Bogey, had his father not rushed to his side, steering him away from the flying stuffing and bits of purple fabric.

Boomer jumped down from the leather chair he had claimed and ran over to the bird, barking. Everyone else watched in morbid fascination, too stunned to move, as Bogey continued his assault on the fiddler crab, repeating his mantra: "Demon's wind! Demon's wind!"

"I've never taught him that phrase," exclaimed a frightened Anne; Eme picked up Boomer, returning him to his chair.

"It's from my parents' last movie, *The Muddy Marauder*, GG." Eme replied as she turned and approached her bird, cooing to him, "Stop, Bogey, it's all right, Bogey."

But the bird was paying no attention to her; he was obsessed with making mincemeat of the toy. When he began eating one of the eyeballs, Anne stepped in and made a grab for the macaw. Bogey stopped for a second, and it looked like he was going to fly to her, but he made a snap at her fingers instead and ate the second eyeball, looking at her all the while, as if he were daring her to try and stop him.

A gasp from the people in the room stopped the bird long enough to squawk, "Whatsa matta wit chu?" Rafe and No wanted to laugh, but were too worried about the possible reaction from Bogey. Everyone else just stared in shock at the scene before them.

Anne could only standby and stare at the bird. "It's from the same movie, GG." Eme explained from her kneeling position three feet away from the unfolding drama.

"His brain must have been addled by what happened to him in cyberspace," cried No. Many cringed and nodded in agreement.

Kala was in tears again, and Camden was sobbing on his mother's lap, while Anne and Bill tried to approach the bird once more. This time Bogey flew to Anne's shoulder, clacked his beak several times, and preened his feathers. Anne cautiously stroked his head and carried him to the makeshift perch Franz had set up for him near the computer desk.

"He's never acted this way before and has never attacked *anything*," explained Anne as she continued to pet the macaw. "I apologize for his behavior, Camden," she told the distraught boy.

"I have a fiddler crab, and he's never even looked at it, let alone try to destroy it, GG," cried Eme. "You can have mine, Camden. I can get it from my closet—if we ever get home again." She broke away from Kala to hug the little boy. He turned to hug her in return, looking up at her with a tiny smile on his tear-streaked face.

"I think you may be right, No; the effects of his trip through cyberspace must have had longer-lasting effects than we thought," said Tim.

"He needs some rest to recover, maybe," offered Helga.

No one knew what else to say, and they watched Bogey continue to preen his feathers, stopping every few seconds to take sips of water and stare at the bits of plush and stuffing scattered over a large expanse of living room carpet. When Kala made an attempt to clean up the mess, Bogey squawked at her, until she stopped.

"He needs to admire his kill for a while longer," laughed No.

Rafe snickered at that, thinking about how vindictive he'd felt, watching Ed and Gun spluttering in the swimming pool while he taunted them with the life preserver. "Yes, revenge is sweet, but why would Bogey feel that way about a toy fiddler crab?"

"Perhaps we'll never know," Anne replied to the many nodding heads. She moved away from Bogey to join Bill and the others in the lounge area of the beautiful living room.

Eme stood and was about to reveal her feelings about fiddler crabs, and then she stopped, thinking about her persistent nightmares and visions on her flight to Bermuda. She shivered and joined the others.

Bill cleared his throat. "I think we *all* need some rest; we have lots to do tomorrow."

"We also must decide how we're going to discover the secrets of that e-mail," exclaimed Eme to a nodding Rafe.

At the confused looks of the others, Rafe continued, "The fair one is correct; one must be a student of history in order *not* to repeat it."

"That's right," added Eme, walking across the room to join the cyberwhiz. "We must learn the origins of the mysterious e-mail if we're to keep whatever happened then from happening again."

"How do you propose to learn about something that happened in the future of a completely different timeline?" asked a confused Tim from the sofa.

Rafe replied, "The best place to start would be at the end."

The group looked around at each other, mouths open in horror.

"St. Bruno's—you want to go to St. Bruno's?" asked an incredulous Anne.

Eme nodded her head, and everyone began talking at once:

"It's too dangerous!"

"Terrorists..."

"Foreign operatives..."

"CIA agents searching for..."

Bill jumped up from his seat, followed by Tim. Bill began pacing the room, and Tim ran to the computer to begin a search of St. Bruno's layout.

"Whoa, everyone, listen to me; somehow, some way, we've got to get to the bottom of this e-mail. Something happened to the world because of me...yes, GG Anne, me," she directed to her great-grandmother who was shaking her head and about to object. "My name is on Tim's program because of something that happened to end the world in 2021. Ed and Gun were involved, but are now in no shape to tell us what they may have done or with whom. It's up to us to find answers and clear our names. We are fugitives—all of us! And we have to get to the bottom of Bruno; what's the significance of that name? Why do we find it associated with everything from the school, to the hurricane, to the odd message Tim found on his computer?"

Anne shifted uneasily in her seat and then rose and joined Bill. "I know you're right, darling, but it's a very dangerous thing that you wish to initiate."

Bill grasped Anne's hand and added, "I agree with Anne, Eme. How are you going to do this undercover work without being discovered?"

"When in Rome—or Switzerland, do as the Swiss do," she answered.

"What Eme is proposing, if I am to understand, is to pose as Swiss students."

"No, No—we can pose as Swiss *workers*. We wouldn't get in as students at this late date, at least not this many of us, and the authorities will be on the lookout for us," replied Eme.

"You've been watching too many espionage movies, Eme," Kala responded from her seat on the floor beside No. "Besides, they have no idea we're off the island."

"How about we split the difference," No responded. "Kala and I can attend as students, and you and Rafe can get jobs."

"Now, wait a minute! I don't like the idea of any of you going off by yourselves to that school!" Bill said.

Anne looked into Bill's eyes. "I agree, so I think we should join them in this venture."

There was total silence after this statement, while they all digested the idea of the six of them working undercover at the school.

Bill was the first to reply, "I like it!"

"So do I!" said Eme.

"Me, too!" agreed Kala

"Cool!" replied No.

"Though this be madness, yet there is method in't."

"Kelly and I can be your base of operations and feed you any information we gather off the net, which means we'll need to get surveillance equipment," offered Tim as he continued scanning St. Bruno's grounds.

Kelly suddenly stood up and grabbed her boys' hands. "Well, if I'm going to be a spy's moll, I'd better get these two little guys to bed and get a good night's sleep."

"I want my Freddy!" cried Camden.

Helga jumped to her feet. "I have just the thing for you, Camden; it's not a fiddler crab, but it's soft and furry." Camden brightened at the possibility of a new sleeping partner, and Helga led the way out of the room.

Kelly paused in the archway, tossing her long dark hair as she turned, then blew a kiss to all assembled. "If I'd only known yesterday, what I know now...hmmm...I don't really know how to finish that!" She laughed at all the nodding heads and followed her boys to their new living quarters, musing about the length of their stay.

Cybersleuth, Inc., Malibu
8:15 PDT/5:15 A.M. CEST

Jim realized what Shae was about to do and checked his watch. After a quick conversion he reported, "It's only 5:15 a.m. in Switzerland, Shae."

"Jim's right, Shae; no one will answer you right away, so let's table this and meet back here tomorrow morning. We can only work on this for a few hours before we leave for Bermuda. Is eight o'clock too early?" asked Kevin.

The teen looked disappointed, but pulled away from the computer and looked at the brothers. "OK, you're right, and eight o'clock is fine with me." She turned and looked at her friend, "How about you, Bailee?" she asked.

Bailee had been standing quietly, anxiously twisting the jade ring on her finger. "It's fine with me, but I may be in trouble for staying out this late. I'll let you know after I get home." Shae left the computer to join the nervous brunette.

"I'll come in with you, Bailee; we'll just tell your parents that we had dinner at another friend's house, if they've checked up on us." Bailee looked at her in surprise. "It's not a lie; they don't have to know that the friend wasn't there," she giggled. Jim and Kevin smirked at the blonde's crafty ruse, and Bailee finally surrendered a small smile.

Shae turned to Kevin, "Back to the e-mail—I guess sending an old joke won't really get us anywhere—will it," she laughed.

"We'll think about what to say tonight and send it off tomorrow, after the four of us discuss it; does that work for you?" asked Jim. Bailee and Shae shared a look, smiled, and nodded at the brothers.

"We agreed not to get anyone else involved in this for a while, since we don't know who's involved and what is going on. That means your parents can't know. So, we'll drop you off up the street from your house, all right?" The girls nodded. "OK, then we'll text you tomorrow before we pick you up at that same spot," Kevin finished.

Another nod from the girls, and then Bailee asked, "What about your families?"

"This is our family!" Jim gestured at the office. "We're married to this place, and all our customers are our kids," he smirked. "That's pretty much what it takes to get a business off the ground these days."

At the surprised looks on the girls' faces, Kevin continued, "Maybe this is the start of our *new* business venture: the Cybersleuth Detective Agency; you two can come and help us run it once we return from Bermuda!"

They all laughed at that as Kevin ushered them out the door and turned off the lights, silently contemplating just where this e-mail venture might lead them. *Tomorrow may be very interesting.*

The Swiss Inn
5:30 A.M. CEST/8:30 P.M. PDT

Meanwhile, the Swiss Family Fugitives had once again moved their planning session to the dining room table. Franz produced pencils and paper for Bill who took over as Commander of

Operations. "OK, let's first tackle this Bruno business. What's with that name?"

Six sets of excited bloodshot eyes were trained on him; when he looked up, he noticed several yawns.

"You know, we can save this for tomorrow," Bill offered. "Tomorrow will be another day. In fact, tomorrow will be the first day of what promises to be an exciting, if not dangerous adventure—one that just might save our world from whatever ended it the first time around."

"How can we sleep after that!" exclaimed No with a grin.

Eme yawned again, followed by Kala, Anne, and Rafe.

"No, you're welcome to stay up, but I think you'll be sitting here alone." Bill laughed while he gathered the pencils and papers and handed them back to Franz.

"And in the dark!" continued Franz, returning the pencils and paper to the desk drawer. "I can't sleep if I know there are lights on in the house. Sorry, I'm going to bed, and he waved to them as he exited the room."

They all stood on that note, leaving No alone at the table.

"Good-night, good-night…" began Rafe.

"Parting is such sweet sorrow…" Rafe grinned at Eme's interruption.

"That we will say goodnight…" began Kala, and then she glanced at Rafe for help.

"…till it be morrow!" prompted Rafe.

"Yeah, what he said," finished the blonde.

"OK, I can take a hint…er, hints." No rose from the table with a groan. Then he snapped his head toward the computer and raised his index finger. "But first I need to check the Atlanta news to see if my parents even know that I'm missing—they almost lost me once before, but didn't take me far enough into the woods," he finished with a sneer.

"More's the pity," replied Rafe and bumped No out of the way in a dash to the computer; he situated himself on the computer bench and reloaded the Atlanta newscast from earlier.

"OK, are we even now?" No asked him while he rubbed his shin after colliding with the computer table.

"Not even close!" Rafe replied with a smirk. Eme scooted in next to him.

No just shook his head. Kala grabbed his hand and whispered, "I told you so."

The others gathered behind the Cyborg, and the video began. Bill rested his hand on Rafe's shoulder while Anne grabbed Bill's arm. Kala and No were side by side, their tired eyes riveted on the screen.

After the news logo, the date and time appeared, and then a hospital room came into view with a news reporter interviewing two men and a bedridden, heavily-bandaged female.

"Hey, that's my dad and...and my stepmom and stepdad, and oh, no, that must be my mom in the hospital bed!" screamed No, his hands gripping the sides of his head.

"Shh, listen to what your dad's saying," said Kala.

"...so don't worry, son, wherever you are, your mom's going to be just fine. And son, I'm on your trail and will find you, mark my words."

There were gasps from those present, and all wide, bloodshot eyes turned to a chagrined No, after the camera moved in for a tight shot of the California politician, his voluptuous blonde wife hanging on his arm, while he made his parting remarks with tears in his eyes. "I promise to find you, my...my son!" He paused to sniff into his monogramed handkerchief and dab dramatically at his eyes. "Dad *will* find you, *Bruno!*"

End of Eme: Book One
The Protocol

BOOK 2

AND NOW IT'S TOMORROW (WORKING TITLE)

BY PJ LAMPHEAR

CHAPTER ONE
SWISS FAMILY FUGITIVES

St. Bruno's Academy, Switzerland
September 1, 2020

Rafe was a firm believer that you should own only what you could carry on your back, or tuck into your pants, at a dead run.

Most of the time it was the Persephone and the various peripherals he was constantly upgrading; other times, this time, it was a pretty girl. *And his fifteen-year-old dilapidated laptop.* Dodging bullets and evading the firefight around him, Rafe slung a wounded Eme over his shoulder and made a mad dash for the door.

If I can just get to the elevator, he thought, *I can make it to the helicopter on the roof.*

Easier said than done; despite her lithe and slim form, Eme was a weight to carry. If not for the adrenaline in his system, caused by the crazed gunfight raging around the e-lab in the heart of St. Bruno's Academy, he would never have managed it.

"Rafe..." Eme gasped, drifting toward unconsciousness.

"Hold on, fair Juliet," Rafe panted, ducking down behind a bank of machines riddled with fresh, smoking bullet holes. "Keep pressure on your shoulder, OK?"

Eme's white blouse was stained crimson with her life's blood, leaking in what looked like sheer gallons from the hole just below her right shoulder blade. Rafe's own coat was soaked in that same precious blood.

The door was only twenty feet away, and the main firepower was concentrated toward the far end of the e-lab. Both forces that had invaded St. Bruno's were after the same thing—the Amazemail protocol—yet for once, none of the bad guys was actively trying to kill Rafe or Eme—they were trying to kill each other. That was a great change of pace, but unfortunately Eme had been caught in the crossfire.

"Is it bad?" Eme whispered; her voice was faint and seemed to travel from a very long way away.

"Just a scratch, sweetheart," Rafe lied. "I'm only carrying you because I can't keep my hands off you!"

Eme chuckled, but it was without humor. Her eyes fluttered closed and her undamaged left hand fell from her wounded right shoulder.

"N-no, Eme, wake up!"

Rafe got no reply.

"Right, then," he said, feeling time ticking away as Eme slowly bled to death. "Once more into the breach—and all that crap."

He ran for the door, feeling the barrels of several weapons zeroing in on his movement, hearing the bullets whiz past his head and slam into the walls and machinery around him. Rafe dove through the maelstrom, shielding Eme as best he could, and threw his back into the e-lab door, hoping it wasn't locked.

The door gave way, and Rafe stumbled into the entrance hall of the old converted manor house. This was the oldest part of the school, the original school, before it became a center for the advancement of technology. He needed to reach the helipad on the roof where Kala and Michael were supposed to be waiting with rescue.

He encountered an immediate problem with his plan. The entrance hall had seen heavy fighting; fire and smoke were crawling up the heavy doors, blood splatters coated the mahogany floorboards, and there were a few unmoving bodies—soldiers in black fatigues and combat masks. No loss there. Yet the elevator doors had been blasted open by some explosion, and two hundred feet of pulley cable had snapped and crashed through the roof of the car. There'd be no ascending in that direction.

Which left the stairs.

The four flights of stairs.

Rafe groaned and set off, knowing time was short and his legs had to carry him. He hoped it was his imagination, but Eme felt colder. Not a good sign.

Two floors up, his legs burning, he heard the wicked sound of pursuit: heavy boots thumping on the stairs below. Rafe thought about abandoning his laptop, but that wasn't really an option; the only copy of the protocol left in the world was stored there, and if it fell into the wrong hands, the hands that belonged to those, who were currently pursuing him, then a lot of people would die. But there was so much blood on *his* hands right now, Eme's blood.

Damn it all! Perhaps I shouldn't have moved her, he thought. *No…then we'd both be dead.* At the moment it felt like all he'd done was delay the inevitable.

Rafe hauled ass as fast as he could, leaping up the stairs, pushing through the pain in his legs and arms. It was just pain, after all, nothing new these days. The terrible scar crisscrossing his face was testament enough to that. Rafe gave his all for Eme and, coming in a close second, for the world, should the e-mail protocol be stolen.

The chase was hot on his heels as he leaped up the stairs on the fourth floor; he was only seconds from the roof. Access there was strictly permitted to staff and faculty, but Rafe had installed his own pass code on his first day at St. Bruno's. He poked it into the keypad at the top of the narrow stairs now.

"Six…nine…nine…one, ha!" he breathed as the door released and cool afternoon sunlight filtered in from outside. There was but a moment to rejoice, however, as a machine gun erupted from the foot of the stairs and bullets chewed through the stone at his feet. "*Shit!*"

Rafe dove through the doorway and onto the roof. He could hear the chopper before he saw it—the roaring rotating sound of the engine. He swung behind the door, on the last dregs of his resolve, and spied the TW-522 Rescue Hawk. Through the glass canopy, he saw Kala's Aunt Mayrah seated in the cockpit, waving wildly for Rafe to hurry the hell up.

The bay doors were open: Michael and Kala were strapped in, looking pale but determined. Their faces lit up with sheer relief as Rafe gave his last and hauled his weary body across the roof toward the chopper fifty feet away.

"*Come on!*" Kala screamed; her voice was a dull roar below the revving of the chopper's engine. Mayrah was mere seconds from take-off.

Rafe stumbled and nearly fell. Fresh bullets tore into the concrete and slate around him, snapping at his heels. It would only take one of those to end his mad, impossible race mere inches from the finish line.

He made it, throwing Eme none too gently onto the floor of the helicopter and clambering in after her, a triumphant, fierce grin spreading across his scarred face.

Something hit him hard in the back—*thump, thump, thump*—knocking the air from his lungs and turning his grin to a frown. The world spun; there was no longer any pain in his legs. Rafe felt himself slipping backward out of the chopper, even as the former Royal Air Force pilot hit the throttle and began to lift off.

Kala lunged forward and gripped the collar of his shirt, pulling him back in, but Rafe was only vaguely aware of that as black dots clouded his vision. In a small part of his mind, he knew something wasn't right, that something had gone horribly wrong.

But he was tired, too tired to care. Why did Michael and Kala look so frightened? He looked down at his feet, at Eme, at the bullet hole in her shoulder, and for the briefest of moments before the darkness claimed him, Rafe's eyes lit up.

"I've been shot," he said, as if discussing the matter over morning tea. "Aw, heck."

He collapsed on top of Eme—broken and defeated.

End of Chapter One
Eme: Book 2
And Now It's Tomorrow

ACKNOWLEDGMENTS

To the ingenious Joe Ducie—his inspiration and many contributions to Eme, through his many e-mails from Australia, were instrumental in keeping me focused and true to the humanity of the story. Please read his numerous novels and short stories, available on Amazon and Kindle—all are fantastic, fast-paced urban fantasies.

Also, if you're a *Harry Potter* fan, you'll enjoy Joe Ducie's wild and imaginative *Harry Potter* stories on Fan Fiction.net.

To my dear friends, Alison Broucek, Judy Brownfield, Kevin Square, Christy Akitiff, Patty Curry, Bill Lamphear, and Kelly Magreevy, who read this story as it morphed through its many stages, giving me positive and not so positive feedback. Your "brutality" helped make this a much better book.

To my wonderful husband, Bill, who detests fanciful books, yet "suffered" through Eme because he loves me, but mainly because he loves my cooking and would dearly miss it.

To Tony Nguyen, my creative former third-grade student, whose Y2K comic strip, featured in our Ducky Village, 1999 classroom newsletter, sparked the idea for a story about traveling by e-mail.

To Trinity, an inventive former student, who inspired the Eme title letters.

To the creators of Incredimail, the amazing e-mail program that inspired Amazemail.

To the brilliant staff at Createspace—their fabulous editing, cover and interior designs gave me a finished project that exceeded my wildest expectations.

Thank you, one and all.

www.ingramcontent.com/pod-product-compliance
Lightning Source LLC
Chambersburg PA
CBHW051445260626
47162CB00001B/251